RAVES F

AMANDA SCOTT

SEDUCED BY A ROGUE

more . . .

more . . .

BORDER MOONLIGHT

BORDER LASS

"4½ Stars! TOP PICK! Readers will be thrilled . . .
a tautly written, deeply emotional love story
steeped in the rich history of the Borders."
                    —*RT Book Reviews*

"Scott excels in creating memorable characters."
                    —**FreshFiction.com**

BORDER WEDDING

"5 Stars! Scott has possibly written the best
historical in ages!"
                    —**FallenAngelReviews.com**

"4½ Stars! TOP PICK! Not only do her characters
leap off the pages, the historical events do too.
This is more than entertainment and romance;
this is historical romance as it was meant to be."
                    —*RT Book Reviews*

"Wonderful . . . full of adventure and history."
                    —*Midwest Book Review*

more . . .

KING OF STORMS

KNIGHT'S TREASURE

"Filled with tension, deceptions, and newly awakened passions. Scott gets better and better."

—NovelTalk.com

HIGHLAND PRINCESS

"Delightful historical . . . Grips the audience from the onset and never [lets] go."

—*Affaire de Coeur*

"A fabulous medieval Scottish romance."

—*Midwest Book Review*

AMANDA SCOTT

TEMPTED BY A WARRIOR

FOREVER

NEW YORK   BOSTON

Copyright © 2010 by Lynne Scott-Drennan
Excerpt from Highlands Trilogy copyright © 2010 Lynne Scott-Drennan
All rights reserved. Except as permitted under the U.S. Copyright Act of 1976, no part of this publication may be reproduced, distributed, or transmitted in any form or by any means, or stored in a database or retrieval system, without the prior written permission of the publisher.

Cover design by Claire Brown

Forever
Hachette Book Group
237 Park Avenue
New York, NY 10017
Visit our website at www.HachetteBookGroup.com

Forever is an imprint of Grand Central Publishing. The Forever name and logo is a trademark of Hachette Book Group, Inc.

Printed in the United States of America

First Printing: July 2010

10 9 8 7 6 5 4 3 2 1

To You, Fearless Reader,
with many thanks and the fond hope that, for a short time,
this book will transport you happily to another time and
place.

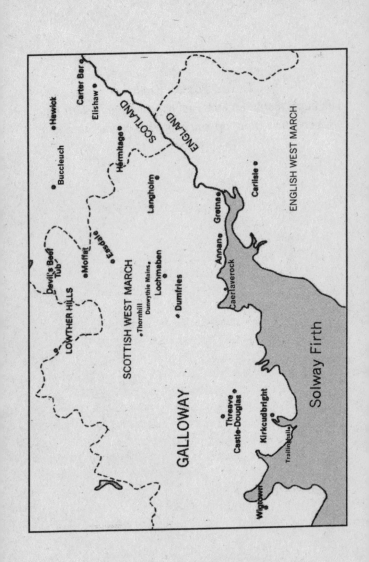

*Author's Note*_____

For the reader's convenience, the author offers the following aids:

Cleuch = CLOO, a ravine, gorge

Dobby = having spikes, prickly

"the Douglas" = the Earl of Douglas only

Dunwythie Hall = "the Hall," the fortified house at Dunwythie Mains

Low tide, or low water = the farthest ebb of a tide

Mains = the primary seat of a lord (from "demesne") as in Dunwythie Mains

Nithsdale = NEETHS-dale

Rig = ridge (Riggshead = a joining of ridges)

The Sands = Solway Sands (a twenty-mile stretch of sand from head of the Firth to the mouth of the river Nith, which occurs when a spring tide ebbs)

Spring tide = tide occurring at or shortly after the new or full moon, resulting in maximum rise (and ebb), occurs twice a month

Prologue

Annandale, Scotland, 5 June 1377

His first slap made her left ear ring.

"*Now* see what ye've made me do!" he shouted over the rush and roar of the river below. A half-moon lit the grassy track and revealed white foam on the water.

Holding a hand to her stinging cheek, seventeen-year-old Fiona Jardine scowled at the tall, powerful-looking man who had struck her and said stubbornly, "Clouting me won't change the truth, Will Jardine. It was your fault, *not* mine!"

He loomed over her, terrifying in his fury. "By God," he snapped, putting the face she had once thought so handsome close to hers, "ye'll no talk to *me* like that!"

"You're ape-drunk," she said. In the crisp night air, she could smell the whisky on him, so powerful that it made her dizzy just to inhale its fumes.

When he drew back his hand to slap her again, she tried to get away, to protect herself. But his left hand shot out then, and with bruising strength, he caught her by an arm and whipped her back to face him.

"Let me go!" she shrieked. But he did not let go, and he was one of the strongest men she knew.

"Aye, I'll let ye go. *After* I've taught ye a lesson."

Struggling frantically and screaming with fear as she tried to break free, she managed to duck the next slap, only to suffer a backhanded blow instead that made her right ear throb with pain.

Before she could catch her breath, he hit her again, a hard smack of his calloused palm right across her mouth. Had he not held her upright, she would have fallen. As it was, she tasted blood and feared that he had loosened a tooth.

He laughed. "Ye should ken fine by now, lass, that what I say, I mean."

His next blow flew at her belly, but by twisting hard, she took it instead on her side just above her waist. Gasping at a pain so sharp that it took her breath away, she continued to fight him anyway, out of pure terror. But the pain was overwhelming, her strength fast waning, and his next blow sent her reeling to the ground.

Her head struck something hard. Blearily, she saw him step toward her.

Then, looming above her, he drew back his foot.

Through the stunning ache in her head, distantly, she heard him say, "Mayhap, *now,* ye'll remember to keep your place, madam wife."

After that, she knew nothing more.

Chapter 1 ————————

Spedlins Tower, Annandale, 20 June 1377

The leather-clad, booted traveler approaching the open kitchen doorway on the pebbled path running behind Spedlins Tower paused at hearing a soft feminine voice inside:

"'I expect I should be spinning, too, aye,' the maiden said sadly. 'But it would be t' nae purpose. I could never finish so great a task in time.'"

The traveler took a step closer as the voice went on, creaking now with age, "'Och, but I could spin it all for ye, aye,' the old woman said."

"Gey good o' the auld crone!" cried several childish voices, as if they had many times heard the story and exclaimed always at the same place.

The traveler smiled, recognizing the tale from his own childhood. He moved nearer, trying to muffle the sounds that his boots made on the pebbles of the path.

He saw the speaker then, seated on the stone floor of the scullery with her back to him. Six fascinated children of various ages sat in a semicircle before her.

Beyond, in the dim, vaulted kitchen, the traveler

discerned bustling movement and heard sounds indicative of preparations for the midday meal.

The storyteller went on in a soft, clear voice—doubtless her own, "So the maiden ran to fetch her lint and laid it in her new friend's hand. Then she asked the old woman for her name and where she should call that evening for the spun yarn."

One child, a dark lad of perhaps eight or nine, looked right at the traveler.

The man put a finger to his lips.

Although the boy obediently kept silent, he continued to stare.

The storyteller continued, "But the maiden received no reply, for the old woman had vanished from where she stood. The lassie looked long for her until at last she became so tired that she lay down to rest."

Three of the children eyed him now as a fourth, the smallest lass—blue-eyed with curly auburn hair—piped up, "Aye, and when she awoke, it was gey *dark*!"

"So it was, Tippy," the storyteller agreed. "The evening star was shining down, and as the maiden watched the moon rise, a rough voice startled her from—"

"Who is *he*?" the same small lassie demanded, pointing at the traveler.

The storyteller, turning, started and winced as she saw him. She began awkwardly to get to her feet, saying, "Good sakes, wherever did *you* spring from?"

He noted first that she had black hair and light blue eyes, and was stunningly beautiful, with delicate features, rosy cheeks, and plump, creamy breasts, their softness rising above the low neckline of her loose, blue kirtle. As she straightened, he saw with a surge of unexpected disappointment that she was heavy with child.

"Forgive me for interrupting you, mistress," he said. "They told me at the stable that I should come this way as it was quicker, and none would mind. But if you will bid someone take me to Old Jardine, I shall leave you to finish your tale."

"This is a good place to stop for a time," she said, raising a hand to the short veil she wore over her long, shiny, thick plaits, as if to be sure the veil was properly in place. "I can easily finish the story later."

To a chorus of indignant protests, she replied firmly, "Nay, then, you must all go now to Cook and ask how you can help him. Davy, you and Kate take care to see that the wee ones know what they must do."

"Aye, we will," the largest of the three lassies said. The dark-haired, dark-eyed boy who had first noted the stranger nodded his agreement, still eyeing him.

As the children scrambled to obey her, the young woman turned her lovely eyes to the stranger again, adding, "Surely, someone must have told you that Jardine of Applegarth lies on his deathbed and refuses to see anyone."

"He will see me," the traveler said confidently, noting that the dark rims of her irises made them look transparent, as if one might see right through to her thoughts.

"Mercy, why *should* he see you? Have you no respect for a dying man?"

"I doubt that the old fustilugs is really dying. But he will see me nevertheless, because he sent for me. Sithee, I am his heir."

Instead of the hasty apology he had every right to expect from a servant who had spoken so pertly to him, she stiffened, saying, "You must have taken *that* notion from a tale of the same sort that I've just been telling the bairns."

His temper stirring, he said, "Mind your tongue, lass, lest—"

"Why should I? Do you dislike being told you are wrong?" she asked. "For so you are if you claim to be heir to Old Jardine's estates."

Doubt stirred. No servant of the old man's would dare speak so boldly.

Despite their kinship, he barely knew Jardine. But if even half of what he had heard about the contentious old scoundrel was true, Jardine's minions would tread lightly and with great care—especially when speaking to another nobleman.

"Who are you, lass?" he asked.

She gently touched her belly. "I am his heir's mother, or mayhap his heir's wife. Whichever it may be," she added, squaring her shoulders and giving him look for look, "I can tell you without hesitation that *you* are *not* his heir."

Stunned, he realized that Old Jardine's lie came as no surprise to him. He had suspected some deception but only in that he doubted the old man was really dying. Ruthlessly stifling the unexpected anger that leaped in response to her near disdain, he said, "I expect, then, that you must be Will Jardine's wife."

"Aye, of course, I am—or his widow," she added. "But who are you?"

"Kirkhill," he said.

She frowned. "Should I know you? Is that all anyone ever calls you?"

"People call me several different things. Some call me Seyton of Kirkhill. But most folks hereabouts know me as Kirkhill. My family has lived in upper Annandale for two centuries. However, as I am Will's cousin, you and I are clearly kin by marriage, so you may call me Richard if you like, or Dickon."

"I will call you Kirkhill," she said firmly, but almost as if her thoughts had briefly flitted elsewhere. "I warrant it must be Lord Kirkhill, though," she added.

"More to the purpose, my mother has the misfortune to be that old scoundrel's sister," he said.

"Good sakes, I did not know that Old Jardine *had* a sister!"

"I think she'd liefer not be one," he said with a wry smile. "But he did send word to me that he was dying and bade me hie myself to Spedlins Tower."

"Then I expect that I should go and tell him you are here and see if he will receive you," she said. "I will get someone to take you to a more comfortable—"

"Nay, my lady—Lady William, I should say—"

"'My lady' is sufficient," she said. "No one calls me Lady William."

"'Tis the usual way, so forgive me if I have irked you," he said. "In any event, I did not come here to kick my heels whilst my crusty uncle takes his time to decide that he does indeed want to see me. You will take me to him. First, though, I want to hear about what happened to Will."

"So do we all," she replied.

"God's troth, do you *not* know? Jardine's messenger told me that my uncle was on his deathbed and that I was to be his heir, so I assumed Will must be dead. But as you have that said you are either the heir's wife or his mother..." He paused.

"Aye," she said, touching her belly again. "I do not

know which it is. See you, Will was here; then he was not. He has been gone for over a fortnight."

"Then I hope you will forgive my asking if you and he were legally married. I am sure that no one informed my mother of such a grand occasion, because she would certainly have told me."

"Aye, sure, we were legally married," she said with a flash in her eyes and deep flush to her cheeks. "If my good-father did not tell his sister of our union, it was through no fault of mine."

"It would not have been your fault in any event," he agreed.

Looking away, she added, "He has plainly called you here to no benefit of your own, sir. Doubtless, you would be wise to turn round and go home."

He waited until she met his gaze again, this time with wariness in her eyes.

"Do I look like the sort of man who would do that?" he asked.

⁓

Fiona did *not* think that Kirkhill looked like a man who would go away just because she'd suggested that course. In truth, she was not sure what to make of him.

He was taller and even more powerful looking than Will was, taller than she was by a head, and he looked as if he might be twice as broad across the shoulders. He had dressed for riding in leather breeks, boots, and a leather jack over a loose, snowy white shirt, similar to clothing that Will and many Border lords wore. But his features were more rugged than Will's, so Kirkhill was not as handsome.

He also lacked that air of menace that Will had worn

so casually, but Will had not shown that side of himself to her at first either. There *was* something unnerving about Kirkhill, though, a sense of power, perhaps.

Will had strutted about like a cock in its hen yard, chin jutting and with an expression that dared anyone to cross him. Looking at Kirkhill, she realized that Will's posturing had missed the mark. His cousin did none of that, but no one could doubt his confidence in himself or his belief that he would get what he wanted.

Despite his kinship with Will and a slight—albeit much neater—similarity of taste in attire, Kirkhill did not look at all like the dark Jardines. His curly hair was the color of dark honey, and his face showed darker stubble, as if no one had shaved him for a day or two. But he moved with feline grace, spoke well, and seemed perfectly at ease with himself. She envied him his air of certainty, recalling a time when she had enjoyed similar self-assurance.

But to ask her if she was "*truly married*"! What a question! A true gentleman would not challenge a lady so— although, in truth, she had not met many gentlemen.

The only ones that came to mind were her deceased father; her sister Mairi's husband, Robert Maxwell; and her cousin Jenny's husband, Sir Hugh Douglas. Sir Hugh was Fiona's maternal uncle as well, although she barely knew him, and she had met Maxwell but once. If Jenny and Mairi had married them, they must be gentlemen, but she certainly did not count her cantankerous good-father as one, or her husband, if Will even counted still amongst the living.

Gentleman or not, Kirkhill did not strike her as a patient man. And, if he was kin to Old Jardine and Will, she knew that she would be wise to do as he bade her.

"Come this way, my lord," she said quietly, and turned toward the kitchen.

They passed through that vaulted chamber and up a wheel stairway to the main entryway and the great hall, crossing the west-to-east length of that hall to the inner chamber entrance near the north end of the dais.

Fiona paused at the closed door, glancing at her unwanted companion. "His chamber is no pleasant place," she told him. "He has a vicious, smelly mastiff with him nearly all the time, and my good-father will be in no pleasant humor, either."

"I'll charm him into one," he said, leaning past her to open the door and gesturing for her to precede him inside.

Grimacing, she did. The room reeked as it always did of sickness, dog, and old man, the combination almost over-powering, and she wanted the business over quickly. The babe moved within her, pushing against the rib that still ached from twisting to see Kirkhill when he'd arrived.

He showed no sign of minding the noisome air of Jardine's bedchamber or the huge, deep-chested mastiff that surged to its feet, growling, when they entered.

The inner chamber was the sort of large room wherein many a laird still held audiences, tended business, and slept with his wife if he had one. Old Jardine's bed frame, large, elaborately carved, and draped with dark blue curtains tied back at its posts, stood at the center of the wall opposite the doorway, its foot end facing them.

The fat old man was awake, propped on pillows, glowering at Fiona through piggy eyes. Hod, his personal servant, hovered at his side, holding out a cup to him.

The mastiff growled again.

"Quiet, Dobby! Hod, take that poison away!" Waving

dog and manservant away, he returned his scowl to Fiona. "What d'ye want, lass? I told ye afore to rap on yon door and wait till Hod admits ye. Ye're lucky the dog didna savage ye."

"That was my doing, Uncle," Kirkhill said, urging Fiona farther into the room with a touch to her back but putting himself between her and the dog.

Jardine exclaimed, "Richard! 'Tis yourself then? But so it must be, for ye're the spit o' your fiendish father, and forbye, ye'd be the only man to call me 'Uncle.'"

"I warrant I was no more than seven when last we met, for I've not been nigh the place since," Kirkhill said. "And now, apparently, I've come on a fool's errand."

"'Tis no foolish thing to answer the cry of a dying man," Jardine muttered, his voice suddenly much weaker.

Fiona nearly rolled her eyes. She did not believe the old man was any feebler than he had been the moment before.

Evidently, Kirkhill agreed, because his voice took on an edge as he said, "But *why* did you declare yourself at the point of death and me your heir when you sent for me? Even if the first part should prove true, the second is patently false."

"D'ye think so? I'm thinking that only God kens if it be false."

Fiona gritted her teeth. She would have liked to remove herself from the old man's presence, but curiosity and a suspicion that Old Jardine might have met his match in Kirkhill bade her stay as long as the two allowed it.

Kirkhill said, "Your good-daughter is obviously with child, Uncle. And she assures me that she and Will were properly wed."

"Aye, 'tis true he did marry her, the young fool, think-ing he could gain much thereby. He should ha' had better ken o' how matters stood."

"From your message, I thought *he* must be dead," Kirkhill went on with a new note in his voice, a harder one that made Fiona look quickly at him and try to judge if a harsh temper was another trait he shared with his uncle and cousin.

Not that she counted herself a good judge of men, for experience had proven she was not. But she *had* learned to recognize certain important things about them. So she studied Kirkhill carefully as he continued to gaze sternly at his uncle.

Old Jardine continued to look at him as if he, too, were sizing Kirkhill up.

The dog growled again, low in its throat.

When the old man's silence made it clear that he had forgotten the question or did not choose to reply, Kirkhill added softly, "*Is* Will dead, Uncle?"

"He must be, aye."

"Even if he is, why did you say that I was to be your heir? I *don't* like liars." As soft as Kirkhill's voice was now, it sent a chill right through Fiona.

Old Jardine said in his usual curt way, "Nor do I *tell* lies. We've no seen my Will now for over a fortnight, so he must be dead. Nowt but a grave would keep that lad away this long without a word to me."

"The English have been restless for more than a month now, breaking our so-called ten-year truce by sending raiding parties across the line," Kirkhill said. "Mayhap Will got himself killed or captured."

"*Not* captured. D'ye think he'd ha' kept his *name* to

himself? He'd ha' said right off that he were my son, and I'd ha' got a demand for his ransom. I'd ha' paid it, too, for Will. He's naebody's prisoner," Jardine added. "It has been too long."

"Even if he is dead, you'd still have an heir or an heiress, and soon, too, by the look of her," Kirkhill said, gesturing toward Fiona.

"Faugh," Jardine snorted. "I'll believe that when I see the bairn. Sithee, her mam lost more bairns than anyone else I've ever heard tell of."

"I won't lose *my* child," Fiona declared.

"Aye, well, whether the bairn comes or no, Richard, I want ye to find out what became o' my Will. I knew that if I told ye ye'd stand to inherit Applegarth, ye'd come here. And so ye did. The fact is, I've willed it so that if Will doesna come home, ye're to look after the place when I die. Ye'll do that right enough, I'm thinking, for a tithe from the rents."

"I will, aye," Kirkhill said. "I'd do that for anyone, tithe or none."

"I've named ye lawful guardian for the bairn, too," Jardine said with a darkling look at Fiona.

Stiffening, she said, "My child will need no guardian but me."

"Even an I believed that, which I do not, 'tis my duty to name a suitable *man* to guard the bairn's interest, aye—and yours, too, lass," the old man said grimly.

Wondering if that were true, she looked at Kirkhill.

He met her questioning gaze with a stern look that somehow reassured her even as he gave a curt nod and said, "That *is* true, my lady. However, you should have someone whom *you* trust to look after your interest, a kinsman of your own."

"Should I?" Fiona said. "My father is dead, and my good-brother lives much of the year in Galloway. My uncle, Sir Hugh Douglas, lives nearer, in Nithsdale—"

"They ha' nowt to do wi' her, and I dinna want any o' them setting foot on *my* land," Jardine snapped. "Get hence now, lass. I would talk wi' Kirkhill alone."

Glancing again at Kirkhill and receiving another curt nod, Fiona obeyed.

⁓

When the lady Fiona had gone, Kirkhill faced his uncle. "I expect you think I should just drop everything else I might be doing and stay here with you."

"Nay, I'm none so daft as that," Old Jardine retorted. "Ye'll ha' your own business to attend afore ye can see to mine. Moreover, for a time yet, I'm still good to look after things here. I just wanted ye to know how ye stand. All of Applegarth will be yours if Will be dead and the bairn also dies. The estates will be yours to run in any event until the bairn turns five-and-twenty. I'd like a *lad* o' Will's to inherit them, but I'm none so sure I'd want one wi' that vixen-lass as his mam. Still, he'd be the heir o' me own blood and Will's, and in the end, God will decide the matter."

"He will, aye," Kirkhill agreed, not bothering to conceal his disgust.

"Aye, sure, but I'll be damned afore I'll see any *daughter* o' hers take Applegarth, so ye'll see to it that *that* doesna happen," Jardine said with a straight look. "I've willed it so that only a male wi' Jardine blood shall get me lands, but others may try to deny my will. I want ye to see that they dinna succeed."

"If I did not know better, I might think you mean me

to do away with the bairn if it's born female, or even to do away with its mother beforehand," Kirkhill said bluntly, noting that every sign of the old man's weakness had vanished.

"Aye, well, if I thought ye'd do it, we might make a bargain, for I've nae use for her," Jardine retorted. "Our Fiona be too hot at hand for any man but Will, and she doesna take well to schooling. Doubtless, a daughter o' hers would be the same. Moreover, I've a strong notion that if my Will's dead, she killed him. Sithee, she were the last to see him alive, and he were gey displeased wi' her, too."

Kirkhill, finding it hard to think of the spirited lass as a murderess, said only, "I'll see what I can learn of Will's whereabouts. I should perhaps seek out someone from the lady Fiona's family, too, to look after her interests."

"Nay, for I've willed it so that ye'll look after Applegarth and after her, too. Mayhap we'll talk more anon, lad, but I'm dead tired now. Ye'll stay the night."

Mayhap he would, Kirkhill decided. He had no interest in talking further with Old Jardine, but he did want to learn more about Will's intriguing lady.

To his surprise, she was waiting outside the door to Jardine's chamber, on the great hall dais. "He thinks I killed his son," she said without preamble.

⁓

Knowing that the old man would have lost no time in expressing the suspicion he had already made clear to her, Fiona had blurted the statement, ignoring a pair of gillies hurrying onto the dais and away again with baskets and platters of food for the midday meal.

Kirkhill heard her declaration with no apparent astonishment.

"He did tell me as much," he said quietly. "But unless Will was weaker than my uncle is now, I doubt that you could have overpowered him, my lady."

"That is kind of you," she said. "I'm nearly sure I didn't kill him."

His eyebrows arced upward, drawing her to note that they were darker than his hair and that his heavily lashed eyes were golden brown. "*Nearly* sure?" he said.

With a shrug, she said glibly, "My good-father has accused me so often that I've almost come to believe him. The reason he sent for you is that he wants to learn the truth before he dies, so that he can hang the guilty person, whoever it is."

"I do understand his wanting that," he said, nodding.

"He will be gey pleased by your understanding, I'm sure. But mayhap, before you inform *him* of it, you should know one thing more."

Pausing, she added, "He also suspects you, my lord."

Kirkhill saw that she expected him to express astonishment that Old Jardine suspected him. In truth, though, he would feel little surprise to hear that his uncle suspected nearly everyone he saw of murdering Will. The old man was even more despicable than Lady Kirkhill had led him to expect, but his disgust stirred strongest when he recalled Jardine's treatment of the lass watching him so intently now.

To be sure, he had seen for himself that the lady Fiona was likely less than dutifully submissive to her good-father. Recalling the angry flash in her eyes earlier when *he* had asked her if she and Will had properly married, and her stiff resistance in the sickroom to accepting a guardian for her child, he suspected that she had a quick temper. But she had also revealed that odd wariness when he had refused rather curtly to let her leave him waiting while she warned Jardine of his arrival.

Still, other than her two brief protests, she had been quiet in the sickroom, so he doubted that she was the temperamental vixen Jardine had described and thought it far more likely that, if the two had a fractious relationship, his uncle was at fault.

Kirkhill found it especially hard to imagine that she would behave insolently when Will Jardine was at hand. Not only had he heard as much about Will as he had about Old Jardine but he had also met Will—several times.

Impatiently, she said, "Have I stunned you to silence, sir?"

"Nay, I was just thinking about the last time I saw Will," he said, recalling that his cousin had greeted him jovially with a plump, clearly willing, and experienced lass on each arm. "How long have you and Will been married?"

She started to answer, for her mouth opened. Then she shut it tight and scowled at him before she said, "Do you ask such things of *every* lady you meet?"

Irritation stirred in him again, although she had every right to object to his quizzing, especially with servants scurrying hither and yon. "Not every lady," he said. "But I do know my cousin better than I know my uncle."

"Aye, sure, and Will is a *man's* man, is he not? A scrapper, ready for any fight and never caring whose side he takes. A devil with the lassies, too, is he not? Doubtless you much admire him."

"Not much," he replied. "I should think he'd make any woman the devil of a husband." Noting that a number of people were eyeing them curiously, he touched her elbow, adding, "Shall we move away from this dais?"

She let him guide her back toward the stairway, but he discerned new wariness beneath her casual demeanor as she said, "Doubtless my husband is no better or worse than any other man."

"Do you love him?" he asked, wondering what stirred him to such bluntness.

Her eyes widened. "My good-father may have named you guardian to all his estates and to my child, sir, not to mention the possible murderer of his son. But *none* of that gives you the right to question me so presumptuously... not yet, at all events."

"Perhaps not," he admitted. "I'm a curious chap by nature, so you are not the first to accuse me of presumption. Pray, forgive the liberty."

If anything, her beautiful eyes widened more, and for a moment, he thought she would not reply. Then she said, "I am unaccustomed to apologies, sir, if that was one. But neither am I accustomed to such questions from a stranger. I will accept your apology rather than delay you any longer, for I expect you will want to depart as soon as you have dined, and I shall not join you at table. With my good-father abed and no proper female companion, it would be *imp*rop—"

"I fear I must irk you again," he interjected. "Old Jardine has bade me spend the night, and I have agreed. Moreover," he added, watching for her reaction, "I see nowt amiss in our dining together at high table. We are kinsmen, after all, and if that old man is truly dying, I will soon be responsible for you and your child. Therefore, I would take this opportunity for us to know each other better."

"To quiz me more, you mean."

"I swear there will be no more quizzing. You may tell me as little or as much as you like, or you may quiz *me* as punishment for my presumptuous curiosity. I will answer any question that you want to ask me."

With a sudden gleam in her eyes, she said, "Good. *Did* you murder Will?"

Fiona watched him narrowly as he said, "Nay, I did not." Then with a slight smile, he added, "Did *you*?"

Hesitating for only a moment, she said firmly, "Of course not. How could I? You noted yourself how unlikely that is." Then, lest he declare that he had changed his mind about that, she added quickly, "Why did you ask me how long Will and I had been married, let alone whether I loved him?"

"Because I wanted to know, of course. Why else would anyone ask?"

"But that is a decision, sir, not a reason. *Why* did you want to know?"

"Do *you* never ask a question just because you want to know the answer?"

"Aye, sure, I do. But I usually know *why* I want to know even if it is only to see if the answer is what I expect it to be. Moreover, one equivocates—as you are doing now— only when one does not want to *explain* one's reason. I think you did have a reason. And you *said* that you would answer any question I asked you."

"Aye, I did," he said ruefully. "I wonder what demon caused me to make such a foolish promise."

"So, now you would forswear yourself, would you?"

"I would not. If you must know, I saw Will twice this past year in such circumstances as would normally preclude a man's having recently married."

"You saw him with other women, in fact."

"You are blunt, too. But, aye, that is so."

She shrugged as she had before to show him that she did not care what he thought of her attitude. But she feared that the effort was less successful than before. She feared, too, that he had guessed she knew of Will's unfaithfulness, and believed that it must upset her. She *had* known, because Will flaunted his infidelity, and in the past there had naturally been times of distress. Of late, though, Will's wandering ways had provided relief to her, but she could hardly say so to his imposing cousin.

"We need not stand here in this archway like two posts," Kirkhill said, putting a too familiar but comfortingly warm hand to her shoulder. "The midday meal was already in preparation when we left the kitchen, was it not?"

"Aye, the men will be in to eat shortly," she said. "You will want to refresh yourself before then, so I will summon a lad to show you to—"

"I can look after myself, my lady. But you *will* dine with me."

"You give orders very easily for one who is not yet master here," she retorted. "Why should I obey you?"

"I am hoping that your curiosity will persuade you," he

said. "Sithee, I have taken your measure now, as I think you have taken mine. I have not taken back my promise, nor will I press you to reveal aught that you do not want to tell me."

She peered into his eyes, trying to judge his sincerity. She could not do any such thing, of course, yet he did seem to meet and endure her steady gaze easily.

At last, wondering if she was making a grave mistake but as curious as he had hoped she was, if not more so, she said, "Very well then. I will dine with you."

Chapter 2 _____

Kirkhill believed in preparing himself for possible trouble, and he foresaw a spate of it ahead where her ladyship was concerned. If Old Jardine was right and Will was dead, she would not take kindly to his returning to run the Applegarth estates when the old man died.

From what he had seen so far of the lady Fiona, she would challenge his authority buckle and thong, especially where her child was concerned.

As a knight with years of experience in battle, despite the so-called truce that had been in effect between Scotland and England for the past eight years, Kirkhill had developed two basic rules for himself in preparing for battle: to learn as much as he could about his opponents and their surroundings, and to figure out the safest way to extricate himself and his men afterward.

He smiled now, trying to imagine the lady Fiona as one of those opponents.

She had gone to refresh herself before they dined, so he used the opportunity to make sure that his man, Joshua, had found suitable stabling for their horses, and to inform him that they would spend the night at Spedlins Tower.

He found Joshua brushing Cerberus, Kirkhill's favorite,

albeit rather aged, destrier. He did not normally ride Cerberus on such journeys. But, having no idea what sort of welcome he would get, and certain that Old Jardine would *not* welcome a tail of Seyton men-at-arms, let alone house or feed them, he had brought only the unimposing Joshua, who had long served as his equerry and squire, and Cerberus, who was still as good in a fight as nearly any man Kirkhill knew.

Joshua might easily have found another position as a knight's equerry, but when Kirkhill had said he would welcome his continued service at home, Joshua had said amiably that such a post would suit him fine.

Now the wiry, bristle-haired Joshua eyed Kirkhill quizzically as Cerberus blew a welcoming snuffle and nosed him, seeking an apple.

Stroking the black beast's soft nose as he gave it the apple he had taken from a basket in the hall, Kirkhill said, "I see that you found good stabling, Joshua."

"Och, aye, 'tis well enough," Joshua said. "Mind your hand, though. The lad be feeling a mite testy, and ye dinna want to lose it."

"You know gey well that he has not nipped me since he was a colt," Kirkhill said. "I'm guessing that you are the one who feels testy. What's amiss?"

"Nowt. But ye dinna look like a man who's had his midday meal and means to depart straightaway. Likely, that would explain why nae one here has suggested that I might take a bite or two... of food, see you."

"Art saying that the people here lack a proper spirit of hospitality?"

Joshua, a man of few words, grimaced expressively.

"They are only now about to take their meal in the

great hall," Kirkhill said. "I came to tell you that Old Jardine has invited me to spend the night, and I mean to do so. You may come in with me now and eat your dinner with Jardine's people, or I can have someone bring you something out here if that would suit you better."

"Thank ye, sir, I'll bide here. I dinna trust these louts around our Cerberus, or even me own lad. I'm thinking I'll bed down here, too, as ye be meaning to stay."

"Shall I taste your food before I let them bring it out to you, just to be sure they have not poisoned it?" Kirkhill asked with a teasing smile.

The only reply was another expressive grimace.

"Buck up," he said. "We'll leave in the morning when I've broken my fast."

"That'll suit me, aye."

"Meantime, though, see if you can make a friend or two here, as we'll likely return when Old Jardine dies. Try to hear what his people say about young Jardine, too. He's been missing for over a fortnight."

"The young master, they call him," Joshua said. "I doubt I'll learn more than that, though. They dinna say nowt but rude comments about Sassenachs."

"And both of us born and raised Annandale men," Kirkhill said.

"Better nor most o' *them,* I'd say."

"I ken your ways fine, Joshua. By morning, I'll expect you to know all about Will Jardine. But I agree that you should also keep an eye on our beasts. Sithee, Jardine men are better known for stealing good horses and kine than for aught else."

"I'll keep our lads safe, sir."

"I know you will." With that, Kirkhill returned to

the house, wondering what Joshua would think when he learned of his master's newest charge.

⌒

Fiona had hurried upstairs to her bedchamber, determined to find at least one gown that would not embarrass her to wear. Summoning her maidservant, she said, "Do my hair in a single plait, Flory, and twist it up in that beaded net with the plain white caul that I brought with me from Annan House. For once, I want to look like Lady Will Jardine. Will's cousin, Lord Kirkhill, is dining with me at high table today, and I do *not* want him to treat me like a child."

"Nay, then, if he's a lord, he willna do that, m'lady," the plump, rosy-cheeked Flory said reassuringly.

"Mayhap he will not, but I've not cared about how I have looked for months, especially since I got so fat with the bairn. Today, I want to look tidy, at least."

"Ye'll look gey fine, m'lady. That sky-blue kirtle we furbished up wi' the lace from Master Will's mam's old gowns looks right nice on ye."

"You must dine at high table with us, Flory."

"I canna do that, m'lady. Old Master would learn of it straightaway, and it dinna bear thinking what he'd do to me, or tell that devil Hod to do."

"Then you must serve me at table," Fiona said. "Old Jardine will not mind that. He will just say that I am putting on airs, but I do not want to dine on the dais alone with his lordship. In troth, I doubt that Old Jardine would like that any better than he'd like you sitting with us, for all that he's had any number of thieves and rascals sit at that table with *him,* not caring a whit that I was dining there, too."

"He'd no like ye dining alone wi' his lordship, nae matter what he does hisself," Flory said. "Nor would Master Will like that neither."

A shiver shot up Fiona's spine at the thought of Will's reaction just to her concern for her appearance while she *prepared* to dine with Kirkhill. But she quickly decided that, having failed to show himself in over a fortnight, Will was unlikely to arrive in time for the midday meal. She did wish that he would show up at some point, though, if only to prove that she had not killed him.

On the other hand, she would not grieve if he failed to return, especially if his absence was a natural result of his own customary behavior.

She would not say as much to Flory, though. The maidservant knew her better than anyone else at Spedlins and was the only person there that Fiona trusted. But some things one did not confide to any servant, no matter how close and trustworthy she might be.

Fiona was soon ready to go downstairs, and Flory declared herself ready after tucking a few straying blond curls under her cap, so they went down together.

Kirkhill, already at the high table, stood as they approached the dais.

Introducing Flory to him, Fiona added, "She has served my sister and me since our childhood, sir. She followed me from Annan House when I married."

"Then I am gey pleased to meet you, Flory," Kirkhill said. "Do you dine with your mistress and me?"

"Nay, sir, the old laird wouldna like that," Flory said, blushing fiercely.

"She ought to stay on the dais with us, though, or

people will talk," Fiona said. "She can serve me. No one will object to that."

"An excellent notion, my lady. Will you take your place now? Those at the lower tables were taking seats when I entered, so I assume that this must be a day when you dispense with the grace before meat at this meal."

She said, "The Jardines dispense with it every day, sir. The men here would likely revolt if their meat were delayed just so that someone could speak words over it. They are not much interested in Holy Kirk or—" She broke off when a thought struck her. "Good sakes, though, with a name like *Kirk*hill, I expect you may be *gey* religious. If you are, then you must do as you please, of course."

He smiled. "The barony's name comes from the fact that my ancestors built their first house on a hill where a wee kirk had stood. That is to say, they thought the ruins looked like the remains of a kirk. Knowing these parts, though, it might as easily have been some pagan hill fort. Some of them did have chapels."

"Aye, Dunwythie Hall has such a chapel hill," she said. "The Hall is my father's primary seat—that is, my sister's primary seat," she amended hastily.

"I know the Hall," he said. "Dunwythie died some time ago, did he not?"

"Just two years ago," she said quietly.

Silence fell between them as gillies began carving the meat and serving the food. Noting scarcely veiled looks from the men at the lower tables, and seeing two of the women and Jeb's Wee Davy peeping through the service stair archway, Fiona felt more vulnerable than usual, sitting there with Kirkhill. She knew the men were muttering about her. Some did not even bother to lower their voices.

The silence at the high table grew heavy before Kirk-hill said abruptly, "Do you not usually dine at this table, my lady?"

"I did before my husband vanished and Old Jardine got so sick," she said. "Since then, I've taken my meals with Flory in the ladies' solar. It lies on the other side of the north wall, to our right, as does the inner chamber. But one cannot enter the solar from here. It opens off the landing, where the porter can keep watch."

Scarcely sparing more than a glance that way, he said, "But there *are* other women here, for I saw them. I saw the children who listened to your stories, too."

"Aye, sure, servant women and their bairns," she said. "But the few women who agree to serve inside stay in the kitchen with their bairns and do not eat with the men. The men prefer it that way, and so do the women, come to that."

"I see. Then I expect you will continue that practice when I leave."

"I'd have continued it today, had you not commanded otherwise."

Silence overcame them again until he said, "A number of those men seem to be looking this way too often for civility. Some even seem to be discussing us."

"Sakes, sir, you are not my good-father's sole confi-dant. He has expressed his view of my husband's disap-pearance to any who will listen to him. Doubtless, most of them believe that I murdered Will. If they are talking of aught else, it is to debate whether you might have done it instead, or have taken a hand to aid me."

"I see." A grim note touched his voice, making her look quickly at him.

Kirkhill was angrier with himself than with anyone else, because he knew he ought to have realized earlier that rumors would be flying and would be more prevalent at Applegarth than anywhere else. That he had not was no one's fault but his. Distrusting Old Jardine's idea of hospitality as he had, he had ridden Cerberus and brought only Joshua instead of his usual tail. But he had failed to learn all he could about Jardine's estates and his people simply because the old man *had* invited him and Applegarth was not enemy territory—and also because of the fine line that existed between gleaning helpful information and encouraging gossip.

Kirkhill loathed gossip, and his people knew it. If he wanted to know what his neighbors were saying, he would ask. Otherwise, he did not want to hear it.

Moreover, because of his mother's connection to the Jardines, his people at Kirkhill were less likely to gossip about what went on at Spedlins Tower than almost anywhere else. He had not even asked Joshua if *he* had heard news of the place before they'd traveled south. Nor would he have done so before he had visited Applegarth and gained an impression of the place for himself.

After hearing Jardine accuse the lady Fiona of Will's murder, Kirkhill now realized, he had dismissed the notion as absurd. Had he considered the likely impact of Will's continued absence and such an accusation on her ladyship, he would easily have deduced that she might be the subject of vicious gossip. The plain fact was that he had not thought beyond wanting to get better acquainted with her before he left, to show her that he was not an ogre who meant to disrupt her life.

The initial silence between them at the table had surprised him, because she had found it easy to talk with him earlier and to say whatever came into her head. Now, sitting beside him, she stared at her trencher except when sipping her ale or politely accepting or rejecting the dishes that Flory offered her.

"I owe you another apology," he said quietly. "I did not expect your own household to treat you with such hostility."

"I told you I ought not to dine with you. You should have listened to me."

"I should have," he agreed, meeting her gaze and this time enjoying the startled look in her eyes. Her face was not only beautiful but also expressive. He wondered how it would express itself in the throes of— Cutting off that thought, he said, "Would you be more comfortable if we left now?"

"Nay!" She looked even more startled, but the look quickly shifted to one of annoyance, perhaps even anger. "If we were to walk out so soon, it would only give people more reason to talk."

"I will pay better heed to such things when I return, my lady," he said. "I promise you that."

~

Fiona did not bother trying to explain to him how little promises were worth to her, men's promises in particular. She focused on the Jardine men's behavior.

"Do you think I run from their scorn and mockery?" she demanded. "See you, only a few of them still treat me so. I was but fifteen when Will married me, and they had cause to scorn me then, for I was young and silly. I knew naught of running a household like this one, with a master like Old Jardine."

"Few people, male or female, would know how to do that," he said.

She gave him a look, wondering if he was patronizing her. She did not like men who treated her like a fool any more than the ones who treated her like a child.

"I did learn to fend for myself," she said stiffly.

"I am sure that you did."

He *was* a bit patronizing. On the other hand, he was listening to what she was saying, which was something of a novelty for her where men were concerned.

She swallowed lingering irritation and said, "Their women and children like me. So, for the most part, the men here behaved better until Will disappeared. But they pattern their behavior on that of their master. To them, even before, I was the young master's wife, no more. Now I'm most likely the witch who killed him."

"Surely, your parents—"

"My father is dead, as you know. You mentioned his death yourself."

"I did, aye. But I was going to say that surely, at the time of your marriage, he made arrangements to ensure that the Jardines would treat you well."

Her cheeks burned, and she looked away, unwilling to meet his steady gaze as she said, "My father died *before* my marriage, so he was not involved in it at all. In troth, I prefer not to talk about that time in my life. Why do you not tell me about your family? Recall that you promised not to quiz me whilst we ate."

"I do recall, and I will tell you all about my family if you like," he said. "However, I would like you to answer just one more question first."

Reluctantly, she nodded.

"From what you've said, I'd guess that your father died about the same time you married," he said, making her stomach clench so that the bairn within her moved sharply in protest. "Did Will Jardine have aught to do with his death?"

The question was not one she had expected. Will did bear some of the blame, but much as she would have liked to blame him for all of it, she could not.

"Will Jardine is guilty of many things, sir," she said. "But not that. And, although I am nearly certain that I had naught to do with *his* death, I *am* responsible for my father's. Now, if you will permit me, I shall bid you goodnight."

As she moved to stand, Kirkhill put a hand on her forearm and said, "Nay, do not go. Turn as if you mean to speak to Flory—order some wine if my uncle keeps any in the house—or you will just draw more of the very attention you dislike."

To his relief, she settled back onto her stool with a slight gesture of her free hand to the maidservant, who came swiftly to her in response.

"What will ye, m'lady?"

"Prithee, have one of the lads fetch us some claret," Fiona said.

When Flory motioned one of the gillies over and relayed the message, Kirkhill took his hand from Fiona's arm, confident that she would not run away.

When they had their wine, Kirkhill said quietly, "Rest easy, my lady. I don't mean to quiz you about your supposed responsibility for your father's death. Some other time we may discuss that. For now, I seek only to learn if these louts might accuse you of wanting vengeance because of aught that Will did. So, sip your wine and tell me where your mother resides."

"I am not sure where she is," Fiona said. "My family does not visit, nor have I seen any of them since my marriage. My good-brother and Hugh Douglas did come to Spedlins once, but Will and I had gone riding, so I did not see them. Old Jardine said he told them not to set foot on his land again, nor have they. My sister, Mairi, and her husband do stay at Dunwythie Hall at least part of each year, but they do not come here."

He saw Flory open her mouth and shut it again.

"Flory, do you ken aught of Lady Dunwythie?"

"Our lady Mairi be Dunwythie o' Dunwythie now," Flory said. "A baroness in her own right, she be. So, see you, when one talks o' *Lady* Dunwythie—"

"I do see, aye," he said. "I was speaking of the lady Fiona's mother."

Flory glanced at Fiona, then back at him. "Folks hereabouts do call her the lady Phaeline, m'lord. I did hear two o' the men say that she were at the Hall. But she doesna visit here. The old master willna let any o' them do that."

"Thank you, Flory," Kirkhill said. "As soon we have had leisure to drink our wine, we will adjourn to another chamber, I think."

"My lord," Fiona said, "if you would talk more with me, pray do so here. The only other chamber where we might be private is the ladies' solar, but it shares a wall with the inner chamber, so Jardine's Hod would hear us there. Old Jardine would dislike any privy talk between us now, and *you* will soon be gone."

He pondered those last words. Surely, she did not fear the old man in his present sickly state. But he could not cross-question her. He had already broken his promise not to quiz her further—more than once.

"We will stay here as long as you think we should," he said. "Shall I tell you about my sisters? I am cursed with three of them."

"Cursed?"

He had diverted her thoughts, just as he had hoped. And, as he described for her the burdens of two older and one much younger sister upon an only son, he saw her begin to relax and enjoy her wine.

"As you are *Lord* Kirkhill, your father must be dead, just as mine is," she said when he paused. "Is your mother still living?"

"Aye."

"Is she such a burden to you, also?" she asked with a smile.

"Do you think that I find all women burdensome?"

"Good sakes, how should I know? You will surely find me a nuisance, and doubtless, running the Applegarth estates and Spedlins Tower a nuisance as well. But you did not answer my question," she added with a direct look.

"It would be *most* impertinent of me to declare my lady mother a burden," he said with a virtuous air. Then, with a wry smile, he added, "Forbye, she is the most submissive of creatures, so one would have to be truly unkind to think her a nuisance."

"Do you mean to say that she submits to your every whim and decree without ever a protest?"

"Aye, *and* submits to anyone else who voices a whim or decree," he said. "She is quite the most obliging woman I know."

"God-a-mercy!" Her gaze met his, doubtful at first and then with a most endearing twinkle. "Do you know," she said confidingly, "I almost believe that you deserve such a mother. Does she *never* make a decision of her own?"

"Never," he said, delighted that she had so quickly caught his meaning and wondering at himself for enjoying such delight at his mother's expense.

"I have met women like that," Fiona said. "Certain friends of my mother's let others make every decision for them, rather than expressing their own preferences. However," she added, "*your* mother grew up as Old Jardine's sister, so one can at least sympathize with *her* and understand why she is as she is. Old Jardine disparages *any* decision that he does not make himself, and they say his father was the same. Imagine how horrid always to have lived with such men!"

"You have lived with such men for two years," he said, realizing that he had never stopped to think about *why* his mother so adamantly refused to express her opinions. It had simply irritated him that she would never do so.

"I've lived here only two years," Fiona said. "Just imagine, if you can, what I'd have been like after twenty or *fifty* years of living with the Jardines." She shuddered and gave herself a shake, as if she, too, were thinking a thought that she had not considered before and was not sure she wanted to ponder any further now.

Deciding that a change of subject was in order, he

described his home to her and then told her about his favorite uncle.

"Uncle James was a dashing knight in his youth and is still a great charmer, but he married young, lost his wife three years later, and has never remarried."

"Oh, how sad," Fiona said. "My cousin Jenny's father could never face marrying again lest he lose the second wife, too. He was also gey shy," she added.

"Uncle James is *not* shy," Kirkhill said with a smile. "Nor is he sunk in misery. He is always paying court to some wealthy noblewoman or other, but he says marriage would kill the fun of courting, so his affairs come to naught."

"Aye, well, mayhap he will meet someone who will change his mind. Does he live at Kirkhill, too?"

"Nay, for he acquired land in eastern Lothian with his knighthood. He does visit us often, and *he* always has opinions to offer me."

"I am sure he provides good advice." She glanced around. "We have stayed long enough, I think. I will take my leave now with Flory, if you will permit me."

She raised her eyebrows as if she were uncertain that he *would* permit it, but he could think of no good reason to keep her. Accordingly, he nodded, thinking he probably looked much as his father might have looked in such a situation.

The thought touched his sense of humor, and he knew he must have revealed as much, because she said sharply, "What is it? Why do you look at me so?"

"'Tis nowt, my lady. I was just feeling a bit paternal, and the realization that I have no cause to do so made me feel foolish."

"Well, you do seem a trifle patronizing at times. In troth, if you treat your youngest sister as you tend to treat me, I feel for her most sincerely."

"Nan is *much* younger than you are."

"I thought you said she was fifteen!"

"Aye, and so she is," he said.

"I am but seventeen, sir, hardly an ancient crone!"

"I expect that marriage matures a woman. My sister is still a maiden."

"You are right to say that marriage ages one," she said with a sigh as she rose to take her leave of him.

He stood, wanting to explain that he hadn't meant any such thing. However, his sister was nothing like the lady Fiona. The two seemed decades apart to him.

Bidding Fiona goodnight, he watched until she stepped off the dais but knew better than to watch her all the way to the stair hall. He would have to start treating her as if he were her grandfather. Anything else would doubtless stir more rumors.

Nevertheless, he had begun to think that accepting Old Jardine's charge was likely to prove more interesting than he had thought, and more of a trial as well.

For the rest of the day, she lingered in his thoughts, but he did not see her again. Nor did he see Jardine or learn much rambling about the yard and stables, other than that there had once been a gated barmkin wall around the tower, which had long since fallen to ruin. The lass even visited him in his dreams that night:

She was slender and laughing, joyous and warm, silky to his touch. Her extraordinary eyes twinkled with delight as her kirtle and shift changed to soft, warm skin beneath his exploring fingertips, inciting every sense to pure lust until the image of Will Jardine rose up, snarling louder than Old Jardine's mastiff had.

Kirkhill's eyes flew open to the reassuring sight of a crescent moon shining through a nearby open window. Lust still flamed through him, but the impropriety of such a dream in the face of his forthcoming duties soon dampened it.

The next morning, when he joined Joshua to take leave of Spedlins, the equerry said as they mounted, "'Tis glad I'll be to see the last o' this place."

"Only for a time, though. Recall that we return when Old Jardine dies."

"Aye, sure, but I did hear that if young Will be dead, ye'll take charge o' the place," Joshua replied. "Ye'll ha' nae cause then to leave our usual tail at home."

"I'll bring them, never fear," Kirkhill said. He had already decided that much, because only a fool would try to assume command at Spedlins—Old Jardine's will or not—without numerous trusted men to support him. "What else did you learn?"

"Nowt o' value," Joshua said. "'Tis plain that the men here canna say what became o' the young master. I heard only that he and his lady had been fratching. They went for a walk, still a-fratching, and nae one has seen young Will since."

"Did no one search for him?"

"Aye, sure, but no till late the next day. See you, it were a habit wi' the man to go off on his own when he were fashed like, so nae one took heed at first."

"I see," Kirkhill said, although he did not see anything useful or new in the information. Old Jardine had told him the lass was the last one to see Will.

"I wager we'll be home afore midday if we set a good pace," Joshua said a short time later.

"We won't be going straight home," Kirkhill said.

Joshua frowned. "Nay?"

"Nay, for I mean to stop on the way, at Dunwythie Hall."

*Chapter 3*_____

Fiona slept late and, when Flory wakened her, she sent the maidservant to fetch a manchet loaf, some sliced lamb, and ale, so that she might break her fast in her chamber. Normally, she did so at the high table in the hall after most of the men had gone outside to take up their duties. But she did not want to take any chance of meeting Kirkhill again before he left. She could not have said why she wanted to avoid him. It just seemed wiser to do so.

She need not have worried, because Flory told her when she came back with the food that his lordship had departed for home an hour earlier.

"They did say that his man had the horses ready as soon as his lordship broke his fast," Flory said. "His lordship took time only to bid the old master farewell, which the old master said was a stupid thing to wish a dying man."

Possessing none of Kirkhill's dislike for gossip, Fiona said, "Did his lordship have aught to say to that?"

Grinning, Flory said, "Hod said his lordship told the old master he might be wise to pray that he did fare well, going wherever he were a-going. Not that anyone doubts where he'll end up," Flory added. "Or where that Hod will, come to that."

Fiona knew she ought to discourage such impertinent comments, but just the thought of finding Old Jardine in heaven if she were lucky enough to get there herself was daunting enough that she just nodded in agreement.

To her surprise, she missed Kirkhill's company. Having been certain she would be grateful to see him leave and would pray that he'd never return, she realized that such was not the case, and for good reason.

The only thing that would prevent Kirkhill's return was Will's, and although she did not go so far as to hope that her husband was dead, the fact was that her marital happiness had not survived the first time Will had taken too much to drink.

Flory set the basket of bread and meat on the table near the window embrasure and said, "That Parland Dow do be in the stableyard now."

"The knacker?"

"Aye, he told Jeb's Wee Davy that he'd brung a nostrum for the old master, summat that might make him well again, Wee Davy did say."

"Does the old master know that Parland Dow is here?"

"Nay, for after his lordship left, that Hod did say nae one should rap on the door again till midday, and that Dow did say he'd no go near Old Master's snarling devil dog, any road. But I'm thinking that Hod may want to talk wi' him hisself about yon nostrum, to be sure it be safe to give the master."

"I think the only nostrum that would help him would be for Master Will to walk into his room, hale and hearty," Fiona said. "Still, someone should talk to the knacker, so I will go to him, Flory. Prithee, cover that food. I shan't be long."

"Ye'll never go down and talk to that man in the stable-yard, m'lady! There be too much talk as it be. 'Twas ever Master Will or Old Master who talked wi' him."

Fiona drew herself up and gave Flory a look. "Master Will is away and I *am* mistress here, Flory, although few choose ever to remember that. In any event, I mean to talk to the knacker. I want to know about this nostrum of his."

"Then I should go wi'—"

"Nay, you stay and tidy up in here. The knacker will not harm me. As for talk, people will talk no matter what I do."

She did not mention that the knacker would also have news. It had frustrated her that Will never allowed her to sit at the high table when the man came to call on them. He had said it was not suitable, but she was as sure as she could be that Will wanted to keep her from hearing news from home. He had said he wanted to protect her from such upset as had ensued when she learned of her father's death, and that it was his decision as her husband to tell her what she needed to know. With Will, it had been easier to submit than to risk angering him, but now...

Hurrying downstairs to the stableyard, she saw Parland Dow talking to Old Jardine's land steward, Evart, doubtless to learn what chores they might have him to do. His skills were many and varied, from butchering cattle, sheep, and aged horses to tanning the hides afterward and fixing various things. But his greatest gift, they said, was his ability to glean and share information wherever he traveled.

She had seen him two or three times a year at Annan House, where her father and even her mother had welcomed him at high table to share news with them.

Dow smiled when he saw her and doffed his battered cap. He was a wiry man with muscular arms and stood just a few inches taller than she did.

"Good day to ye, m'lady," he said, making her a sweeping bow. "How may I serve ye today?"

The steward said bluntly, "Old Master wouldna want ye out here like this, m'lady. I can see to this man."

"I'm sure you can, Evart," Fiona said. "But I want to know more about this nostrum that he has brought for the master. You may safely leave me with Parland Dow, for I have known him since my childhood. He will do me no harm."

The steward hesitated. But she stared at him until he turned away, only to look back and say, "Nae one must disturb the master, Hod said, till midday."

"I did hear that, aye," Fiona said, adding pointedly, "thank you, Evart."

He glanced at Dow as if he would say more to him but evidently decided against it, strolling into the stable instead.

"'Tis good to see ye, m'lady," Dow said. "I see that ye'll soon be a mother."

"Aye, but I want to hear news of Annan House and Dunwythie Hall, if you please. I did just learn that the lady Phaeline is staying at the Hall."

"Aye, sure," he said, "Or so they tell me. They do say her coming surprised everyone, because she does prefer the view o' the Firth from Annan House to that o' the river Annan from the Hall. Mayhap she just wants to see that all is in order for the lady Mairi's return to Annandale next month."

"Mairi is coming so soon?"

"Aye, before the end o' July wi' her husband, the Laird o' Trailinghail, and doubtless their bairn as well. Sithee, they do live at the Hall most o' the year now. They spent a month at Annan House last winter and a fortnight again in April, afore they left again for Trailinghail. That be his lordship's estate in Galloway."

"I do remember that, aye," Fiona said, as an image of Robert Maxwell rose in her mind. She had teased Mairi about him when the man had visited the Hall with Will. That had been the first time either had laid eyes on the two men and the only time Fiona had seen Maxwell. Certainly, neither she nor Mairi had thought they were meeting their future husbands that day.

"The baroness and her lord husband mean to return to celebrate Lammas here, same as they did last year," Dow told her. "That be the first o' August."

"Did they do so last year? No one told me."

He frowned. "Someone *ought* to ha' told ye, m'lady."

"Did you say they have a child?"

"Aye, sure, a braw little lad they named Thomas after your lord father."

"Do you go up the dale from here or down?" she asked next.

"I ha' come from Annan, m'lady. I mean to visit the Hall from here."

She looked around and saw no one near enough to overhear her. "Then, prithee, would you take a message from me to the lady Phaeline?"

"I would, aye," he said, nodding. "What would ye have me say to her?"

Fiona had not thought that far ahead. What could she say after two years of silence? She wanted to say she was sorry, that she had made a dreadful mistake, but surely, one did not confide such personal messages to the knacker. She could write a little if she could acquire the necessary materials, but she had never seen such items at Spedlins. Moreover, if they existed, they were in Old Jardine's chamber.

At last, she said, "Prithee, tell her that we are...that is, that I am in good health here and...and hope she is the same," she said at last. "Now, perhaps you had better tell me about this nostrum you have brought for my good-father."

Kirkhill had not visited Dunwythie Hall before. He thought it an imposing pile, perched as it was atop a low hill overlooking a sharp bend in the river Annan. Woodland covered the base of the hill, but the woods ended well short of the high curtain wall, and the round castle keep was tall enough to command a panoramic view of the Roman road a mile away and any other possible approach.

No one could get near it from the river at this time of year, because the Annan tumbled in a heavy, frothy boil down to the Solway Firth, some fifteen miles or more to the south. He knew of a ford north of the castle and another one south of Spedlins Tower, both doubtless well guarded in these days of recurring unrest.

As he and Joshua approached the tall gates, Joshua drew ahead to announce him to the guardsmen on the wall-walk above. The name Kirkhill of Kirkhill was sufficient. The gate swung slowly open, and they rode into the yard.

Gillies came running to meet them and see to their horses.

As Kirkhill dismounted, he said to the most senior of them, "Prithee, inform your porter that I should like a word with her ladyship if it is convenient for her to receive me. Tell him also that I have ridden here from Spedlins Tower."

"Aye, me lord, I'll tell him straightaway if ye'll come wi' me. Our baker has fresh buns on the hob if your man there would like one. One o' these other lads will show him round to the kitchen."

Kirkhill glanced at Joshua, who had dismounted, and knew that he would likely learn more in the kitchen than Kirkhill would in the great hall or solar.

After consultation between the obliging gillie and the porter at the door, the latter escorted him to a pleasant chamber with sunlight streaming through two tall, narrow, southeast-facing windows. Announcing him to the lady Phaeline, the porter added briskly that his lordship had come to them from Applegarth.

Phaeline Dunwythie sat on a cushioned bench in the window embrasure to his left, but she rose gracefully to her feet and curtsied as he made his bow. "I knew your father, my lord," she said in a lilting voice similar to her daughter's. "That is to say, I knew the late Lord Kirkhill and assume that you must be his son."

When he assented, smiling, she added, "I believe that I have met your lady mother, too, although I confess that I do not recall her as well."

Her eyes were darker blue than her daughter's, but he could not tell if her hair was as dark and glossy, because the lady Phaeline followed prevailing fashion for plucking out every facial hair, right up to the edge of her beaded caul.

She wore plenty of jewelry after the fashion in the Borders, where women wore most of what they owned to declare their husbands' wealth or—more likely in these lean days—their sad lack of it. He recalled then that she was a Douglas and kinswoman of both the Earl of Douglas and Archie the Grim, Lord of Galloway.

He would have recognized her easily as Fiona's mother, although she looked to be no older than perhaps five-and-thirty and had retained much of her own youthful good looks. Her face was plumper than Fiona's, her chin more rounded, and her hands were plumper, too. But she was still a notable beauty.

She said, "Won't you take a seat, sir, and tell me what brings you to us."

Blinking, he pushed memories of Fiona away and concentrated on her mother. Pulling up a back-stool, he sat, saying with a smile, "I thought you might like to have word of your daughter, my lady."

"My porter did say that you came here from Applegarth. Do you mean to say that you *saw* our Fiona?"

"I did, aye."

"Faith, sir, you are the first person I have met who owns to having done so. I had begun to think they must keep her locked up in Spedlins Tower. My good-son, Robert Maxwell, and my brother, Sir Hugh Douglas, rode there shortly after Fiona was taken. But Old Jardine spun them a tale—said Fiona and Will had gone riding. As anyone can tell you, if that *were* the case, she would have got word to me or to her sister straightaway afterward. But never a word have we had from her."

"You said 'taken,' madam," Kirkhill said with a frown. "Do you mean to say that Will Jardine abducted the lady Fiona?"

"I am sure that he must have," Phaeline said. "See you, Rob Maxwell has never denied that *he* abducted our Mairi, *which* he did! Moreover, he and Will were friends then and met both of my daughters when they called on my husband here together, so clearly Will Jardine *must* have got the notion from Rob."

"That must have been difficult for you," he said. "Two daughters abducted at much the same time, and losing your husband as you did—gey suddenly, I believe."

"It was horrid," she said with a sigh. "Such a shock for my lord . . . first Mairi, and then just a month later, our dearling Fiona. I regret to say that *he* believed Fiona had run off with Will Jardine . . . eloped with him, in fact. He even dismissed her maidservant, insisting that the girl had helped Fiona meet Will secretly."

"Was the maidservant's name Flory, perhaps?"

Phaeline's eyes widened. "Have you seen her, too, then?"

"Aye, for she still serves her ladyship, even now."

Phaeline was silent, apparently digesting that information, before she said, "Then my lord may have been right. He did say that Flory had admitted aiding Fiona, and he was not a man to tell falsehoods. But I did not want to believe him. Still, if she did elope with that scoundrel and marry him of her own free will, why did she not come home for her father's burial? Or get in touch with me since or with our Mairi, who spends much of each year right here at Dunwythie Hall?"

"That I cannot tell you, my lady, for she told me only that Dunwythie died before she married," Kirkhill said.

"Aye, well, he died the evening of the very day she left," Phaeline said. "He collapsed whilst he was summoning horses and men to fetch her back."

"I do think Fiona would like to see you," Kirkhill said, suspecting that he now understood why the lass blamed herself for her father's death. "You must have heard by now that Will Jardine is missing. Old Jardine believes he must be dead."

"I shan't mourn his loss if he is, or that of any Jardine," she said. "But unless Old Jardine is also dead, his men will not permit any of our people on his land."

"He is not dead, but he is gey sick, so I think he soon will be," Kirkhill said.

"Forgive me, sir, but what has any of this to do with you?"

"Old Jardine sent for me," Kirkhill said. "As you may know, my mother is his sister, and he wants me to learn what became of Will." He did not think it wise then to tell her that Old Jardine had also named him guardian of her forthcoming grandchild, protector of his estates, and trustee for her daughter.

"Do you think you *can* find out what became of Will Jardine?"

"Someone will, in time. You should know, too, if you do not, that the lady Fiona is big with child," he said.

Phaeline's pale cheeks grew delicately pink. "I did hear about that," she admitted. Then, in what was clearly a burst of unaccustomed personal candor, she said, "'Tis, in troth, why I made the journey here. I...I was hoping that I might hear from her if I stayed nearby at such a time."

"Mayhap you will," he said. "At all events, someone

will send for me when Old Jardine dies. I will take a message to her for you then if you like."

She agreed, and he took his leave, finding Joshua in the yard with a bag of warm bannocks.

"I thought ye'd be ready to leave by now," Joshua said. "They be a-fetching out our horses straightaway. And I ha' summat for ye to munch on the way."

"I hope you've collected information as well as the food," Kirkhill said, accepting a still-warm bun.

"I learned some things, aye," Joshua said. He said no more until they were on the road, heading north. Then, without prompting, he said, "The baroness, Lady Dunwythie of Dunwythie, be married to Maxwell o' Trailinghail, who be likewise brother o' the Sheriff o' Dumfries. *He* would be the same villain who were making such a stir two years ago about his right to govern all the dales o' Dumfriesshire, instead o' just his rightful jurisdiction o' Dumfries and the rest o' Nithsdale."

Kirkhill, like most noblemen in Annandale, knew that the sheriff's efforts had failed, in large part due to the efforts of the late Lord Dunwythie. Dunwythie's ancestors having been hereditary stewards of Annandale, his lordship had taken understandable umbrage at the sheriff's attempt to usurp his proper authority.

Kirkhill said, "Once a man grows hungry for power, he rarely loses his taste for it. Mayhap he expects his brother to exert influence with Baroness Dunwythie."

"That's as may be," Joshua said. "Robert Maxwell's land be in Galloway, though. *I'm* thinking that he'll take good care no to stir up Archie Douglas."

Already Lord of Galloway, the appropriately named Archie the Grim had declared his intent to control all of southwest Scotland, as his cousin, the Earl of Douglas, controlled the Scottish Borders. The Douglases were more powerful than the royal Stewarts were, so Kirkhill agreed that Rob Maxwell would tread carefully.

Even so, if Kirkhill had understood the lady Phaeline, and the sheriff's brother had *abducted* the lady Mairi before wedding her, the Maxwells might still hope to force her to influence her neighbors in Annandale.

As Kirkhill finished his tasty bun, he recalled that Fiona had also mentioned her cousin Jenny, Baroness Easdale, who had married Hugh Douglas of Thornhill. So the Dunwythies had more than one strong tie to Clan Douglas, and he knew Hugh.

As Dunwythie Hall vanished into the distance behind him, Kirkhill reminded himself that kinships were complex and politics even more so. Pondering that reality as he and Joshua continued to talk, he realized that having bowed to Old Jardine's will, he might soon find himself bemired in conflict from all sides. In any event, it behooved him to learn more about the Dunwythies *and* the Jardines.

Meantime, he had a few kinship issues of his own to settle at home. He just hoped that he could get the primary one resolved before Old Jardine's promised messenger arrived to demand his return to Applegarth.

Fiona had spent most of her morning as she usually did, making sure that the kitchen ran smoothly, so that Old Jardine would not complain that his midday meal was late or inedible. Before adjourning to the solar to take her own meal there with Flory, she retired to her bedchamber to tidy herself.

As she entered the room, a pain gripped her lower back, and she reached quickly to try to ease it with her hands. It lasted only a half minute or so, but she wondered if she or the bairn had suffered more injury.

She had felt heavy and cumbersome for a sennight or more and wished the babe would make its appearance. A hefty kicker, it was doubtless healthy, but the thought of its coming was both wondrous and terrifying. She knew naught about babies or birthing. Even so, she looked forward eagerly to its arrival.

She had no sooner shut the door behind her and taken a step toward the bed than another pain came. It was stronger, lasted longer, and took no ease from the hand she put to the small of her back.

As she drew a breath and let it out, the door opened and Flory entered.

"What's amiss, m'lady?" she demanded at once.

"Nobbut an ache in my back," Fiona said. "But I'm carrying this great weight in front of me, so doubtless my back has a right to complain."

"Aye, well, one o' the women did say she had pains in her back for more than a fortnight afore one o' her bairns came," Flory said wisely. "I ha' nae doots it be summat natural and nowt to fret over, but I can rub it for ye if ye like."

"It has gone now. But, Flory, do you really think you know enough about such things? How can you? You told me yourself that although you have a younger sister, you were not at home when she was born."

"I never *seen* nowt about it, but I ha' been asking Jeb's Jane and Eliza, and any other woman who will talk o' such things to tell me all I must know. All o' them ken summat about it—them what ha' bairns, any road. How hard can it be, if folks ha' been birthing bairns ever since there ha' been folks? Ye do be looking pale though. Mayhap that Lord Kirkhill did upset ye more than we knew."

"Nay, why should he? I am just tired, that's all. It is hard at night to find a comfortable way to sleep. No sooner do I find one than the wee one starts kicking me, so I'm sure it must be a lad. No lass would kick so hard."

"Then ye should rest after ye ha' your dinner," Flory said. "Your mam did rest often whenever she were with child, nigh onto every afternoon, she did."

"I don't like to rest in the daytime," Fiona said. She did not elaborate, but the fact was that she tended to dream when she napped, and her dreams too often replayed the little she did remember about her last night with Will.

"Ye do ha' bad dreams, I ken that fine," Flory said, gazing steadily at her.

Sighing, Fiona said, "I have not told you about that night, because I do not like to talk about it. But you must have heard that Master Will and I argued."

"Aye, sure," Flory said with a grimace. "I hear far too often from his own louts what *they* think. But they be fools and rascals, every one, so dinna ye be listening to their blethers, m'lady. They dinna ken nowt."

"No more do I," Fiona said. "I cannot even tell you how I got back to this room that night."

"Hoots, ye never said *that* much to me about it afore now."

Fiona sighed. "I did not tell anyone, because . . . Sithee, when I awoke, I was alone in that bed of mine and Master Will's, and . . ." She hesitated.

"Ye told me as I came in that ye'd just wakened, and

ye asked where Master Will was," Flory said. "Ye nearly always do that, though, whether he has been a-sleeping wi' ye or no. That morning it were the same. What were no the same were them bruises on your face and your ears being all red, as they were…and—"

"And pain all through the rest of me, too," Fiona said. "I remember how you looked when you saw all the bruises. But you did not even ask me about them."

"I didna ha' to ask," Flory said. "It were no the first time, after all."

"Nay, it was not," Fiona agreed. "Then you said that no one had seen Will, that he must have gone out gey early. And you tried to help me dress."

"Aye, but though ye insisted on getting up, ye could scarcely move," Flory said with a reminiscent grimace.

"Because my head hurt so, and my side. Sithee, he had hit me there, too."

"Sakes, me lady, I could *see* what he'd done," Flory said, turning abruptly away to open a kist near the service door. As she bent over it, sorting through the clothing inside, she added, "I could see how much he'd hurt ye and that ye were fretting that he might ha' hurt the bairn, too. But the way that wee one were a-kicking ye, we decided he were fine. Ye, though…ye were none so fine. Sakes, but ye still be a-trying to hide how much he did hurt ye."

"I could not and cannot let on to Old Jardine," Fiona explained. "He would say I'd deserved it, because he always takes Will's part. Moreover, he would have gone on and on about it whenever he got the chance. Will can do no wrong."

"According to the old master only," Flory muttered.

"Aye, but then, when Will stayed away, Old Jardine

began to suggest that I'd done something to him. I didn't dare tell him then how much Will had hurt me. I know he's just worried about Will. But when he quizzed me about what happened, I could not bring myself to talk about it. I still don't want to."

"Well, ye needna talk to me about it," Flory said. "I ken all I need to ken. Ye did nowt to harm a hair on that man's head, although God kens fine he'd ha' deserved it if ye'd clouted him a good one afore he clouted ye."

"I do wish I could recall how I got to bed," Fiona admitted.

"Sakes, ye were out o' your head! Where else would ye go?"

Fiona did not answer. The recurring dream she had suffered sporadically since that night had never proceeded beyond the moment of her unconsciousness. Never before had she considered that she might somehow, unknowingly, have got up after Will had knocked her down, and walked back inside to their bedchamber.

Kirkhill arrived home late that afternoon as clouds gathered in the western sky. He loved the approach to the house, the way the steep track emerged from woodland to reveal the sprawling edifice set in the high meadow amidst lush grass and wildflowers. Behind it, cliffs rose in the distance, over one of which the picturesque waterfall called Cat Linn tumbled all year long to feed a nearby burn.

The weather was clearly still trying to decide if the long winter had entirely relinquished its hold on the land to spring. By the time he and Joshua rode into the courtyard at Kirkhill House, gray clouds hid the sun and the air had turned decidedly chilly.

Nevertheless, his welcome was warmer than expected, for as he dismounted, two men emerged from the house to greet him. One was many years older than he, the other two years younger. Both were broad-shouldered and brawny.

Kirkhill was not noticeably delighted to see either one.

"What the devil are you doing here, Tony?" he demanded of the younger one, who was grinning at him. "And, you, Uncle James! Was I expecting you?"

"Nay, then, you ken fine that you were not," Sir James Seyton declared jovially as he strode down the steps to shake hands. His fair hair showed touches of gray, but his powerful body was still that of a man ever ready for battle. "When young Tony here gave me the good news about his forthcoming betrothal to our Nan, I decided to ride here with him to help everyone celebrate in proper style."

Kirkhill shot a menacing look at his hitherto longtime best friend, Sir Antony MacCairill, saying, "I fear that Tony presupposes a happy outcome, sir. We have barely begun to negotiate."

The dark-haired, dark-eyed MacCairill met his stern gaze blandly.

A fierce feminine voice from the shadows of the entryway behind MacCairill declared, "*Your* friend Tony hopes for an outcome that will *never* come to pass!"

Kirkhill's youngest sister, the fifteen-year-old lady Anne Seyton, followed her declaration into the open. Arms akimbo, she glowered at Kirkhill.

Watching her, he said sourly, "I do not suppose it will

do any good to point out that you ought not to be out here without our mother or your maidservant, Nan."

"None at all," the fair-haired, green-eyed damsel declared. "I am gey happy to see *you,* however, Dickon, because mayhap if *you* tell Tony I won't have him, he will not inflict his presence on us overnight."

Kirkhill, sighing deeply, almost missed hearing Joshua's low-voiced, "Welcome home, sir."

Chapter 4 _____

Kirkhill House, having begun as a small dwelling, had grown over its two centuries to a sprawling, rather confusing tumble of rooms and vast chambers to which its various owners had added as it suited their whims and income.

Kirkhill's family had descended from a good-brother of Robert the Bruce's who ended unhappily on the gallows. Thus, they had long valued privacy, and their home in the secluded, burn-fed declivity in upper Annandale, near the line dividing it from Eskdale, had provided privacy, more often than not allowing them to avoid depredations of reivers and English raiders, and other military upheaval.

At present, however, his lordship felt overrun with unwanted visitors. Shepherding his sister, his uncle, and his erstwhile best friend inside to the great hall, the oldest and largest chamber in the house, he noted with pleased anticipation the wafting aroma of roasted meat that presaged their approaching supper hour.

He did not suppose, as Nan had, however, that he would rid himself of his visitors quickly. In truth, he was relieved to see his uncle.

Therefore, he suggested to the two gentlemen that they

prepare themselves for supper and then join Lady Kirkhill, whom he assumed would by then be in her solar, awaiting the proper moment to take her place at the high table.

"Be a good chap, Uncle James, and first tell my lady mother that if I find time I shall see her before we sup. However, Joshua and I ate little more than bread and cheese for our midday meal, so I do not want to delay supper. Nan, I do want a word with *you* before I change my clothes," he added sternly.

"Aye, sure," his sister replied. "Shall we talk here?"

"We will not," he said, putting a hand to her elbow. "I want to be more private than this with you."

"Art furious that I was rude to Tony, Dickon?" she asked as she walked with him to the stairway. "Sithee, he deserves rudeness, declaring to Uncle James that we are to be married and bringing him here as he did. I don't *want* Tony, Dickon, and I know you will not be so cruel as to force me to marry him."

"I won't force you to do what you don't want to do, Nannie," he said, using her childhood nickname. "But you are gey young, so neither will I let you spurn such an eligible offer without due consideration. Let us use Mam's sitting room," he said then, pushing open the door to the quiet chamber that his mother used only when she was ill and did not want to risk the narrow, twisting, stone stairway.

Nan passed him with a near flounce. "We can use any room you want," she said. "But you will not persuade me, Dickon. Tony wants everything to be his own way and believes that he is all that is great and wise. Moreover, he wants me only because I'm *your* sister, and he thinks it will benefit him to link his family with ours."

"Wherever did you get that notion?" Kirkhill demanded. "And *where* did you get that gown?" he added when she whirled grandly to face him and the silk scarf that she had carefully pinned across her bodice slipped aside to reveal a décolletage so low that her pert young breasts threatened to pop right out of it.

Looking down at herself, she wrinkled her nose. "Is it too low? Mam was afraid you might not like it, but I was sure that Tony would. I think it will do him good to see what he disdains to appreci—"

"That will do," Kirkhill said quietly, but in a tone that made her eyes widen.

She swallowed visibly but knew him well enough to keep still.

"I can see that you did not expect me to return so soon, Nan," he went on. "But openly teasing a man with your body is not behavior that I want to see in my sister or, indeed, in any woman bearing the Seyton name."

"Then I shan't do it again," she said. "But neither will I marry him, Dickon. You must reconcile yourself to that, for it is plain fact. You told me long ago that I might choose where I wed, and our lady mother has said the same thing. I know that Tony is your friend and that you think he will suit me, but—"

"You will not find anyone more suitable unless you were thinking perhaps of the royal family, Nan. I hope you have not set your sights on one of our royal earls."

Again, she wrinkled her nose. "Don't be a dafty! They are horrid, all of them. But there are other men in Scotland, even men with Tony's impressive lineage and ability to support me. I mean to be expensive, however, and he told me that his father still controls the MacCairill purse strings. So I would have to ask him—Tony, that is—before I could buy anything or order clothes made for me."

"Just as you have to ask me now and as any wife has to ask her husband. Rarely do females control the gelt in their families, Nan."

"Well, the man I wed must agree to give me a generous allowance to spend as I please," she said. "Mam does not beg you for every penny she spends."

"I will raise the matter with him whilst we negotiate the contract," he said, knowing it would serve no purpose to remind her that their mother never made any purchase without discussing it with all and sundry. "But I am going to continue those negotiations, Nan. Allying our two families will benefit all of us in the future. I will hear your complaints, and I will take each one up with Tony, but I'd need better reasons than I have yet heard from you before I would reject his suit."

"No one *ever* listens to me, least of all you, Dickon," she said. "But you told me yourself that no one can force a Scotswoman to marry against her will. So, do your worst. It will avail you naught and Tony *less* than naught!"

Kirkhill felt his temper rise as, with chin high, she swept past him out of the room. But she would fly into the boughs if he stopped her and doubtless would next treat him to a flood of tears. He was not in the mood.

Moreover, he knew that she would change her dress before rejoining the others. As a man who liked to pick his fights when and where he could, he was able to content himself with a small victory in this one.

The rest of Fiona's day passed much as it had begun, in a vague fog of frustration. The days since Will's disappearance had all passed in a similar manner, but she had not suffered such a sense of disorientation until now, after Kirkhill's visit.

Before, she had just wondered where Will had gone and wished that someone would report something, anything, to explain his prolonged absence.

Underlying those feelings, however, was a sense of unease, even guilt.

Old Jardine's continued assertions that Will's absence was her fault had rung strangely true to her. But as Flory had pointed out more than once, one could not deduce much from that, because Fiona *always* felt guilty after she and Will argued, as if she ought to have done something differently, something to avoid the quarrel.

She remembered having once accused her older sister, Mairi, of feeling such guilt simply because Mairi preferred peace to conflict. Mairi felt guilty if anyone disagreed, as if she might have prevented the hostilities if only she had intervened in just the right way before they had begun. When Mairi did try to intervene, she got upset if her intervention failed.

Fiona had always deemed such quick assumption of responsibility for others' actions to be a stupid way of managing one's life...until she had married Will and learned that she was automatically responsible for any disagreement between them.

Mairi was like their father, who had been a man who preferred peace at almost any price. But Mairi—now Dunwythie of that Ilk rather than Mairi Maxwell of Dunwythie—had also managed to keep her own name and title just as their cousin Jenny Easdale had after marrying Sir Hugh, so perhaps Mairi had changed.

Fiona had certainly changed after *her* marriage. But she had never been like Mairi and never would be.

If Mairi were going downstairs in response to a curt summons from Old Jardine, as Fiona was now, Mairi would not be *striving* to appear calm and resolute. Mairi was calm by nature. She never lost her temper, never threw things, and never behaved in a manner other than that of a lady born. She had, after all, known from birth that if her father had no son, she would inherit his title and estates.

Fiona had always had a hot temper and had frequently given it free rein. Now, however, she quaked at the thought of facing Old Jardine for the second time in one day. She loathed and feared him even as he lay on what he had assured everyone was his deathbed, and she feared his enormous, fierce, badly trained dog even more. She had intended to go to bed right after supper, but Jardine's summons had come before she had left her solitary table in the solar.

His man, Hod, stood waiting for her at the door to the inner chamber, watching insolently as she walked the length of the hall to the dais.

"Ye took your time about it, lass. The master doesna take kindly to waiting."

"Then pray stand aside and let me in," she replied, refusing to react to his disrespectful greeting. She was pleased that her voice was steady and did not reveal the sad state of her nerves. It was rare for Old Jardine to summon her like this unless he meant to wreak vengeance for something she had done or failed to do.

She could not imagine how she might have vexed him this time. But she forced herself to wait calmly until Hod pushed open the door for her and declared loudly, "Here she be, master—at last."

With a wary eye on the dog sprawled across the foot of Jardine's bed, Fiona moved to stand at the old man's left. She thought he looked smaller than he had that morning, and frailer, as if he had lost a stone of his weight during the intervening hours. His face seemed thinner, too, his cheeks more hollowed.

"Dinna stand gaping at a man," he said sourly. "D'ye no ha' the good manners to say good evening? Stay, Dobby," he added as the dog shifted itself to watch her.

"You sent for me," Fiona said. "In this household, I have found it safer to hold my tongue in the presence of a Jardine until he bids me speak."

"I had not noticed that, m'self, but if it be true, at least ye've learned summat here at Spedlins. Leave us, Hod."

"Ye may need me, master."

"Nay, then, I'll do. Dobby will look after me, so go on now."

Visibly reluctant, Hod left but sent Fiona a warning grimace as he did.

Fiona breathed easier when he was gone. Fixing her attention on Jardine, while trying to keep at least an eye and an ear on the dog, she waited.

"Ye're gey meek of a sudden," Jardine said.

"I'm curious to know why you sent for me."

"Then ye havena heard aught, have ye?"

"I rarely do hear things," she replied. "You and Will have seen to that."

"Aye, well, we keep our family close, but ye canna trust

folks to keep their tongues behind their teeth *all* the time. What did ye think o' Kirkhill?"

Raising her eyebrows in surprise, she said, "Good sakes, sir, I scarcely know the man, certainly not well enough to venture an opinion of him."

"Nay, now, dinna be telling me lies, lass. I ken fine that ye dined wi' him at me own high table. Ye surely didna think nae one would tell me."

"I knew that someone would, but he commanded me to eat with him," she said. "To my mind, he is much like Will. He assumes that the world will bow to his commands, whatever they may be."

Jardine frowned. "Now why would he be issuing such a command to ye?"

Not wanting to repeat what Kirkhill had said about seizing the opportunity to get acquainted with her, she said, "I am sure I do not know."

"He canna ha' been flirting with ye, as puffed up as ye are wi' your bairn, and being his own cousin's wife. Mayhap, he kens fine that my Will be dead, though. That would explain it. Still, Kirkhill's given me his word that he'll look after the place, and the bairn. And men do say that God's cursed the man wi' strong integrity. Nobbut what I take that to mean more than it would for any man. Every man *gives* his word easily enough and changes his mind just as easily when the circumstances change. I dinna ken one who can keep it longer nor that."

"Many do, though," Fiona said. "My father always kept his word, and I have heard it said that the Lord of Galloway always keeps his."

"Aye, sure, when it be expedient, he does," Old Jardine said with a knowing chortle. "Ye'd be wiser never to trust any man farther than ye can see him, lass. Only a fool trusts blindly."

She had certainly learned that only a fool would trust Old Jardine or Will any farther than that, so she held her tongue, still wondering why he had summoned her. Surely, he did not care what she thought of Kirkhill.

"I expect ye ken that there ha' been rumors about our Will and what became o' him," Jardine said, eyeing her narrowly.

"You told me yourself that there were," she reminded him.

"A man doesna recall all he says to a female. But Hod tells me them rumors ha' spread all up and down Annandale. He says many agree wi' me that the likeliest person to ha' done our Will in be his bonnie bride."

"So *you* have said, many times," she said. "Does it not occur to you that Hod himself is the man most likely to be spreading those rumors?"

"Aye, well, if he is, other men do believe him."

"Men who do not know me," Fiona pointed out, wondering how it was that she could remain calm in the face of such accusations. Was it possible that she *had* killed her husband? She had loved him once, or had thought that she did.

"We'll ken more when they find Will," Jardine said. "Nae one could believe that ye'd bested him in a fair fight, that's sure. But if ye clouted him over the head with a club, or poisoned him…" He paused, eyeing her narrowly.

"Why do you look at me so?" she demanded, feeling her temper rise and not caring anymore if it did. "Do you think I'd tell *you* if I *had* killed him?"

"Nay, I do not, but I be a good judge o' liars," he said.

"I expect you are," she said, looking right into his eyes.

"Watch that tongue o' yours," he warned.

"I doubt you'd beat me for agreeing with you, or order Hod to do it when he might endanger your grandson's life," she said.

"So ye think ye're carrying a lad, do ye?" He actually looked pleased.

Fiona shrugged. "I am not a witch, so I cannot know. Will wanted a son, so he always talked as if only a son would do. I expect I've come to believe that, too."

"If it do be a lad, ye're to call him William," Jardine said. "'Tis a grand notion, that, to call him after his da."

Fiona remained silent.

"Promise me," he said more fiercely.

"Nay, I won't make such a promise," she retorted. "If Will comes home, he'll decide what name the child should have, just as he decides all else."

"Aye, that be true enough. But if he doesna come home, ye'll do it then."

"Mayhap I will," she said mendaciously.

His eyes narrowed to slits, and he struggled to sit up. His face reddened with the effort, and he gasped for air. The dog turned its head briefly to watch him, then turned back toward Fiona, baring its teeth.

Fiona stayed where she was, watching the old man. She could do nothing to help him, nor—if experience was any guide—would he or the dog let her try. And she did not trust Old Jardine to keep his hands to himself or protect her from the dog if she did try to aid him.

His gasping grew worse, and he fell back hard against the pillows.

"Shall I call Hod?" she asked.

The gasping grew harsher, frighteningly so, as if he were trying to talk.

"I'll get him," she said, turning but keeping an ear cocked toward the dog.

As she reached the door, the old man said clearly, "Ye'd best have a care."

She stopped with her hand on the latch but did not turn.

The harsh voice continued, still gasping but not so dreadfully. "Them rumors... will reach the sheriff's ears. Nae one will stop him *then*... if he decides to flex his authority in Annandale... to hang a murderess!"

Having changed from his riding dress to fresh clothing, Kirkhill hurried down to join his mother, his sister, and their guests in the great hall for supper.

Annis, Lady Kirkhill, reed slender and with some forty-five years behind her, but still pretty in a pale yellow kirtle and a colorful wrap, her fading blond hair concealed beneath a white veil, had already taken her place beside his own when he strode across the hall to the dais. Sir James and Tony MacCairill were also there.

Kirkhill went to his mother at once and bent to kiss her cheek. "Forgive me, my lady," he said with a warm smile. "I am a most undutiful son."

"You will always have your joke, my dear Dickon," she said, smiling back at him. "I know how busy you are. You have done naught to require my forgiveness."

"You should give him a good scold nevertheless, Annis," James Seyton said, breaking off his conversation with Tony MacCairill. "It would do him good."

"Oh, no, James, how can you say so? Dickon is always so kind to me! By my troth, he has never given me cause to scold him."

"Don't tell me that," Sir James said with a laugh. "Why, I can recall any number of pranks he pulled as a youngster. His father certainly had cause to scold—aye, and often to do more than scold, come to that."

Lady Kirkhill beamed at her son. "I do not recall any such event, sir. Dickon has always been the best of sons."

"Madam, enough," Kirkhill said, chuckling. "We all know which of you is right and which of you has chosen to forget my many misdemeanors." He glanced around the great hall. "Is Nan not here yet?"

"I am sure she will be here directly, my dearling," Lady Kirkhill said hastily. "Doubtless, she lost track of the time."

"Nay, I did not," Nan said, sweeping toward the dais from the hall entryway. "Dickon sent me to change my dress—and after I had chosen it especially to sup with Tony, too," she added with a roguish look at that gentleman and a more challenging one for her brother.

Lady Kirkhill nibbled her lower lip and glanced nervously at her son, but Kirkhill would not play the villain's role that his sister so clearly intended for him.

"We are glad you have come, Nannie," he said, meeting her gaze. "Do take your place, so we may eat. You cannot want our guests to starve."

"Mercy, no," she said. "Only look at Tony, practically at his last gasp."

The stalwart MacCairill grinned at her.

"Surely, my dearling," her mother said, shooting another wary look at Kirkhill, "you should address Sir Antony more properly."

"Oh, he does not care," Nan said, tossing her head. "Do you, Tony?"

"*You* may call me anything you like, my lady," he said with a slight bow.

"Likely, I shall take base advantage of that offer," she said with a twinkle. "I think of you as merely a second odious brother, after all."

He clutched his chest dramatically. "You wound me to the quick, lass."

"Tony," Kirkhill said evenly, "*don't* encourage her. She must learn to behave more courteously before either of us takes her to Stirling or anywhere in company."

"Faith, Dickon, you cannot mean for me to go to Stirling with Tony! Only think what a scandal *that* would cause—a young innocent girl traveling alone with a man of his scurrilous reputation, and to join the court!"

"Sit down, Nan," Kirkhill said, giving her a look to warn her that he had had enough. "They are carving the meat."

Returning his look speculatively, Nan put her chin in the air but obeyed him.

Kirkhill turned to his uncle. "I'd like a word with you after supper if you don't mind, sir."

James Seyton nodded amiably.

"Me, too?" Tony asked.

"You and I will talk later," Kirkhill assured him grimly.

"I want to hear all about your trip to Spedlins Tower, Dickon," Nan said as gillies scurried about, serving them, while others served in the lower hall. "Is our uncle as unpleasant a man as everyone says he is?"

"He is dying, so it will soon cease to matter what sort of man he is."

"Pish tush," Nan said. "Of course it matters. Men like Old Jardine influence everyone around them. Moreover, I have heard that Cousin Will Jardine is just such another, so things will remain as they are at Spedlins, will they not?"

"Will Jardine has been missing for more than a fortnight," Kirkhill said. "No one seems to know what became of him, so Spedlins is in a muddle. Our uncle has asked me to sort things out after he dies, and to find out what happened to Will."

Because his mother sat between him and Nan, he had been talking across her to his sister, but if Lady Kirkhill was paying heed to them, he saw no sign of it, although they discussed her brother and nephew.

Kirkhill realized again that, until the lady Fiona had drawn his attention to the possible reason for his mother's lack of interest in her own family, he had not questioned it. Now he noticed that her right hand, on the table near his left one, clenched her eating knife so tightly that her knuckles had whitened.

His sister turned her attention to a platter of sliced roast beef that a gillie was holding for her inspection, so Kirkhill rested his hand atop his mother's, leaned close, and murmured for her ears alone, "I tell you, madam, after seeing my uncle, it astonishes me anew that so gentle and kind a lady sprang from that nest. It proves yet again what extraordinary judgment my father showed in choosing his wife."

Her hand lurched under his, releasing the knife it clenched. Then it turned over and gripped his tight. She looked at him silently, tears glistening in her eyes.

As he met that look, his thoughts shifted abruptly back to the lady Fiona.

Whatever else he did after Old Jardine's death, he would do all he could to protect her against the old villain's ridiculous accusations.

As he ate his supper, it occurred to him that if he left Tony behind in order to talk with his uncle James, Lady Kirkhill would be obliged to invite the young man to sit with her and Nan in her solar, which would only lead to more of his sister's mischief. Accordingly, when they had finished the meal, he said, "You might as well come with us, Tony. You may possibly have an idea or two to aid me."

"I am full of good ideas," Tony said cheerfully.

"You are full of something, at all events," Kirkhill replied.

They adjourned to the room at the back of the house that he used to deal with matters of business. Someone had lit a fire on the hearth there, and it was warm. A large table took pride of place, and Kirkhill drew up a back-stool to it, motioning the other two men to do likewise.

As they sat down, he said without preamble, "I want to find out all I can about Will Jardine, which means that I need to learn what the Jardines have been up to these past few years. I've heard talk, of course, but I'm not interested in rumors or insinuations. I want to know the truth."

"A tall order, lad," Sir James said.

"Aye, well, you keep your ear to the ground, sir, so I'm hoping your men can help. I'm also going to need you here at Kirkhill for a time when Jardine dies. He has named me guardian of his unborn grandchild and trustee for the child's mother as well as steward for his estates until the child reaches its twenty-fifth birthday."

"Will Jardine eloped two years ago with the lady Fiona Dunwythie," Sir James said. "But I've heard nowt of his having disappeared."

Kirkhill explained what he knew, adding, "Annandale is rife with rumors about his disappearance. If they've not spread to Lothian, I count that to the good."

"What sort of rumors?" Tony asked.

"Primarily, that the lady Fiona killed him. I am sure that cannot be true, though. Will is young and strong, and the lass is with child and near her time. She is also much smaller than Will is."

"Aye, she would be," Tony said. "Will prefers them small."

Ignoring him because he did not want to dwell on the lady Fiona or Will, Kirkhill said, "I'll search through everything at Spedlins when I take over there. I have a notion I won't find many documents, because Old Jardine does not seem like a man who keeps good accounts. However, perhaps I've misjudged him."

"I doubt it," his uncle said. "That old man is a scoundrel, and his son is no better. I'd wager that much of what they have done does not bear accounting."

"What do you want *me* to do, Dickon?" Tony asked.

"I want you to stay away from Nan until we get a few things sorted out," Kirkhill said. "You are mistaken if you think constant attention will win her heart. She reminded me that I promised years ago that I would let her choose her husband, and she insists that she'll have none of you. She said that you always want your own way and want only to ally yourself with our family, not with her."

"Do you mean to say our negotiations are off?" Tony demanded indignantly.

"Not at all. But if you want her, my lad, you'd do better to keep your distance. Neglect her. If my sister believes she can wind you round her thumb, you will never win her. You'd be wiser to tell her you agree with me that she needs to grow up before she thinks of marrying, and then leave in the morning." Turning to his uncle, he said, "As I mentioned before, sir, I'm hoping that you will return to keep an eye on things here when I am recalled to Spedlins. My lady mother will be more comfortable with you here, and you can also keep an eye on Nan."

"Now hold on, lad," Sir James said. "I've nae experience with misbehaving lassies. Mayhap you should take Nan with you when you return to Spedlins. Nae doots, she'd be good company for Will Jardine's lady wife."

Kirkhill rejected that suggestion. The last thing he wanted was to have to contend with *two* defiant young women while taking charge of the Jardine estates.

~

Fiona spent the next ten days, the last days of June, doing her best to keep out of Old Jardine's way. She focused instead on finishing her preparations for her baby's arrival and ignoring the recurrent but unpredictable pains in her back. A number of women on the estate, and even a few of the children, came in to help with cleaning, and several brought small gifts they had made for her child.

Jeb's Jane, one of the women who helped in the kitchen, brought in a cradle that she said her husband had sanded, oiled, and polished for her ladyship's baby.

"It belonged to Lady Jardine's family, me lady," Jane

said. "My Jeb did say that Master Will thought it were foolish to furbish it up, but Jeb did it anyway and finished it last month just afore he died." Tears sprang to her eyes. "He did say the wee heir to Spedlins ought to ha' a bed o' his own."

"Thank you, Jane," Fiona said solemnly. "It was a gey thoughtful thing for Jeb to do. I will think of him whenever I lay my bairn in this cradle."

She supposed that Parland Dow had taken her message to Dunwythie Hall, but no message had come to Spedlins in return. So, either her mother had not cared enough to send one, or—and much more likely, Fiona was sure—Old Jardine's men had not allowed anyone arriving from the Hall to deliver it to her.

In either case, Fiona was glad that she had sent her message. Doing so had given her a sense of victory, of outsmarting the fat old man in the inner chamber.

By the first day of July, a Wednesday, her back pains were occurring daily. Flory would rub her back, trying to ease them, but Fiona soon learned that until they eased of their own accord, there was little that anyone could do.

That Saturday, midafternoon, Hod burst into her chamber without knocking.

Whirling at the intrusion, she swiftly noted his pale face and shaking hands.

"What is it?" she demanded. "Is he dead?"

"Nay, but he wants ye, and ye'd best come quick," Hod said. "He can scarcely breathe, and he's been a-clutching at his chest. Says he'll do for the nonce, but I'm thinking that he canna ha' but a few hours left to him."

"Then what does he want with me? He cannot want my comforting."

"Nay, but he insists he must speak wi' ye, to make things clear, he said."

"He's made things clear enough."

"Aye, well, ye'll come if I ha' to carry ye," he snapped.

She went without further objection.

Chapter 5 _____

The mastiff growled as usual when Fiona entered. It lay beside the old man on the bed, showing its teeth, clearly on guard.

Old Jardine's face was gray, but whether it was his skin or just the stubble of beard on his jowls she could not tell. His glower was as fierce as ever.

"Ye'll ha' to walk softly now," he muttered, one hand on the dog, his voice so weak that she could barely hear him. But she would not move closer to the bed.

She did not understand what he'd meant. "Why must I walk softly?"

"Because God will see that ye'll pay for what ye did to my Will," he said, his voice sounding stronger. "And ye willna ken where or how. Mayhap ye think our Kirkhill will be kind, that he'll look after ye as if ye were his own family. But he'll do nae such thing. Soon or late, the fact that he inherits all o' this if your bairn dies, or turns out to be a wee vixen like yourself, will be more than the man can stand."

"Even my daughter would inherit," she retorted, "just as my sister did."

"Nay, for I told the man that I'd willed it so that only a

male o' Jardine blood shall get me lands. I'd be damned afore I let any woman run Applegarth."

"I expect you told him that he will inherit if my child dies, too."

"Aye, sure, because if Will be dead and the bairn likewise, Kirkhill *is* my heir. I warrant he already knew as much, for ye can be sure that me sister has long known it even if her son has not. Sithee, wealth be power, lass, and these lands be more than what most men own. Ye'll see. He'll prove to be a man like any other."

"Kirkhill is not like you," she said. "Nor like Will."

"Well, ye'll find out, won't ye? Ye killed Will, but even so, I did tell Kirkhill that I didna mind a *lad* wi' your blood inheriting Applegarth, because he'd ha' me own blood in him, and Will's, too. God will decide the matter, but it be on your head, too, to keep me grandson safe to claim his inheritance. Mayhap ye can do that. I warrant ye'll want to, because ye'll hope to control him. That be how women think. But Kirkhill will still take charge here, and I'm thinking ye'll no like that."

That was true enough, Fiona thought, whatever happened.

"I'll haunt ye," Old Jardine muttered.

"What?" She focused on him again.

"Are ye no listening, woman? I said, though ye'll think me dead and buried in me grave, I'll haunt ye, come what may, for doing away wi' my Will."

She was silent, aware that further protest would be useless, especially as she could not be sure what *had* happened to Will.

An irksome memory stirred of someone in the past

telling her about the extraordinary strength a mother could display if her child were in danger.

Jardine's eyes had narrowed to slits, as if he hoped to read her thoughts. In his earlier agitation, his face had lost some of the gray. His breathing was shallow though, lacking the harsh sounds to which she had grown accustomed.

"Ha' ye nae more to say for yourself?" he asked.

She said then, "You will not haunt me, and God will do naught for you, but He *will* protect my babe because a child is innocent." Gently stroking her belly, she added, "This wee lad may be half Jardine, but he is also half Dunwythie with a good bit of Douglas as well. He will thus be strong, and I mean to see that he grows up to be good and kind, not cruel and deceitful like his father and you."

"You watch that mouth o' yours," he growled. "If I ha' to get up—"

The dog growled, baring teeth again, but it did not move away from Jardine.

"You don't scare me anymore," she said. "You're just a sick old man."

"How dare you!" he snapped, struggling in his fury to sit up, clutching the dog until it turned abruptly toward him. But although he fought so hard to raise himself up off his pillows that his face grew purple with the effort, he was too weak.

Fiona watched him, feeling no fear or sympathy, only curiosity about whether he would manage to sit up. He fell back instead, gasping again but with gasps much weaker than when she had last stood before him.

His mouth opened and closed like that of a landed fish,

making her realize that he could not get air enough to speak. With an abrupt turn, she went to the door.

"I think he wants you now," she said to Hod.

He pushed past her without a word, but she had not expected a reply.

Returning to her chamber, she found Flory at the window, closing a shutter.

"It be growing dark, me lady," the maid said. "I've put out a fresh shift for ye." She paused, looking closely at Fiona. "Ye look queer. Be summat amiss?"

Fiona put a hand to her belly, feeling it tighten strongly. "The old master has taken a bad turn, but I...I think something else is happening, too," she said.

"More pain?" Flory asked sympathetically, stepping nearer.

"Nay, or at least not the same—" She broke off, gasping. Through a wave of agony, she managed to say, "Oh, Flory, this is *much* different. Could it be my time?"

"Aye, it may be starting," Flory said. "But mind, me lady, them other women did say that wi' your first, it be bound to take a long time. I do think ye should be getting into bed, though. I'll help ye. Then I'll fetch Jeb's Jane. She did say she'd be that pleased to help ye through it, and she kens gey more than we do."

The pain eased and then vanished as if it had never been. Drawing a long breath, Fiona said, "Aye, send for Jane. But I don't want to get into bed yet, especially if this is going to take a long time."

Flory sent at once for Jeb's Jane, but it was more than an hour later before Fiona felt another contraction. Wrenching pain, followed by nothing.

"Just a wee warning o' things to come, I'm thinking,"

Jane said two hours later. "They'll come closer together afore that bairn will show itself, m'lady. I'll go back to the kitchen to help set out things for supper. Send for me an ye need me, but I'm thinking the wee one willna be ready afore sometime tomorrow."

She opened the door to reveal Hod, standing at the threshold.

"He's gone," he said. "The old master be dead."

~

After seeing Tony MacCairill and Sir James Seyton on their way back to their respective duties, Kirkhill had enjoyed a fortnight's peace. That is, he had if one did not count his younger sister's irritatingly relentless attempts to talk him into taking her to join the royal court at Stirling or—a notion that had taken a more tenacious grip on her imagination—to invite a host of family friends to Kirkhill House.

In vain had he explained that he might be called away at any moment.

"A messenger could find you at Stirling as easily as he could here," she began coaxingly that Sunday morning as they broke their fast together.

"Stirling is nearly a hundred miles northeast of here, whilst we are just ten miles north of Spedlins," he pointed out, striving for patience.

"Then the thing to do is to invite people here, as I've also suggested."

"How would it look if, the minute our guests began arriving, I received word that Old Jardine had died? I should have to leave at once."

"I don't know why you could not wait a day or two. But

if you could not," she added generously, "Uncle James could—"

"No, Nan, and that is my final word on the subject," he said.

"But—"

"I said no, and that must be the end of it if you do not want to spend the next three days in your bedchamber to give me some peace."

An hour later, his mother, clearly prompted by Nan and just as clearly wary of his likely reaction, approached him in his room at the rear of the house to suggest that if Nan was not interested in Sir Antony, it would behoove Kirkhill to arrange for her to meet other eligible young men.

He said curtly, "No, madam. I understand that Nan persuaded you to speak to me, but I have given her my answer. Prithee, tell her that she may now take her dinner in her bedchamber. Tell her, also, that I do not want to see her again until tomorrow morning at the earliest."

"Aye, dearling, I will tell her. I warned her that this was a mistake."

So it was that when a gillie entered the chamber to tell him that Sir Antony MacCairill had returned and was in the courtyard with a large number of other riders, Kirkhill greeted the news with near exasperation.

Getting abruptly to his feet, he muttered, "By heaven, if he thinks to make progress this way, he'll soon learn his error." He strode past the gaping lad only to meet his porter hurrying to find him.

The porter, wide-eyed, announced, "The Lord o' Galloway, me lord."

Archie Douglas strode past the porter with a hand held

out to Kirkhill. Tony MacCairill followed, grinning as usual.

A tall, lanky man in his fifty-ninth year, Archie the Grim, also known as the Black Douglas because of his dark hair and complexion, was bareheaded, doubtless having left helmet and sword on the porter's bench in the entryway, though he'd kept his dirk in its sheath at his hip. His still mostly black, shoulder-length hair framed a long, hawklike face, and his dark eyes glinted brightly as he met Kirkhill's gaze.

Archie's long stride was that of a younger man, and his arms and torso still looked muscular enough to wield the two-ell sword that had made him famous.

"I left all my lads save Tony in your courtyard," he said as he shook Kirkhill's hand. "I hope you keep enough food in this pile to feed at least me and my captains. Tony told me that you do."

"I think we can manage," Kirkhill said, shooting a look at his friend. "Tony, mayhap you can make yourself useful by conveying those orders to the kitchen."

"Aye, sure," Tony said, turning to follow the porter out of the chamber.

Archie raised an eyebrow. "You send one of my best knights to give orders in your kitchen? Have you no lesser minions at hand to send on such an errand?"

Kirkhill smiled as he gestured toward two chairs by the hearth, on which a small but cheerful fire crackled. "Won't you sit, my lord? 'Tis nobbut punishment for Tony's having turned up again so soon after I thought I'd got rid of him for a spell. See you, he wants to marry my sister Nan, but she will have none of him."

The second Douglas eyebrow went up. "He did mention

such intent, but I expected the match would be to your liking. 'Twould be a good one."

"Aye, sure, but the lass is contrary, and Tony is too avid in his pursuit. I'd hoped to put distance between them for a month or more."

"I won't keep him here long, for I mean to be off again after we dine," Archie said. "But as I was nearby, I thought I'd come myself to tell you I'll likely need you before long with as many men as you can muster. The Earl of March seems determined to take control of Annandale. Such is his right; however..."

When Archie paused, Kirkhill said, "March has been Lord of Annandale for years but has kept to his estates in the east and shown no interest here before now."

"I ken fine that you must wonder who will come along next, wanting to irk the dale's pricksome inhabitants," Archie said. "But bordering right on Solway Firth as it does, Annandale is strategically important. The blasted English, by occupying Lochmaben Castle, have made nuisances of themselves here for three-quarters of a century, and Sheriff Maxwell of Dumfries laid *his* claim to its rents two years ago." He shrugged. "Maxwell has shown no interest in resuming that debate after his failure, but I doubt that he is any less ambitious now than he was then."

"But...forgive me, my lord," Kirkhill said. "Are you not also intent on extending *your* rule from Galloway to all of Dumfriesshire?"

"I am," Douglas said. "But that won't alter March's rights as Lord of Annandale, and so I have told him. Even now, he gets his share of the rents when they are paid. But he hopes to take personal charge of the dale by ousting the English and does not seem to know he cannot do that alone, or without Douglas help."

"Do you *support* him then? He's a gey ambitious man, I'm told."

"I've had no time even to think about that," Douglas said. "But if he means to invade Annandale with a large force and lay waste these lands, I *must* take notice. I won't have petty strife here, no matter who stirs it. And the way things are going in Stirling and throughout the Borders, I'll need more men soon, and lots of them."

His mentioning Stirling reminded Kirkhill that the increasing Douglas power was becoming a thorn in the side of the royal family. The royal Stewarts believed they were the premier Scottish clan, but Clan Douglas was far more powerful.

Together, the Earl of Douglas—as chief of that clan—and Archie as Lord of Galloway ruled not only the Douglases but also the Scottish Borders, Galloway, and most of the land, from coast to coast, between the Borders and the Firths of Forth and Clyde. Together, they were at least three times as powerful as the Stewarts were. It was therefore unlike the prickly Archie to give the flip of a finger for what the Stewarts might want—or the Scottish Earl of March, come to that. However, at least one more powerful faction would also enter any dispute over Annandale.

"The English have been restless," Kirkhill said as he reached for the jug of whisky that always sat on the table by the hearth. He poured a mug of it for his guest and another for himself, saying, "England's Earl of Northumberland will surely object if March leads troops into Annandale."

"Aye, sure," Archie agreed, taking the proffered mug.

"Northumberland's men have been flitting back and forth across the line to stir trouble all the way from Berwick to Roxburgh, and that blasted March only makes matters worse by thinking *he* can end the damnable English occupation here."

"I heard that whenever March stirs a step westward from his seat at Dunbar, Northumberland sends raiding parties across to divert him elsewhere," Kirkhill said.

"Aye, and so far, that ploy has kept March busy in the east, but their antics are annoying the Douglas, and when that happens, the Douglas sends for me."

"And when the two of you respond, March returns to Dunbar and the English hie themselves back across the line," Kirkhill said with a slight smile.

"That amuses you, aye, and would doubtless make a charming pattern for a courtly dance," Archie said. "But I don't mean to put up with it much longer. Ridding Annandale of the English would help, and that is why I have come to you."

"You must mean to besiege Lochmaben then," Kirkhill said. "I can think of no other way to get them out. That castle has proven impregnable for sixty years."

"Aye, but thanks to the Annandale folks who have kept its English garrison well pent up these past years, they cannot build an adequate store of supplies. Nor have their masters in England been able to replenish those supplies or pay the men with any regularity. A successful siege should take no longer than a fortnight but requires more men than I can spare at present. I'll need more just to aid the Douglas."

Tony returned then, assuring them both that Kirkhill's kitchen had all in train and that dinner would shortly be ready. Helping himself from the jug of whisky, he said as he took a seat, "Have you learned aught more about Will Jardine, Dickon?"

Kirkhill glanced at Archie.

"Och, I ken all about it," that gentleman said. "I've little use for the Jardines. But if you take over there, as Tony says Old Jardine wants you to do when he dies, I'll expect to see his men under your command when I need them."

"I'll do my best, sir, although one cannot swear how loyal they will be."

"They'll be loyal, or we'll hang the dearling bastards," Archie said.

Smiling, Kirkhill turned to Tony and said, "My men have searched the dales, but we've learned nowt of Will's whereabouts that we did not already know."

"Aye, well, the man's vanished then, because the best any of my sources could suggest was that either he was carried off by wee folk or the devil flew away with him. I'd opt for the latter, myself."

Kirkhill chuckled. The three men talked desultorily for another quarter hour before a gillie came to tell them that the midday meal was ready to serve.

Adjourning to the hall dais, Kirkhill had taken his place, and Archie was paying his respects to Lady Kirkhill, when Nan, in blatant defiance of Kirkhill's order, swept into the hall and onto the dais. She wore a becomingly modest rose-pink gown with a front-laced bodice of exquisite tapestry work, and she made a deep curtsy to Archie, bringing a rare smile to that gentleman's dark face.

Kirkhill's good humor, on the other hand, darkened grimly.

"Be the laird really dead, mistress?" Jeb's Wee Davy asked, looking up at Fiona as she paused, put both hands on her sides, and waited until the pain eased. She had met the boy as she took the air in the courtyard after her mid-day meal, and they were strolling back to the tower.

The pains had begun again that morning and had been coming regularly but were still about an hour apart. When the contraction eased, she looked down into Davy's anxious little face and said, "Aye, the master is dead, laddie. We must not be sorrowful though, for he is no longer sick and suffering as he was."

"Me da weren't suffering or sick. He just died."

"Your father was a good man, Davy. I'm sure that God is looking after him now, just as Jeb is looking down with pride as he watches you."

"Be me da in heaven, then?"

"Aye, sure. That is where all good men go, so if you are good, you will join him there one day."

Davy frowned. "I'm no always so good, sithee."

Fiona put a gentle hand on his head, stroking his dark silky curls. "God doesn't mind a bit of mischief now and again, laddie. He looks for kindness and such things as the way you look after your sister, Tippy, and the other little ones."

"Aye, well, some'un has to watch over them or they'd be in the suds every day." After a pause, he added, "Be the old laird in heaven, d'ye think?"

Fiona hesitated, because one could scarcely talk of God with a child and lie to him in the next breath. At last, she said, "I don't know. What do you think?"

"Me da didna like the laird," Davy said. "Were that wrong o' him?"

"Nay, we cannot always choose whom we will like or not like."

The boy nodded. "Then I hope the laird be somewhere else and no wi' me da."

"He *must* be somewhere else," Fiona said. When they reached the hall, she sent him to find his mother, and while she waited for Jeb's Jane to come to her, she found her thoughts drifting as they so often had of late to Kirkhill.

She had not sent a messenger for him yet, although she knew that she ought to have sent one as soon as she learned that Old Jardine had died. Guilt stirred over the delay, but the truth was that she was in no hurry to send for Kirkhill. When he arrived, she would have to answer to him and apply to him for aught she needed, just as she had with her father, Will, and Old Jardine.

After managing the Jardine household for two years, despite the Jardines, she resented knowing that Kirkhill would have the right to undo things that she had done and would doubtless order her about with everyone else.

Jeb's Jane hurried in minutes later, but when Fiona admitted that the pains were still far apart, Jane shook her head, albeit with an understanding smile.

"I ken fine that ye be in a hurry for the wee one to come, me lady, but he'll get here in his own good time." Pausing briefly, she added, "They say that Lord Kirkhill will be a-coming soon. D'ye think he'll be a kind master?"

"I don't know, Jane. I haven't even sent for him yet, but he seems to be a gentleman, so I expect he'll be reasonable enough." She hoped he would be more persuadable than the Jardines had been. After all, she had often persuaded her father to see things her way when Dun-wythie had seemed at first to be intractable.

Kirkhill had seemed affable enough, except for the few times she had noted an edge to his voice or a glint of ice in his eyes.

Another pain struck then, and Fiona stopped thinking about Kirkhill.

⌒

Kirkhill was sorely tempted to order his defiant sister back to her bedchamber. He did not, but only because Archie's captains were taking places at the lower hall trestle tables, and he did not want Nan to create a scene that they would likely describe for the entertainment of others wherever they traveled.

He would, instead, make Nan sorry later for her defiance.

As she took her place at the table beside their mother, who was still chatting with Archie, Kirkhill glanced down the table at Tony, conferring with two of the captains. If Tony had observed Nan's grand entrance, he gave no sign of it.

Nan stood at her place, looking annoyed and impatient as she waited for her mother to sit. Kirkhill signed to the gillies to begin serving and took his seat, nodding when Tony motioned that he would like the two captains to sit at the high table with him so that they could go on talking.

Archie held Lady Kirkhill's chair for her and then took his seat beside Kirkhill. "Your lady mother is as charming and beautiful as ever," he said.

"Aye, she is, my lord," Kirkhill agreed.

They talked more of what Archie expected to take place in the next few weeks, but the meal did not take long. The Lord of Galloway was eager to be off again, so as soon as good manners allowed, he signed to his men to depart and lingered only long enough to make his adieux.

Tony, Kirkhill noted as they all stood to bid Archie farewell, had paid no heed to Nan. As the younger knight prepared to follow Archie, he stopped briefly at Kirkhill's side and said, "If I learn more about Will Jardine, I'll send word, Dickon, but I'm thinking that the damned fellow has vanished into thin air."

"As you'll most likely be traveling south, if you do send a messenger, warn him to look for me at Spedlins before he rides all the way to this end of the dale."

"Aye, sure," Tony said. Then, with a bow, a polite farewell to Lady Kirkhill, and an equally polite but sober nod to Nan, he strode from the hall.

Nan's look of astonishment might have stirred Kirkhill's amusement had he not still been so annoyed with her. As it was, he said, "You will come with me, my lass. I should think you'd know by now how little tolerance I have for defiance."

She put her chin in the air but, looking at him, held her tongue. When he stood aside and gestured for her to precede him from the hall, she went meekly.

Her meekness availed her little in the next quarter hour and might have availed her less, because her brother was reaching for a good supple switch when a sharp double rap sounded on the chamber door.

He opened it to find a gillie at the threshold with news that a man riding a lathered horse had come to Kirkhill House in search of its master.

By evening, Fiona's pains were close together and fierce.

She was sure that if the baby did not come quickly, she would go mad with the pain, for she had never felt anything like it before. With every breath, she cursed Will Jardine for ever coming into her life.

Flory and Jane had persuaded her to get into bed, but she could not get comfortable, and when Flory moved to try to straighten the bedclothes, Fiona snapped, "Don't do that! Find someone who knows how to make this stop!"

Flory backed away and looked from Jeb's Jane to the other two women that Jane had summoned for advice.

"My lady," Jane said quietly. "There be nowt we can do till the bairn starts to come. That will happen only in its rightful time."

"Don't *tell* me that! Someone needs to *make* it come before I die of this. Go find some—" Her words broke off in a scream of pain just as the door opened and Kirkhill walked into the room.

Gasping, she shrieked, "What are *you* doing here? Get out!"

"Jardine sent for me," he said calmly.

"You must be daft. Jardine is dead!"

"Aye, but he arranged to send me a message lest you forget to do so."

"Well, I don't care. Get out! You cannot be in here!"

He turned to the women, all four of whom were looking frazzled, one even wringing her hands. "Who amongst you knows most about birthing?" he demanded.

"We've all had bairns," Jeb's Jane said bravely. "But I

canna say we ken gey much about it, me lord. Our bairns just came when they were of a mind to."

"Madam," he said then over his shoulder, "mayhap you had better come in at once, without waiting for an invitation. First, tell that lad I saw on the landing to run and fetch your midwife to us."

"Who are you talking to?" Fiona demanded. "Are there not enough people in this room? I don't *want* anyone else, so—" She broke off with a scream when another contraction struck hard.

"Hush now, that's enough," Kirkhill said firmly. "You do yourself no good with that noise. Here, look at me," he added when she cried out even louder.

"No, get out! I don't want you here! I don't want anyone!"

Instead, she heard him ask Flory how long she had been having the pains.

"Sakes, m'lord, she's had some o' them for weeks now, but these big ones only since yestermorn."

"Do you not understand that I don't *want* you here?" Fiona demanded. Angry tears streamed down her face. "I don't want anyone! Does no one hear—?"

When she cried out again, Kirkhill caught her firmly by the shoulders and said, "Calm yourself now and breathe. If you keep this up and your babe hears you, you may frighten its wits out of it before it is even born. Moreover, the pain will ease if you can make yourself think about something else."

"As if *you* would know!"

"Believe me, I do know. Now, do as I bid you and look at me. Fix your eyes on my face and grip my hands. Squeeze them as hard as you can to vent your anger and ease your pain. Meantime, you might welcome the visitor I've brought you."

"Visitor! Are you mad?" She had shut her eyes tight rather than look at him, but curiosity overcame fury, and she opened them.

The lady Phaeline stood just behind him, smiling at her.

"Mam? Is that really you?"

"Aye, my dearling," Phaeline said in a loving tone. "Now, do as Kirkhill bids, for I begin to think he knows more about birthing babies than all the rest of us together, although I cannot imagine how *that* could be."

Chapter 6 _____

Kirkhill wished he had as much confidence in his abilities as Lady Phaeline had. But at least the lass had forgotten her pains in her surprise at seeing her mother.

To the other women, he said, "You may stay, Flory, but you others must go when the midwife comes unless she sets tasks for you. Sithee, the lady Phaeline brought the woman with her from Dunwythie Hall."

"I don't want a stranger here," Fiona said, still breathing hard from the previous contraction.

"Mother Beaton is the midwife who aided Mairi," her mother said gently.

"Aye?"

"Aye."

"I sent you a message," Fiona murmured.

"Aye, sure, with the knacker Parland Dow," Phaeline said. "And a gey good notion that was, too. But why did you not send one long ago?"

Fiona grimaced, but another contraction came just then, so Kirkhill could not tell whether the grimace was for the question or the pain. She took hold of his hands, though, and squeezed them tightly enough to cut off the circulation in both of them. But at least, he thought with relief, she had ceased her shrieking.

"Try to breathe more deeply and much more slowly," he told her. "Think about each breath and inhale as deeply as you can. Then let it out slowly."

"How do you know that will help?"

He nearly told her just to trust him, but he knew that her pains had frightened her, so he said evenly, "Someone gave me that advice when I got hurt. It helped me, so I think it will help you."

"Were you having a baby?"

"You know I was not."

"Do you mean to deliver *my* baby?"

"Nay," he said. "I have never done so before, although I have delivered or aided in the delivery of a number of calves, foals, and lambs, and I believe the process is similar. But your mother told me that this Mother Beaton of hers delivered your sister's son gey handily."

Fiona gritted her teeth as another pain struck. This time a keening wail escaped her that sent a shiver up his spine.

When she could talk again, she said, "Where have you hidden this midwife?"

"She probably went to bed," he said. "I warrant the woman sleeps whenever she can, and the lad who came for me did not tell me that your pains had begun. Your mother just thought you would want a midwife when your time did come."

A rap sounded on the door as he spoke, and Flory opened it to admit a plump, motherly woman who gazed around the room with widening eyes. "Good sakes," she exclaimed in a melodious voice, "a birthing's no a grand entertainment! Ye there, Jeb's Jane? 'Twas your lad, Davy, who fetched me, aye?"

"Aye, Mother Beaton," Jane said.

"I sent him to tell them in the kitchen that I'll want pots o' hot water. Mayhap ye should go and see that they do as I bade, and take them other two lasses wi' ye." Turning next to Flory, Mother Beaton said, "If ye be her ladyship's woman, ye'll stay and help me when I need ye. But ye, me lord, must leave us. A birthing chamber be nae place for a gentleman."

Fiona's grip on his hands tightened.

Giving her a reassuring look, he said calmly to the midwife, "Now that you are with her, Mother Beaton, I'll go. But I *am* legally responsible for her ladyship's interests, and responsible, too, for her bairn. If it is a lad, it will inherit all that its grandfather had except the funds left in trust for her ladyship's keep. It is quite customary in such a case, as you must know, for the child's appointed guardian to witness its birth in the event that he ever has to testify to the validity of its claim."

As Mother Beaton nodded, Phaeline exclaimed, "Do you mean to tell me only *now* that Old Jardine named *you* Fiona's trustee and *my* grandchild's guardian?"

"Aye, madam, and I apologize, because I should have told you before," he said. "I am also trustee for the estates until the child reaches five-and-twenty."

"Mercy," Phaeline said.

A cry escaped Fiona.

"Get thee hence now, sir, do," Mother Beaton said gently. "I need to see if this bairn be truly on its way. Ye'll see soon enough if it be a lad or no."

"I'm going, but send for me as soon as it's born," he

said firmly. "'Tis my duty to see it. I don't believe that anyone here has cause or intent to switch babies, but I'd prefer that no one in the future find excuse to suspect such a thing, either."

She agreed, and he left. The midwife was right in that a birthing chamber was no place for a gentleman, especially one unrelated to the new mother except by a dead scoundrel's command and a few legal documents.

Nevertheless, those documents meant that the child would be in his charge for its first twenty-five years, and just being at Spedlins, knowing that it was about to be born, had increased the already deep sense of responsibility he felt toward it.

Seeking out Old Jardine's chamber, he found the manservant Hod stuffing clothing into kists. Others stood nearby, strapped and ready for removal.

Numerous items sat on a large table against the wall near the doorway where Kirkhill stood: a cresset lamp, a few winter caps and gloves, and other oddments, including something of brassy-looking metal that peeked from one of the gloves.

Kirkhill's gaze swept the rest of the cluttered room.

The mastiff had curled itself by the cold hearth and barely lifted its head. Even so, as its gaze met his, it bared its teeth.

"Nae doots, ye'll be wanting this room for yourself," Hod said gruffly.

"Not until it has been well cleaned and aired out," Kirkhill said, wrinkling his nose. He looked back at the table, picked up the glove, and saw that the thing inside it was a brass key. Holding it up, he said, "What does this key fit?"

When an answer was not immediately forthcoming, he looked up.

Hod shrugged and his eyes shifted focus back to the kist he was packing. "I dinna ken," he muttered. "I found it amongst his things, like them caps and such."

"Then I expect I should keep it until we find out what it fits," Kirkhill said, slipping it into the leather pouch strapped to his belt. "Sithee, Hod, if I do use this room, I'll keep this big table here. When you've cleared out his clothes, see that they'll go to folks who can make good use of them. Then throw out all his old bedding, have the floor well scrubbed, open all those window shutters, and order a fire built with pine logs in the fireplace. To get rid of the odors in here, you'll need to keep it burning for a while. Then I'll decide if I'll sleep here."

Hod stood where he was, resentment plain in his expression.

"What is it?" Kirkhill asked.

"I ken fine that the old master put ye in charge here, but I'm no used to taking orders from any save himself."

"Then you have a choice to make," Kirkhill said evenly. "You will take your orders from me, as every other man, woman, and bairn on these estates will, or you will find a home elsewhere."

"Aye, well, laird or no, ye're nobbut one man," Hod said.

"One who came here with a tail of forty more, well armed," Kirkhill said in the same tone. "I can summon a hundred more with a signal fire, and if necessary, I can call the Lord of Galloway and his thousands to my aid. I don't want to have to do either of those things, because these estates will run more smoothly if the people who are used to running them go on doing so. But neither will I suffer defiance or insubordination, Hod. I don't tolerate it at home, and I will *not* tolerate it here."

Hod stared at him, clearly taking his measure.

Kirkhill let the silence lengthen for a count of ten before he said, "Your decision is a simple one. Stay or go. I would prefer that you stay, because I'll wager you know more than most folks do about this place and its people. But if you cannot stomach me as your master, I'll not hold that against you. I ken fine that you took good care of Old Jardine, and I shall write a letter for you, saying so."

"What of the young master then?"

"Do you know where he is?"

"Nay, but although Old Master did think he were dead, he may yet live."

"Well, I mean to find out what happened to him," Kirkhill said. "Recall, if you will, that he is my cousin, so 'tis nobbut one more family duty."

"Ye'll also be heir to all here if Master Will be dead and her ladyship's bairn dies at birth or doesna live long enough to take his grandsire's place."

"That is true, but hard as it may be for you to accept my word, I do not covet Applegarth or any of its dwellings or estates. I came here because Old Jardine left me no choice. You will not believe that, and I can understand why. Doubtless you have a strong fondness for this place and for the Jardines."

"I do, aye."

"Well, I own Kirkhill in upper Annandale, and my family owns lands in Lothian as well. Sithee, man, my plate was full before your master summoned me here. I'll need any help I can get, but I will be master of Applegarth, its lands and tenantry, until Will Jardine returns or his child comes of age. Reconcile yourself to that, Hod, for when I give an order, I'll expect compliance. Anyone who fails to obey me will quickly learn the nature of my temper. Now, what say you?"

"I'll see to the room, sir, and I'll do nowt to undermine your authority here," Hod said. "More than that I canna say till I ken ye better than what I do now."

"Fair enough," Kirkhill said. He turned to leave, bethought himself of one more thing, and turned back, saying, "That dog goes outside. If it is dangerous—"

"I'll look after it, sir," Hod said hastily.

"See that you do. I don't want to see it inside the tower again."

⌒

"Ye've a bonnie wee son, me lady, and once he decided to come along, he came quick and easy," Mother Beaton said in her comfortable way hours later. She held the tiny, wrinkled, healthily squalling creature so that Fiona could see him, then turned to wash him in a tub of warm water that Jane had brought up to her.

He continued to cry, albeit not so lustily.

Exhausted, Fiona looked at her mother. "He's so tiny and so red."

"He will grow before you have time to turn around, my dearling. To think that you have produced a son with your first attempt. How proud you must be!"

"I don't feel proud," Fiona said. "I just feel tired."

"That, too, will soon pass," Phaeline assured her. "But you should rest now, so that you will feel more the thing in the morning."

"Beg pardon, me lady, but she should suckle the bairn first," Mother Beaton said. "He'll get little from her this first time, but they need to get acquainted, and she'd best be a-doing it afore she falls asleep and afore his lordship comes back."

Despite the good advice he had given her and her brief reluctance to release his hands, Fiona felt a surge of anger now. "His lordship has no business in here."

"Aye, dearling, he does," Phaeline said. "It is not only his right but also his duty to see that all is well with your son. Doubtless Jeb's Jane is right outside the door, or her Wee Davy is. In any event, I'll find someone to send for him."

Mother Beaton said, "His lordship need not come into this chamber if her ladyship objects to his presence, madam. I can carry the bairn out to him."

"No," Fiona said curtly. "You will not take him out of my sight without my consent. Do you hear me, all of you? I do not know Kirkhill, but Old Jardine said that he is as likely as anyone to have killed Will, if anyone did. Also, Kirkhill will inherit Applegarth if..." Her breath caught. "He must *not* be alone with my baby!"

Seeing Flory frown, and Phaeline and Mother Beaton exchange a look, Fiona said urgently, "You must promise me, *all* of you, or I swear I won't sleep a wink."

Phaeline had opened the door, but she turned back to say, "We cannot make such a promise, Fiona. Kirkhill is master here now. If he wants to be alone with the child, he need only command it."

"He could not be such a beast as to snatch a newborn babe from its mother," Fiona snapped. "Nor could any of you. If he must see my son, let him come in."

"I will come in then, thank you," Kirkhill said as Phaeline stepped aside to let him pass. "Jane's Wee Davy ran to fetch me as soon as the babe squalled."

He paused halfway to the bed when his gaze came to rest on the baby.

Mother Beaton had finished rinsing him and was wrapping him in a blanket that Flory had handed to her. "We'll just see if this laddie recognizes his mam," the midwife said. Then, to Kirkhill, she said, "He's a fine, lusty lad, sir. He has all his fingers and all his toes, his mam's dark hair, and the right male equipment, too. But if ye'd like to see it all for yourself..." She held out the babe toward him.

Glowering, Fiona moved to object, but seeing the awe-struck look on Kirkhill's face, she kept silent.

Phaeline, still near the doorway, caught her eye and smiled. "Your wee laddie is gey handsome," she said. "He looks more like a Dunwythie than a Jardine."

"Good," Fiona said.

Kirkhill seemed to give himself a shake, and her gaze snapped back to him as he stepped almost hesitantly toward her child.

"D'ye want to hold him, my lord?" Mother Beaton asked.

He nodded silently, his eyes on the baby.

It stopped crying and seemed to stare back at him.

Fiona did not realize that she was holding her breath until she let it out as he accepted his tiny ward from the midwife and cradled him close to his broad chest.

The room was still. No one spoke as Kirkhill gazed down into the baby's solemn little face. A tiny fist escaped the blanket and clutched at his shirt.

Fiona's breath caught again, but when Kirkhill looked

at her, radiating his delight, something turned over inside her, leaving a warm feeling in its place.

After what seemed to be an extraordinarily long moment, Mother Beaton said, "Ye should give the laddie to his mam now, sir. He needs to suckle."

Kirkhill nodded again, still silent, but his gaze still held Fiona's warmly as he moved toward her. When he reached her bedside, he bent to give her the baby, but before he did, the midwife spoke again:

"Lay him atop her first, so that one of his ears lies next her heart, sir. He'll hear it beating and ken fine that he be wi' his mam."

Obeying her, Kirkhill leaned nearer than necessary and murmured for Fiona's ears alone, "I'd never snatch a child from its mam, lass, unless I knew it to be otherwise in mortal peril. This child is in no danger from me."

Realizing that he had overheard at least a portion of what she had said about him before he'd come in, and feeling guilty now, even sorry, she looked him in the eye and said, "I believe you, my lord. However, unless you mean to stay and watch me suckle him, I wish you would go away."

"I would fain watch you, lass," he murmured with the new, warmer look still in his eyes. "But I ken fine that you'd liefer be alone with him this first time. Moreover, you do need to rest." He glanced at Flory. "Did it occur to any of you to seek a wet nurse for this babe?"

Flory hesitated, glancing at Fiona, before she said, "Jane's sister, Eliza, did say that she has plenty o' milk for her wee bairn and this one, too, m'lord, so—"

"He is *my* son, sir," Fiona interjected, giving him a look that dared him to cavil. "As I told Old Jardine before he died, my child needs no one but me. So, if anyone is to seek a wet nurse, I will. Meantime, I will nurse him myself."

"You will need to keep to your bed for a time though, to recover your strength," he said. "Surely, it would be better to let someone else—"

"I will be up and about tomorrow or the next day," she said. "I know many women who give birth and take *no* time afterward for themselves."

Mother Beaton said, "They be but common folk, my lady. Noblewomen do seem to need more rest, not being as accustomed as them others be to—"

"Just how long do *you* think I should stay abed?" Fiona asked her, striving to keep her voice level but feeling as if everyone in the room had allied against her.

Phaeline said hastily, "There is naught amiss in getting all the rest you need, my dearling. Giving birth, as you have just learned, is a painful and exhausting business. Why, I stayed in bed nigh onto a month after you were born."

"Well, I have no intention of doing anything so daft," Fiona said. "A month! Why, I should be bored to lunacy. Moreover, just who do you think will look after this household if I stay in bed? Do *you* mean to remain at Spedlins to do so?"

"I will look after everything," Kirkhill said, "whether you stay in bed or not."

"Will you, sir?" she said. "Have you ever run a household before?"

"No, but I need only tell the housekeeper to act as she is accustomed to act when you are up and about."

"Aye, perhaps that would suffice if there *were* a

housekeeper. However, as my husband and good-father decided that I should serve in the place of one, we have none. I have run this household myself these two years past, so I would suggest that you let me continue lest you find that you are not up to the task."

"Oh, I rather think that I—"

"Moreover," she went on, ignoring his interruption, "I think you will find that looking after the estates is enough to do without troubling yourself over what goes on in the kitchen and bake-house or how often the floors need scrubbing."

"Then you may tell me what orders to relay to your people, and I will see them carried out," he said, apparently undaunted. "But you *will* remain in bed until Mother Beaton says that you are fit enough to get up."

She opened her mouth to tell him what she thought of his giving her orders as if she were just another servant in the house, but Phaeline said hastily, "You must think only of feeding your babe now, my dearling. I am sure that Kirkhill must be longing for his bed, just as I am. I do hope they have arranged to accommodate us, my lord. Mayhap you would be kind enough . . ." Pausing pointedly, she smiled.

"Aye, sure, my lady," he said. "I'll find out where they have put you. I warrant you'll want to stay until the lady Fiona is her usual self again."

Phaeline's expression suggested that she was not as sure about that as he seemed to be. But Fiona meant to get up as soon as she could manage it in any event, Mother Beaton or no Mother Beaton, and without any advice from a man who so mistakenly thought he could order her behavior as he chose.

Kirkhill had seen the same mutinous look on his sister's face far too often to misread it now on Fiona's, but he knew better than to comment.

He had meant to ask her about the key that he'd found on the inner chamber table, but instinct warned him not to do so just then with others in the room. Having declared herself mistress of the household, Fiona would want to keep it, and he rather thought that he ought to keep it himself.

So, instead, he bade her goodnight, thanked Mother Beaton for her ongoing services, and promised to make sure beds were available for her and for the lady Phaeline. Then, lighting a taper from a nearby candle, he left the room.

As the hour was well past midnight, few candles were still alight outside her ladyship's bedchamber, but his emitted a sufficient glow to light his way down the stairs. Or so he believed until he nearly stumbled over a small figure sitting, arms around knees, in a deep shadow on the next landing.

The figure gave a grunt of surprise, and as it scrambled to its feet, Kirkhill recognized the lad who had told him of the baby's birth. He was also the lad who had stared so intently at him the day that he had interrupted the lady Fiona's storytelling.

"What the devil are you doing there so late?" Kirkhill demanded.

"I thought ye might need summat for her ladyship or the wee bairn," the boy said warily. "I didna mean nae harm by it, sir. Also, me mam—"

"You're Jane's Davy, are you not?"

"I be *Jeb's* Davy. Jeb's Jane be me mam, though."

"Which of the men is Jeb, then?"

"Me da's dead."

"I'm sorry to hear that. Has he been dead long?"

The candle's glow revealed a glint of sudden tears in the boy's eyes. "Nay, none so long," he muttered.

"When?" Kirkhill asked quietly.

"Nobbut a short while afore ye came here that first time."

"I see. I lost my father just a year and a half ago," Kirkhill said. "I warrant you must miss yours as much as I miss mine."

"D'ye still miss him then, even after so long a while?"

Gently touching the boy's shoulder, he said, "Lad, I'm told that one never stops missing the people one loves when they are gone. But I'll tell you something I've learned for myself about *my* father, if you like."

"What, then?"

"Sithee, when I wish that I could ask him a question or just hear his voice, I nearly always have a memory that serves almost as well. It makes him seem closer to think that way—for me. I don't know if it works as well for others, but you might give it a try." Then, matter-of-factly, he said, "Meantime, I hope your mam has not gone to bed yet. I do not know where the lady Phaeline and Mother Beaton are to sleep, or where I should, come to that."

"Och, I near forgot," Davy said. "Hod did say he's had the old master's room swept out and the shutters open to let in the wind these hours since he saw ye, and he built a roaring fire, too, so it smells gey fine, he said, if ye'd be wanting to sleep there. He ha' cleared out his own room for your man, too. And me mam said the lady Phaeline should sleep in the room over Lady Fiona's. She's made up the bed there, she said, and if the lady needs help, she can send me to fetch Mam."

"Then, I think you should fetch your mam now and tell her that the lady Phaeline will welcome her help," Kirkhill said. "Also, prithee ask your mam to render what aid she can to Mother Beaton as well."

Davy nodded and hurried off ahead of him down the stairs.

Reaching the hall, Kirkhill wended his way among the men sleeping there, crossed the dais, and opened the door to the inner chamber.

Joshua, kneeling by the hearth and encouraging the small fire there with a poker, looked over his shoulder. Then, taking a last look at the now leaping flames, he stood and leaned the poker against the wall nearby.

"So, you've decided that this is where I am to sleep, have you?" Kirkhill said. "What have you done with Hod?"

"'Twas Hod came to fetch me, sir," Joshua said with a wry smile. "Said he thought this room would do for ye now and that I should take the small one that shares the service stair landing for myself, if that would suit ye."

"If that room is also well aired, it will."

"Aye, it is. Hod said he even had all these curtains down and aired outside, and the feather bed as well. Them's all fresh bedclothes, too, he said."

The change was startling, because Joshua or perhaps Hod himself had lit every candle in the chamber, so that the place looked almost welcoming. The room was spacious and seemed more so now that it was tidy and smelled pine-fresh. With Joshua to look after it, it would be a pleasant place, Kirkhill decided.

"I should be comfortable enough here," he said. "But what of Hod? Did he say aught about leaving—or about staying, come to that?"

"Nary a word," Joshua said. "He did seem a mite more hospitable than before. I dinna ken whether that means summat or nowt, though."

"I'd like him to stay if only because he knew Old Jardine well, and likely knew Will just as well. We've a mystery on our hands here, Joshua, and I want to get to the bottom of it."

"Ye'll be wanting to do that as soon as ye can, I'm thinking," Joshua said.

"Why is that?"

"'Cause them rumors be growing louder hereabouts, they say. Many folks here seem to think her ladyship— aye, or ye yourself—must ha' put an end to young Will Jardine. Nae one else would ha' cause, they say. It be clear, too, that others here think her ladyship had good cause to be rid o' the man."

"I doubt he was a good husband to her. Sakes, I ken fine he was not. The man chased every skirt that flitted past him. But why do the local folk talk so about her? The women here seem to like her—those I've met, at all events."

"Aye, they do like·her, but that doesna stop their wee tongues from clacking. Since folks think she had reason, many also think she most likely did the man in."

Kirkhill said, "That's plain daft. The lass was big with child and half Will's size. She could not have done it."

"Mayhap not alone," Joshua said. "But with help, she could."

Kirkhill felt a chill and wondered why he had not drawn that conclusion for himself. For all he knew of her or Will, someone else *could* have helped her. The lass was a beauty, pregnant or not. She also had a mind of her own—and a temper.

What if she had decided she'd had enough of her wayward husband and had persuaded some doltish but besotted male, servant or otherwise, to kill him *for* her?

Chapter 7 ⸺⸺⸺⸺⸺⸺

Fiona did not sleep well, because the baby cried twice during what little remained of the night and required nursing. He also required frequent nursing all day Monday and through Monday night as well. And he cried whenever he awoke, so that she began to think that she would never sleep soundly again.

Mother Beaton, having requested a cot for herself in Fiona's room Monday afternoon, had sent Flory to her own small room across the service-stair landing to sleep and had looked after Fiona and the baby herself in her quiet, competent way.

The sun was just beginning to shine through the east-facing windows Tuesday morning when the midwife took the baby after his latest feeding, changed him, and laid him in his cradle near Fiona's bed.

"Be ye hungry, me lady?" Mother Beaton asked as she rocked the cradle with a foot. "Ye've had two gey busy nights, and ye scarce ate a morsel yesterday. I'm thinking some creamy porridge or the like might suit ye well."

"Not porridge," Fiona said. But she was hungry. "Flory kens fine what I like, and she should be along soon." She felt sleepy and fretful, so she was grateful when the midwife merely nodded and fixed her attention on the gently rocking baby.

He was sleepy, too, his eyes already closing.

Fiona could hear her son softly breathing and muttering baby noises, making her wonder if he was uncomfortable in his cradle.

"I'm awake now, Mother Beaton," she said quietly. "Surely, you must be tired and wanting to sleep or to eat breakfast, yourself."

"I'd no mind a few minutes to rest me eyes in that wee solar downstairs, where your Jane did put another cot for me," the woman said. "But I'd best no leave ye till your Flory comes in."

"Nay, then, for you must be nigh to sleeping where you stand. Prithee, do go. He'll sleep now for at least an hour or two, will he not?"

"Aye, sure," the midwife said. "But—"

"Not another word," Fiona said. "You won't be of much use to anyone if you drop from exhaustion. Flory always comes just after sunrise, so I'll wager she is dressing now. I thank you most kindly for all your help, but do go now and sleep."

"I'll go along then," Mother Beaton said with a warm smile. "Ye'll make a good mother, me lady."

"I hope so," Fiona said, wishing the woman would just go.

First, she smoothed the blanket in the cradle and made sure the washstand ewer and the jug on the table by Fiona's bed had water, but at last she did go.

Immediately on hearing the latch click into place, Fiona slid out of bed. To be sure, she was tired and still plagued with some of the aftereffects of giving birth, but she was glad to be alone and hoped that Flory would not come too quickly.

Aside from aching breasts, some slight bleeding, and lingering pain, she felt normal. Putting a hand to her belly, she marveled at how flat it was after months of growing larger by the day. It was softer than before, but she had a waist again! She could hardly wait to try on clothes that, for months, she had been unable to wear.

She would start with her favorite silk robe, which was one of the few things she had brought with her when she'd eloped with Will. But it had stopped going all the way around her nearly three months before.

Taking it from the kist where it lived, and finding a fresh shift there as well, she made use of the chilly water in the washstand ewer for her ablutions, and then slipped the shift over her head.

"Mistress, what be ye a-doing up so soon?"

Fiona started so violently that she tangled herself in the shift, emerging from it at last to find Flory a few steps away with a fierce frown on her face.

"Mercy, you startled me nearly out of my skin!" Fiona exclaimed.

"And so I should think," Flory hissed, clearly aware of the sleeping baby even as she put fisted hands on her hips. "I came in here as quiet as a mouse so as no to wake ye or the bairn, and here ye be wi' your shift over your head." She glanced again at the cradle. "Aye, he is a precious wee thing, though."

Fiona smiled. "He is, isn't he?"

"What d'ye mean to call him?"

"Faith, I don't know. I might have called him Thomas after my father had Mairi not already given that name to her son. And, in troth, I ken fine that Father would not thank me for giving *his* name to a Jardine. His father's name was Robert, but so is Mairi's husband's, *and* the King of Scots and one of his dreadful sons."

"I dinna expect ye'll be calling him after his own da, any road," Flory said.

"I will not. Nor will I call him after his horrid grandsire, even if I knew what Old Jardine's name was."

"I think someone once told me it were John, or mayhap they said Gilbert," Flory said with a shrug.

"I wish you knew which one," Fiona said. "I rather like Gilbert."

"Aye, but everyone would call him Gil, would they no? Gil Jardine."

"God-a-mercy, you're right! I don't want him to have any name that even *sounds* like Will Jardine. What about Archie, after the Lord of Galloway?"

"His name be Archibald," Flory said. "Makes me think of a bald man."

"I'll have to think," Fiona said, wondering if Kirkhill thought *he* would be deciding her baby's name. She almost hoped he would so that she could set him straight. He might be her baby's guardian, but the baby was *her* son, not his.

"Ye'll be getting back into bed now, m'lady," Flory said.

"Will I?" Fiona said, giving her a challenging look.

"Ye should, aye," Flory said less forcefully. "I only just crept in to see if ye'd be awake yet, but I ken fine that the lady Phaeline has gone down to break her fast, and if I should tell her—"

"You'll tell her naught if you do not want to vex me

sorely. I want beef, bread, and ale, as usual, but I'd liefer my mother not visit me yet a while. I sent Mother Beaton to rest, and I shall rest myself *after* I break my fast, for I've had no sleep these two nights past. But then, I will get up. I'm not sick. I just had a baby."

Flory gave her a speculative look, as if she might say more. Then, evidently judging it wiser to keep silent, she nodded and left the room.

Fiona knelt beside the cradle then, and sat back on her heels.

"Good morning, my wee laddie," she murmured to the sleeping baby. "'Tis your second dawning, and we're alone at last. I wonder what you'll think of me."

He was so tiny. And what did she know about being a mother? It was not as if she had her own mother to emulate. Phaeline had spent more time being pregnant and yearning to present a son to her husband than she had spent mothering her daughters.

Fiona was determined to raise her son, if only to protect him from growing to be like his father and grandfather, or worse, but she knew that servants and wet nurses customarily did more to raise noble children than their parents did. Phaeline's notion of mothering had fixed solely on her duty to bear her husband a son.

Even now, other than expressing pleasure that her grandson looked more like a Dunwythie than a Jardine, Phaeline had shown only mild interest in him. She did not coo over him or beg to hold him, as others did.

Fiona sighed, recalling her mother's uncertain expression when Kirkhill had assumed she would want to stay at Spedlins until Fiona was herself again. Phaeline had often declared a preference for the comforts of Annan

House over the more rustic amenities at Dunwythie Hall. Spedlins was more rustic than the Hall and smaller.

Fiona wondered if Mairi had thought about similar things when *her* son was born. She wondered, too, just when Mairi and Rob would return to the Hall.

Taking a deep breath, she carefully picked up the sleeping baby, fearing on the one hand that he might waken and begin squalling, and on the other that he would not waken at all. He was breathing evenly, though, and if he realized that his mother was holding him, she could see no sign of it.

Moving carefully back to her bed, she laid him gently on it and climbed in, plumping pillows behind her and then gathering him up again and holding him, enjoying his warmth against her body. As she looked down into his face, at the way his dark lashes curved against his cheeks, she tried to decide whom he resembled most. His hair was dark like her own, and her mother had said he had a lot of it.

Fiona thought it rather sparse, not nearly as thick as hers or Will's. It looked straight like hers, though, rather than curly like Will's. As for the rest of him, he just looked like a baby, albeit a fine, bonnie one.

When she touched one of his palms with a finger, his own tiny fingers curled around it, and she recalled how he had clutched Kirkhill's shirt. She could hear her heartbeat, and a rush of warmth spread through her as she gazed lovingly at her son.

Hearing a light rap on the door, she quietly said, "Enter," not looking away from the baby but smiling, thinking that Flory had feared to startle her again.

Surprised that she had not asked who it was, Kirkhill opened the door quietly and stood still, enjoying the sight of the lady Fiona smiling at the baby in her arms.

"Just put it on the table, Flory," she said softly without looking up. "I'll get up in a moment and eat there as I usually do."

"I'm not Flory," he said.

She looked up then, her smile changing instantly to a frown. "Good sakes, sir, do you frequently enter a lady's bedchamber without announcing yourself?"

"I rapped," he reminded her.

She opened her mouth to speak but shut it again as color suffused her cheeks.

"Why do you blush, my lady? You are properly covered."

"I thought you were Flory."

"Does Flory usually knock on your door before entering?"

"Nay, but she startled me before when she came—" The color in her cheeks deepened, and she looked down again at the baby. Then, looking right at Kirkhill, she said evenly, "She just went to fetch my breakfast."

He held her gaze for a moment before he said, "Do you know, you remind me most forcibly sometimes of my youngest sister, Nan."

"Do I? Is she nice then?"

"She is a damnable nuisance most of the time, particularly when she thinks she has persuaded me that she has *not* been up to mischief."

"Mercy, sir, what mischief do you imagine I have been up to?"

Injecting a touch of sternness into his voice, he said, "I suspect that Flory caught you out of bed, which is how she startled you, and that she did not fetch the bairn to you before she left, as I first thought. I recall now that when I saw her in the hall a few minutes ago, all she said to me when I asked how you were faring was that you were awake and the babe was asleep in his cradle."

"Oh."

Detecting the wariness in her expression that he had noted a time or two before, he abandoned sternness and said, "I did not come to ring a peal over you, only to see if all was well and to learn what orders I should issue for the household."

"Then I hope you won't be vexed when I tell you I mean to get up today."

"I cannot promise I won't," he said. "I don't know much about the rules for women after childbirth, but because I don't, I mean to take advice from your mother and Mother Beaton. If you do not want to vex me, you will do as they bid you."

"Tell me more about your sister."

"Nay, for I am sure that you will soon meet her, and I've a notion the two of you will get along well. Moreover, Flory will soon return with your breakfast. I did want to ask you, though, if you and Will had chosen a name for the lad."

She nibbled her lower lip.

"'Tis not a difficult question," he said. "You need only say aye or nay."

A slight smile touched her lips. "It is only that Flory asked me the same question," she said. "I do not know yet what I want to call him."

"Did not your husband suggest a name?"

She shrugged. "He took little interest in the fact that I was with child, except as my condition affected him."

Her cheeks reddened again. "In troth, I think he expected people to encourage him to name a son after himself. But I'd liefer not."

"Nay, 'tis better if names skip a generation. Mayhap your mother will have some suggestions. Would you like me to put him back in the cradle now?"

"Flory will do it when she comes. I want to hold him for a while."

"Then I'll take myself off. But you look after yourself as well as the bairn."

"How long do you mean to stay at Spedlins?"

"As long as necessary," he said. "I must look over Jardine's accounts and the estates, of course, and decide if Evart, his steward, knows his business well enough for me to leave him in charge when I cannot be here. He is getting on in years."

"He and Old Jardine knew each other from childhood, so Evart is used to doing as he's told. I expect you have your own good steward looking after your affairs back at Kirkhill."

He smiled, thinking of his uncle. "I do. My uncle, Sir James Seyton, should be there by now, because I sent for him as soon as I received word from Spedlins. My mother likes to have a member of the family in charge, and Uncle James will keep his eye on my sister, too."

"Does your mother not do that?"

"She does try. But Nan's determination is usually greater than our mother's ability to stand firm, so Mother finds it difficult to keep Nan out of mischief."

"And you think I am like Nan?"

"Do you think you are not?"

She frowned. "I think I may have been mischievous

once, in a way, but I have not felt at all so since coming to Spedlins."

"You just do not like it when others tell you what to do."

"Not when I don't think they should," she replied soberly.

"We're likely to fratch then," he said. "I *am* accustomed to being obeyed. But I meant what I said to you the other night, Fiona." Catching the slip, he said hastily, "I hope you don't mind if I call you so when we're alone. To address you so formally when we'll be living almost in each other's pockets seems unnecessary."

She said evenly, "What did you mean, my lord?"

For a moment, he thought she meant they should retain their formality, but then he noted the twinkle in her eyes. He also noted again what a beautiful woman she was, especially sitting as she was with the baby cuddled in her arms and her hair parted in the middle and hanging in simple, glossy black plaits over her shoulders.

He had dreamed of her again the night before, and had wakened in a sweat.

Collecting his wits, he said more sharply than he'd intended, "I meant it when I said that your child has nowt to fear from me, lass. Nor do you."

"Good sakes, sir, I don't fear you."

"That's fine then. I think I hear your Flory coming now." He stepped to the door to open it, and if Flory looked surprised to see him, she looked only grateful when he took the tray from her. "Put the bairn in his cradle," he said to her. "Then you can arrange this tray on your mistress's lap so that she need not get up again."

Flory's eyes widened, but she said only, "Aye, m'lord."

When Fiona looked mutinous, he smiled at her and said, "Pick your fights carefully, my lady. This isn't a good one. I'll come back later to see how you do."

He waited a few beats to see if she would reply, while Flory leaned over her to take the baby. Then, as the maid was settling the child into his cradle, he stepped nearer with the tray of food.

Fiona watched him but said nothing.

Flory turned to take the tray from him, saying, "Thank you, m'lord. I'll look after them now."

Smiling at the still silent Fiona, he turned and left the room, wondering what they would fight about next.

Fiona waited after the door had shut to be sure he would not return before she said, "He ought not to come into my room the way he did. He just walked in."

Flory looked astonished. "Without knocking?"

"He did rap, aye, but lightly. I thought he was you."

"'Tis a good thing he did not come before, when it *were* me. Only think what he'd ha' seen then if he had!"

Remembering how startled she had been, and how she had tangled herself in her shift when Flory had spoken so sharply after entering quietly, Fiona chuckled. "I expect I'd have been just as startled to hear his rap then, and I might have thought he was you anyway. Sakes, Flory, gentlemen do not just walk into the bedchambers of women they scarcely know."

"Your father would ha' done the same," Flory pointed out.

"Kirkhill is *not* my father!"

"Aye, sure, I ken that fine. But does he no stand in much the same place to ye, thanks to the old master's will?"

"Mayhap he thinks he does," Fiona said sourly. "He will be sorry if he tries treating me like a daughter, though. I'll have none of that."

The thought that he probably did look upon her as a cross between a daughter and a younger sister did not sit well at all. She would rather fight with him.

That thought brought another one, that he was kin to the Jardines. He did not look like them or act like them (except in his apparent penchant for issuing orders right and left). But the men of any given family were often much alike, and she did not want to learn that he was, after all, like Will and Old Jardine.

Kirkhill spent the bulk of the morning interviewing Old Jardine's steward and looking over Spedlins Tower. He was not favorably impressed with the place—because its late master had not maintained it well. Nor was he impressed with Evart, a timid, elderly man who seemed unwilling to express any opinions but who had answered all of Kirkhill's questions willingly if somewhat vaguely.

Warning the man that he would expect his company again the following morning to look over the rest of the tower's demesne and as much of the rest of the Applegarth estates as they could easily cover in a day's time, he retired to his chamber to write the letter he had promised to give Hod. He had not seen him all morning but was sure the man would not depart without telling him he was going.

Finding a gillie outside his chamber door on the great

hall dais, he said, "Do you know where to find Old Jardine's Hod?"

"Aye, sure, me lord."

"Fetch him for me, will you?"

When Hod came to him, Kirkhill read him the letter and said, "I want you to keep this, Hod. If you find work with another nobleman, he may not be able to read it himself. But you may tell him that Sir Richard Seyton, Baron Kirkhill, will speak for you and will recommend you for any position that the man deems suitable."

Hod gave him a long look before he took the letter from him. "D'ye mean to say that ye've changed your mind, m'lord, and dinna want me to stay?"

"I do not mean that," Kirkhill said. "I say what I mean, Hod. I would be grateful if you would agree to stay for at least a month or so, or as long as you like. But whether you go or stay is up to you. The letter is yours in either event."

A wry smile touched Hod's thin lips. "What if ye change your mind about what a grand chappie I be?"

"Then I'll tell you so, and I may alter some of what I might say to any man who came here asking about you. But I won't change what I've written about how well you served Old Jardine. That is plain fact and will not alter now that he is gone. Nor," he added with a smile, "do I think that you will serve me ill."

"I'll stay then, m'lord, but what would ye ha' me do? Ye've your own man, such as he is, so ye've small need o' me."

"I believe that Old Jardine lacked a household steward as well as a housekeeper," Kirkhill said. "I think you would do well as my steward."

After a pause, Hod said, "Her ladyship runs the house, m'lord. Mayhap ye didna ken that, things being what they be wi' her just now. But she'd no like seeing me in charge o' this household."

"Would she not? Does she have cause to dislike you?"

Visibly taken aback by the direct question, Hod grimaced. "Aye, sir, she may think she does. Would ye be wanting to hear why?"

Shaking his head, Kirkhill said, "That lies between you and her ladyship. You should know, though, that I will expect you to take your orders from her and to serve her as well as you will serve me. However, I will also expect that if you think she is acting unwisely, you will tell her so. If she persists in an unwise course without apparent good cause, you will bring the matter to me."

"Ye dinna want me to spy on her, do ye? I'd no like doing that."

"No, I want you to help me protect her. I ken fine that you are aware of Old Jardine's suspicions about her, and I believe that you also know that rumors stirred by those suspicions have been flying the length and breadth of Annandale."

"Aye, sir, I did hear that."

"Tell me this then. Did you start them?"

"Nay, sir. Old Master told anyone who would listen to him, though, so many here did ken what he thought. Them rumors could ha' started here, right enough, but I dinna talk about Old Master, nor about aught he said to me. I doubt ye'll believe that, for I ken fine that the lady Fiona blames me—"

"You have given me no cause to disbelieve what you say, Hod. Until you do, your word is good enough." He put out his hand. "Thank you for staying. You can begin your new duties straightaway. If you have any questions, ask me."

"There be one or two that come to mind, sir."

"And what would they be?"

"Do I tell her ladyship that I am now house steward, or will ye tell her?"

Kirkhill chuckled. "For my sins, Hod, I will tell her. May God help me."

"Aye, sir, ye'll need His help if ye're to come off wi' a whole skin. Ye should be prepared to duck, too. She does like to throw things now and now."

"In that case, I had better tell her straightaway. It would not do for her to find out from someone else before I tell her myself. But you said one or two questions. Have you another?"

"One, aye, about the old master."

"What about him?"

"Folks be a-wondering when we should bury him," Hod said.

Kirkhill stared at him. "Bury him! Sakes, I thought you'd have done that straightaway. It's summer, man. Where have they put his body?"

"In one o' the outbuildings, m'lord. Nae one dared take responsibility for the burial, wi' her ladyship birthing and us thinking that ye'd want to see to it yourself."

"You thought wrong," Kirkhill said. "See that he is properly prepared and we'll bury him at dawn. Would he have wanted a priest?"

"Nay, he didna hold wi' priests or wi' the Kirk."

"Then we'll have a simple ceremony at dawn tomorrow. Anyone can attend who has a mind to, but you see that it gets done. That can be your first task as house steward. Why the devil didn't you tell me at once that he was still aboveground?"

"I didna think it were my business to tell ye. I thought Evart would."

"He should have, aye, especially as I asked him to show me everything here. Odd that it did not occur to him to show me where Jardine's body lay. But I imagine that you can work with Evart to see the thing done properly."

"Aye, sure," Hod agreed, nodding.

"I'll go and see her ladyship now," Kirkhill said. Although he did not think Fiona would be pleased to learn of his decision with regard to Hod, and did not want to debate it with her, he was disappointed when Flory answered his soft rap and told him that both her ladyship and the bairn were sound asleep.

He was glad that Fiona was resting and had apparently decided against testing him yet, but he did not want to leave the revelation of Hod's new position to just anyone. Accordingly, he said, "When she wakens, Flory, prithee send a gillie to tell me. I have news for her that I'd liefer she not hear first from anyone else."

Flory's eyes narrowed. "It'll be summat she'll dislike, I'm thinking."

"I'm afraid so, but she should hear it from me. I'll be at the high table."

"Aye, sure, sir. I'll send for ye when she wakes up."

⁓

"The laird be here to see ye, mistress," Flory said as she plumped pillows on a bench in one of the window embrasures. "Ye'll be more comfortable here, I'm thinking, whilst he's wi' ye. It dinna be fitting for ye to receive him in your bed."

Stifling a bubble of astonished laughter, Fiona said, "You are quite right, Flory. Tell him to wait."

"Now, mistress, it willna take ye a moment to shift to this window seat."

"I don't move as quickly as I'd like yet," Fiona said. "But hear me, Flory. Although I have slept most of today away, I shan't do so tomorrow. I shall get up at my usual time, and I'll break my fast in here. Then I mean to walk about and see to my usual duties. I'm fidgety and tired of staying in bed."

"Aye, mistress, we'll see. D'ye want me to stay?"

"Unless he sends you away, aye," Fiona said. She could not imagine what Kirkhill might say to her that she would not want Flory to hear, but she scarcely knew the man, after all. He might say anything.

The baby was sleeping but would wake soon to nurse, and her breasts were sore. She forgot about them when Kirkhill walked in.

The searching look he gave her was warning enough that he was uncertain about how she would react to what he wanted to tell her.

"What is it?" she asked. "You look as if you expect trouble."

"Do I?" he said. "Then it must be so. I'm thinking that you will not like the decision I've made. Is it all right if we talk normally, or will we wake the bairn?"

"He sleeps like he's deaf, but Mother Beaton says such sleep is proper for newborn babes. He'll awaken starving, though, and I think it must nearly be time."

"Then I'll just say what I must say quickly. I've told Hod that I want him to serve as steward of this household."

"Hod! Nay, I won't have that." She glanced at Flory.

Kirkhill said mildly, "You will still have charge of the household, my lady, but Hod can make that easier for you. I have told him he is to seek his orders from you and to discuss any conflict with you. If something arises on which the two of you cannot agree, I will expect you to come to me."

"You don't understand," she said tensely, wanting to shout at him but fearing that if she gave way to temper, she might also give way to tears. At that moment, her emotions seemed entirely unpredictable.

"Perhaps *you* would explain the difficulty to me," he said gently.

She shook her head. She couldn't.

"Then we'll give him a try. After Old Jardine died, Hod thought of leaving, but I'd like him to stay because he knows much about this place and its people, much more than you can know after just two years here."

"He hasn't been here much longer than that," she said.

"Hasn't he? He did work closely with Old Jardine, though. Moreover, if he does not give satisfaction, he will go."

"I don't know why you say I'm in charge. You're not giving me a say in this."

"Not unless you give me reason," he said. He hesitated then, eyeing her thoughtfully. Then he took the small pouch he wore from his belt, opened it, and extracted a key. "Do you chance to know what this key fits, lass?"

She shook her head. She had never seen it before.

"Well, you do command this household. Have you a chatelaine?"

"Aye, sure, yonder on that hook by the door." She pointed to the silver-linked girdle, or belt, that she had worn at her waist until it had gotten too small. Attached to it on short chains were the various articles of household use that she usually carried, including her keys, a cork-screw, scissors, and her thimble case.

Taking one ring of keys from its chain, the one with the pantry key, he added the key he'd shown her. "I found it in Jardine's room. You should keep it with these others until we learn what it fits. There is one other thing," he added as he hung the belt back on its hook.

She felt wary again, but this time he seemed only wryly amused.

"What is it?" she asked.

"Old Jardine is still aboveground. Evidently, in the hurry to send for me, and with the birth of the *newest* Jardine, no one got round to burying the *old* one."

"God-a-mercy! He died on Saturday! It has been nearly four days!"

"He died Saturday evening, so it is barely three days," Kirkhill said. "And it has not been hot. They are digging his grave now, and we'll bury him at dawn tomorrow. I told Hod to arrange it with Evart and let everyone else know so that anyone who wants to attend may do so. He said Jardine would not want a priest."

"Nay, he would not," she agreed. "He would spin in his grave if he heard a priest speaking over him. But why did Hod not tell you before now?"

"He thought it was Evart's business to do so, but Evart strikes me as an old man afraid to speak to his own shadow."

"Aye, he worshipped Old Jardine but feared him, too.

And doubtless he is terrified of you. But Evart suited Old Jardine because he never said nay to him."

"Well, I want my steward to speak up," Kirkhill said. "Now, lass," he added, "your mother has not seen you or her grandson today, and she asked me to say that she would like to do so if you are not too tired. May she come up?"

"Aye, sure," she said, trying to match his tone but fearing she sounded sullen.

When he'd gone, Flory said, "Ye should tell him why ye canna abide that Hod."

"Nay, I cannot. 'Tis too humiliating. And don't you dare tell him, either."

Flory grimaced but she said, "Nay, then, ye ken fine that I won't."

Phaeline soon joined them and seemed for once truly to dote on her grandson. But Fiona was tired and found her mother's ready advice on nearly every subject that arose only irritating.

At last, Phaeline said, "I can see that you are not feeling yourself yet, my dearling. Truly, I want only to help you in any way I can."

"I know that, madam," Fiona said tightly as the baby stirred and began making noises that she recognized as a prelude to loudly announcing his near starvation. She would have liked to ask her mother why she had not attempted to help her during the two years since she had left home, but she was afraid that if she broached that subject, she would lose her temper altogether.

When Phaeline left the room, Fiona felt only relief.

*Chapter 8*_____

The next morning, when Kirkhill arrived at the Sped-lins graveyard, pale gray dawn mist rising from the river Annan lay thick on the hillside. It gave the place an eerie look, with headstones sticking up through it like posts through a soft cloud.

Two shovel handles showed above the dense, low mist, about six feet apart.

Kirkhill wondered if Hod had thought about a head-stone for Old Jardine. He had purposely delayed his arrival, not wanting to look as if he were there for any reason other than to pay his respects to the dead. In truth, he did not care how they buried the old man, as long as the interment was respectful. And with Hod in command of the proceedings, he was sure that it would be.

A group of perhaps twenty people had gathered at the gravesite, looking like dark shadows looming out of the mist. He saw Joshua first, because he had expected to see him there. His man was employing his usual skill at mak-ing friends to good purpose. Kirkhill had not, however, expected to see the maidservant Flory standing beside Joshua. Surely, she should be looking after...

His gaze stopped when he recognized the figure next

to Flory as her mistress. He felt a surge of irritation bordering on anger before he recalled that he had not forbidden Fiona to attend the burial. Moreover, if she was fit enough to get out of bed, as she had doubtless insisted, the Jardines would expect her to be there.

She looked at him, and he nearly smiled to see the challenging look she shot him. Controlling the urge, he gave her look for look instead.

It would be unwise to let her see that her stubborn determination to defy those who cared for her well-being rather amused him, but he admired her courage.

He walked over to stand beside her, noting that she was wearing a hooded cloak, warm gloves, and leather boots.

Her chin rose at his approach, but she said coolly, "Good morrow, sir."

"Good morrow, madam," he said with a slight nod. "Is everyone here?"

"I think so, aye. We were just waiting for you."

He looked for Hod and saw him talking with Evart. Then Hod saw him and stepped nearer the space between the shovels, as his gaze drifted over the onlookers.

"There being nae one else here wha' may wish to speak for the old master, unless his lordship has words to say . . ." He paused until Kirkhill shook his head. Then, drawing a breath, Hod said, "We all ken fine that ye didna ken him well, sir. Sakes, but I served him three years, m'self, and in that time he scarce spoke to any save the young master n' me. 'Tis Master Will as ought to be speaking for him now."

Kirkhill noted that two or three men in the group nodded, but most showed no reaction. As he scanned the group, he realized that the mourners were all gillies and house servants, plus a dozen or so men-at-arms, half of whom were his own.

Hod spoke briefly, relating what he knew and admired of Old Jardine.

Kirkhill realized as the mist began to dissipate that the shrouded body was already in the grave, with a mound of dirt waiting at one side to bury it. When Hod stopped speaking, he motioned two men to the shovels, and the ceremony was over.

Fiona, standing beside Kirkhill, gave a shudder, and he offered her an arm. As they turned toward the tower, he saw another, smaller figure a short distance away.

"Is that not Jeb's Wee Davy?" he asked her.

She looked and nodded, frowning. "He should not be here, watching," she said. "His own loss is too new."

"'Tis nobbut life in the Borders, lass," Kirkhill said. "Nearly all bairns suffer loss by the time they are his age."

"He's barely nine," she said curtly. "His sister, Tippy, is only six."

"Even so," he said, wishing she would look up at him. "How did Jeb die?"

"A stupid accident. He was helping saddle horses one evening, because Will wanted to ride along the river, and one of the beasts kicked him in the head as he tried to remove some thorns that had lodged in its hoof. It did not even seem as if the horse kicked him hard, but Jeb died less than an hour later."

"That's a shame," Kirkhill said. "A lad needs a father."

She gave him a look. "My son will do gey better without his, I think."

He put his hand over hers on his forearm and urged her toward the boy, who seemed to be staring at bare ground, looking at nothing in particular.

As they approached, however, Davy looked up and said, "They put him here, me lady. I ken the place, 'cause the ground be still bare. Me mam said that one day mayhap we can make a stone for him. I'd do it m'self, but I dinna ha' the ken."

"Jeb will have his stone, Davy," Fiona said. "We will see to that."

Kirkhill said, "Her ladyship is right, lad. If you want to help with it, I'll arrange that for you. But for now, prithee run ahead to the great hall and tell them we're coming in hungry. Also, ask Lady Phaeline if she wants to break fast with us."

"Aye, sure, me lord," Davy said, running to obey.

"That was kind of you," Fiona said, looking up at him with approval.

"I'm a kind chap," he said, "when people do not defy me."

She looked swiftly down, but he was nearly certain that she smiled.

⟿

Fiona stifled the bubble of laughter in her throat. Not only did it seem inappropriate to laugh at such a time and in such a place but also she did not know where the bubble had come from. Surely, she did not *want* to defy Kirkhill.

Someone with more power than she possessed had to protect the Jardine estates for her tiny son until he was of an age to take them over himself. Kirkhill seemed eminently qualified for the job. So why did the man annoy her so much?

Glancing at his handsome profile, she looked down again before he could feel her gaze on him. Her boots were wet from the damp grass of the hillside, but the dawn mist was dissipating. It was easier now to see where they stepped.

Earlier, as she and Flory had followed the others downhill to the graveyard, she had wondered nervously if someone might fall into the hole that the men had dug there. The image had sent shards of ice up her spine, and she had turned her thoughts abruptly to her child, wondering if he might get hungry before she returned.

As they neared the tower entrance, Kirkhill slowed and looked back over his shoulder to say, "Flory, I want a word with my man before I break my fast, and he is yonder with Hod. I'll leave you to see your mistress safely inside from here."

Fiona lifted her hand from his forearm and walked on ahead, not waiting for Flory. She had a sudden fierce yearning to see her baby.

She was hurrying up the twisting stairway beyond the hall landing, when she heard a deep growl above, followed by a gasp and a sudden outraged squall that she recognized as her son's. The sounds giving wings to her feet, she flew up and around the curve, only to come to an abrupt halt just below the landing outside her bedchamber at the sight of her mother with the baby in her arms, staring at Jardine's great mastiff, crouched to spring, on the stairs just above them.

"Don't move, Mam," Fiona said evenly.

At the sound of her voice, the dog sprang.

Kirkhill, having wanted only to see if Joshua had learned anything new in the graveyard and hearing that he had not, followed Fiona and Flory at once. Entering the tower a few yards behind Flory, he saw her skirts whisk around the curve of the stairs above the great-hall landing, then heard the baby's cry and a shrill scream.

Taking the stairs two by two, he pressed the shrieking Flory hard against the stairway wall and pushed past her, striving to see what was happening above. At first, all he saw was a swirl of skirts. Then he recognized Fiona's dark cloak, heard a canine snarl, and moved faster. But he was not fast enough. As he reached for Fiona, she thrust herself between Phaeline and Old Jardine's mastiff just as the dog, still snarling, leaped.

Terrified for Fiona, and realizing that Phaeline held the baby and that they might all plunge down the stairway under the dog's great weight, he braced himself with one hand to the wall to hold Phaeline steady while he tried to grab Fiona with his free hand. Phaeline suddenly shifted away, having managed to regain sense enough to open the bedchamber door and stumble inside with the baby.

Fiona had not made a sound, but as she fell back under the weight of the dog, it was all Kirkhill could do to retain his footing and catch her. She grew abruptly much heavier, and as he strove to hold fast, blood spurted all over him.

Fiona cried out, and more terrified than ever, fearing that she had sustained a mortal injury, he clutched her to him, trying to shove the dog off her as he did.

His mind was still on pushing the heavy dog up and

away from them when a calm young voice from just above his eye level said, "D'ye think he's dead, laird?"

Lifting his gaze from the blood soaking Fiona's breasts and torso, he looked past the dog's head into Davy's face. It looked as if the lad were straddling the dog.

"Where did you come from?" Kirkhill demanded.

"Yonder," the boy said, jerking a thumb toward the stairs above them as he clambered awkwardly off the dog and tried to help drag it off Fiona. "Sithee, I thought the lady Phaeline were still in her chamber, so I went up to tell her that everyone were a-coming in to break fast. She were no there, but that fiendish devil-dog were a-sitting on the stairway. He paid me nae heed, but when I rapped on Lady Phaeline's door, he bolted down the stairs. Be the lady Fiona hurt bad?"

"I don't know," Kirkhill said, forcing himself to speak as calmly as the boy did. "The dog is dead, though. It looks as if someone slit its throat."

"I did, aye. I saw him leap at her, and I kent fine that I couldna stop him or pull him off her, so I jumped atop him. I had me da's dirk in me hand when I did, and it stuck in his neck when I landed on him. I just wiggled it around, is all."

An icy chill swept through Kirkhill at the thought of how easily the lad's knife might have plunged into Fiona instead, but he said only, "Good lad."

"You saved us all, Davy," Fiona said, gasping.

Kirkhill, working from an awkward angle as he supported her and tried to move the dog, was having little luck with the latter task, even with Davy's help.

"Are ye bad hurt, me lady?" the boy asked. "Ye're all over bloody."

"Nay, I twisted as he leaped. And, although he did sink his teeth in my shoulder when he struck me, my cloak is thick and his lordship kept me from falling. I think he also eased the force of Dobby's impact," she added, still gasping for breath. She looked up at Kirkhill. "He *is* heavy, sir. Cannot you shift him off me?"

"Aye," he said, helping her sit against the wall and then leaning over her to move the dog. Hearing the chamber door open, he looked up to see Phaeline in the opening. He could hear the baby crying inside. "Are you all right, madam?"

"I am, aye, although I don't mind telling you that that beast frightened the liver and lights out of me. Is it truly dead?"

"It is. I'll have some of our lads come and remove it. I'll also have them bring food to you up here. The babe is hungry, and her ladyship would do well to rest. I shall rely on you to keep her here in her chamber."

"Help me up, my lord," Fiona said sharply. "I have some few things to say, and I don't want to say them whilst I'm sitting here on this landing."

⁓

Fiona waited only for Kirkhill to get the dog off her before getting quickly to her feet and confronting her mother.

"What demon possessed you to take my son out of his cradle?" she demanded. "Faith, to take him out of my chamber! I told you never—"

"Moderate your voice, Fiona," Phaeline interjected. "I heard him wailing, and when he did not stop, I came to see what was amiss. He was in your room all alone save for that child, Tippy, so I sent her away and decided to take him downstairs to Mother Beaton until you returned, thinking she might prepare a sugar tit or some other sustenance for him. I no sooner shut the door behind me than that beast dashed around the corner, crouched, and growled at me. Where *were* you?"

"At Old Jardine's burial, of course, but you had no right to take him from his cradle, Mam. He was safe there and—"

She broke off with a sob when Kirkhill gripped her arm and urged her into her bedchamber. As he released her, she whirled to face him. "What do you mean—?"

"Calm yourself," he said. "Your bairn is hungry. Go and feed him."

She opened her mouth to tell him how much she disliked his arbitrary orders, but something in his expression deterred her.

"Before I leave and shut that door to the landing," he went on quietly. "You might want to thank Wee Davy again."

She nodded, collecting herself enough to say, "Prithee, Davy, come in here. Flory, go and look after the bairn, will you? Likely, he needs changing."

As Flory hurried to obey her, the boy came in, looking wary. "I didna let that devil dog inside, me lady, if that be what ye're a-thinking. The door downstairs were open when I came in, but I shut it behind me, and he were already inside."

"I ken fine that you would not have let him in," she said. "But his lordship is right to remind me that I did not properly thank you for your swift action. You saved us, and I did not even know that you carried a dirk."

"Nay, and me mam doesna ken that neither," he said

with a wry look. "Likely, when ye tell her, she'll say I'm no to carry it anymore."

"I'll see that she does not forbid it," Fiona said, giving Kirkhill a look that dared him to gainsay her.

He did not.

"But, Davy," she added, "what you did was gey brave. I dare not think what might have happened had you not thought and acted so quickly."

"I didna *think* at all," Davy said. "I just flew to stop him the only way I could. I kent fine he were too strong for me, but me da's dirk be ever sae sharp."

"A good thing it is, too," she said. "But I want you to know something more. I have been trying and trying to think what to name my wee son, and now I know just what I shall call him. He is to be David Jeb Jardine, Davy, after you and your father. Do you think my David Jeb will grow up brave enough to suit his name?"

Davy stared at her. "Ye be a-naming the new Jardine after *me*... and me da?"

"I am," Fiona said, this time not even looking at Kirkhill. *Just let him object*, she thought fiercely.

Kirkhill said, "'Tis a great honor, Davy-lad, and well deserved. Go now, find two stout men below, and tell them I want them to remove that beast from the landing and give it a decent burial—*not* in the graveyard."

"Aye, sir, I'll do that straightaway," Davy said, squaring his thin shoulders.

"Oh, and, Davy," Fiona said as he turned to leave, "now that we shall have a much smaller David, no one will call you *Wee* Davy anymore. They will have to make do with plain Davy, or Jeb's Davy, or our fierce Davy from now on."

"Coo," Davy said, grinning at her. Still grinning, he hurried away.

⁓

Kirkhill watched Fiona, wondering if she had forgotten that she was awash in the dog's blood. She had talked to the boy as if she dealt with such things daily, but he knew from her display of temper with her mother and the slight sob when he'd ushered her into her bedchamber that the incident had much disturbed her.

After the boy left, instead of following him, he shut the door and said, "That was a frightening experience for all of us, lass, and particularly for you. Moreover, Mother Beaton has warned me that it is normal for a new mother to tire easily, so—"

"You are about to issue orders again," Fiona interjected. "But I have been looking after myself now for some time, sir. If you think that either Old Jardine or Will ever looked after me, you are much mistaken. I am also capable of looking after my son," she added with a darkling look at her mother.

Kirkhill said, "I will leave you to look after him then, but before I go, I do have one more thing to say."

She hesitated, visibly bracing herself, still facing her mother. But when he did not continue, she turned at last and met his gaze. Although she strove to look as if nothing he might say could affect her, he knew as if he could taste them that her lips were dry, that she was dying to lick them but would not do so because such a reaction would reveal her uneasiness to him.

Gently, he said, "Davy is not the only one who showed courage, lass. You put yourself between your mother and that vicious beast. You may say that you did it only to save your bairn, but had that been your sole purpose, you would have snatched him from her and let the dog attack her."

"Nay, I would never—"

"Just so," he said.

After a reflective pause, she said, "How did Dobby get inside, anyway?"

"I told Hod to keep him out, but I expect that whilst Hod was attending to the burial, what with folks coming and going, someone just left the door open," he said.

"Aye, they often do," she said with a nod. "And Davy said it was open."

"I should have spoken to the porter as well as to Hod about the dog," he admitted. "But now, lass, go and feed your babe. I'll have them bring food enough up for you and Lady Phaeline to break your fast. I expect Flory has already eaten."

"Aye, m'lord, hours ago," Flory said.

Nodding, he waited only to see if Fiona would argue with him. When she did not, he turned toward the door.

"I will go with you, my lord," Phaeline said. "I am not needed here."

He glanced back at Fiona, but she had turned toward her child. With a nod to Phaeline, he opened the door, drew it shut as he followed her onto the landing, and politely preceded her down the stairs, as a gentleman always did on such stairways lest the lady in his charge trip and fall. At the hall landing, he offered his arm.

"You might want to send someone to invite Mother Beaton or your woman to join us at the high table, my lady, so that you are not the sole female in the hall."

"Aye, sure," Phaeline said. "See you, Mother Beaton stayed with Mairi only three days after Wee Thomas was born, so doubtless *she* is ready to depart now, too."

"You are thinking of leaving us then," he said as he waved a gillie to them.

"Aye," she said. She fell silent while he sent the gillie for Mother Beaton and then to have someone take food up to Fiona. When the lad had gone, Phaeline said, "Fiona is thinking only of her child now, sir, and that is as it should be, I expect. In any event, I shall be nearby at the Hall if she wants to send for me."

"You don't mean to return at once to Annan House, then."

"Nay, for Lammas quarter day is nearly upon us, so Mairi and Rob—aye, and our Jenny and Hugh, and their children, too—will soon be arriving at the Hall. All of us mean to stay with Rob and Mairi until the end of August. Mairi wants to celebrate Lammas Day with minstrels and feasting for all who will come."

He nodded. "Fiona will miss you long before then, I think, madam."

"Do you? I doubt it. I was not a good mother, sir, but I did not realize that until my lord husband died. See you, I was his second wife, and I had failed to give him a son. I could give him only Fiona, and I fear now that because of my desire for a son, my daughter felt so unloved that she ran off with that scoundrel Will Jardine in search of love. I doubt she found it with *him,* but mayhap someday, she will."

"I am sure she will," Kirkhill said, wondering why the thought should irritate him. To be sure, he'd dreamed of possessing her himself, but that was lust and nowt more.

Ignoring the sensation, he gestured for Phaeline to precede him to the dais.

He broke his fast quickly, explained that he had arranged for Evart to show him as much of the Jardine property as he could, and left Phaeline to finish at her own pace, assuring himself that she would not depart until afternoon.

With that in mind, he cut short his time with Evart to join her again at high table for the midday meal and wondered if Fiona would join them. When she did not, he motioned Hod over and learned that she had ordered a light meal in her chamber. Wondering if the lass, despite having shown her courage that morning, was avoiding him or her mother, he exerted himself to get to know Phaeline better.

He was still enjoying hearing what Fiona and her half sister Mairi had been like as children when his porter entered to tell him that guests had arrived.

"'Tis Sir James Seyton and the lady Anne Seyton, my lord."

"Then you had better fetch them in," he said. To Phaeline, he said, "You are about to meet my younger sister and my uncle, madam. I shall endeavor not to throttle them both until after we have finished our meal."

"Why, I look forward to meeting your sister, sir. I believe I may have met Sir James at Stirling some years ago."

"Then if *you* speak well for him, mayhap I will spare him. I have no doubt whose idea this visit was, in any event. However, before they come in, I beg of you, madam, do not hurry away this afternoon as you had planned. I have many duties to attend each day, and it would be most unsuitable for Nan to rattle around here by herself when

I am out or away, or to be the sole lady at meals in this hall full of men even if I am here. I cannot expect the lady Fiona always to bear her company."

"Nay, for Fiona is not fully recovered yet," Phaeline said. "I would gladly oblige you, my lord, but this tower is small. Unless you mean to turn the room that Fiona calls the solar into a bedchamber, my room is the only one that that would be suitable for your sister. But if you think she'll agree to share it with me, I'll stay."

"We will get through one hour at a time, madam," he said. "You are right, though, about Spedlins' size. It is beginning to feel most confining. Good afternoon, Uncle," he added with a wry smile as Sir James and Nan entered the hall. "What—or should I more accurately say *who*— brings you to Spedlins on this fine day?"

Sir James bowed deeply to Phaeline, saying, "You *know* who brings me, lad, but I'd nae notion that I'd find *this* lovely lady acting as your hostess. You will not remember me, Lady Dunwythie, but we met at Stirling Castle some four years ago."

"I remember you quite well, Sir James," Phaeline said, smiling demurely.

Kirkhill had not noted before how much her smile resembled her daughter's.

Nan shifted an astonished gaze from her flirtatious uncle to her brother and said, "I'm starving, Dickon. Are you not going to invite us to dine with you?"

He said, "You, my lass, would be well served if I did now as I was about to do when Jardine's messenger arrived at Kirkhill, and gave you a good skelping. So heed me well. If I let you stay, I'll expect you to behave."

"But, Dickon," she said, dimpling, "I *always* behave."

After tidying herself, changing her clothing, and spending most of her morning confined with Flory and the baby, Fiona looked forward to an even more tedious afternoon. She told herself that she was looking after her baby but let Flory do most of the tending while her mistress paced or stared out one of the windows.

As she picked at food a gillie had brought up for her midday meal, she had heard the commotion of riders arriving. But although she strained to see who had come, she saw no person or banner she knew. She did, however, see a beautiful, fair-haired young woman gracefully dismount from a dun-colored palfrey.

An older man offered his arm to her, and they walked together to the entryway below Fiona's window and disappeared from her view.

Curiosity overwhelmed her, but apparently, it occurred to *no one* to send word of the visitors upstairs. She hadn't felt like going down to eat with everyone in the hall, but now, fuming, she replied curtly to Flory's suggestion that she could simply go downstairs to see who had come.

"Or I could go and see for ye, mistress," Flory added diffidently.

"It is just *like* him nearly to order me to rest and then refuse to send word to me when we have visitors," Fiona said. "He's just like all Jardines."

"Nay, he is *not* like them! And ye've been pacing more than ye've rested."

Fiona looked out the window again. In truth, she did not know what to make of her own emotional state, especially where Kirkhill was concerned. One moment she wanted to challenge the man, the next to please him, even to touch him. She could still feel the warm touch of his hand atop hers on his arm. But such thoughts irked her. Why should she care if she pleased him or challenged him?

One moment he seemed to like her, even to want to protect her, and the next she managed somehow to irk him. There was no understanding the man!

And why, she asked herself then, should she *want* to understand him? First, she would do better to understand herself.

"Mistress?"

"What is it?" Fiona said. Then, when Flory bit her lower lip, she added ruefully, "I'm as much a beast as that awful dog was, to talk to you so, Flory. In troth, I do not know myself anymore. I begin to say something, and before I know what I'm doing, my words come out in a snap, or I suddenly want to cry."

"Aye, sure, me mam gets snappish and moped after she has a new bairn, too. Likely, everyone does," Flory added sagely.

Biting back a retort, Fiona said, "What did you want to say to me?"

"Only that ye never said if I should go and see who has come."

"Nay, I'll go myself, and you were right to suggest it. I'm behaving badly to everyone because I need to be *doing* things, attending to this household and the like. And do *not* be telling me that Hod is seeing to all that, because he has never heeded anything beyond the old master's needs before now, so he cannot *know*."

"Aye, that be true enough," Flory said. "Will ye change your clothes?"

"I'll just wear my red shawl over this gray kirtle," Fiona said. "If Kirkhill does want to be of use here, I wish he would arrange for me to get new clothes."

"Aye, sure, he ought to. Ye've had nowt to speak of since we came here."

Reassured by Flory's always devoted support, Fiona soon felt ready to go downstairs and remind everyone that *she* was mistress of Spedlins.

Halfway down the stairs, she met Hod coming up.

"There ye be, mistress."

"What is it?" she asked, striving to sound only curious and not irritated that he was only just now coming to inform her of their visitors.

"I wanted to tell ye I be sorry Dobb got back in. The laird were gey fashed after what happened, and so he should be. But I did also want to warn ye that them rumors about ye and Master Will be flying everywhere, likely even to Dumfries."

"Mercy, rumors have been flying ever since he vanished," she said. "What difference could it make if they reach Dumfries?"

"Why only that the Sheriff o' Dumfries has authority here, too. And the man has a passion for hanging murderers, even women, if they've killed their husbands."

Chapter 9 ————————————

Kirkhill was chafing to get outside and back on a horse again. He had seen less of the Jardine estates with Evart that morning than he'd wanted to see. But although he had decided that it behooved him to soothe Phaeline after the incident with Old Jardine's dog, he had realized, too, that he had felt uneasy about leaving things as they were with Fiona.

His uncle's arrival with Nan ended his plans to rejoin Evart after the midday meal. Instead, he and his guests lingered at the high table, chatting about all and sundry. Sir James had met briefly with Archie the Grim and shamelessly used that meeting as his excuse for letting Nan persuade him to journey south to Spedlins. At least, Nan seemed to be getting on well with the lady Phaeline.

Although he had yet to be private with his uncle, he did not mean to spare him when the opportunity arose. Clearly, Nan had wound the older man around her thumb to get her way. Doubtless, she had been dying to see the place her brother had taken in charge and was even more curious to meet its mistress.

"I do think you should send to tell the lady Fiona that

we are here," Nan said for the third or fourth time. "Surely, it is her duty to make us welcome."

"Do *I* not make you feel welcome, Nannie?" Kirkhill asked gently.

Giving him a speculative look, she tossed her head a little. But whatever she might have said he would never know, because Fiona swept into the hall, wearing a bright red shawl casually over a simple gray gown, and looking magnificent. She strode briskly toward them, her head high, her eyes sparkling, her cheeks revealing nearly as much color as her shawl did.

Only as that comparison struck him did he realize that she was in a flaming temper. Wondering if she had overheard the exchange of comments with Nan and decided to take umbrage, he stood politely as she approached the dais.

When her angry gaze collided with his cool one, he said, "As you see, my lady, we have visitors. Allow me to present my uncle, Sir James Seyton of Lothian, and my youngest sister, the lady Anne Seyton."

"Welcome to Spedlins," Fiona said, giving each of them a polite nod. "I am pleased to meet you both. But I would like a word with you, Kirkhill, if you please."

"Good sakes, but you look furious," Nan said. "Whatever is amiss?"

It was only then that Kirkhill took his eyes from Fiona long enough to see Hod hovering in the doorway of the great hall, looking ruefully perturbed.

Fiona looked daggers at Nan but said only, "It is a private matter, I fear, and not one for general discussion. Kirkhill?"

"Aye, sure, I'll come," he said. Excusing himself to the

others, he followed her swift stride to the doorway, enjoying the view as her hips swayed enticingly.

Hod waited for them, unmoving and silent.

The lower tables had been cleared, so the hall was empty except for those on the dais, and was likely to remain so until servants began setting up later for supper.

As they neared Hod, Fiona said in an angry undertone, "He has spread those dreadful rumors about me all the way to Dumfries and now taunts me by informing me that the sheriff there delights in hanging women who kill their husbands. I won't have him in this house, Kirkhill. He *must* go."

Kirkhill said, "You heard her ladyship, did you not, Hod?" When the man nodded, he said, "What have you to say to her complaint?"

"I can do nobbut beg her ladyship's pardon, m'lord. I must ha' been gey clumsy wi' my words for her to take such dire meaning from them. I meant only to pass on news I gleaned from some o' the men: that them false accusations may ha' reached Sheriff Maxwell's ears. They say he often tries cases on nae more than rumor, and I fear that the ones against her ladyship may attract his attention."

"I see," Kirkhill said, noting that Fiona was bristling with indignation at the admittedly glib explanation. Even so, Hod looked and sounded sincere, and she had been reacting emotionally to nearly anything anyone had said to her since his arrival. Had he not noted her cool demeanor at their first meeting, he might have thought her a female who simply lacked self-control. But he had seen her competence and her warmth for the children. He had witnessed her temper then, too, but even it had seemed more contained than it did now.

She looked grim. Tersely, she said, "That is *not* how it was."

"We will talk more of this later if you like, my lady," Kirkhill said. "For now I will say this to *you,* Hod. Her ladyship will remain safely under my care, sheriff or no sheriff. I am grateful for your concern, and I am sure that she will be, too, when she has had time to consider your words. However, in future, if you have other such concerns, do not trouble her ladyship with them. Come to me."

"As ye wish, m'lord," Hod said, bowing. Then, to Fiona, he said, "I do apologize, m'lady, if I offended ye. I tell ye true, I never meant to upset ye."

"I don't believe you," Fiona retorted.

"You may go, Hod," Kirkhill said. "But do not forget what I said."

Bowing again, Hod turned on his heel and left them.

"You said I needn't keep him as house steward if he proved to be unsatisfactory," Fiona said. "But I don't want him here at all now."

"I'm not going to dismiss the man over what may easily have been a misunderstanding," Kirkhill said. "I do agree that he should not work closely with you, but we can avoid that if you will relay your orders through me. In fairness," he added, noting her disapproval, "the man has not tried to interfere with the usual routines. I think he is trying to learn his way, but *you* must not think that I am recklessly dismissing your concern, lass. I saw how you reacted to his explanation, and I believe that you described the incident accurately, as you believed it to be. But you should know, too, that when you fly into the boughs over such things, even over outright insolence, you diminish the effect that your words have on others."

"I become a hysterical female. That is what you mean, is it not?"

"It is," he said, meeting her gaze. "You'd do better to keep a calm demeanor, something that I know you possess but that you find difficult of late to present."

She sighed. "'Tis true enough, that is. Sometimes I do not recognize myself. It is as if I am standing aside watching some strange virago-Fiona snap at people."

"You have had several great changes in your life," he said quietly. "It will take time yet to accustom yourself to having lost your husband and good-father and gained a trustee and wee son all in the space of a month or so. At risk of having you snap my head right off, may I suggest that it would help to let Jane's sister Eliza act as wet nurse, if only for nighttime feedings, so that you can sleep more soundly."

She looked down at her feet, then back at him. "I'll think about it," she said.

"Fair enough. You should come and offer a proper welcome to my too-persuadable uncle and my impertinent sister. But first, tell me if you would like Nan to apologize for asking you such an impudent question. Sithee, she says such things only to see how people will react."

"Does she?" Fiona said dryly.

"Aye. My father would have punished such behavior in me at once, but he thought she was amusing. By the time he no longer thought her so, she had acquired the habit. I have sought to curb her and believed I was making progress. But, now that I am not at home, my mother and uncle will give her full rein again."

"Good sakes, sir, you have been gone for only a few days!"

"And you see how faithfully Uncle James followed my instructions. Not that he has ever felt bound to obey me, head of our family though I am. He'd already achieved fame as a warrior when I sought my knighthood, so I was duty-bound to obey him. You see my dilemma now. I asked him to keep an eye on Nan and my mother. Instead, he brings Nan straight to me. The man is hopeless in such a case."

To his surprise, she smiled, seeming genuinely amused. And when he raised his eyebrows, she said with her delightful, albeit rare chuckle, "My sister would say that I am getting my just deserts by having your sister as my guest."

"How could she think you deserve such rude treatment?"

"Because saying things to get a reaction was once a favorite pastime of mine. Sithee, I often felt like an observer, rather than a participant at home. No one paid much heed to me there, because I wasn't the son they wanted."

"Did your sister feel like that, too?"

"I don't know how she felt. Mairi rarely shows her feelings, but I was as outspoken as your sister is, and I'm afraid I thought it was a fine thing when *I* was doing it. I can see now that it is not such a good thing when the words fly from someone else's mouth. But Nan needn't apologize, sir. Nor should you."

"Perhaps you will have better luck with her than I have had," he said.

Her eyes twinkled, and she smiled again. "Perhaps I will," she said.

He offered his arm, and as he escorted her to join

the group on the dais, he hoped he was gaining a better understanding of her. He wanted her to trust him, but he knew that she did not yet do so. In truth, he doubted that she trusted anyone, and having known her husband and met her good-father, he could not blame her for that.

It did make it hard to get close to her, though, and he wanted to do that. Not only would it make things easier for both of them, but he found her conversation—even their verbal jousts—stimulating.

⁓

Fiona exerted herself that afternoon to enjoy their visitors and liked Sir James immediately. He was clearly a practiced flirt and was practicing his art on Phaeline. Phaeline's chuckling responses clearly delighted him, but he also flirted mildly with Fiona and twice made her laugh.

As for the lady Anne—or Nan, as Kirkhill called her—Fiona reserved judgment. She had taken an uncharacteristic dislike to the girl the instant she had seen her dismounting in the yard but could not imagine why she had, since she had not even known then who Nan was. That she had mistakenly assumed that Nan must be a friend of Kirkhill's was hardly a sensible reason for dislike.

As she watched the younger girl at supper that evening, Fiona had a discomfiting notion that she had been just as silly at the same age. The realization that, when she had eloped with Will, she had been exactly Nan's age told her that she had been much *more* foolish. Nan also delighted in discussing current fashions with Phaeline, and Phaeline smiled often while chatting with her. Fiona had enjoyed similar talks at one time, but she no longer knew anything about current styles.

She was still angry about Hod, and despite Kirkhill's reassurance, she felt as if he had taken Hod's word over hers. Still, she could not fault him if he had.

He had been right to take her to task for flying into the boughs. When he'd described the behavior he preferred, she had thought of Mairi, who was always calm and never flustered. But Fiona knew that she could only be herself and strive to regain her own occasional, determined calm.

The next three days passed without incident, and she learned with pleasure on Saturday afternoon that Nan enjoyed riding as much as she did.

"I cannot take a horse out yet," Fiona said as they strolled together in the yard that afternoon. "But I seem to be having fewer physical difficulties than anyone expected, so mayhap I will be back to my normal activities soon, too."

"You have recovered your figure right speedily," Nan said, eyeing her. "My sisters took *much* more time to recover theirs, and indeed, Margaret has increased considerably in size with each of her children."

"How many does she have?"

"Just three so far, but I doubt that she can wear anything she wore before she began increasing with her first."

"Well, it is a good thing that I can get into the clothes I wore before I increased," Fiona said. "I have no others to wear."

"Mercy, then why do you not send for a seamstress to come and make you new dresses? 'Tis what I do whenever I get tired of my old ones. Then I tell dearest Dickon, and he rages at me, but he always pays for them just as Father did."

"You should not tell me such private things about your brother, you know," Fiona said, stifling a chuckle at the thought of Kirkhill being so easily managed. "I warrant he would not like it."

"Oh, piffle, Dickon won't mind. He knows I just say whatever I think."

"Do you like others to say whatever *they* are thinking to you?"

Nan wrinkled her brow. "Not when Dickon does it in a temper. He has a way of speaking when I have displeased him that always makes me wish he would just stop. However, I prefer him to rant than to do aught else," she added with a grin.

Fiona was dying to ask her what else "Dickon" might do, but she decided she ought to practice the behavior she had just recommended, and contain her curiosity for once. In any event, whatever Kirkhill might do to his sister, he would never dare to do to her. He might be trustee for whatever Old Jardine had left for her upkeep, but that was all he was to her.

Early Tuesday evening, six men rode into the yard at Spedlins as Fiona, Nan, Phaeline, and Sir James were taking the air before supper. They were walking up the gently sloping hill above the tower and could see the riders plainly.

To Fiona's surprise, Nan stared hard at them. Then, a certain light came into her eyes, as if she had recognized someone. However, as she turned toward her uncle, her expression altered ludicrously to irritation and she said in a long-suffering voice, "Do you *see* him? I ought to have *known* he would follow us here!"

"Now, now," Sir James said. "Likely, he has come at Archie's command."

"Who is it?" Fiona asked.

"Sir Antony MacCairill, that's who," Nan said. "He is the most annoying man I know, *and* the most odiously persistent."

"Faith, do you dislike him as much as all that?"

"I don't dislike him at all," Nan said, putting her nose in the air. "I just don't want to *marry* him and have him ordering me about for the rest of my life. Still, I expect we ought to go back now, or Dickon will send someone to fetch us."

Kirkhill had been sitting at the large table in the inner chamber, trying to create an accounting of the past several months from what little information he had gleaned, and learned of his newest visitors with mixed emotions. Tony was still his best friend, but Sir James and Nan had now been at Spedlins for nearly a week, so he was beginning to think the tower contained far too many people.

Therefore, when his porter showed Tony in, Kirkhill greeted him with a curt demand to know what the devil had brought him to Spedlins.

"Archie sent me," Tony said. "He thought you might want help persuading Jardine's men to ride with us, or might find cause to return briefly to Kirkhill House, and would want a captain you can trust to stay here and look after things."

"Mighty thoughtful of Archie," Kirkhill said dryly.

Tony grinned. "Well, I *may* have said something to stir his thoughts in that direction. You've taken on great responsibility here, after all, and you do still have an obligation to provide men of your own to help defeat an invasion of the dales, no matter who leads it. There was fighting in Roxburgh last week, and Douglas—the earl, that is—would rather fight the English than fight a fellow Scotsman like March, who *should* go home to Dunbar. Instead, he has angered Northumberland, and the English would much rather fight March than fight the Douglas. So there we are."

"What about Archie?"

Tony had moved to help himself to whisky from a jug on a nearby side table and looked over his shoulder to say, "Our respected Lord of Galloway is recalling men from his barely begun siege. Whilst the English raids have stayed well east of here, Archie thinks they are trying to draw *him* east so they can take Annandale."

"He is likely right," Kirkhill said. "He usually is."

"Aye, for if they control Annandale, they cut off Niths-dale and Galloway from the Borders and Douglas. If Archie is *with* the earl ... well, you see how *he* is thinking. I thought I could help more here, mayhap even aid you in looking after Will's young widow. Everyone is saying he must be dead, and I hear that she is gey easy on the eyes. If our sharp-tongued Nan gets word that I'm looking else-where, mayhap—"

"Nan is here," Kirkhill said.

"So much the better," Tony said, grinning again.

"If you stay, I'll put you to work, but you will treat the lady Fiona with due respect. I mean to persuade Uncle James to return to Kirkhill, and if he goes, Nan goes. But I have learned—not much to my surprise—that Old Jardine and Will were sadly derelict in maintaining their land and looking after their people. The cottages on the estates are makeshift shacks, the thatch is old and bug-ridden, and except for the apple orchards, the few crops they grow are poorly tended."

"Hold on, Dickon. I'm no farmer. My father still runs things at home. He and our steward would reject any advice that I might be brave enough to offer."

"Then see what you can do with Jardine's men. They are good fighters, I warrant, so you need only get it through their thick skulls that we do not call Archie 'the Grim' for nowt. He said straight out that he'll hang any man who crosses him. If you can get them to understand that, I wager they'll serve him well."

"How many men are there?"

"About two hundred. Jardine lands lie on both sides of the Annan, and much of the land is arable. But either Old Jardine knew little about planting aught save apple trees or he stopped tending his other crops during the long years of conflict with England. In any event, the English occupation of Lochmaben, less than five miles southwest of here, makes planting west of the river too dangerous."

"I'm guessing that Jardine kept few accounts then."

"Nearly none," Kirkhill said. "He had a partial list of his tenants but apparently confided in none of them, including his personal manservant."

"If he was close to Old Jardine, I'll wager he knows more than he admits."

"Aye, sure, and that is why I've kept him on as house steward. Mayhap I can eventually persuade him to talk of what he *does* know." Kirkhill left it at that, seeing no good reason to tell Tony how much the lady Fiona disliked Hod.

"Will Jardine was always well dressed and carried fine weapons," Tony said thoughtfully. "There must be gelt somewhere."

"I agree," Kirkhill said. "Moreover, run properly, the estates should turn a handsome profit if we can prevent English raiders and March from laying waste to the entire dale. There is little ready gelt to spend on seed or seedlings, but we have plenty of apples, plenty of cattle and horses, and even a few sheep for shearing. A judicious landlord could make something of this place."

"Aye, sure, as long as the rightful owners don't come to reclaim their beasts."

Kirkhill chuckled, but he knew the Jardines, so Tony's point was a good one.

"Nan encouraged the lady Fiona to apply to me for new clothes," he said. "In troth, she deserves some, because she got gey little from the Jardines and is now reduced, Nan says, to rags. It may be that Jardine was just tightfisted or that Will was so expensive that he had no gelt to spare. I told Fiona she can send for fabrics and a seamstress but that she must be gey frugal until I get things sorted out. I haven't told her exactly how things stand, because I don't know that myself yet."

"Well, I'll do what I can to help," Tony promised. "If Nan is staying here in the tower, however, you might prefer that I camp elsewhere with my men."

"Nay, your coming will give me good opportunity to send James and Nan home. She persuaded him to come here to satisfy her curiosity about the place, but they have been here for nearly a sennight. That is long enough."

"Sakes, have you room for me?"

"Aye, sure. You can have them bring your things in here

if you like. Your men will bed down in the hall or out in the yard if they prefer, but you can sleep in Joshua's room. He sleeps in the stables most nights anyway, being one who shares your belief that the Jardine men prefer stolen horses to those they must breed or purchase. They'll serve supper in an hour. You might like to tidy up before then."

Although Fiona had expected Nan to go at once in search of the new arrivals, that young lady informed her that she had decided to make an entrance at suppertime that would make Sir Antony MacCairill sit up and stare. Therefore, she said, she would change her gown and descend to the hall in her own good time.

Fiona had changed her dress before joining the others for their hillside stroll, but she did exchange her stout boots for slippers more suited to taking supper in company, before opening her bodice to nurse wee David. Then, leaving Flory to rock him to sleep in his cradle, she tidied herself and went downstairs to see that all was in readiness for their increasing number of guests.

As she entered the hall, she noted first a number of scurrying gillies. They had set up more trestles to accommodate Sir Antony's men, and seeing breadbaskets on all the tables, she decided that the kitchen had things in hand.

A sudden cry from behind her, near the great fireplace, startled her. She turned to see Davy jump between Hod and Tippy, his dirk at the ready. Tippy backed hastily away to the chimney corner as Davy confronted Hod.

Hurrying toward them, she heard Hod say, "Ye'll take a good skelping for this, ye wee villain. Ye're nae better than what your da' were. Now give me that blade or by the Rood, I'll take it from ye, and then see what ye'll get."

"Ye should no ha' hit me sister, ye great ape," Davy snapped. "She were just a-doing what me mam told her to do, and ye've nae right to interfere wi' her."

Lightning quick, Hod snatched the dirk away with one hand, grabbed the boy's knife hand with the other, jerked him forward, then let go and slapped him hard enough across the face to knock him down—all in a single brief flurry of movement.

"Leave him be, Hod," Fiona ordered as Hod stepped toward the boy.

"Ye keep out o' this, m'lady. This be nae affair o' yours, for *I'm* the steward here and this lad wants skelping." As he spoke, he jerked Davy up again, clearly intending to mete out his punishment then and there, but Fiona sprang forward, pushed Davy back with one hand, and shoved Hod away from him with the other.

Startled, the big man stumbled backward but, by releasing Davy and flinging the dirk aside to clatter against the chimney stones, he managed to grab Fiona's arm and used it to steady himself. Then, jerking her toward him much as he had done with Davy, and ignoring her furious struggles to free herself, he slapped her, striking the side of her head and sending her stumbling away from him.

He started toward her, but before he could grab her again, he encountered an obstacle in the shape of Kirkhill's fist and took no further interest in Fiona.

She had not seen Kirkhill coming, but he loomed above them all now.

Hod landed on his back near Davy, who scrambled to

his feet and ran to Tippy, still crouched in the chimney corner, weeping.

"Get up."

Fiona, still dizzy from Hod's blow, thought that Kirkhill was issuing the order to him and realized only when Kirkhill grasped her upper arm and hauled her upright that he had been talking to her. She stared at him in shocked dismay.

Expressionless, he said, "Davy, fetch me your dirk."

"Aye, laird," Davy said, picking it up from the hearth-stones and handing it to Kirkhill with tears welling in his eyes. "He broke the blade, hitting them stones."

"So he did," Kirkhill said. "I'll see if someone can mend it. Meantime, I'll show you how to use one properly. Threatening a man like Hod with it was the act of a fool, so you must learn to choose your opponents more wisely. For now, take Tip downstairs to your mam and tell her I said the hall is no place for a wee lassock like her. She should stay with your mam in the kitchen. Do you understand me?"

"Aye, sure. Are ye sore vexed wi' me, laird?"

"Nay, laddie, but we will talk more of this later," Kirkhill said.

Davy looked uncertainly at Fiona, but she judged it wisest to say nothing.

When the boy had gone, Kirkhill approached Hod, now sitting up and rubbing his jaw as he looked ruefully at Kirkhill.

Kirkhill stood over him. "Don't try to explain your actions this time, Hod. Just be grateful that I don't order you flogged before you go. Striking the lady Fiona is reason enough for that as well as for your dismissal."

"Aye, sure, *now* it is," Hod said with a grimace. "I just lost me temper wi' the both o' them, but I'll go. I expect ye'll want yon letter back, after all, then."

"I told you I would not take it back, and I meant what I said. You should have no trouble finding another place, but you will leave here at once, today."

"I will, aye," Hod said, getting to his feet and leaving without further ado.

"Your mother and my uncle are just coming in," Kirkhill said to Fiona. "You should go with them to the high table now. But you and I will also talk later."

His tone was cool enough to send shivers through her.

She was still trying to figure out why he was angry with her when she had simply tried to protect Davy. But she held her head high as she joined Phaeline and walked to the dais with her. Sir James followed them.

Only as they approached the table did Fiona see the muscular, dark-haired man standing in the open doorway of the inner chamber, watching them. His eyes twinkled, and she could have sworn he was laughing as he went to meet Kirkhill.

The two men approached the high table together, and Kirkhill formally made Sir Antony MacCairill known to both Fiona and Phaeline.

"By the Rood, that was the bravest thing I ever saw, jumping in to protect that lad the way you did, Lady Fiona," Sir Antony said. "Not many women—"

"Enough, Tony," Kirkhill said austerely. "I'll thank you not to encourage such foolishness. Indeed, if you mean to encourage Nan in such—"

"Nan!" Tony snorted. "I should like to see that!"

"See what, Tony?" Nan said clearly as she swept into

the lower hall and made her way alone toward the dais, oblivious to those men-at-arms and castle servants who scrambled out of her path. "Did Archie send you, sir, or could you just not stay away? It makes no difference which it is, for I'll have none of you."

"God's troth, look at the lass!" Sir Antony exclaimed. "Did you set out to make yourself look forty years old, Nan? That purple silk makes you look sallow, my lass. You'd do better to wear a paler color and a simpler style. All that lace spoils the lines of the dress. You must speak to her, Dickon."

"I'm going to speak to both of you in a moment in a way that neither of you will like," Kirkhill said in the same voice that had sent shivers up Fiona's spine. "Stop acting like a doxy, Nan. Take your place at the table and be silent."

She obeyed him quickly, and Sir Antony made no further comment.

They sat in the customary formal order, with Kirkhill and Fiona at the center, facing the lower hall tables. Lady Phaeline sat next to her daughter with Nan at her left, while Kirkhill had Sir James on his right and Sir Antony beyond Sir James.

After the gillies had served them, Nan said casually across Phaeline, "What was Tony talking about, Fee, when he said that he'd never seen anything so brave?"

"It was naught to talk of here or now," Fiona said, hoping that Nan would drop the subject. However, she had known the other young woman long enough not to be surprised when Nan only laughed and turned to Phaeline.

"What was it that she did, madam? Or did you not see, either?"

"Nay, I did not, but I confess I am as curious as you are to hear about it."

Sir Antony, clearly straining to hear them, said, "I can tell you what I saw as Dickon opened the inner chamber door to step out here. A big fellow struck a small lad and clearly meant to do worse, but her ladyship darted between them. The big chap had a dirk in one hand, but he hit her with the other. The dirk went flying, and so did her ladyship. That was when Dickon put an end to the matter."

"Merciful heaven, Fiona, what will you do next?" Phaeline demanded.

"Hod knocked Davy down after slapping his little sister," Fiona said. "He is the lad who killed Dobb, the dog that tried to attack you and my bairn."

"Nevertheless," Kirkhill said in that unpleasantly chilly tone, "*you* should have kept out of it. It was not the brave act that Tony calls it. It was daft. You had no hope of besting Hod. In fact... But we'll talk more of this anon."

"Nay, we will talk now," Fiona retorted. "You said yourself that I acted with great courage when I jumped between that vicious dog and my mother and child. How was *that* courageous if what just happened was daft?"

"What is this then?" Sir Antony exclaimed. "What vicious dog?"

"Never mind," Kirkhill said. "As I said, my lady, we will discuss it later."

"But why not explain it now?" Nan asked. "Fee's question sounds perfectly sensible to me. I'll wager you just don't want to answer it, Dickon, because—"

"Nay, he does not, and *I'll* tell you why," Fiona said hotly. "Because he is just like all Jardines, *that's* why. He orders people about and seeks to govern their lives. Faith, but he even makes up the rules as he goes along, so that one never knows when one is going to put a foot wrong. Well, I'm tired of it!"

She stood up.

"Sit down," Kirkhill said curtly. "You will hush now, both of you, and eat your supper unless you want to answer to—"

"I don't *want* my supper," Fiona said. "You can have it!" With that, she picked up her trencher and dumped its contents onto his. "I will now bid you all—"

That was as far as she got before Kirkhill stood up and caught hold of her. When she fought to free herself, he picked her up bodily and carried her from the dais into the inner chamber, kicking the door shut behind them.

Chapter 10 _____

Kirkhill had borne enough. His temper was high, and he meant to make it clear to the lady Fiona that such tactics with him were dangerously unwise. Once the chamber door was shut, he strode with her to the back-stool near the table.

Seating himself, he draped her across his lap and raised his right hand.

"No! Don't! Oh, pray, sir, don't!"

The panicked note in her voice caught him by surprise, because he had intended to give her only a few smacks hard enough to get her attention but not hard enough to hurt her. She sounded truly frightened, even terrified. Moreover, she was trembling like an aspen and practically sobbing.

Nan frequently tried to beg off punishment, but never like this.

"Easy, lass," he said as he lowered his hand to the small of her back, his fury gone. "Here now, sit up and tell me what this is all about."

She remained utterly still for a long moment before he realized that he still held her arm, and let go. Then she squirmed sideways and slid off his lap to the floor, where she sat back on her heels and looked up at him, her face pale.

"Sakes, what did you think I was going to do to you?" he asked.

"You know what you were going to do."

"I do, aye. I was going to give you a few well-earned smacks on the backside in the hope that they would teach you better manners."

Color flooded back into her cheeks then, and she looked quickly down, but not before he saw the glitter of tears in her eyes. He leaned toward her, his hand moving to her shoulder and then to touch her cheek. He wanted to pull her close, give her a hug, and tell her again that she need not fear him. He could not do most of that, however, as he had so impulsively carried her into the inner chamber.

That the room was where he conducted much of his business did not matter a whit. It was also his bedchamber, and the only way he could deal with the situation now without raising a scandal was to continue as he had begun.

He was, after all, her trustee. Considering her age, that put him in the same position as any guardian, a point that was beginning to irk him sorely.

"Get up from the floor," he said.

She obeyed slowly, looking small and uncertain. But once she was on her feet, she straightened and gave him one of her direct looks as she said, "If you are not going to beat me after all, sir, I will bid you goodnight."

With that, she turned away.

He let her take a few steps toward the door before he said, "Not just yet, lass. I still have some things to say to you."

She stopped where she was, visibly stiffening.

However, his resolve had stiffened, too.

~

Fiona stood still, wishing that her heart would stop hammering so she could hear herself think. She did not understand her behavior, let alone his, but she did not trust him any more than she would trust any other man in that situation.

She deserved punishment for what she had done and more than the few smacks Kirkhill had intended. Her father would have said so, and Will would not have hesitated for a moment. Sakes, if she had dared to dump her food onto Old Jardine's trencher, he would have ordered her flogged. Not that she had ever done such a thing to anyone before Kirkhill, for she had not.

Kirkhill had meant to do only what any man would do to a naughty child. He had said so, and she believed him, which only made the situation worse. The very thought was as humiliating as anything the Jardines had done to her.

"Come back here and sit down."

His voice, still chilly, interrupted her tangled thoughts, but the last thing she wanted to do was to go back and face him. He made her feel small and vulnerable, much more so than her father or the Jardines ever had.

"I'm waiting, and my patience is *not* limitless."

Swallowing hard, she turned back to see that he was standing.

"In troth, sir," she said hastily, "I do not know what led me—"

"Sit down, Fiona, and be glad that you can do so

comfortably." He moved away from the stool and gestured to it as he leaned his hips against the big table.

"If you're going to rant at me, I'd rather stand."

"Sit down," he said. "You are not fully recovered yet, and I don't rant."

"Aye, well, Nan said—"

"We will not bring Nan into this. Sit."

She sat.

He said, "You are seventeen years old, are you not?"

"Aye, you know I am."

"Do I? I'd have thought you ten years younger by your behavior tonight."

Tears welled in her eyes, but she ignored them. "I swear, I don't know why—"

"I don't want to hear your excuses, lass. I've heard them, and although I do understand that having a baby can make some women behave oddly, enough is enough. Not only was your behavior at the table tonight childish, but your behavior earlier, with Hod, was downright dangerous."

"But—"

"Do *not* interrupt me," he said coldly. "For once, you will just listen. You asked me what the difference was between what you did when the dog attacked and when you leaped to Davy's defense tonight, so I will tell you exactly what it is."

Somehow, she was certain that she no longer wanted to hear the explanation, but he gave her no choice.

"It is one thing to thrust yourself between certain danger and your own mother and child," he said. "The danger to them was imminent and fierce. Phaeline, holding the babe, could do nowt to defend it or herself. You did not know that Davy was there or that I was nearby. Flory was behind you on the stairs and thus useless to aid you. So you did the only thing anyone could have done. Most people—male or female—would have hesitated to challenge that dog. You did not. You flung yourself into its path without sparing a thought for your own safety. *That* was courageous."

His words warmed her to the core, making her feel more in charity with him. She even felt an urge to thank him for the compliment.

He did not give her the opportunity. Instead, his voice chillier than ever, he said, "What was *not* a matter of courage or even good sense was rushing in between Hod and young Davy. Don't argue," he added when she opened her mouth. "It is one thing to act swiftly and instinctively to protect your own, another to leap between your house steward and a junior member of your household. It is especially daft when the steward is twice your size, armed with a dirk, and angry. You surely ought to have noted how swiftly he disarmed the lad. What you thought you could do if Hod turned on you, as he did, I cannot imagine."

"I didn't think about that. There was no time! I just acted, as I did before."

"Then you must learn to tell the difference between doing the only thing you *can* do and interfering in a dispute when you do not know the facts. Young Davy had no business pulling that dirk on Hod under any circumstance, and Hod was right to chastise him. You were wrong to interfere, and even had you been right, you went about it the wrong way. Others were at hand, my men and yours. If you feared for the lad's life or limbs, you should have let out a screech. You do have the authority to order our men to intervene when anyone behaves dangerously."

"But I did tell Hod not to—"

"You are thinking that he should have obeyed your order," he interjected in that maddeningly calm, icy tone. "He should have, but he did not. And *when* he did not, you, being much the smaller, should have thought hard before you acted."

She grimaced, knowing he was right, but again he did not give her a chance to tell him so.

"It is time for you to take yourself in hand, Fiona," he said. "Indeed, it is more than time. You are not taking care of yourself, and you have behaved badly to nearly everyone here at Spedlins, in one way or another, since my arrival. Tonight you went beyond what anyone should have to tolerate, particularly your guests. You often snap at Flory. You snap at me. I have heard you snap at your mother, as well as Mother Beaton and heaven knows how many others. Had I spoken to my mother as I've heard you speak to Phaeline, my father would have made me smart long and sharp for it. You should be smarting, too, even without a good smacking."

The too-ready tears sprang to her eyes again, but she dashed them away, determined not to let him make her cry.

He certainly had the knack. That was clear enough.

"You must apologize to them all, lass."

The urge to cry vanished in a blink. "*All* of them?"

"Aye, and quickly, because I suspect that most of them will be gone by this time tomorrow."

"Gone! Because of me?"

"Nay, because I mean to send James back to Kirkhill to

look after things there as we'd arranged for him to do, and he will take Nan with him. Your mother was ready to go back to the Hall the day they arrived and agreed to stay as hostess only so that you need not assume that role before you were ready. I have no doubt, though, that she will go when they do. Your sister will arrive soon—before Lammas Day, Phaeline said—but Phaeline will return to us if you need her."

"Must I apologize to them all at once?" The very thought was daunting.

"Nay, but neither should you rejoin them until you are ready to make amends. You may take the service stairs from here to your chamber and use what time you need before morning to decide what you want to say to them."

She stood, hoping he had finished. She felt battered as it was, and did not know how much more of that cold, cutting tone she could stand. He had made her smart, all right, and he had made her sorry, all without once raising his voice.

Most of all, she was sorry that she had pushed him to such a point and hoped fervently that she would never do so again.

She drew a breath and faced him. "May I apologize to you now, sir? I—"

"No, Fiona. Think about the others first and the behavior that led us here. I don't want your apologies when they come on the heels of a well-deserved rebuke. Come to me when you are truly apologetic, not merely chastened."

Feeling as if he had slapped her, she searched his face for any hint of compassion and found none.

Abruptly, she turned away, not waiting for dismissal,

and went swiftly to the service stair door. Jerking it open, she stepped onto the dim, unwelcoming landing.

"Fiona!"

She barely heard him call to her as she pulled the door shut behind her and stumbled up the stairs, blinded by tears she could not stop.

⁓

Kirkhill nearly went after her but fought the urge, remembering similar dramatic moments with Nan and also Fiona's admission that she had been much like Nan at the same age. He wondered if anyone had ever held her to account for her actions before. But even as the thought crossed his mind, he corrected it. He had seen clear signs since his arrival that Will Jardine—and Old Jardine, too—had taken her to task, and roughly. Still, she seemed to have developed little respect for either of them, and he could scarcely blame her for that.

He recalled Hod's saying that "*now*" striking her was grounds for dismissal, as if it hadn't been before. It had seemed an odd thing to say, but perhaps he had spoken only the truth in that the rules had changed with Jardine's death. Mayhap the old man had actually *let* Hod strike her. If he could believe that of anyone, he could believe it of Jardine, so it was just as well that he'd sent Hod away. Had he learned first that the man *had* struck Fiona before, even at Jardine's command, he'd have throttled him.

In any event, he could not sit thinking about Fiona all night, although she had been invading his thoughts more and more often of late. She continued to invade his dreams, too, although those were not to be thought of now...or lingered over.

His uncle and sister and the others were doubtless still waiting at the table, eager to hear what had happened. He would tell them nowt, but he could not ignore them, especially as he wanted to get rid of a few of them. Therefore, he put Fiona firmly out of his head and returned to the dais.

Before anyone could quiz him—although, surprisingly, no one seemed eager to be the first—he said quietly, "James, I'm going to have the infernal impudence to ask you to return to Kirkhill tomorrow with Nan. I am always glad to see you, but I need to concentrate on things here if I'm to have the place in order and the Jardine men trained for Archie when he calls us to arms. I depend on you to see that my men at Kirkhill and your own in Lothian are also ready. Also, I expect that by now my lady mother feels as if her entire family has abandoned her."

His uncle's eyes twinkled, but he said only, "I am yours to command, lad, as always. Nan, dear—"

"But I don't want to go home," Nan said. "I like Fiona, and I want to stay."

"Nevertheless, you will go," Kirkhill said in a tone that brooked no debate.

He got none from her, but Phaeline said quietly, "If it please you, my lord, I would be most grateful for Nan's company at the Hall. She is welcome to stay until my daughter Mairi returns, and indeed, longer if she likes. We have plenty of room, and I am sure that she would much enjoy the Lammas Day festivities."

"Oh, Dickon, prithee, say I may!"

"You would be doing me a great favor, my lord," Phaeline said. "I have missed the company of my daughters. I promise you, I would welcome Nan's."

"Then there is no more to be said, madam," he told her. "Your invitation clearly delights Nan, so I'd be a cruel fellow to deny you both. But, Nan, I beg you, save your gratitude and promise me instead that you will behave."

"I'll be utterly angelic, Dickon. You are the very *best* of brothers! But prithee, excuse me now. I must find someone to help me pack!"

He shot a rueful look at Phaeline. "She did not bring her woman with her, madam. I hope you can cope."

"I am sure that we can, sir," Phaeline said with one of her demure looks. "As you know, yourself, I did not bring my woman here, either. This place is too small to count on finding suitable accommodations for one's servants."

Kirkhill was not certain that Phaeline would be able to cope with Nan, but at least he would be nearer if Nan got into a scrape at Dunwythie Hall than he would if she were to go home to Kirkhill and get into one there.

As Nan left the great hall, he turned to his uncle and met Tony's amused gaze just beyond. Ignoring Tony, he said to Sir James, "I doubt you will miss Nan, sir."

"That's a fact," Sir James said. "She's a handful, that one. Nobbut what her ladyship will manage her well enough. Still, the sooner you get the baggage married and off your hands, the better it will be. If Tony still wants her..."

"Tony is having second thoughts," that gentleman said more loudly than was warranted and with a nod toward the doorway, where Nan had paused. "What that lass wants, Dickon, is a good sound...There, she's gone, so I'm wasting my breath. But, speaking of just deserts, dare I ask what you have done with the lady Fiona?"

"Not if you want to stay at Spedlins," Kirkhill said.

"Aye, sure, then I'm mum. Are *you* leaving us, too, madam?" he added, getting hastily to his feet when Phaeline stood.

"I must also pack, sir. Kirkhill will do much better, I'm thinking, with fewer guests. Mayhap Sir James will lend us his escort as far as the Hall."

"It will be my pleasure, madam," Sir James assured her, also standing.

Within moments, Kirkhill was alone with Tony at the high table. But if Tony hoped for further enlightenment, he got none.

Kirkhill, realizing that he had not finished his supper, ordered a fresh trencher and did so. However, keeping his thoughts off Fiona was not so easy.

⁓

Fiona flung open her bedchamber door and stopped at the threshold when she saw Flory with the baby in her lap, rocking it. She had been so full of her woes that she had not thought once about wee David since going downstairs. Guilt washed over her, and the hour or so that she had been away seemed suddenly ages long.

"Oh, Flory, is he hungry again already?"

"Nay, mistress, ye fed him afore ye went downstairs, and he's been making noises to hisself and such. But he's sleeping now. I'll put him in the cradle, shall I?"

"Aye, do," Fiona said on a surge of relief. "I've had a dreadful evening, and then he refused to accept my apology and sent me upstairs like a child."

"Who did? His lordship?"

"Aye." As she said it, Fiona wished she had kept silent about the episode.

For lack of anyone else to talk to, she had fallen into the habit of confiding everything to Flory, even private things about her life with Will and Old Jardine. However, talking so freely about Kirkhill seemed not only wrong but also something of a betrayal, although she was not certain why it should.

"Why did he send ye up here?"

"Oh, it was naught," Fiona said, striving to sound casual. "I did a stupid thing, and he was displeased…as in troth he should have been," she added with a sigh. "I don't want to talk about it, although I should tell you that he dismissed Hod as our household steward."

"Well, that be a good thing, that," Flory said bluntly. "Bad cess to the man!"

"Aye, but I want to think, Flory, and then I need to sleep. Do you suppose that Jane's sister Eliza would still be willing to act as wet nurse to David at night?"

"O' course she would," Flory said. "Sakes, but I could keep him wi' me, and ye could ha' this chamber all to yourself, mistress. I'll just tell Eliza that I'll carry the bairn down to her when he wakes, shall I?"

Fiona had become used to the baby's soft sounds during the night, to hearing his quiet fussing before he demanded sustenance, and to cuddling him while he nursed. She knew she would miss him sorely, but she knew, too, that Kirkhill was right. It was time to take herself in hand.

So she said, "Aye, take him, Flory. I'll help move the cradle to your room, and I'll sit with him whilst you go down and tell Eliza."

They moved the baby, and as Fiona sat with him, she recalled every word that Kirkhill had said to her. He had made her feel foolish, even reckless in her actions on young Davy's behalf. She could not feel sorry about intervening, though. She knew only too well the sort of brutality of which Hod was capable. Still, Kirkhill was right to point out that she had had other means at hand to stop him.

Flory returned, saying, "Eliza will be pleased to have our David whenever he needs her. She has more milk than she needs, she says, so he be welcome to it."

Thanking her, Fiona said, "I must apologize to you for being so curt of late, Flory. I know you say that such behavior is normal, but it does not feel normal to me. And *you* should not have to put up with it, not after all you have done for me."

"Sakes, mistress, it were nowt," Flory said, flushing deeply.

"Not to me, Flory," Fiona said. *And not to Kirkhill.* The thought was strangely warm, considering all that he had said to her. But she knew that he had not just protected her from the brutish Hod; he was trying to protect her from herself, as well.

Leaving Flory with the baby, she returned to her own chamber and closed the door. Then, going to the bench in the window embrasure, she pushed the shutter wide and stared out at the setting sun, trying to imagine how she would make her apologies. It came to her quickly that apologizing to Sir James and Sir Antony would be relatively easy, and she did not think that Nan would be much harder.

Phaeline was another matter. The moment Kirkhill had said that she had to apologize, she had thought of Phaeline. The woman was her mother, and she hardly knew how to talk to her. How could she, when Phaeline had not cared enough to come and rescue her from the Jardines or arrange for someone else to do so?

A rap on the door was the only warning before it opened and Nan walked in.

"Are you alone?" she demanded. "Where is your baby?"

Fiona had barely explained when Nan said, "Well, I don't care about all that. What I want to know is what Dickon did to you. Was he furious?"

"You know he was," Fiona said. "What I did was outrageous."

"Aye, it was," Nan agreed with a grin. "But it was a pleasure to see the look on his face when you upended your trencher onto his. You are braver than I am, Fee, but I'll wager that he did not use you as he would have used me."

"He just told me what he thought of what I'd done," Fiona said.

Nan winced. "I know how *that* can be, coldly logical and *very* long-winded. And then, just when you think he has finished at *last,* he says something that…well… that…" She shuddered dramatically.

"Aye, it was just like that," Fiona admitted. "I must apologize to you, though, and to everyone else for creating such a scene. It was discourteous of me."

"Aye, but you need not apologize to me. I've done worse, I'm sure."

She bade Fiona goodnight soon afterward, and took herself off to the room she shared with Phaeline; whereupon, Fiona returned to her contemplations. She had already reduced by two the seemingly daunting number of apologies, but it occurred to her then that Phaeline's would not be the most difficult one, after all.

Kirkhill had rejected her first attempt out of hand. At once, it became of the utmost importance that he accept her second one, but what could she say to him?

When another knock sounded at the door, she had a dreadful premonition that it would be Phaeline and did not even want to open the door.

Calling herself a coward, she marched over and opened it with a jerk.

Kirkhill stood on the landing.

Everything she had been feeling and thinking when she had rushed out of the inner chamber earlier returned in a wave of embarrassment and a sudden urge to slam the door and burst into tears. She could not think of a single thing to say.

"I came to make sure that you are all right," he said quietly. "I was too hard on you, and I think I was mixing your behavior up with that of my sister."

"I'm not your sister," she said, staring at his broad chest.

"No."

Something in the way he said the single word made her look up. As her gaze collided with his, she felt a rush of unfamiliar heat through her body and could not seem to look away. "I...I apologized to Flory, and...and to Nan."

"So Nan was here, was she? Well, I'm not surprised. I warrant she gave you much unmerited sympathy. Did you tell her what a brute I was?"

"Nay, for you were no such thing. I did not tell her much at all."

"Didn't you?"

"Nay, that...that was just between you and me."

"It was, aye," he agreed. "But I was harsher than I should have been."

"You were right, though," she said with an unexpected little sob at the thought of his rightness. "And I'm truly sorry for dumping my trencher onto yours, sir. I do wish you would accept my apology, because, by my troth, I—"

But she said no more, for his arms had gone around her and pulled her close. She had feared she was about to cry, but instead, with a sigh, she rested her cheek against his hard, muscular chest. Then she put her arms around him, too.

Chapter 11 _____

Kirkhill held Fiona, calling himself all sorts of a fool. She was in his care, so he had a responsibility to keep her safe, and that included keeping her safe from him. But the fleeting attraction he had felt on first meeting her, an attraction that he had thought at the time vanished in the face of her obvious pregnancy, had returned almost the moment he saw her again. His dreams had exacerbated the problem.

As a result, the attraction was stronger than ever.

Standing at her doorway, where anyone might see them as they held each other, he knew he cared for her more than he had let himself imagine. He did not want to harm her, and although his men would keep silent, any Jardine member of the household who saw them would likely speak widely of it.

Accordingly, he gave her a hug, set her gently at a slight distance, and said again, "I just wanted to know that you were all right and to tell you that Nan is going to stay at Dunwythie Hall with your mother for a time, mayhap until after the Lammas Day festivities there. Phaeline has invited us to take part in them, too."

She looked up at him, her expression softer than he had

yet seen it. "You...you still have not said whether you will accept..."

When she paused, he was still so full of his feelings for her and the resulting concerns that he nearly asked what she meant. Then it came to him, and he smiled reassuringly as he said, "I do accept your apology, lass. I shan't offer one in return, because you did need to hear what I said to you. But I hope the fact that you have more apologies to make will not keep you awake all night."

"It won't," she said. "Flory is keeping my wee David with her, and Jane's sister Eliza will see to his night feedings for me. So I should sleep well tonight."

"Good," he said. He fell silent as he looked down at her, wishing he were not a man who took his duty so seriously. She stirred a hunger in him that was...

She licked her lips, looking wary, and he realized that he was frowning.

"Aw, lassie, don't look at me like that," he said. "I'm not angry, I swear. I'm just...oh, may God forgive me!" He caught her by the shoulders, pulled her close, and kissed her tantalizing lips.

She stiffened in surprise, but her lips softened against his, and she leaned into him, moaning as she responded with unexpected passion of her own.

Thinking he heard a noise on the stairs, he urged her farther inside without releasing her or ending the kiss, and eased the door nearly shut with his foot.

Then his customary good sense righted itself.

With a sigh, he pulled back and said, "I should not have done that."

"No," she said, gazing at him solemnly. "Nor should I. But—"

"Aye," he said dryly. "But I wanted to, and I've imagined what it might be like from the day we met. 'Tis a harsh burden Old Jardine laid on me."

"Is it?" she said, looking at him as if she were trying to decide just what he meant. "We should not have kissed. Indeed, I do not know why I did not resist you. Less than an hour ago, you made me feel so ashamed of myself that I was in tears, and now . . . By my troth, sir, I do not know *what* to think now!"

"Nor I, lass," he said. "'Tis a dilemma, this overwhelming attraction I feel for you. But mayhap you should call me Richard now, or Dickon, if only because we have got to know each other better. I will strive not to confuse you so again."

"But I did not mean that it was your fault only, sir. I did *not* resist . . . or just at first, because I did not expect such a thing after you were so displeased with me. Also because I thought you did not like me much," she added softly.

"I like you just fine," he said gruffly. "My feelings . . . Sakes, lass, I could not *get* so angry—not the same way—with someone I did *not* care for, and care deeply."

"I have never known anyone to get angry the way you do, so coldly," she said. "You just kept talking and talking, and every word made me feel worse about what I had done and how daft I had been."

"Not daft, Fiona, just thoughtless and gey reckless."

"Well, don't start *again,*" she begged. "I could not bear it now, after . . ." She looked up at him hopefully, but he shook his head.

"We must not let that happen again," he said. "Certainly not until I learn what happened to Will Jardine."

"He must be dead," she said.

"I confess that I hope he is," Kirkhill said ruefully. "He would not approve of my being in your bedchamber like this, let alone kissing you."

She shuddered, and he added brusquely, "Sakes, I don't approve of it myself, and I hope you will never tell Nan. She would fling this in my teeth every time I called her to account for *her* behavior. That would never do!"

"You'd deserve that she should fling it at you, but I won't tell her."

"I must go," he said, still brusque for the simple reason that his behavior had astonished him even more than it had her. He had long taken pride in his ability to separate duty from personal feelings, but his behavior—taking base advantage of his position as her trustee—in his eyes, was unacceptable. None of it was her fault, but he had given her a weapon of sorts, whether she knew it or not.

"I felt so powerless," she said abruptly.

"Just now?" *Little did she know!*

"Nay, before, and for the past two years, come to that. Men wield all the power in this world. Women have none."

He chuckled. "Lass, you have more power in one finger than any man I know has in his whole body. You don't know the will I am exerting now, or how much I fear that you may learn the vast power that *you* wield."

"I do?"

"Aye, but we will not talk about it now, and *not* in your bedchamber. You want to go to bed, so I am going downstairs to have a mug of whisky with Tony and try to keep him from prying into my personal affairs."

"Have I become a personal affair?"

"From the minute Old Jardine told me what was in

store for me, aye. Now, I'm going." Resisting the urge to kiss her again first, he went quickly.

—⁓—

Fiona stared at the closed door, pondering what had just happened and wondering why the kiss had not shocked or surprised her. She felt now, instead, as if she had been hoping he would kiss her, and more. Not that she had consciously wished that he would or that she could have asked him to kiss her, but...

What would he have thought if she had? As it was, he was berating *himself* for it. And what if Will *were* still alive? She shuddered.

Will would be furious that Kirkhill had been living at Spedlins, and would assume at the least that he had flirted with her and she with him. The rest of what Will would assume was even more frightening. She was glad that Old Jardine was dead and hoped fervently that Will was, too. Crossing herself, she looked upward, hoping that she had not just offended God with such evil thoughts.

She decided the wisest thing she could do would be to sleep, as Kirkhill—Richard—had advised. She could not call him Dickon. Only his family did that, so if she did, too, people would talk. But she could certainly think of him so if she liked.

Sakes, they were already talking about her, and about him, too, if Old Jardine was right. If they learned that Kirkhill had kissed her, that one fact would convince everyone that the two of them had murdered Will just so that they could be together.

Shoving Will out of her mind, she saw to her ablutions and got into bed. But it was long before she slept, because fear had entered her thoughts and would not leave. Why could she not remember what had happened that night? Until she did, she could never be sure that she had *not* had something to do with Will's disappearance.

The next thing she knew, it was Wednesday, Flory was at her bedside, and sunlight was pouring into the room. "Ye've slept later than usual, mistress," Flory said. "But his lordship did say that ye'd want to be wakened afore everyone leaves."

"Thank you," Fiona said. "How long ago did wee David feed? My breasts are aching, and I've leaked milk all over myself."

Flory grinned. "It has been hours now, because Eliza did say ye'd want to feed him yourself when ye woke, but he still sleeps. Shall I wake him?"

"Nay, help me dress, so I can go down and bid my farewells. I'll come back and feed him before I break my fast."

Making her apologies proved easier than expected, because everyone was in a cheerful mood and eager to be off to their various destinations. Even so, she made them sincerely, even to Phaeline.

"I thank you, too, Mam, for coming here with Kirkhill as you did when my wee David was born," she added. "Mayhap I did not seem glad to see you, but I was prodigiously grateful that you had come and even more so to know that I could rely on you to see to our guests whilst I was recovering. I...I have missed you."

The last words were out before she knew she would speak them. She was not even sure that it was wise to speak so openly.

"I missed you, too, my dearling," Phaeline said. "Old

Jardine would not let any of us see you, or even ride onto Jardine land, and Will never communicated with us at all. I always wondered, though, why *you* did not send any message to us, other than to say you could not attend your lord father's burial."

"By my troth, Mam, I wanted to be there," Fiona said, suddenly aware that Kirkhill was watching them. "Will forbade me to go. He was sure that you would find a way to prevent my returning here if I went. And when I did not hear from you or from Mairi again, I thought you were both too angry to *want* me back. I never knew that he and Old Jardine were keeping even your messages from me."

Phaeline looked hurt, and Fiona could say no more. She had agreed to elope with Will, and she would not make excuses for that or blame him for all that had happened since. She still thought that her mother or sister, or one or another of the powerful men in their family, could have tried harder to learn the truth and save her.

Turning with relief to Nan, Fiona said, "I hope you will visit me."

"Just try to stop me," Nan said with her mischievous grin. "I have already told the lady Phaeline that I mean to ride here next week to visit, if only for the day. She agreed that I might, but she did say that I would have to bring one of the maids with me *and* a proper armed escort."

"I am sure that Kirkhill will agree with you, madam," Fiona said to Phaeline. "I have not ridden as much here as I did at Annan House, but I do know that folks here worry more than we did about raiders. In Applegarth, we always have to remain aware of how near we are to the English at Lochmaben Castle."

"Well, I want to see as much of this part of Annandale

as we can see," Nan said. "So you must take care to be entirely recovered by the time I do return. And, prithee, do *not* annoy Dickon, lest he decide to forbid us our outing together!"

◦

After the visitors had gone, Kirkhill and Tony spent the rest of the morning working with their men-at-arms. They took their midday meal at the high table, but Fiona did not join them, making Kirkhill wonder if she might be avoiding him. Only when Tony asked if she were no longer going to dine with them, now that her mother had gone, did it occur to Kirkhill that the departure of the other women had condemned Fiona to taking her meals privately again in her solar.

He explained that likelihood to Tony, who said, "But how unfair! We are not barbarians, Dickon. What harm can come to her with us? Sakes, man, have her bring her woman with her. Surely, you can decree it so."

"You are, for once, a source of unexpected wisdom," Kirkhill said as he motioned to a gillie. When the lad ran to him, he said, "Prithee, fetch the lady Fiona to dine here with us and tell her to bring her maidservant with her."

Fiona soon joined them with Flory hurrying in her wake. "Do you think this is wise, my lord?" Fiona asked, casting a pointed look beyond him at Tony, who grinned so infectiously at her that she grinned back.

"I shall doubtless acquire the reputation of a capricious man determined to order things as he pleases," Kirkhill said. "In any event, Tony declared it unfair to banish you to solitary meals, and I agree with him. He and I will be spending too much time together for our own good, and will be glad of your company at meals."

"Then I thank you, sir," she said, gesturing for Flory to sit beside her.

Leaning forward to speak across Kirkhill, Tony said, "Most folks will think he's just being a strict guardian, my lady. But you wait until he starts receiving offers for your hand. He won't *let* you be alone then, lest one of your suitors rides off with you across his saddlebow."

Kirkhill winced inwardly at the abrupt introduction of what could prove to be a delicate subject, but he knew he'd gain little by hushing Tony now.

Clearly amused by the absurd picture Tony had drawn for her, Fiona said, "Even if it were at all likely that any man might try such a feat with Kirkhill at hand, sir, it cannot happen until we learn the fate of my husband."

"Och, aye, I keep forgetting that you've got one," Tony said. "Careless fellow he must be, though, to leave a lass like you on your own without a word from him about where he's got to. Likely, he's dead, and his body will turn up in some odd place or other. Then Kirkhill will be fighting off your suitors with both hands."

"Surely *I'll* have more to say about them than he will," Fiona said, darting a challenging look at Kirkhill. "If I do marry again, be sure that I'll do the choosing."

Tony opened his mouth, met Kirkhill's warning look, and shut it again.

Kirkhill said, "You may certainly express any preference or objection you have, my lady. But I will have much to say about your reply to any such offer."

"But why would you?" she asked.

"By law, I must approve of any man you marry unless

you decide to leave your child to my sole guardianship. I could not allow you to take him from this household unless I strongly supported your choice of a husband. Of course, if you were willing to leave the laddie behind—"

"You would not be so cruel!"

"Sakes, I'm not threatening any such thing," he said, stung. "Nor are you likely to receive any offers as long as those fiendish rumors are flying about."

"That's true, aye," Tony said. "To marry a woman who has already killed one husband would incur rather more risk than most chaps— What?" he demanded when Kirkhill caught his eye again. "*You* mentioned the rumors, not I!"

"But *you* have no business to be making light of them," Kirkhill said. "I was simply explaining the facts with regard to any offer that her ladyship might receive *after* the details are known and we have established her innocence. I did think you ought to know the facts of my authority, lass, that's all," he said to Fiona.

Tony looked from one to the other then but, for once, kept his mouth shut.

"I should have known that you'd control all," Fiona said, ignoring Tony. "I can certainly understand your sister's refusal to marry a man who insists on controlling everything *she* does and ordering *her* every move and thought."

"Here now, I don't do all that," Tony protested.

"You certainly try to do it all," Fiona said roundly.

Tony looked to Kirkhill for help, but Kirkhill said, "That will teach you to stir coals, my lad."

When Fiona, having eaten little, stood to leave, Kirkhill did not attempt to persuade her to linger. He knew

she was upset and that he had been the one to upset her,
but he had known that the subject would arise at some
point. And now it had.

～

After six days of seeing Richard and Tony occupied with
accounts, estates, and men-at-arms, and the household
running smoothly, Fiona found herself missing their visitors sorely and yearning for activity.

Her life with Will and Old Jardine had been one so full
of tension and criticism that she had learned to keep quiet
most of the time and busy herself with household tasks.
Such pastimes no longer sufficed, though, and with Flory
taking over much of wee David's care, and the servants'
children busy in the kitchen with so many more men to
feed each day, Fiona had begun to feel like a prisoner
again.

Thus it was that on the Tuesday afternoon following
their visitors' departure, she greeted the announcement of
the lady Anne's return with a cry of delight.

Nan strode in, grinning. "I knew you'd be bored to dis-
traction by now, and your mam agreed. So here I am with
an escort of armed men and a maidservant who could talk
the feathers off a chicken. Can you ride in that dress, or
must you change?"

"I must change to one with a wider skirt, but will you
not get enough riding just coming here and riding back to
the Hall in one day?"

"Pish tush," Nan said. "'Tis nobbut three miles each
way, and I want to see Annandale. Indeed, I'd like to see
that so-notorious Lochmaben Castle."

"We cannot do that," Fiona said. "'Tis too dangerous,

and your brother would likely have the hide off both of us if we got within a mile of the place."

"We won't tell him then," Nan said cheerfully. "Is Tony still here?"

"Aye, of course, he is, but they are not here at present, either of them. They took a large group of men-at-arms out to some field or other to practice their skills with bows and arrows, I think, and mayhap swords. So it is every day!"

"Good, then they need not trouble us," Nan said.

Fiona, on the brink of admitting that she had no idea which direction the men had gone, decided that before she entered into what was certain to become a debate, she would do better to learn what orders Kirkhill had left. She had seen enough of that gentleman to be sure he had left orders of some kind with regard to her ordering a horse for herself. Will had never let her do so. If he had not ordered the horses and gone with her, she had not ridden at all.

Taking a more positive view of Kirkhill, she hastily changed her skirt and went with Nan to the stableyard.

Joshua strolled out of the stable as they approached.

Fiona went to him and said, "The lady Anne and I mean to go riding. Will you tell someone that I want my bay gelding?" Hoping she sounded more confident than she felt, she waited with bated breath for his reply.

"I'll see to that myself, m'lady," Joshua said. "I ken the beast ye like."

She had no idea how he could know which was her horse, but he brought it out quickly, along with another that was clearly for himself. Glancing at Nan, she noted that that young lady was displeased to see Joshua but also that Nan refrained from voicing an objection. Nor did she again mention Lochmaben.

It was just as well, too, because although they did go south, riding downhill past the graveyard and then along the boundary of several apple orchards near the river, they had ridden for less than an hour—and more sedately than either Nan or Fiona had hoped—when they met Kirkhill, Tony, and the men they'd been training.

"What have you done with the lady Phaeline, Nannie?" Sir Antony demanded as soon as they were within earshot of each other.

"I cannot imagine how that is any concern of yours," Nan snapped back.

"Dickon, did you grant your sister permission to career about the countryside on her own like this?"

"She is hardly on her own," Kirkhill said, briefly meeting Fiona's wary gaze as he gestured toward Joshua and the four Dunwythie men who followed them.

"I brought a maidservant with me, too," Nan said with a virtuous air that made Fiona want to laugh and hope at the same time that neither gentleman learned of Nan's fascination with Lochmaben. Nan, oblivious, went on to say, "But the poor lass had had her fill of riding by the time we reached your tower, so I left her there."

"Thoughtful of you," her brother said. "Tony, why don't you ride ahead with Nan, and continue your exchange of compliments where they will not stir my wrath. Joshua, you head on back to the tower with this lot and the rest of the lady Anne's escort. I'll escort the lady Fiona myself. I want to have a little talk with her."

As the others sorted themselves out, Fiona said to him, "I hope you are not vexed with us for riding out here as we did, sir. Despite our snail's pace, I have enjoyed myself more today than on any I can recall since leaving Annan House."

"Nay, lass, I'm not vexed. The boot is on the other foot. I have not made time to see you alone this entire sennight and feared that you might still be vexed with *me* over that business Tony brought up about finding you a new husband."

"I *was* vexed at the time," she admitted. "But I've given it some thought, and my judgment of men being clearly flawed in some way, I have decided I should be grateful that someone *must* take a hand to protect my son."

"You won't make another mistake, lass. I won't let you."

She looked at him, wondering if he could really be thinking about finding her another husband. But she said nothing.

Although it had irked her to learn that she'd need his approval if remarriage became possible, she doubted that it would for a long time, if ever. To be sure, she *had* thought about it, but the man who came to mind when she did was Kirkhill himself. He had admitted his attraction to her and had likely deduced hers to him, but after Will, she did not trust her own feelings, let alone Kirkhill's.

They rode in silence until they reached the graveyard again. When she shuddered as they passed it, he said gently, "Do you fear ghosts, lass?"

"Nay, but this place always makes me shiver, and more now than ever."

"It is a pleasant hillside."

"Perhaps, but the view from here is just another dull

hillside. I want a better place for my grave, overlooking the river or the western hills, perhaps."

He stiffened visibly, but he said in his usual even tone, "I hope it will be a gey long time before you require a grave, my lass."

She smiled then and, in return, received a smile that warmed her all through.

Meanwhile, she could hear Tony and Nan enjoying their usual differences ahead. Their debate continued through the midday meal until Kirkhill ordered Tony back outside with the men. He then told Nan that Fiona had ridden enough for her first day in months on a horse and sent Nan and her escort back to Dunwythie Hall.

Fiona, in a much more cheerful frame of mind after her day's outing, spent a pleasant afternoon with Flory, deciding what clothes wee David would need and compiling a list to give Parland Dow when the knacker returned. Since Dow had known at his previous visit that the baby's birth was imminent, Fiona was sure he would have at least a few things to sell her that he had collected in his traveling.

Kirkhill ordered his supper served in the inner chamber so that he could continue to attend to estate business while he ate, and Fiona took hers with Flory in the solar. Afterward, she spent an hour with David, nursed him, and put him in his cradle. By the time she slipped into bed that night, she was weary but beginning to think that life at Spedlins Tower had greatly improved.

The forested hillside overlooked a vast green valley, its floor covered with splendid wildflowers. Birds sang from the trees, and a soft breeze rustled leaves overhead. She lay with her head on his shoulder beneath a tall chestnut, feeling drowsy until he shifted beside her and his free hand sought her bodice laces.

In a trice, they were open, and his palm slid lightly over her exposed breasts, his fingers teasing her nipples. She gasped but did not open her eyes, wanting to savor the sensations he stirred throughout her body.

A full moon drifted above the canopy of trees, and she wondered idly why she did not recall opening her eyes again or that darkness had fallen.

His face was in shadow as he leaned toward her, his head haloed in moonlight. He kissed her, deeply, his tongue thrusting into her mouth, the very taste of him stirring her soul. She put a hand to his warm cheek, and then stroked his muscular chest and taut belly, reaching lower.

He turned his head slightly, as if he had heard a noise. Now she could see his features. His deep gaze met hers, and his smile warmed her heart.

Then his face melted away in so puzzling a way that she squeezed her eyes shut. When she opened them, she was no longer lying with him or looking at him but was standing, looking down at something on the heavily shadowed ground.

Darkness hid all but the full-sacklike shape of it, six feet long and lumpy.

A shiver of fear shot through her, and she took a hasty step back before she realized that whatever it was, it just lay there, unmoving. Nevertheless, she stood frozen for such a long time that she began to wonder if she could move.

She would have to. She was alone in a dark forest.

Dickon had vanished as if he had never been there at all.

The woods were silent. The moon had gone behind a cloud or had otherwise vanished, because the area around her was as black as ever a forest night could be. The stillness was eerie. She heard herself breathing… too loudly, too quickly.

She inhaled and exhaled slowly to steady herself, then looked down again and realized that although she was unable to see even shapes of the nearest trees in the blackness around her, the long shape on the ground was clear, ominously so.

For some reason its lifelessness disturbed her. She dared to prod it with the toes of one foot, gently. When it did not stir, she nudged harder. No movement.

She started. Surely, there had been a sound, someone coming!

What had she done?

Trying to remember, she put a hand to her side, stirring a sharp pain and a recollection just as sharp that Will had punched her there. Then he had knocked her down, and blackness had enveloped her. Apparently, darkness still ruled, because she had regained consciousness in the unnerving stillness of the eerie forest.

Listening hard, she thought she heard a night bird's peeping cry. She wanted to run but could see no path. And she could not leave her burden where it lay.

It did belong to her. She was sure of that, although she could not say why or how. What would people think if she abandoned it here? Surely, someone would know that she had it, that she was responsible for its being here.

The enormous, long sack looked unwieldy and unbearably heavy, but she had to get it away. Hiding it was urgent. The reason for keeping it secret was not clear to her, but it could not stay where it was. Too terrifying to think that someone might stumble over it in the heavy darkness and touch it as she had had to touch it.

The cries grew louder, as if the birds were fussing at each other, wailing. Hearing the sound increased her sense of urgency until it overruled all primal fear.

Pulling, tugging, rolling, pushing—she did everything she could do to make the sack move up the hill. Slowly, slowly she began to make progress. She knew where it had to go, over the hill and down. The other side would be easier, she hoped, because only one place was suitable. But never had it seemed so far away.

The moon had reappeared. She saw its beams diving through the woodland canopy when she crested the hill with her burden. But, as she emerged into the open, the moon evaporated. One moment it was there in the dark sky, as clear as could be. The next it was brittle-looking, diaphanous mesh, and then gone.

Still, she had seen enough. The oblong opening in the ground ahead was perfect for her purpose, just the right size. Her burden seemed lighter, too. Moving it downhill was easier, despite certain upright, deeply shadowed obstacles in her path. Twice she had to move quickly to keep up with the sack as it rolled.

The moon took form again, casting its pale light on the deep hole, warning her an instant before the great sack tumbled into it, or she'd have fallen in, too.

She peered down into the hole. The sack had vanished,

and all that lay there in the moonlight now was Will Jardine, fiendishly grinning up at her.

Fiona screamed…

…and awoke still screaming, her cries distantly echoed by those of the now squalling baby in Flory's room just across the service-stair landing.

Chapter 12

In the inner chamber, Kirkhill heard Fiona's screams and those of the baby, leaped up from his chair at the large table where he had spread his version of the Jardine accounts, and ran up the service stairs with his heart pounding. As he rounded the stairway curve, he saw Flory ahead, crossing the landing. She shoved Fiona's bedchamber door back on its hinges, then hesitated at the threshold.

Gently urging her on into the room, Kirkhill saw Fiona sitting bolt upright in her bed, looking blindly toward the open, moonlit window, still screaming.

"Look after the bairn," he told Flory as he moved swiftly to the bed. "I'll call for you if I need you. She has only suffered a bad dream, but the bairn will calm more easily if you shut your door and do your best to soothe him back to sleep."

"I should stay near so I'll hear if you call for me, but I could send for Eliza, m'lord. Likely, the wee laddie be hungry."

"I'd liefer have no one else up here yet. Just do what you can."

"Aye, sir, I'll give him a sugar tit to suck on until her

ladyship be calm again. He'll be that hungry then, and when she settles, nae doots she'll want to cuddle him."

"Likely, you're right," he said, having no notion whether she was or not.

Fiona had stopped her shrieking, but she still faced the window, eyes shut, sobbing in a mixture of short cries and gasps. He barely waited for Flory to shut the door before he gripped Fiona firmly by both shoulders and gave her a shake.

"Wake up, lass," he said calmly. "'Twas nobbut a bad dream."

Her eyes snapped open, and she looked right at him, her mouth still agape, her breath drawn in as if to scream again. Her gaze met his, but her eyes focused only briefly before she looked around as if she felt disoriented.

"Faith, I'm in my own bed," she said. "Again!"

"You had a bad dream."

"Horrid," she agreed, nodding fervently. "So real!"

"Sometimes, it helps to talk about such dreams," he said.

Her darting gaze found him again but slid away before he finished speaking.

"It was dreadful," she muttered, looking down at the coverlet. "I...I don't want to talk about it at all, let alone try to describe it. Faith, but I cannot even bear to think about it. I'm sorry if I woke everyone up."

"You didn't," he said, searching for some clue to what was troubling her. "I was poring over the accounts I've assembled below, so Flory got here before I did. She is looking after the bairn, but she says he is likely hungry."

"Poor wee chappie," she said. "I must have frightened him witless."

"I doubt that his wits are formed enough yet to suffer from being startled by loud noises. Do you feel up to feeding him, or shall I send Flory to fetch Eliza?"

"I'll feed him. I just had a nightmare. There is naught else amiss with me."

He did not believe her. She had not met his gaze again, making him wonder what sort of dream could have frightened her so. She was trembling, too. On the thought, it occurred to him that she might be shivering instead.

"Art cold, lass?"

"Nay, and I wish you would go," she said. "Old Jardine may have made you responsible for me, but as you yourself have pointed out, because of that charge and... and because of what happened before, you should *not* be alone here in my bedchamber with me."

"Flory is just across the landing."

"Even so..."

"Aye, sure, you are right. I'll go." But he did not move. She looked so vulnerable, so alone with her fears, whatever they were, and he wished she would confide in him. But he could not make her do so. Nor could he blame her for not yet trusting him. Trust was neither instinctive nor something one person could demand of another. One had to earn trust, and he wanted more than ever to earn hers.

He saw a blanket folded at the end of the bed and picked it up. Shaking it out, he draped it around her shoulders, rubbing them gently as he did until she put a hand up to touch one of his.

Quietly, he said, "I do not always heed my good sense, lass, but I would do nowt to harm you, alone or in company. Still, you might feel more comfortable with your mother here. If so, I'll ride to the Hall in the morning and fetch her for you."

"Pray, do not, sir! She would be most *un*comfortable. It is but a testament to how badly she wanted to see her grandson born and to provide a proper hostess for your sister and Sir James that she stayed as long as she did. I am grateful that you brought her here, though, so that she *could* see my David born."

He did not want to talk about Phaeline or the baby. He knew he had no business in Fiona's bedchamber. It was dangerous even when his conscience reminded him of his duty to her. Even so, he was loath to leave her in her current state.

"Shall I send for Flory now to bring the bairn in to you?"

"Aye, sure," she said, her tone softening. "He *must* be starving to have set up such a fuss. I think I heard him in my dream before I started shrieking."

"Lass, are you sure that you would not like to talk about that dream? I'd wager it would not seem so dreadful if you could bring yourself to do that."

"I can't!"

"Aye, well, mayhap Flory should sleep in here for a time. Since Eliza is taking some of the bairn's feedings, you could just let him stay with her at night. Surely, that would be more convenient for all—"

"You mean well, sir, but no. I want him near so that I can feed him whenever I can do so without exhausting myself. Sithee, I want to make him as much mine as I can. He is Will Jardine's son, and Old Jardine's grandson. And Spedlins will belong to him one day. I cannot change any of that, nor do I want to deny him his birthright. But I do want to fill him full enough of his mam that he has no inclination to heed such traits as he may have inherited from his father or grandfather."

He wanted to take her in his arms and reassure her that no son of hers could be like Will Jardine. But without knowing what had become of Will—in fact, without proof that Will was dead—he could not promise her any such thing. He would do all he could to see that her son grew up strong and honest, but family traits did have a way of asserting themselves, no matter what one did to prevent it.

"I'll get Flory and the bairn now," he said, stepping back from the bed.

She was silent, but she did relax against her pillows, and her normal color seemed to be returning, so he went to the door and called Flory.

Waiting until she appeared with the baby, he held the door for her and then shut it again. He wanted to linger, to ask her when she came out if her ladyship had confided any details of her nightmare to her.

Fiona Dunwythie Jardine did not strike him as a woman likely to let a bad dream terrify her. It had to be something more. But he knew, too, that he could not apply to Flory. He'd be far wiser to let Fiona tell him herself, and in her own time.

She was safe with Flory and the bairn, and he had no good reason to wait outside her door. He would make it his business, however, to be patient and try to win her confidence. If he could persuade her to tell him what it was that had frightened her so, he was sure he could ease her fears.

Fiona was certain that Kirkhill still stood outside the
door, because she had not heard his footsteps departing
down the service stairs. But she let Flory settle the baby
into place and smiled down at him as he rooted feverishly
for her nipple.

"He's famished, poor laddie," Flory said. "He were
content wi' yon sugar tit whilst we waited, but I be glad
ye be yourself again, m'lady. It must ha' been a fright-
ful bad dream. I canna recall ye ever waking with such a
screeching afore."

"I do not want to talk about it, Flory, and I hope you
will not be talking about it either," Fiona said evenly. "To
anyone."

"Nay, then, I wouldna talk o' such a thing," Flory said
virtuously, as if she had never gossiped in her life. "Still,
it were gey scary to hear ye, and nae mistake."

Fiona was satisfied that Flory would pursue the subject
no further, but she was just as sure that she would not
silence Kirkhill so easily. He had said he was a curious
man, and as one who would do almost anything to satisfy her own curiosity, she recognized in him a kindred
spirit in that regard. He might bide his time, but in the
end he would do all he could to make her tell him about
her nightmare.

He contained himself in relative patience for two days,
although Fiona caught him gazing speculatively at her
more than once.

Each time he did, she held her breath, waiting for him
to speak. But each time, he managed to hold his tongue or
to introduce a harmless topic.

That Friday morning dawned clear and warm, and
when Fiona descended to the hall to break her fast, she

found Kirkhill putting two manchet loaves in a cloth sack from the basket on the high table.

"I thought we might like to break our fast on that hilltop overlooking the river just north of here," he said. "'Tis a splendid view that I came upon only yesterday whilst I was exercising Cerberus. I saw at once that it would make a fine place to eat, and I am hoping you will agree to join me there this morning."

"I'd like that," she said impulsively. "I know the hill you mean, but I have never been to the top of it. Will didn't—" She broke off, feeling herself flush.

"Then you must see the view," he said as if she had not spoken those last two words. "Can you ride in that dress, or must you change it? Come to think of it," he added before she could reply, "you have not been out riding since you went with Nan. Did you try the exercise too soon? *Should* you be riding yet?"

"Aye, I should," she said, grateful that he had not demanded to know what she had so nearly said. "Lying about has never been my notion of pleasure. As for my dress..." Looking down at it, she grimaced. "This skirt is full enough, and I have few clothes that I consider too fine to wear for aught that I do. As I told you some time ago, I've had to make do with what I could manage."

"I did say you might send for a seamstress," he reminded her.

Color tinged her cheeks. "I have been waiting for Parland Dow to return. I know not how otherwise to summon one."

"Aye, well, that is something that I can see to," he said. "I have learned enough about the state of things here that I can do so in good conscience. If you will tell me what you need to outfit yourself as a lady should, I will see that you have it."

Feeling suddenly like crying again, and knowing that the tears were already welling in her eyes, she turned hastily away, murmuring, "Thank you. Did you put apples in that sack? Applegarth folks rarely go anywhere without a few, you know. It would be practically sacrilegious."

"I did put some in," he said. "There will be a stiff breeze on that hill, though, so you will want your cloak. How long since your wee lad last took nourishment?"

"Just a few minutes ago. I am free for at least two or three hours . . . not that we'll want to linger as long as that," she added hastily.

"But we need not hurry," he said.

She looked at him then, and for a moment, she thought he looked pleased. Then he smiled at her. It was a particularly charming, almost mischievous smile.

"Nay," she said. "We need not hurry."

She fetched her cloak and followed him out to the stable. She expected to find Joshua waiting for them, but he was nowhere to be seen.

When Kirkhill asked which horse was hers, she indicated her gelding, and since she rode astride as most Border women did, he put her on it before saddling his big black destrier.

"He's gey beautiful," she said of the great steed.

"He is, aye, but don't you trust him until I say that you may," he warned. "Cerberus is a warhorse, and although he can be quite civil when he chooses to be, he is unpredictable with people he does not know."

She nodded and watched how deftly he worked, as if

he did it often. She also thought the destrier behaved better than any Jardine horse she'd seen ever had.

Joshua still had not appeared when they rode out of the
yard, and although several stable lads were going about
their duties, Kirkhill invited none of them to go with them,
and Fiona was glad. He chose a course that took them
along the river.

Will had often followed the river route with her, but
riding with Kirkhill was entirely different. Unlike Will,
he liked to chat about the things he saw, pointing out odd
rock formations, swirling eddies in the river that he said
must harbor salmon just yearning to be caught, and birds
in the trees, sometimes recognizing the birds by their
cries or songs before he spotted them.

Fiona felt herself relaxing to a degree that had become
unfamiliar during her two years at Spedlins Tower. Only
as the tension melted away did she recognize the sensation for what it was and realize how tense she had been.

"Yonder is the trail I followed up the hill," he said sometime later, his voice just slightly louder than the soothing
sounds of the Annan tumbling by and the chirping and
chattering of birds and squirrels from nearby trees and
shrubs.

Fiona nodded, urging her gelding ahead of Cerberus,
eager to see the view from the top. They did not speak again
until they reached a large clearing just south of the western-
most brow of the hill. Kirkhill dismounted there, dropping
his reins to the ground while he moved to lift her down.

When she stood beside him, he guided her with a touch
to her shoulder along a path until they stood near the steep
drop to the river Annan, beyond which lay the western
half of Annandale.

"Look there to the southwest," he said, pointing. "You can see all the way to Lochmaben. Those are the castle's towers amidst what looks like one vast loch."

"Is it *not* a loch?"

"'Tis two small lochs surrounded by a series of burns and rills that feed into them. All that water is what makes the castle impregnable."

"The English don't bother us much," Fiona said. "I doubt that I've ever seen an Englishman at Applegarth, or at Annan House, come to that."

"They are a nuisance, though," he said. "But look to the northeast now. The highest hill you see in the distance is the southern boundary of Kirkhill. The hill where the ancient chapel perches lies about three miles north of that."

Fiona's stomach growled loudly.

Kirkhill chuckled. "I'll wager you'd like to eat."

His eyes twinkled and looked softly golden in the early morning light.

She found it impossible to resist smiling as she said, "Aye, I would."

He unstrapped the basket and a blanket from his saddle. Setting the basket aside, he spread the blanket on the ground, where they could enjoy the western view.

Fiona picked up the basket and handed it to him. As he took it, she realized that, although she had been glad that he had not asked one of the gillies to ride with them, they ought perhaps to have brought someone for propriety's sake.

It had seemed so natural to be riding alone with him and to stand at the brink of the hill and enjoy the view together. But now, about to share a blanket and food, she felt isolated, vulnerable, and as if she ought not to have come alone with him.

"We should have brought Joshua or Jeb's Davy or someone else with us," she said with a slight frown. "Mayhap we should go back."

"Not till we've broken our fast," he said as he set the basket on the blanket.

"But *you* should have told someone," she said. "Why did you not?"

"Because I want to talk to you alone," he said over his shoulder. "But first we should eat. I don't want to fratch with you on an empty stomach."

She stood stiffly, glowering at him until he straightened again and faced her.

"Come and sit down," he said.

"Nay, I won't. I ken fine what you want to discuss. But now you've spoiled this wonderful morning, and I don't *want* to talk to you."

She turned toward the horses, but his hand shot out to grip her arm. "We're going to talk, lass. Do not forget that *I'm* responsible for you and your child."

"For my child, aye, but you are only trustee for whatever Old Jardine left for my keep. If he left naught, as I do suspect, then you are likewise as naught to me."

He held her gaze, and she knew she was trembling. "Are you sure about that?" he asked quietly.

She could not speak. The sudden, *stupid* urge to cry made her throat ache.

"Trustee or guardian, it is my duty to protect you both and keep you from harm, Fiona. Moreover, I know you well enough now to believe that no ordinary nightmare could terrify you into a fit of screaming. I want to know what did."

"Let go of me. My dreams are none of your business."

He released her, saying in the icy tone she hated, "You are being childish again, but it will do you no good this time, either. I mean to get the truth from you."

"Well, I don't mean to tell you." She turned again, but he caught her again and forced her to face him, giving her a shake as he exclaimed, "By God—!"

Gasping, she tried to wrench herself free. "No! Let me go!"

Kirkhill felt her stiffen and saw the color drain from her face.

"What is it?" he exclaimed. "Surely, I did not hurt you with that little shake!"

She shook her head. But her body remained tense, and her gaze riveted on his face as if she would peer through it to his thoughts.

They stood like that long enough for him to have counted to ten, had he thought of counting. But his thoughts were racing, and amongst them flashed myriad details that he had seen or heard about her since his arrival at Spedlins.

He could no longer deny the most likely answer to the puzzle that was Fiona.

He had known that Will Jardine had kept his wife close, had known that neither he nor Old Jardine were men who would tolerate insolence from a woman, and he had suspected that Jardine had even ordered Hod to strike her when *he* could not. But Kirkhill had assumed that Fiona's occasional wariness, even fear, of *him* stirred only because she did not yet know him well enough to trust him.

As the bits he knew all clicked into place, the truth made the breath stop in his throat. He carefully released her, but as he did, his hands clenched into fists.

When he could speak calmly, he said, "You are safe, Fiona. I won't hurt you, but I'm beginning to think that you have had reason to fear any angry man, even me. You seemed to fear Old Jardine even whilst he lay on his deathbed. And I recall now that when we met, you moved as if you were in pain. I supposed then that your pregnancy had made you awkward, but that was not the case, was it?"

She kept still, eyeing him much as a frightened woodland creature might.

"Ah, lassie," he said, drawing a long breath. "When you look at me like that, you make me feel like a scoundrel. But, truly, you are safe with me."

"You would have beaten me for dumping my food onto your trencher," she said. "Men are all the same."

"Nay, we are not," he said. "Putting a child or a stormy woman across one's knee and awarding her backside a good smack or two is justice for misbehavior, not cruelty. I'd wager your father did it to you more than once, unless he was cut from the same bolt as Will and his father, and you feared him, too."

Her eyes filled with tears as she shook her head.

Gently, he put his hands back on her shoulders and drew her close, looking into her eyes as he said, "I won't ask you to trust me, Fiona-lass, although you can. I will just ask you to tell me some things, if you will. First, did you dream about Will?"

She nodded, still watching him.

"Thank you," he said. "Here's the next question. I'm

right, am I not, in believing that he badly mistreated you?"

She shut her eyes.

"I have heard that you and he argued that night. Is that true?"

She nodded.

"Did he hurt you?"

She chewed her lower lip but said nothing.

"Tell me, lass. I must know all that you can recall if I am to protect you."

For a long moment, he thought she would refuse. But, at last, staring at his chest, she muttered, "First he slapped me, at least twice. Then he drew back his fist to hit me in the belly. I turned, and he hit me in the side instead. The pain was fierce and sharp. It lasted for weeks, but my turning away made him angrier. He knocked me down, and I must have hit my head, because when I woke, I was alone in our bed and my head ached as much as my side did. I don't know what became of Will."

Kirkhill drew her closer until she rested a cheek against his chest. Her hair tickled him under his chin. "I'll tell you one thing," he murmured to the top of her head. "If Will Jardine is not dead, I'm gey likely to kill him myself."

"I do truly think he must be dead," she replied. "Naught else would keep him away now. Everyone for miles must know of Old Jardine's death and the birth of Will's son. He would come back if he could, to claim both David *and* Applegarth."

Drawing her toward the blanket, he said, "Is that why the dream terrified you so, because you believed Will *had* come back?"

She shook her head. "Prithee, do not ask me about that

awful dream, Dickon," she pleaded. "I cannot talk about it. It was too real. I cannot tell anyone."

"You can tell me anything without fear," he said, relieved to hear her use his nickname, although he was sure she had done so without knowing it. "I'll protect you, whatever the risk. When you are ready to trust me, I'll listen, and I will help. Now, however, I do recall that we came here meaning to break our fast."

Releasing her, he turned away to open the basket. As he did, a barely audible sob escaped her that nearly spun him back to her. But instinct warned him that she had tried hard to stifle the sob and just needed a moment to collect herself.

It was the first time that he could recall being truly thankful for three sisters.

Fiona had come nearer to flinging herself into Dickon's arms than she had come with anyone since some childhood scrape or punishment had sent her into her father's arms for consolation. Not that there was anything the least bit paternal about Dickon, for there wasn't. But he did provide a sense of safety that she had not experienced since her childhood... and a sense of danger that she had never known and could not clearly define.

They ate silently, and then he moved to tend the horses.

She looked into the western distance, trying to focus on the forested ridge that divided Annandale from neighboring Nithsdale. But she was conscious of every move that Dickon made behind her, doing whatever it was that he was doing. His boots crunched twigs and leaves, and the great black destrier made a snuffling sound that indicated welcome, followed by the familiar equine crunch of an apple.

A moment later, the gelding made similar sounds.

Drawing a breath and letting it out, Fiona turned to find Dickon standing between the two horses, watching her. The look on his face sent a wave of heat through her, but it was not the familiar heat of embarrassment or shame. It was closer to what she had felt the night he had come to her bedchamber and they had agreed that she was *not* his sister.

She vaguely recalled a similar but lesser feeling when she had first met Will and had fallen for his flirtatious manner, handsome face, and powerful torso. Will had also stirred her sense of adventure, her love of mischief, and a certain daring that had made her feel all grown up at fifteen.

But this…with Dickon…seemed to flow from deep within her. Part of it was a sexual attraction similar to what she had felt for Will when he had made no secret of wanting her. But the semifamiliar sensation seemed now to rest on much more. She had never felt *this* before with anyone. It was as if she knew Sir Richard Seyton of Kirkhill through and through, knew him better than she knew herself.

Such a sensation had to be false, but even that thought did not disturb or weaken it. The moment seemed timeless, as if she might study it and consider it from every angle before she need move or speak.

Then he smiled the soft, encouraging smile that she had come to look for, and held out a hand to her.

She went to him and put her hand in his, looking up at him.

"Better now?" he said.

"I think so, aye. In troth, though, I thought I had got over being so unpredictably emotional."

"I am not sure that females ever get over that," he said with a tender smile and a squeeze of her hand. "I will admit, though, that I doubt if you ever *threw* yourself at any one of your kinsmen and beat on his chest to make your point."

She looked up at him from under her lashes. "Does *Nan* do that?"

"She has done it only once with me, but I did see her try it on my uncle once, and he's told me of other times. And she has done it to Tony at least once."

"Why only once with you?"

"Because I have little tolerance for such behavior."

"Good sakes, what did you do?"

"I smacked her backside and sent her to her bedchamber to contemplate her ills in solitude."

She grimaced, and he knew she was remembering again how she had nearly suffered the same fate.

Recovering, she said, "Well, I have never beaten on any man's chest. But, in troth, I do not know whom I might have treated so. My father would have reacted as you did. I have met my good-brother, Robert Maxwell, only once. I know my uncle, Sir Hugh Douglas of Thornhill, a little better—the one married to my cousin."

"I know Hugh Douglas," he said.

"Well, I cannot imagine pounding on him. In troth, I cannot imagine anyone doing so with impunity."

"I find him amiable, but mayhap he's a sterner gentleman with his family."

"He is, aye," Fiona said with feeling. "Sithee, he is my mother's younger brother. She once said that when Hugh makes up his mind, he never changes it. I doubt he behaves so with Jenny, though," she added thoughtfully.

"I doubt he does," Kirkhill agreed, giving her hand another squeeze. "Would you like an apple, lass?"

His gaze met hers again, and she realized that the mood between them had altered, leaving her hungry for something other than food. She licked suddenly dry lips, unable to look away from him as he slowly leaned closer and kissed her.

The kiss was different this time, softer, tenderer. But her body reacted as it had before, with passionate yearning to be closer to him. She dared to slip her tongue between his lips and felt a surge of delight when he let her.

Then, with a low hum in his throat, he pulled her close again and kissed her more fervently. His hands moved caressingly over her back and sides, then to her buttocks to urge her closer yet. She felt him stir against her, and he made the humming sound again in his throat.

She slid her arms around his waist and hugged him, but his hands moved then to cup the sides of her head, as with a sigh he ended the kiss.

"Don't look so sad, lass," he said. "I promised to protect you, and that means protecting you from me, too. I do feel strongly about you, and you seem to have feelings for me. But we both need to be sure that our feelings are genuine. If they are, then it becomes more imperative than ever to know what happened to Will."

"Just hold me," she murmured. "I *don't* want to think about Will Jardine!"

Putting his hands to her shoulders again, he said, "You will have to think about him, however, because you are going to tell me all about him."

Chapter 13

Kirkhill saw the light go out of her eyes and wished he could say something that would bring it back. He would not force her to relive her nightmare, for heaven alone knew where that might lead. But if he was going to learn what happened to Will Jardine, he needed to know as much about the man's habits as possible. So far, despite sending men to search all of Annandale for Will, he had learned nothing about where the man might have gone, or why.

Fiona stood silently before him, making no effort to step out of his grasp but making no effort to respond to his comment, either.

"Tell me about Will, lass. I know what I saw. What do you know of him?"

"Will was..." She paused to think, but when he raised his eyebrows in surprise, she said, "What is it?"

"Was?"

She gave him a look. "Do you want to know about him, or are you just seeking signs that I know he is dead?"

"I want to know," he said. He was glad to hear her sound more like herself.

Fiona saw that his eyes looked greener now than golden, with calmness in them and a warmth of expression that she found reassuring.

"I swear to you," he said, "I do not believe that you killed your husband or took any part in his death, if he is dead. Not only is it impossible to believe that you could overpower him, as I have said before, but I know you well enough now to be sure that you are incapable of having aught to do with killing *any* man. However, I do believe that things may have happened that you do not remember."

"Do you mean that Will could have died whilst I was with him and that I might somehow know how it happened without *knowing* that I know?"

"Perhaps. It is possible."

She shuddered, recalling her horrid dream. "But how could I *not* remember his dying—however it might have happened?" *Let alone burying him myself whilst big with child, and in such a place that no one has ever found him?*

"I have seen a strong man clouted on the head in the heat of battle, who went on to fight with great skill and bravery only to collapse from his wounds, senseless, at battle's end, then awaken later with no memory of any battle taking place. I have heard similar tales from others, as well—more than one."

"Such men have *no* memory of their actions? None?"

"None," he said firmly. "The chap I know did recover some of his memory in time, but he still has not recalled being hit or fighting afterward. He insists that the rest of us who were there are jesting when we describe his feats of bravery."

"How does he think he came by his injuries?"

"At first, he said that he must have got drunk and been drawn into a brawl. He has no memory of fighting, although he recalls that we were preparing for a battle. He believes that he fell soon after it began and we are making up all the rest."

"But you are not."

"Fiona-lass, I saw him fight with my own eyes, for he saved my life that day, striking down a man who waved a Jedburgh axe at my head whilst I fought another with my sword. As it was, I suffered a deep cut on my left shoulder. It was whilst they stitched the cut together that I learned the benefit of squeezing someone's hands, focusing on his face, and trying to breathe deep and evenly to ease pain."

"I'm sorry you were hurt, but I'm no soldier," she said. "I cannot speak for what soldiers might do in the heat of battle. Still, I do think that I would remember if I had killed my husband or seen him die."

"Tell me about Will," he said again. "I want to know as much about him as you do. It may help me learn what became of him."

She nodded, then fell silent, thinking about Will, trying to decide how best to let Dickon see what Will was like. Deciding that all she could do was tell him how Will had seemed to her, she said, "He was funny and charming at first—flirtatious."

"Where did you meet him?"

"At the Hall. He had come with Robert Maxwell to see the place when the Sheriff of Dumfries was trying to collect Annandale's rents and royal taxes. You will doubtless recall how hard the sheriff fought to extend his authority into Annandale."

"I do, aye. And I know that Rob Maxwell is the sheriff's younger brother, and husband now to your sister, Mairi. 'Tis an odd match, I thought, in view of your father's strong opposition to the sheriff's unsuccessful efforts."

She nodded. "Mairi and I were together when we met them. Will flirted with me, and...and I flirted back. Mairi told me I was a fool. I...I should have listened."

"We rarely listen when people tell us we are behaving foolishly," he said. "We never want to believe that it might be true."

She wondered what foolish things he had ever done. He did not seem like the sort of man who would ever behave foolishly. He always seemed to be in complete command of himself and of everyone around him.

"When did you next see him?" he asked.

She remembered that easily. "He followed us home to Annan House, where we lived most of the year then. We had just visited the Hall. Then Rob and Mairi...You must have heard about what happened with them. Everyone did."

"I heard something about his abducting her, aye. But at present, I am interested only in Will. Your father was not friendly with the Jardines."

"Nay, for they were Maxwell allies, and he did not like the Maxwells, either. Also, the Jardines feuded constantly with the Johnstones, who live just north of the Hall. That's why we lived at Annan House, to avoid being always between them."

"I ken Lord Johnstone fine," he said. "A crusty man, but a good one."

"I don't know him," Fiona said. "I thought it was romantic for Will to follow me home. He sent a message, asking me to slip out and meet him in the woods near Annan House. I did, and Mairi nearly caught us. That made it even more exciting," she added, grimacing. "Sithee, I had never had an adventure all my own. My cousin Jenny seemed to have them all until then, so I thought that I should enjoy just one."

"But why did you run away with Will?"

She shook her head. "Do you know, I can hardly remember what I was thinking. Looking back, I expect it was no more than an impulse, because Will made me feel special when no one else ever had. Before I met him, I was just the unnecessary daughter. My parents wanted a son, so I was a disappointment to them both. And Mairi was four years older, which is a great span when one is young."

"Aye, twice what it is between you and Nan."

She smiled. "Aye. Mairi was always kind but not interested in me or in things I liked to do. I was just someone she had to watch over, a nuisance who wanted to be with her all the time. Also, she was the one who would inherit our father's estates and title. Will thought *that* was wrong. When I told him how it was, he said he was sure I would get land, too. I was supposed to inherit Annan House, because it was part of my mother's tocher when she married. But Father was so angry when we eloped that he changed his will, so that house went to Mairi with everything else."

"I suspect that Will was unhappy about that," Kirkhill said.

"He was *furious*. He had not believed that I would get only Annan House. Then when I got nothing..." She shuddered, remembering. "He said it was all my fault, but he would fix it. He said he would *get* me my inheritance."

"And did he?"

She shook her head, feeling fire in her cheeks.

"What did he do?"

"I don't know exactly. He would not tell me, but I heard that he tried to capture Mairi. He...he told me that I would inherit everything if Mairi were dead."

"She has a son now who would inherit."

"Aye, but this was before she married Robert Maxwell. Will was furious when she did marry him. But his anger grew even stronger with me then," she added. "I could do naught to please him. Everything was my fault."

"He must have been glad to learn that he was going to be a father."

"He paid little heed to my condition," she said. "I warrant he would be pleased now to know that he has a son, but he had only one use for a woman then, and he did not like it when I began to increase. Old Jardine grew surly even with Will sometimes, too, and whenever he did, Will would visit *his* anger on me."

"I see."

"Do you?"

"I think so, aye. Will was a violent man and a powerful one."

"He said power lies more in one's allies than in oneself, that the trick is to choose the right side to support. He thought we should be placating the English. In troth, so did I. Before I came to know Will, I thought it was foolish to fight, that if people would just talk to each other, they could resolve any problem."

"That tactic works only if both sides *want* to resolve the problem," he said with a wry smile.

"It certainly did not work with Will. But we all want

peace, don't we? We just want to grow our crops and know that our families are safe from attack."

"I'm afraid that, although many of the common folk—and doubtless most women and children—would prefer peace, men in power nearly always want *more* power, whatever it takes. It sounds to me as if Will was more interested in attaching himself to the most powerful side than he was in protecting his family or his land."

"He thought he could protect everything if he just sided with the right faction," she said. "He also thought that the more wealth he could accumulate, the better. And he thought that if he could take control of Dunwythie Mains and add it to Applegarth, he would put himself in a strong bargaining position when he negotiated with the winning side, whoever won."

"I doubt he'd have found Archie sympathetic if he had sided with the English," Kirkhill said. "Or the other way around, come to that. If Northumberland were to take Annandale, he'd be more likely to award land here to loyal Englishmen than to a Scot known for switching sides each time the wind shifts."

"Aye, perhaps, but Old Jardine believed the same as Will did. He said the English already had such a strong foothold at Lochmaben that taking Annandale would be easy for them when they got their forces together and stopped fighting the Earls of Douglas and March miles east of here."

"Then Old Jardine was a fool," Kirkhill said roundly. "Northumberland would have exploited that foolishness, too. He would have promised the Jardines whatever they wanted, used up their men in the fighting, and then he would either have hanged them or taken their land with the rest of Annandale and left them to fend for themselves any way they could."

"Does any of this help you to know Will?" she asked after a brief silence.

"I don't know," he said. "I need to think about it all. But it is always better to know as much as you can. Information is often worth more than gelt."

"Do others in Annandale think as Will and his father did?"

"That is a good question," he said. "I know most of the barons hereabouts, of course, and I'd trust almost any one of them in a fight. Old Johnstone is as loyal a Scot as any who breathe, and your lord father enjoyed the same reputation. That your sister married a Maxwell must still trouble some folks."

"Mairi would not let a Maxwell sway her from her principles, sir. And if Robert Maxwell were untrustworthy, she would not have married him."

"Mayhap it was an arranged marriage, lass. She might also have been mistaken in him."

"Nay, because although Mairi is quieter than I am and does not show her feelings as easily as I do, she is strong, sir. Moreover, Will was a friend of Rob Maxwell's, or thought he was. And Will told me that *Mairi* proposed to Rob."

Kirkhill looked at her in astonishment. "That sounds most unlikely," he said. "Art sure, lass?"

"Nay, of course I am not sure, but Will *did* say so," she assured him. "Mayhap we should ask Mairi when she returns to the Hall."

"Aye, perhaps," he said. "But for now, we should pick up our things and start back to the tower. If you will hold the basket for me, I'll fold up the blanket."

She helped him and they were soon mounted and on their way. As they neared the base of the hill, they saw Joshua and Davy riding toward them.

Visibly worried, Fiona said, "Why have they come, do you think? Could something be amiss at home? We've been gone longer than I'd expected."

"Nay, lass, Joshua is obeying my orders," he said. "Few people can have seen us leave, but many will see us return, so I told him to follow us and wait nearby. If anyone asks questions, he will deal with them. As for young Davy, he has been aiding the men by cleaning their weapons and such, and Joshua has been teaching him to see to their horses. The lad is quick to learn, Joshua says."

"I hope you were not too stern with Davy over that confrontation with Hod," she said. "I never thought to ask you what you'd said to *him*."

Color tinged her cheeks, and he knew that she was remembering what he had said to her about her part in the incident.

"Davy knew that he was in the wrong," Kirkhill said, trying to think how to explain the lad's attitude to her. "He told me he got angry when Hod hurt Tippy, but sithee, I could tell him that that had angered me, too. I explained then that a man cannot let his temper rule his behavior. I also made it clear to him that Hod was the house steward, and that household servants must obey their steward, just as Davy must obey Joshua if he is working with Joshua, or me if I give him a command."

"I do not think Davy would disobey you, sir," Fiona said.

"Unlikely, I'll agree," he said with a smile. "The only ones who defy me are young women who should know better."

She dimpled, and he was glad that Joshua and Davy were near. Their presence stifled the strong desire he had to snatch her off her horse and carry her with him on Cerberus so that he might teach her that flashing her dimples at a man could lead to unexpected consequences.

As it was, he glanced at her from time to time as they rode, trying to judge her mood. He thought she looked more relaxed and that it had helped her to talk about Will Jardine, especially to admit to him that Will had frightened her and hurt her physically. But it concerned him that she would still not talk about her dream.

If the nightmare had frightened her only because it seemed terrifyingly real and she had feared that Will would hurt her again, surely—having at last found the courage to disclose his brutality—she ought to have found it easy enough to discuss her dream. That she had not, and was now casting Kirkhill a wary, speculative look, told him there was more to Will's being in the dream than just his presence there.

It also told him that she still did not trust *him* enough to reveal the details.

Fiona was well aware of Dickon's flickering glances, and she was sure she knew the reason for them. Images from her nightmare loomed large in her memory, so large that it would not have shocked her to hear that he could see them in her mind as well as she could. A part of her wanted to tell him about it, because she had found it surprisingly easy to tell him about Will once he'd got her started. But the nightmare was different. How could she be sure it was just a dream? What if it was a returning memory such as his friend had experienced after that battle?

Dickon had not said that the soldier had had nightmares first, but he might have had some. Dickon might not even know about them.

Joshua and Davy had fallen in behind them, as if they had been escorting them all day. Both rode without talking. She knew it was a habit with Davy to keep his thoughts to himself. The lad had done so even before his father's death, but since then, he had rarely spoken unless someone addressed him directly.

And Joshua, although always respectful, was a taciturn man by nature.

Dickon, too, seemed lost in thought except for those fleeting glances. Not once did he point out vistas or draw her attention to a birdsong. Even so, his very presence was pleasant, companionable, and calming. She felt safer with him than she had felt with anyone for a long time. She knew that he was merely giving her time to think and hoping she would decide to confide in him. If she did not, she also knew that it would not be long before he demanded a full recounting of her dream.

Therefore, when he arranged for private speech with her on their return by the simple expedient of dismounting and motioning away the gillie who would have helped her dismount, she was unsurprised.

Lifting her off, Dickon held her with her toes barely touching the ground long enough to say quietly, "It does disappoint me that you cannot yet put your trust in me, lass. Sithee, truth is elusive. Until we can separate suspicions and fears from the facts, we'll not learn what happened. I can be patient but not for long."

With that, he set her solidly on her feet and politely offered her his arm.

She hesitated, feeling as if she had vexed him again and been rebuked. But when he said no more, she let him escort her inside. He excused himself then, saying that he had duties to see to before their midday meal.

She found it easier to breathe when he had gone, and hurried upstairs to find Flory with wee David, changing him.

Fiona tidied herself, dismissed Flory, and spent a pleasant half hour with her son until his eyelids drooped and he dozed. Then, she took him into Flory's room, where she found Tippy patiently waiting on a cushion by the cradle.

"He's asleep," Fiona murmured as she laid the baby in it. "If he wakens betimes, shout for someone to fetch me."

"I ken what to do, m'lady," Tippy said with a smile that revealed two missing teeth.

"I know you do, Tip. You're a good watcher."

"Me and our Davy both be good watchers, m'lady. Me da told us we ha' to watch over each other and them we do love. 'Tis wha' good folks do, me da said."

"Your da was a good man," Fiona said. "We all miss him."

Tippy said, "He has been dead more than six weeks now, Davy says. It seems a gey long while t' me."

"It does to me, too," Fiona said.

Leaving the little girl to keep watch over David, she went down to the kitchen. It had been easy to take up the reins of the household again, easier than before Dickon had come, when Old Jardine or Will had criticized almost anything she did, or—even more often—had complained just to complain.

The rest of the day passed without incident, but thoughts of Kirkhill continued to trouble her. Seeing Tippy in the kitchen with Jane just before supper, Fiona remembered the little girl's confident words: "I ken what to do, m'lady."

Fiona knew what *she* ought to do, too. She just wished that she had the child's cheerful confidence in doing it.

"Mistress," Jane said, approaching her diffidently.

"What is it?" Fiona asked. "Is aught amiss?"

"Only that one o' the big pots as Cook uses has cracked, and he says it needs mending. Shall I send for a smith to see to it?"

"Aye, sure," Fiona said. "Send someone tomorrow and ask him to come straightaway. We don't want the pot to split and spew its contents across the floor."

"I'll see to it then, aye."

At suppertime, learning that Dickon and Tony had ridden out and not yet returned, Fiona ordered her meal served in the solar and, for once, rather enjoyed her solitude. It no longer felt as if she were an exile. Looking around her, she decided that the little room could become cozy with just a few new touches.

Remembering that Kirkhill had recommended frugality but then had said that she must have a seamstress and a wardrobe suited to her station in life, she decided that he would understand that other new things were also necessary.

Leaving the remains of her supper, feeling sure that Dickon must have returned, she went upstairs to look in on David and then back down to the hall.

Dickon was not at the high table, and she did not want to draw undue notice to what would be a private conversation by entering the inner chamber from the dais, so she hurried back up to her own chamber and down the service stairs.

Rapping softly on the service door to the inner chamber and receiving no reply, she rapped again more loudly.

Still nothing.

Turning with a sigh to go back upstairs, she hesitated.

Curiosity urged her to have a look at Dickon's sanctum. She had been inside the room only once since Old Jardine's death, and that inauspicious occasion had not been one that tempted her to take much interest in her surroundings.

Putting the memory aside, she returned to the door and knocked once more.

Still hearing only silence within, she listened for noises on the service stairs but heard only more silence. Accordingly, and very carefully, she lifted the latch and eased the door open.

Someone had lighted a fire not long before, because it crackled merrily. A branch of candles on the table by the door to the great hall was also alight, casting flickering light over some documents spread there.

Stepping inside, keeping an ear cocked for the sound of approaching footsteps, she gazed around and saw that Dickon had evicted every remnant of Jardine's ghost. She saw nothing of the old man in the chamber. Even the huge carved bed now stood in one corner, like a cupboard bed, with new silken bed curtains of a soft, mossy green. The washstand and candle-stand were also new.

Taking in the changes, smelling the citrus scent of him

mingled with the peaty aroma of the fire, she moved idly to the table and glanced curiously at the documents. Even to her less than practiced eye, it was clear that most of the amounts noted were expenditures. Only a few small sums looked like income.

Deciding from his notations that she was looking at expenses for the stables and kitchen, she went on until she found what appeared to be accounts for the orchards and fields. They, too, appeared generally to be expenditures.

The click of the latch startled her, and she whirled from the table to see Dickon entering with Tony at his heels.

⁓

Kirkhill's first reaction to seeing Fiona in his chamber was anger. Clearly, she was snooping and had no right to be there without his permission. Moreover, she had to have sneaked in from the service stairs, because had she entered from the great hall, he'd have seen her as he and Tony were hastily eating their late supper. If she had entered earlier from the hall, someone else would have seen her and wondered what she was doing there.

Before he expressed his displeasure, however, he saw that the documents spread across the table had drawn her attention. He wondered if she could read.

Most women could not, but she was smart and she was curious. Also, although their entrance had startled her, as she looked up, he had detected irritation in her expression, if not anger.

A twinge of guilt stirred within him at what she might have deduced.

⁓

His eyebrows had risen alarmingly when he'd seen her, but although Fiona had detected the initial glint of anger, he did not seem angry now. He looked rueful. In any event, he said over his shoulder, "Forgive me, Tony. I forgot that her ladyship had asked to speak privately with me. I'll send someone for you when we have finished our talk."

"Aye, sure," Tony said, vanishing as Dickon shut the door.

Fiona held her breath. But when he did not demand to know what she was doing in his chamber... when he said nothing at all... she said, "He kens fine that you had no appointment with me here. At least, I hope he does, because the sort of appointment he must be thinking—"

"Just so, lass," he interjected. "Tony will say nowt, but I trust that you have good reason for being in here."

"I did, but first I want to know about these." She gestured to the documents. "I do not know much about such accounts, but I do know when numbers are to the good and when they are not. These appear to be nearly all expenses."

"They are, aye."

"You told me I had to be frugal until you'd discovered how things are here. But then you did tell me that the estate could bear my expenses, did you not?"

"I did, aye."

She waited, but he did not continue.

"Is there any money?" she asked at last.

"Nowt to speak of," he said.

As a chill swept over her, he added gently, "The land here is good enough for barley, mayhap for oats, and, of course the apple orchards thrive. With better management, I hope to show a good profit here in a year or two."

"A year or two! Then how am I to meet household expenses until then? Jane just told me we need to have one of the big pots mended, and I told her to send it to the smith. How will we pay him for mending it?"

"You will have him present his reckoning to me, of course," he said calmly.

"But you—" She stared at him. "Are *you* paying for the things we buy? Do you mean to pay for fabrics for my new dresses, for my bairn's clothing? Good sakes, sir, you say that you worry about scandal! What do you think *that* will stir?"

"It will stir nowt to concern you," he said. "My responsibilities for you, your bairn, and the Jardine estates give me broad discretion. The reason you found these documents here is that I am keeping careful accounts—unlike the Jardines, I might add. I did not reveal the full state of their finances for two reasons. I did not yet have a clear picture of them, and I saw no reason to frighten you. These estates will be profitable with good management, and it is my duty to provide that."

"You should have told me," she said. "It is unfair to encourage me to act as mistress here and *not* tell me that we have no gelt to pay for things."

"Had you asked questions, I'd have answered them honestly," he said. "I did not lie to you about anything. I just asked you to be frugal, and then, when I realized that things would soon improve, I encouraged you to replenish your wardrobe."

"How very reasonable you are," she snapped. "How logical you sound! Well, let me tell *you* something, my lord. If I *am* mistress here, I have a right to know the truth. You say you did not tell me because you did not want to frighten me. You tell me with one breath that you want me to trust you and then, with the next, you admit that you keep things from me. I will tell you what being mistress here means to *me,* sir. It means being free to make decisions for this household and for myself. It does *not* mean letting you protect me from the truth. Being wrapped in cotton wool is just as stifling and just as demeaning as never being allowed to make a decision *at all*!"

As she flung the words at him, she saw his lips press together until tiny muscles in his jaw twitched, giving her a feeling that his teeth were grinding and that she was making him angrier with every word she spoke. But she did not care.

Then, in the same even, carefully controlled tone she had endured when he'd scolded her, he said, "Would you have dared to speak to your husband like that?"

Heat flooded her cheeks, and she bit down on her lower lip to keep from snapping a rude reply. Then, meeting his gaze, she said, "I did, aye, more than once, and suffered painfully each time until I learned to mind my tongue."

"Well, *don't* mind it with me," he said. He grimaced and then smiled wryly. "You were right, lass, and I apologize. I *should* have told you how things stand."

Fiona stared at him in astonishment, wondering why in the world a simple apology should make her feel like crying again.

Chapter 14

Kirkhill watched Fiona, wishing she would go on speaking her thoughts aloud. In particular, he wanted her to explain what had brought her to his chamber.

At last, he said, "You did say that you had reason to await me here, lass."

Her cheeks flushed, and her gaze slid away from his. Then, taking a breath, she looked him in the eye and said, "I *was* looking for you, but the truth is that when I rapped and no one answered..."

She paused, looking down, wetting her lips with her tongue.

Suppressing a grin, he said, "Curiosity, lass?"

She nodded and raised her head but still avoided his gaze as she said, "I hated this room because it was Old Jardine's, and whenever I had to come in..." She stopped, nibbled her lip, and then added in a rush, "I just wanted to see how you had altered it. When I was here with you that other time..."

"You'd prefer not to think about that, either, I expect."

She shook her head. "It isn't that. What with all you were saying to me then, I just did not heed the changes you had made in here."

"By that time, as I recall, I had just had Hod get rid of Old Jardine's bedding and the chests of his clothing. Why were you looking for me tonight?"

She shook her head. "Not now or here. Someone else might come in."

He wanted to protest, but he knew Joshua would be along soon. The man would not talk about anything that Kirkhill did, but Fiona did not know that.

Even so, he had let her keep her secret long enough, and he suspected that she had looked for him to tell him at last about her dream.

In any event, he could not wait indefinitely for her to decide to trust him. He was losing patience with the mystery of Will Jardine.

Moreover, if Will was *not* dead, it could mean that he and his obstreperous father had again decided to support the English. If *that* was so, the sooner they found Will the better it would be for the Scots.

Accordingly, he put both hands on her shoulders as he had on the hilltop and said firmly, "I'd prefer that you confide in me because you feel safe doing so. But before much more time goes by, I am going to insist that you tell me all about that dream of yours whether you want to or not."

"Faith, do you think you can force me?"

"Do you think I cannot, even though I swear I'll do nowt to harm you?"

She glowered at him, telling him clearly that she knew he could.

"I'll not press you further now," he said, "because Joshua will be along soon to see to his duties. So I'll say goodnight and send you up the service stairs as I did before. You did come in that way, did you not?"

She nodded, watching him as if she did not want to hear what he'd say next.

"Tomorrow, Fiona. We can walk by the river or take horses out again as we did today. You decide what will make it easier for you, but we are going to talk more about Will, and you *are* going to tell me about your dream."

She licked her lips again, then blurted, "I'm afraid it is just as you said about your friend...a...a way of remembering what I don't want to remember."

Nodding, he said bluntly, "It may *be* something of that sort. But it might just as easily be nowt but a bad dream suggested by things people have said to you, or something that your mind made up out of summat or nowt, as Joshua would say. We cannot know until we get it into the sunlight, lass, and look at it together."

When she grimaced, his hands tightened briefly on her shoulders before he let go of them to embrace her.

For a long moment, he held her close, enjoying the sense of her head against his shoulder. When she shifted so that her breath warmed his neck as she sighed, he moved a hand to her chin and tipped her face up more, making her look at him.

"If *we* are going to get anywhere, lass," he said, "*you* must help me learn what happened to Will. Until we do, we'll have to go on hiding our feelings for each other. Before tomorrow morning, you must decide if yours are strong enough for you to trust me, because if we *don't* find him, and continue to feel this attraction we feel, my spending time here, as I must, would become torture for both of us."

"I have to think," she said. "I must go."

⌒

Fiona hurried up the service stairs, her emotions in turmoil. She could still feel the warmth of Dickon's body, but she thought that he might at least have tried to reassure her that she was not beginning to remember something she didn't *want* to remember instead of practically agreeing with her that she might be.

Halfway to her bedchamber, she recalled that she had twice ridden past the graveyard shortly before she'd had the dream, first with Nan, then with Dickon. Mayhap it was just a horror put into her mind by her usual reaction to graveyards.

She had loathed *all* graveyards since the day that Will had told her of her father's death. Will had said that Dunwythie's own temper had carried him off, but Fiona had known that by eloping with the son of an enemy, she had acted in a way that her father would see as a betrayal. She had no doubt, even now, that it had been the shock of that betrayal that had killed him.

Her failure to say a proper farewell to him had tortured her dreams with graveyard images long before the nightmare about dumping Will into *his* grave.

She had nearly persuaded herself that seeing the graveyard had put the notion into her head of burying Will by herself. Thinking about it gave her shivers, though.

Not only did she not want to think about it but she also, *definitely,* did not want to tell Dickon about it. At best, he would think her mad. At worst, he would believe her a murderess.

⌒

Kirkhill arose early Saturday morning determined to win Fiona's confidence, but by the time he finished breaking his fast, she had not yet come downstairs.

He did not wait for her but, seeing Davy at one of the lower tables, left the dais to speak to him.

"Don't rush yourself, lad," Kirkhill said when the boy jumped to his feet. "I want you to stay here until the lady Fiona comes downstairs. When she does, I want you to run and find me so that I may join her here."

"Aye, sure, laird," Davy said. "Ye'll tell Joshua I'll be a bit behind time?"

"I'll tell him," Kirkhill promised. "Mayhap this afternoon I'll have time to show you a few more things about using a dirk properly."

"Aye, sure," Davy said, his face clouding. "'Tis no the same though since Hod broke me da's dirk."

"I might have an idea about that, too," Kirkhill said, ruffling the boy's fine hair. "You just eat enough now to build some muscle in you."

"I will, aye," Davy said, smiling again.

Taking an apple for himself from the basket on the high table, and another for Cerberus, Kirkhill found Joshua in the stables brushing the destrier and told him Davy would be late. Then, casually, he added, "I may ride out later with her ladyship. If I do, I'll want the pair of you to escort us as you did yestermorn."

"From the start this time but at a discreet distance, I'm guessing," Joshua said without looking up from his currying.

"Aye to both, but I'll have no more of your sauce, my lad."

"'Tis a dangerous game ye play, m'lord."

"Perhaps, aye, but we still have much to learn, Joshua, and I'm hoping that her ladyship can help."

But Davy no sooner ran out to tell Kirkhill that her ladyship had descended to break her fast than a rider arrived from Dunwythie Hall.

"M'lord," he said to Kirkhill, "Baroness Dunwythie, Baroness Easdale, and their lord husbands arrived at the Hall late yestereve. They mean to ride here to Spedlins to take their midday meal wi' ye and the lady Fiona unless I go back at once and tell them that such a visit today wouldna suit ye."

"Such a visit would suit us gey fine," Kirkhill assured him.

"That be good, as they'll be starting soon," the gillie said. "Our lady did say to tell ye she's gey eager to see the lady Fiona and to know that all is well wi' her."

"Get yourself some ale in the great hall, lad, and food if you need it. Then you may ride back to meet your mistress and tell her that she and anyone she chooses to bring with her will be welcome at Spedlins as long as I am master here."

"Thank ye, sir, I'd be grateful for a morsel and a sip." Jumping down from his horse, he found Davy in front of him. "Here now, lad," the gillie said, squinting down at him. "Be ye big enough to handle this beast o' mine?"

"Aye, sure," Davy said. "If ye want to see a true beast, ye should see our Cerberus, yonder by the stable door."

The gillie followed Davy's pointing finger and his eyes widened at the sight of the black destrier. "That be a fine animal, indeed," he said.

Davy nodded solemnly. "Sithee, I'll take good care o' yours, too. The great hall be that way, so just go as your nose tells ye to keep a-going."

"I'll find it," the gillie said. Thanking Kirkhill and assuring him that he'd be off again as soon as he had refreshed himself, he strode toward the tower entrance.

Kirkhill, making a hasty adjustment in his plans for the day and, once again, giving thanks for sisters, followed in the gillie's wake. He entered the hall in time to hear Fiona exclaim, "Gerrard's Eckie, is that really you?"

"Aye, m'lady," the gillie said as he strode past the lower hall trestle tables to the edge of the dais, where Fiona and Flory sat at one end of the high table.

Pulling off his cap, he made a creditable bow.

~

Fiona stared at the young man with mixed emotions. Delight warred with hesitation and wariness, but curiosity overrode all.

"Do you come here from Annan House or from the Hall?" she demanded.

"From the Hall, m'lady. I ha' been serving her ladyship—Lady Dunwythie, that be, no the lady Phaeline—these past two years."

"Then Mairi is at the Hall?"

"Aye, at least she were when I left, but she did expect to be away as soon as everyone had broken fast. They be a-coming here to take midday dinner wi' ye."

"Everyone? Is Lady Easdale there, too, then?"

"Aye, and his lordship and Sir Hugh."

"His lordship?"

"Aye, m'lady, the master. I dinna ken if ye ha' met him. He married the lady Mairi after—"

"Aye, sure, you mean Robert Maxwell. But surely, they do not call him Lord Maxwell!"

"Nay, nor does anyone call him Lord Dunwythie. Most folks still think o' that being your da. But the lady Mairi did say it were proper for us to address him as his lordship and m'lord, so most folks do refer to him as the lord Robert."

"Do they," Fiona said. Movement beyond him diverted her to Dickon's approach. She said, "This is Gerrard's Eckie, my lord, who serves my sister. His father is captain of the guard at Annan House. Eckie tells me we are to have guests for dinner—a fair crowd, I expect, because I'll wager that my mother and Nan will come with the others. I shall have much to do to prepare for so many."

She gazed at him expectantly, even hopefully.

Knowing just what she was thinking, Kirkhill dismissed Eckie to his "morsel and sip" and went to pour himself a mug of ale from the jug on the high table.

Then, to Fiona, he said, "The kitchen has been in almost daily anticipation of such a visit from the moment we learned your sister would be returning to the Hall. I own, I did not expect her to come *here* so soon, but she is certainly welcome."

"Even if the kitchen is prepared, sir, I must go and tell them what to expect."

"Knowing that you were breaking your fast, I sent a lad to warn Jane."

"But I must—"

"Fiona-lass, I ken fine that you will want to attend to all manner of things, to see that everything is as it should be to receive them. But young Eckie did say that your sister's party would not be leaving until they had *all* broken their fasts."

"Which they may well have done at the crack of dawn," she said.

"I doubt that," he replied. "Sithee, lass, I do not know them all, but the larger the party the less likely it is that their departure will take place as expected."

"Sakes, m'lady," Flory said. "Your mam won't even be out o' her bed yet."

Fiona gave her a fierce look, but Kirkhill intervened, saying, "The journey will take them at least two hours. So you should have plenty of time to do *all* that you need to do before they arrive."

At the emphasis he put on the word "all," she looked sharply at him.

He held her gaze until her cheeks grew pink. Then he smiled, saying, "Now that that is settled, the sooner we have *our* discussion, the sooner you will be able to get to everything else."

"But—"

"We can talk in your solar as soon as you are ready. I will await you there. You may bring Flory with you if you like." Giving her a look that warned her he would not be put off, he turned and headed for the solar.

Fiona watched him go with increasing irritation. She had hoped that with so many guests arriving and so little warning, he might agree to postpone their discussion. Instead, he had exploited the situation to further his own ends.

Sorely tempted as she was simply to go about her own

preparations, that last look he had shot her warned her that she would probably be sorry if she did.

Dickon's way of making people sorry was unlike any she had known before, but in its own way, it was no less discomfiting.

"Will I go wi' ye then, mistress?" Flory asked diffidently.

"Nay, you will not," Fiona said more sharply than she had intended.

"But I ken fine that your mam would say ye should no be alone wi' him!"

"Mayhap she would," Fiona replied, reminding herself that she had sworn not to snap at people. "But I am mistress here, Flory, not my lady mother, and Kirkhill is responsible for us all, so there can be naught amiss in my being private with him from time to time, just as I was with my father or... or with Old Jardine."

"Aye, but his lordship be neither your father nor your good-father."

"Nay, he is not, for all that he sometimes *acts* as if he were."

When she said no more than that, Flory gave her a speculative look before she said, "I'll just go and order ye some water and a tub for a bath then. I warrant ye'll want to wash your hair, too, will ye no?"

Fiona nearly told her that there would not be time for all that, but she knew that Flory and Dickon were likely both right in saying that Mairi's party would not get off as soon as they'd hoped.

Therefore, she said only, "I'll be as quick as I can, Flory."

"Be the laird sorely vexed then?" Flory asked.

Fiona gave her a quelling look, but it failed, because Flory looked right back at her until she said, "He is not vexed, Flory. He is just curious about something, and in troth, I do not blame him. But I do *not* want to talk to him."

"Aye, well, nae doots ye'll feel better after ye do," Flory said comfortably.

Fiona gave no response to that, but neither did she have any appetite left.

Rising from the table, feeling much as she *had* felt when facing a stern interview with her father, she left the dais and headed for the solar.

He had left the door open for her, and she could see him inside, kneeling by the hearth, stirring flames to life.

Just watching him, Fiona felt her mood lift.

Kirkhill sensed her approach before he heard her light footsteps. Giving a last poke to the fire, satisfied that it would burn well for a time, he straightened and turned to greet her.

She came in and reached to close the door.

"Leave it open, lass," he said. "We'll talk over here, and no one will hear us. I think this is where we should talk whenever we want to be private. Anyone seeing us together through an open doorway is less likely to think aught of it."

"Before we say more, sir, I owe you an apology."

"What for?"

"For entering your chamber last night without your permission."

"Nay, then, you have no need to—"

"But I do," she interjected firmly. "I would be furious if I'd walked into *my* bedchamber and found you snooping through *my* things."

"So you are hiding things from me, are you?"

"Nay, I am not. I have naught worth hiding, and I'd liefer you not jest about this. It *would* anger me, and when you first came in I could *see* that it vexed you."

"Aye, it did at first," he admitted. "Then I saw that you'd been looking at the accounts, and my first thought was to wonder if you could read them."

"Aye, sure, I can... well, most of them. I am not as good at keeping my household accounts as I ought to be. But that angered Will, so I did try to learn."

"I will teach you anything you want to know," he told her, itching again to have just five minutes with Will Jardine. "You were right to call me to account, though, just as I said you were. Even before you took me to task," he added, "the fact that you were interested enough to be looking at them told me that I ought to have explained the situation clearly from the start."

"Aye, but I should not have taken you to task as I did, either," she said, gazing at a point somewhere beyond his left shoulder.

He put a finger under her chin and drew it back so that she had to look at him before he said, "You may always speak your mind to me, Fiona. We may fratch. In fact, I'm sure that we *will* fratch, many times. But you need never be afraid to say what you are thinking to me. I often speak bluntly, lass. I always have. It would be most unfair of me to deny you that same privilege."

"But you said that I was being childish when I did speak my mind."

"Aye, well, you did behave childishly, more than once," he said.

With a wry grimace, she said, "I expect I did at that."

"Sit down, lass," he said, gesturing to a back-stool near the window embrasure. "Do you think you can tell me now about that dream of yours?"

"Perhaps, but may we not talk about some other things first?" she said as she obediently took the indicated seat.

"Do you have other things that you want to discuss with me?"

"Nay, but I thought you might…about the Jardines or Spedlins or…"

"Look here, Fiona, this is not going to get any easier if we keep talking around it or if you keep trying to change the subject. The only thing that will make it easier is getting it out of your head and into the open. So, now, what do you say?"

She stared out the window without speaking.

Impatience stirred, but he forced himself to wait.

At last, she looked at him and said, "I dreamed that I buried Will."

~

Hearing herself say it aloud, Fiona cringed inside. But the words were out now, hanging in the air between them.

"Suppose you begin at the beginning," he said. Pulling another back-stool out, he straddled it, facing her and resting his forearms atop its back. "What is the first thing about the dream that you remember?"

She stared at the point where his arms met the chair back, trying to remember the only part of the dream that had grown hazy in her memory. "I was on a hillside in a forest," she said. That was right; she was sure. "I think it was daylight at first, because I remember wildflowers, colorful ones. It was pleasant there."

She fell silent again, trying to remember what came next.

"Was Will there?" he asked quietly.

"Nay." She glanced at him. "I remember that it was most agreeable. I would not have thought that, had Will been with me. There were birds, songbirds."

"Then you were alone."

Her memory cleared abruptly, flooding her cheeks with heat. "Someone else was there, but it was dark then and there was a moon, a full moon," she said rapidly. "Then everything melted into something else, the way dreams do, and suddenly I was standing in pitch darkness, looking down. I'm quite sure I was alone then."

"Who was with you before?"

"I ... I'd rather not say." She met his gaze, praying that he would ask her something, anything, else.

He held her gaze for a moment, frowning. Then, rather curtly, he said, "Are you sure that this other person had nowt to do with Will's disappearance?"

She could answer that one honestly. "Aye, quite sure."

"And he would have no reason to want Will out of the way?"

That question was another matter. She hesitated, but the answer was there nevertheless. "He may have had reason," she said. "I cannot speak for another's thoughts. But I am as sure as anyone could be that he did nowt to Will."

He nodded. "What happened next?"

She heard the quaver in her voice as she described the

sacklike burden she had pushed up hill and down, the vanishing moon, the darkness. She let it quaver, exerting herself to remember details that might help her decide if the dream had been a horrid memory turned into a dream or just a terrifying, pointless nightmare.

When she told him about the sudden pain she had felt where Will punched her and that she had remembered that he had, in the dream, Dickon just nodded.

But she saw his right hand clench.

He noted the direction of her gaze, too, because he straightened his fingers as he said calmly, "Go on, lass. What happened next?"

Letting out breath she had not known she was holding, she said, "I seemed to know where I was going, that I had to go up the hill and then down. The sack was gey long and heavy, but I felt an urgency to hide it that did not go away until the thing fell into the hole."

"What hole?"

"One that was just there in the ground, waiting for him," she said.

"So it *was* Will in the sack," he said, frowning again.

"Aye, though I did not know it until I looked down into the hole," she said, shuddering. "The sack was gone then, and Will just lay there in the moonlight, grinning up at me. That's why I woke up, screaming."

"Sakes, lass, anyone would have screamed, seeing that. But you say that you knew where you were going. Where were you standing at the time?"

"I don't know," she said. "I just knew in the dream where to go, and when I got there, the hole was there, waiting."

"Like a grave, then."

"Aye. After we talked before, I thought that riding with Nan past the graveyard that day and then doing it again with you had put the idea in my head of me burying Will. But you'd said that bit about parts of a memory returning to someone who had forgotten much after a clout on the head. And I did get such a clout."

"I can see how you might think as you did, aye, but your dream was nowt but a dream. You cannot have done all that by yourself. Will had to weigh at least twelve or thirteen stone. You don't weigh more than eight."

"I weighed more than that at the time," she said, remembering.

"Carrying the bairn, aye, but that just proves my point, Fiona-love. I'd defy you to have picked up a sack of apples weighing a quarter of what Will weighed, as close as you were then to birthing your wee David."

She stared at him, memory of the dream evaporating in the face of what he had just called her. He was frowning though, staring over his folded arms at the floor. She was as sure as she could be that he was unaware of the endearment.

Perhaps he often added "love" to women's names, just as a sign of friendship. Some people were overly generous with such tender words.

He looked up then, and she felt sudden fire in her cheeks.

~

Kirkhill noticed her blushes but gave them little thought, knowing how hard it had been for her to confide in him. Hoping to reassure her, he said, "Look here, lass, I am not going to tell you that there is nowt of substance in such a dream, because neither of us can know that yet. But I *am* certain that you never did any such thing awake as you did in that dream. The notion is preposterous. You saw someone else bury Will, or otherwise cause him to vanish or die, or the whole thing is pure imagination, dreamed up because of all the rumors against you."

He stood up and held out a hand to her.

Taking it, glad of its warmth, she said, "Are you sure? Might I not have *helped* someone else?"

"Is that what has been troubling you? If so, then prithee tell me who is so important to you that you would protect that person with every fiber of your being."

"I don't know anyone like that!" Her thoughts seemed to whirl. Letting go of his hand, she tried to think sensibly, saying, "Mayhap if Mairi had killed him, but she was not here. Nor was Mam, and until you... Sakes, I don't *know* anyone else!"

"Then, you see, the whole thing is a tale that your imagination has spun, doubtless a result of making up stories to entertain the bairns. This one was not at all entertaining, however."

"Nay, it was not. But you were right, sir... Richard."

"How is that?"

"It *has* helped me to tell you about it."

"Good," he said, hoping he sounded casual but refraining from touching her again. He knew that if he did, he would grab her and hold her tight until all memory of the awful dream had faded from her memory.

Chapter 15 _____

The party from Dunwythie Hall arrived little more than an hour before the midday meal. Besides their armed escort, it included the two baronesses, their husbands, the lady Phaeline, the lady Nan, and surprisingly, Sir James Seyton.

As that gentleman assisted Phaeline to dismount, he grinned at his nephew.

Both Kirkhill and Tony had met them in the courtyard, and Kirkhill, moving to help Nan dismount, had failed to notice his uncle until that moment.

Seeing him turn with a much warmer smile for Phaeline, Kirkhill began to wonder if Sir James had found a new interest there. As he pondered the thought, he found himself rudely thrust aside as Tony passed him to lift Nan from her saddle.

"I like that dress," Kirkhill heard him say. "You should wear that soft pink color more often. It makes your eyes look even darker green."

"Why, Tony, how sweet," Nan said with a teasing grin. "You are learning courtesy, sir. But it is too late, for I have decided to wed another... or I would, were he not already married."

"*Now* who the devil are you making sheep's eyes at?" Tony demanded, looking around fiercely enough for Kirkhill to put a curbing hand on his shoulder.

"Peace, fool," he muttered. "She is baiting you."

"I ken that fine, but she refers to *some*one, Dickon. You know that she does."

"Aye, and judging by her usual flirts, it is most likely Sir Hugh, who can deal with her silly infatuation much more easily than you or I could."

"Hugh Douglas?"

"Aye, but dampen your anger, my lad. He is just steps away from you, helping his lady wife, and he would lay you on your back before you could put a finger to him. I've seen him do it, and you are no match for him. Moreover, no one would delight in the sight more than my mischievous sister would. So, peace now."

"Aye, sure," Tony said. "I've no wish to embarrass you or myself."

"Good, now let's herd these folks inside. They will want to tidy themselves before we dine. Davy, lad," he called, seeing the boy run to help with the horses. "Go back inside and tell the lady Fiona that her guests have arrived."

"Joshua already sent up to tell her, laird," the boy said.

Kirkhill nodded, noting that the ladies had dismounted and were already moving toward the tower. He went to his uncle before Sir James could follow them and said, "What brings you back to this part of the dale so soon, sir?"

"Nowt to speak of, lad, but I did think I ought to see that your sister had been behaving herself. We'd not want her being a nuisance to so kind a hostess as the lady Phaeline. Moreover, her ladyship did invite me to stop by if

I felt concern for our Nan's well-being. One could not be concerned whilst Nan is in her care, but..."

Kirkhill raised his eyebrows. His usually unflappable uncle was babbling. Had Sir James really worried about Nan?

"How does my lady mother fare?" Kirkhill asked.

"In fine fettle," Sir James said, grinning. "All is well, lad. Annis does not fret as much as one might expect when she's alone, and I promised to return by week's end. As for your lads, they await Archie's call to battle, as do mine own at home."

Kirkhill nodded. If his mother was content and the men ready, he would not protest their abandonment. His uncle had every right to an interest of his own.

Fiona hesitated at the hall entrance. She had had her bath before a cheery fire, had dried her hair, and had taken as much care as possible with her appearance. But lacking new gowns, she felt at a disadvantage when she saw how finely her sister, their wealthy cousin Jenny, and Nan were all dressed.

Not seeing her mother at first, Fiona looked closely at the group on the dais, then around the rest of the chamber. She found Phaeline near the great hall fireplace with Sir James, chatting and laughing with him as if she had known him for years.

Returning her attention to the dais, Fiona saw her sister looking right at her.

Mairi smiled, and Fiona's anxiety vanished. Hurrying to greet her, she found herself enveloped in a warm and hearty hug.

"You look wonderful, dearling," Mairi said, her gray eyes twinkling as she released her. "Motherhood must agree with you. But where is my wee nephew?"

"Upstairs, sleeping," Fiona said. "He sleeps hours and hours each day, but I'll take you to meet him after we dine. Oh, Mairi, it is good to see you!"

"You, too," Mairi said. "I hope you remember Robert Maxwell," she added, drawing the tall, dark-haired, smiling gentleman nearer. "You met him only that once at the Hall, but we have now been married for two years. You will soon meet our wee Tammy, too. But now here are Jenny and Hugh wanting to greet you."

Jenny Easdale, her soft, golden-brown hair confined in a simple net, hurried forward with a smile. Her stern-looking, dark-haired, hazel-eyed husband followed right behind her. But Hugh Douglas embraced Fiona, giving her a bearlike hug.

"I'm glad to see you looking well, little niece. We worried about you."

Fiona looked him in the eye. "I wish that you had worried enough to come and take me away from here, sir."

Mairi, overhearing, said calmly, "We did try to see you, Fee, but although Old Jardine did once admit us, he said that you and Will had gone riding and that you did not want to see us. Then he ordered us off his land. You had made it clear that you were strongly attracted to Will Jardine, so what were we to think other than that you had chosen to stay with him and did not want to see us?"

Fiona stifled a gasp. It had never occurred to her that they might think she would stay away so long of her own volition.

But just as she might have said something—most likely something she ought not to say—a large, warm hand touched her shoulder, and Kirkhill said, "People do tend to think the best of a situation until facts prove otherwise, my lady. Fiona-lass, you have not yet presented me to your sister or to her husband."

"Forgive me, sir," Fiona said, feeling calmer at once and perfectly able to perform the introductions graciously. As she introduced Dickon to Rob and Mairi, and learned that he had already met Jenny, she began to feel much more relaxed.

Aware of Dickon's calm voice as he chatted with Hugh Douglas, whom he clearly knew well, and with Robert Maxwell, whom he had just met, she felt safer than she had felt for two years. When Sir Hugh reached out and gently squeezed her shoulder sometime later, she smiled up at him.

He said, "I'm sorry you were unhappy, lassie. Had you let us know—"

"I . . . I couldn't. They would not let me."

"We can talk about all that later, Hugh, if you like," Dickon said. "At present, though, I see that the carver is ready for us to take our places."

Fiona looked at Dickon, wondering how much he would tell Hugh and the others, but as her gaze caught his, he said quietly, "You and I will talk first, lass. I'll tell them nowt without your say-so. They thought that you had chosen Will *over* your family, because you knew they would object to him as your husband. But you should know, too, that it is lawfully almost impossible to interfere between a man and his wife. Had they done so, Will could have got a magistrate's order to get you back."

"I . . . I see," she said, knowing then that she had brought about her own fate.

Kirkhill said no more but gently urged Fiona to her place beside his at the table. She sat between him and Mairi Dunwythie, who took precedence over Lady Easdale only because Mairi was Fiona's sister. But Jenny sat next to Mairi with Phaeline on her left. Nan was at the end of the ladies' row.

Sir Hugh was next to Kirkhill, but Kirkhill's thoughts were on Fiona and all that she had told him that morning. A notion had struck him in the yard as the others were arriving, and he wanted to look into it, but he knew he would have to wait until their guests had departed.

When the ladies adjourned with Fiona to see her little son, Hugh said, "Archie expects trouble within a fortnight if not sooner, Dickon, but suggests that we move our men quietly. This place and Dunwythie Mains are good places to gather them, but you don't have as much room here as Mairi and Rob do."

"We've plenty of land," Kirkhill said. "They can camp east of us in the hills and forest there. I'd liefer not advertise their presence, lest we still have English sympathizers at Spedlins. But if they come in quietly, few will heed them."

"That would be the best solution for us, too," Rob said. "We'll have guests for Lammas, but we can put troops on land between Chapel Hill and Dryfe Water. No trails pass through there. Your minstrels, Hugh, will want to camp nearer the Hall."

Kirkhill looked at Hugh. "*Your* minstrels?"

Hugh grinned. "Mine and Jenny's, aye. I'll tell you all about them one day, but it's a long story and better suited to another time."

Kirkhill nodded, and the discussion turned to tactics and strategy. Apparently, it was going to be a race to see if the Scottish Earl of March would arrive in Annandale with his army before the English Earl of Northumberland invaded the dale with his. Archie meant to defend it against either of them.

"But he's praying the English will get here first," Rob Maxwell said. "He'd rather hang Englishmen than Scots, but he means to govern all of Dumfriesshire as well as Galloway, and he won't let either a Scot or an Englishman get in his way."

"March is lawfully entitled to rents from Annandale," Kirkhill said.

"Much Archie cares about that," Hugh scoffed. "He doesn't want March laying waste the whole dale, which is what will happen if March roars in with an army, determined to force the English out of Lochmaben."

"Then Archie should get rid of them before March comes," Kirkhill said.

"He won't have enough time, which is why he wants to muster our men."

Rob said, "Our task is to keep Northumberland out, whilst the Douglas keeps March fighting raiders east of here long enough for Archie to gather a force large enough to deter them both and rout the English from Lochmaben."

Kirkhill nodded, hearing all they said and already planning how he might provide space for a significant portion of Archie's army. But thoughts of Fiona and the mystery of Will Jardine's disappearance kept intruding.

"He is beautiful," Mairi cooed, looking down into her wee nephew's face. "Oh, Fee, how proud you must be to have such a handsome son!"

"Who would not be?" Jenny demanded. "He's going to be a handsome man."

Fiona might happily have listened for hours as her sister and cousin exclaimed over David had her curiosity not awakened when Phaeline and Nan retired to the solar... to chat, Phaeline had said. But Fiona had seen Mairi talking with Phaeline just after the meal and suspected that her sister had purposefully arranged it so.

Signing to Flory to leave them, Fiona said, "What is it, Mairi? Why did you ask Mam to take Nan to the solar?"

Mairi looked up from the baby and said in her usual calm way, "I expect you know that people are talking about you, Fee, and about what happened to Will."

"What they *say* happened," Jenny interposed. "You and I both know, Mairi, that things are not always as people surmise them to be." She turned to Fiona. "I, too, have heard the rumors and did not believe them for a minute. Nor have I let anyone prate such nonsense to me without telling them how foolish it is. Hugh does not believe the rumors either. But we could do naught for you before now, Fee. One cannot lawfully interfere between a man and his wife."

"I know that now," Fiona said. "Kirkhill explained it to me."

Mairi said, "Rob and I heard the rumors before we reached Dumfries, and learned of Old Jardine's death from Hugh at Thornhill. We had not planned to come on to the Hall until next week, but when we heard what people were saying, we put forward our journey. Sithee, Fee, one reason for making such a festival of Lammas this year was that I'd hoped to prevail upon you and Will to come. Last year, when we invited you, you did not even send to decline, so I wondered then if Will had forbidden you to leave just as he'd forbidden us to visit." She sighed. "Mam always did believe that he'd abducted you."

"He didn't," Fiona said. "I went willingly and even stayed willingly for a time. But he would not let me go home for Father's burial. We were not married yet, and he was sure you'd keep me there. Had I known what the future held, I'd have fought harder to go. You do know he hoped to gain your lands through me."

"I ken that fine," Mairi said grimly. "He told me so himself."

"Surely, you did not believe that I supported him in that!"

"Nay," Mairi said. "Not for a minute. I suspected that he had kept you from attending Father's burial. I could not imagine that you would stay away unless Will had commanded it. And Father suspected the Jardines of more than an elopement. He left Annan House to me because he did not want any Jardines living there."

Fiona said, "What am I to do, Mairi? I am as bewildered by Will's disappearance as anyone else, but I cannot prove that."

Jenny said, "What about Kirkhill, Fee? Does he believe the rumors?"

Feeling heat in her cheeks, knowing that she was blushing at the very thought of Kirkhill, she said quietly,

"Nay, he has never believed it. Indeed," she added without thinking, "he believed in my innocence before I did."

The two other women gaped at her. Jenny said, "Would you like to explain that statement, Fee? Surely, you *knew* that you were innocent."

"Nay, I did not," Fiona said. "I'd liefer not explain the whole to you now, but I will in time. Kirkhill has been all that is kind...mostly," she added reminiscently.

"I am sure he has," Jenny said. "Hugo has great respect for Kirkhill and says he is one of the finest warriors he knows."

Fiona was aware that Mairi was watching her closely as Jenny spoke, so when Mairi stood abruptly and gently handed the baby to Jenny, Fiona braced herself for a sisterly scold. Instead, Mairi turned to the bed, picked up an odd-shaped bundle she had brought upstairs with her, and handed it to Fiona.

"Heaven knows if you will be able to make these things fit, because we guessed at nearly every measurement, but you are much the same size that I remember, so mayhap they will. Flory can hem up the skirts easily enough."

Fiona gaped. "Do you mean to say you've brought some of my own gowns?"

"Nay, I had two new skirts and bodices made up for you, and also brought a few accessories I thought you might like," Mairi said. "It was Mam's notion. When she told me that she had seen you, I asked if you needed anything, and she said she thought you had no clothes suitable for our festival. So I've got fabric, too, and I told Parland Dow when I last saw him that we'd need a seamstress at the Hall."

"Kirkhill did send for a seamstress and fabrics," Fiona

told her. "But he says there is no gelt from the Jardines, so he was going to pay. I don't—"

"I don't think he should do that, either," Mairi interjected crisply. "You are my sister, Fee. I will gladly provide anything you need."

Fiona nodded gratefully, unable to speak.

～

Their guests departed late Saturday afternoon with reminders that everyone at Spedlins was expected to arrive at Dunwythie Hall by Thursday to settle in before the Lammas Day festivities on Saturday, and to stay as long afterward as they liked. Kirkhill stood by Fiona in the yard until the last rider disappeared. She said then that she was sure David was hungry and vanished into the tower.

Kirkhill watched her go, thinking she looked happier than he'd ever seen her.

Tony, on the other hand, wanted to talk. "Your sister is driving me mad, Dickon. One moment she is all smiles, the next she is telling me I'm a fool. And today, she hid in the solar with the lady Phaeline until it was time for them to leave. I know you said to stay away from her, but the lass comes *here*—twice now! And if she speaks to me, it is only to fratch."

"Have you changed your mind about her then?"

"Nay, I'm still of the same mind. God spare me, but I've wanted her since I first laid eyes on her, and do what she will, I still want her. Moreover, you—"

"Tony, I won't order her to marry you," Kirkhill said. "Either you must let her think you've lost interest in her, to spark *her* interest, or you will have to do as Will Jardine did with the lady Fiona and elope with her. Be warned, though, that if you do the latter, I'll likely strangle you with my own bare hands."

"Aye, sure, now *there's* a choice for a desperate man!"

"A devilish one," Kirkhill agreed. "But you'll have to forgive me. Take a few men and seek out some locations for campsites. If you begin now and continue tomorrow, you should know where to put everyone when the time comes. Meantime, you can ponder your problems. I want to talk to young Davy."

He found Davy with Cerberus, handing the destrier an apple.

"Take care he doesn't nip your hand off instead of taking that apple, lad."

"Aye, sir, I will. He's gey gentle for such a big 'un, I'm thinking."

"He is when he's of a mind to be gentle, but although he likes you, a warhorse is no lamb for petting. I've been wondering about something," he added.

"Aye, laird? Ha' I done summat I shouldna?"

"You have not. I think your father would be gey proud of you, lad. I was just wondering if you can recall exactly when it was that Jeb died."

Davy frowned. "I dinna ken much about dates and such, laird. The days just go by and I do what I do. Then the next one comes wi' the dawning."

"Mayhap something else of note happened about the same time," Kirkhill suggested quietly.

The frown vanished. "It did, aye! 'Twere when Master Will went a-missing."

"Your father died that same day?"

"Well, as good as, I'm thinking. Master Will didna

come to me da's burying. I recall that right enough. He were there when me da got kicked though. Sithee, it were Master Will's own horse as kicked him. He were always a troublesome brute wi' nae manners, and me da were a-trying to pull a thorn from his hoof. Some said Master Will didna come to the burying 'cause he felt bad. Others said he didna care nowt about me da, only about the horse. But he did ought to ha' been there, I think."

"You're right about that, lad. What time of day did Jeb's accident occur?"

"'Twere no so long after supper, laird."

"I see. Thank you, Davy. Mayhap you'd like to ride Cerberus one day."

The boy's eyes gleamed. "I'd like that gey fine, laird. Tomorrow?"

"We'll see," Kirkhill said. He knew that many would say he ought not to let such a lad near the great steed, but Kirkhill had ridden his own father's destrier at much the same age, without permission. He recalled the day with great fondness, despite the inevitable consequences when his father learned what he had done.

More important, as far as he was concerned, the suggestion had—for a moment or two—banished the bleakness from the boy's eyes. Kirkhill went out into the yard, where he found Joshua and told him that he had as good as promised Davy that he could ride the destrier the next day.

The glint of amusement in his man's eyes as he nodded told Kirkhill that he was not the only one who remembered his youthful escapade.

As he returned to the tower, however, his mood darkened. Davy's information reinforced his hunch, so he had little choice in what he had to do next.

Leaving Flory happily hemming one of the skirts that Mairi had brought, Fiona tucked the baby into his cradle and went to ask Tippy to help Flory. As she descended the service stairway toward the kitchen, she met Hod coming up.

Halting abruptly on the landing outside the inner chamber, she said, "What are *you* doing here? I thought you left nearly a fortnight ago."

"I did, aye, but I'm gey pleased to see ye, mistress. I've had nae opportunity to apologize properly for letting me temper get the best o' me that day."

Striving to conceal her dismay at meeting him in the dimly lit service stairway, Fiona said, "Does Kirkhill know you are here?"

"I dinna ken, mistress." His gaze shifted downward to a point somewhere near her waist. Then, glibly, he said, "I came to fetch summat I must ha' mislaid afore I left and to warn ye that I'd heard the sheriff be a-coming from Dumfries to look into Master Will's disappearance."

"Why would you warn *me* about the sheriff?" she asked him. "You were the one who started those horrid rumors in the first place."

"I ken fine that ye believe that, m'lady. But ye're wrong about me. I feel bad about what happened and just want to make amends."

She did not believe him. "Just *what* did you leave here?"

A muscle twitched high in his left cheek. Recognizing it as a sign of suppressed anger, she felt a responsive tremor in her stomach. But his tone remained even as he said, "'Twas nobbut a wee wooden box wha' the old master gave me. I thought I'd put it in wi' me clothes and such, but I were in such a hurry, see you, that I must ha' left it in me room."

"That is most unlikely," she said. "Kirkhill's man is in that room now."

"Now?" The notion seemed to dismay him.

"Aye, sure, for where else would he sleep?"

"But I just saw him wi' the laird out in the—"

He broke off, frowning, and Fiona said, "I meant only that he sleeps there now. But if you took note of his whereabouts, you must have wanted him out of—"

Tippy's voice wafted up the stairs to her. "Mistress, the laird did say I—"

"Tippy, shout for the laird! Tell him I want him at once!"

Pushing roughly past her, Hod ran up the stairs.

Fearing for her son, Fiona fought to keep her balance and shouted at Tippy again to get the laird, and hurry. Then she snatched up her skirts and followed Hod.

⌢

After talking with Joshua, Kirkhill headed to the kitchen, where he found Jeb's Jane and Tippy with the cook. To Tippy, he said, "Unless your mam needs you, lass, run up and ask the lady Fiona if there is aught you can do to help her or Flory with the new clothes that Lady Dunwythie brought her."

Tippy looked eagerly at Jane, who nodded.

When the lass had crossed the kitchen far enough not to overhear him, Kirkhill said, "Jane, I want to ask you a question about Jeb's burial."

The woman's face clouded, but she said, "I thank ye, laird, for sending Tip away afore ye asked me. She's missing her da summat fierce."

"I ken fine that you all miss him," he said quietly. "Davy told me that Will Jardine did not attend Jeb's burial. I'd doubt that Old Jardine did, either."

"Nay," Jane said. "He were too sick, but I doubt he'd ha' troubled hisself, any road. The only one o' the family that did attend were her ladyship."

"So she was there, was she?"

"Aye, sir, and Flory, too. They both came, though her ladyship looked as sick as the old master did, and Flory were more concerned wi' her than wi' the burial. Sakes, we all worried about her ladyship. She said she ha' just strained a muscle or some such thing, but . . ." Jane pressed her lips together and did not go on.

Kirkhill nodded but said only, "When did you next see Will, then?"

"Never, sir. Nae one saw him that morning, and nae one has seen him since, but I tell ye true, sir. Nae matter what the old master said, or them rumormongers, either, her ladyship didna ha' nowt to do wi' his vanishing. She could scarcely get out o' bed that morning, but she got herself out to that graveyard to pay her respects to my Jeb. And so I'll tell that sheriff, too, if he comes here a-looking for her."

"Good, Jane, you do that," Kirkhill said. "Meantime—"

But just then Tippy shrieked, "Laird, laird, the lady Fiona says come quick!"

~

Rounding the curve before her landing, Fiona saw that the door to Flory's room remained closed, just as she had left it, but the one to her own room stood wide. Flory was inside, standing with a half-hemmed skirt in her hands, staring toward the opposite corner of the room, at the door to the main stair landing.

"Flory, where did he go?"

"It was that Hod, mistress! He charged through here like an angry bull and then off again down the main stairs."

Quick footsteps behind Fiona on the service stairs heralded Kirkhill's arrival. "What is it, my lady?" he asked her. "Tippy said you shouted for me."

"Hod is here," Fiona said. "He said he'd left behind a box that Old Jardine gave him. He said he must have left it in his old room."

"He left nowt in that wee room," Kirkhill said. "Joshua would have found anything that was there, and he would have brought it to me."

"I know," Fiona said. "Hod was acting strangely, too, because when I told him that Joshua was in that room, he misunderstood me. He thought that I meant he was there now. Hod said he'd seen him with you in the yard. I think that, knowing Joshua was *not* there, he meant to search that room. Moreover, when I shouted for Tip to fetch you, Hod pushed past me up the stairs and through this room, then down the main stairs. Should you not stop him?"

Kirkhill frowned. "Art sure he was going into Joshua's room, lass?"

She nearly said she was, but thinking, she said, "He could as easily have been going into the inner chamber, I expect. But how did he get inside at all?"

"Through the scullery door and up the service stairs," he said. "He could easily slip past the kitchen. People are working there now, talking, and clattering pots and such. No one else would have paid heed to a man going up the stairs."

"But would not someone in the yard have seen him?"

"Lass, we have my own men, Jardine men, and a few of Hugh Douglas's men here. None of them knows Hod, and only a few of our own lot know that I dismissed Hod. It was not my intention to ruin the man, just to get rid of him."

"That may have been a mistake," she said.

"It might, aye," he agreed. "But just now, I'm more interested in what he came back to retrieve, and for whom?"

"Good sakes, do you think Will might have sent him?"

*Chapter 16*_____

Kirkhill hesitated before answering Fiona's question. The question itself strongly indicated that, despite her dream, she believed or perhaps feared that Will was still alive. He, on the other hand, was nearly certain that Will Jardine was dead, and if he was right, he would soon prove it. However, until he did...

"I don't know who might have sent Hod," he said. "Come to that, I don't *know* that he is lying about his reason for coming back."

"Sakes, we do know that he's up to no good, sir, or he would not have run away as he just did. Moreover, he would have approached you openly in the yard. When he said that he had seen Joshua there, he also said that Joshua was with you."

He grimaced. If Hod had seen them both, then one of them should have seen Hod. They had apparently grown complacent at a time when they needed to keep all their wits about them and stay alert for trouble.

"You are right, lass," he said. "The man is behaving deceitfully, and therefore we must trust nowt that he says. If he said he came here looking for a box—"

"A 'wee box' is what he said," she interjected. "He said it was a wee box that Old Jardine had given him."

"Well, if Old Jardine ever gave anyone anything of value, he gave it to Will, not to Hod. And, from all that I've seen, there was nowt of value here."

"But there must have been gelt somewhere," she protested. "I may not have had new clothes, but Will dressed well and always had silver groats to spend on himself. And lest you wonder, there is no wee box in our chamber. But the Jardines did have horses and cattle that they sold at Langholm, and apples, too. Old Jardine said the apples had long kept Jardines from starving when many other families did."

Kirkhill said, "Do you still have that key I found on Jardine's table?"

"Of course," she said, touching the chains on her chatelaine that held her keys.

"Did you ever chance to ask Hod what lock it might fit?"

"Nay, why should I? You said that you had found it, so I assumed that…"

"I did ask him," he said. "He said that he'd just found it. Sithee, when I searched for documents, he disclaimed knowledge of those, too, although he did find a list of folks who live here and work the land, and another with Spedlins' costs for a few months past. I doubt if he can read, but he did recognize the list as an accounting. He also told me that he recognized Will's hand, so Will must have written it."

"Unless Hod was lying about that, too," she said.

He smiled. "He would have no reason to lie about that. Moreover, although Old Jardine told me that first day that he was still running things here, I doubt that he was up to keeping accounts or working with pen and ink in his bed even then."

"I never saw him with such implements," Fiona said thoughtfully. "It *was* Will who got angry with me, too, for not keeping the household accounts properly."

"I have not found them, either," Kirkhill said. "Mayhap I should take charge of that key for now, though," he added. "It may be more important than we know. And, if it is, it may not be safe for you to keep it on you as you do."

Nodding, she detached one of two key rings from its chain on her chatelaine and thumbed through its keys. Frowning, she let that ring fall and, finding the right one on the second ring, she detached it and gave it to him.

Having expected to find it next to the long pantry key, Fiona had found it instead near one nearly as long to the buttery and wondered how she had mixed them in her memory. She understood that Dickon worried lest Hod or someone else try to take the key from her. But why it might matter to anyone else, she could not imagine.

Mayhap it fit the small box for which Hod had said he was looking. But if it did, and Old Jardine had given both items to him, surely Hod would have said as much to Dickon when Dickon asked him about the key.

Perhaps Old Jardine had *not* given him the box. Perhaps the old man had kept his gelt in that box and Hod had meant to take both away with him.

But how, she wondered, could he have forgotten something so valuable if he had *meant* to steal it in the first place? Surely, just the thought of stealing Jardine's money would have taken precedence over anything else the man had been doing.

But what if it wasn't a *wee* box at all? What if it had been too large to take with him, too heavy with gold and silver, or jewels, or whatever else it was that the old man had hidden away? Then where, she asked herself, was that big box now?

Shaking her head at her fancies, she decided she would be wiser to concern herself with her own affairs. Only four days remained until Thursday, when they would leave for Dunwythie Hall. If she was going to look anything like a stylish lady by then, she'd do better to see to her bairn and help Flory with the hemming.

Whatever Old Jardine had left would go to her son, and although she might not quite trust Dickon completely yet, she knew she could trust him to see to that.

Accordingly, she spent a pleasant afternoon with Flory and took supper at the high table with Dickon and Tony, while the maidservant ate quietly beside her for propriety's sake. The men took turns reminiscing about adventures they had enjoyed together, and when Fiona burst out laughing at something that Tony said, she realized that she was enjoying herself hugely.

⁓

Kirkhill smiled at Fiona's laughter, but he knew that if he was right, it would not last. He had talked to Joshua and would take Tony into his confidence after supper. Joshua would select four of their own well-trusted lads to help as well.

Bidding the lass goodnight, he wondered how angry

she would be that he had said nowt to her about what he had deduced or how he was going to handle it. That Hod still took enough interest in something at Spedlins to risk returning to find it had decided Kirkhill to keep his notion to himself until he learned if he was right.

Inviting Tony into his chamber to dice with him, he voiced the invitation loudly enough so that anyone nearby would overhear him. But when they were in the chamber with the door shut, he said, "We have work to do tonight, and it won't be pleasant. But it must be done in full secrecy if we can manage that."

"What are you up to now, Dickon?"

"Grave robbing," Kirkhill said brusquely. "We'll need shovels and rope."

They waited until well after midnight, taking care meantime that Kirkhill's men took guard duty. Then, leaving the tower silently and on foot, with light from only the misty moon and the stars above, they made their way to the graveyard.

"Yonder, lads," Kirkhill said quietly, knowing how easily voices carried on such a still night. He pointed to Jeb's grave. "Dig, there. It should still be soft."

Half an hour later, by slipping ropes carefully under the well-shrouded body, they were able to lift it out without incident and set it gently beside the open grave.

Pale light from the occluded moon shone faintly into the hole.

"There's nowt there," Tony said. "What did you expect to find?"

"Help me down into the hole," Kirkhill said, drawing his dirk from his boot.

"Sakes, d'ye expect to find demons down there?"

"Be silent, Tony," Kirkhill muttered. "This is no time for levity. And keep careful watch. That moon is casting too much light on us here."

With help from Tony and Joshua, and by digging out precarious footholds in the side of the grave with his dirk, Kirkhill managed to find footing on the bottom, well to one end of the grave.

Squatting on his heels, taking care not to move about, he began carefully digging with the tip of his dirk.

Jeb's shrouded body had packed the dirt beneath it, but he realized straightaway that the soil was looser than it should be. His heart pounded. He was not a superstitious man by nature, but graveyards were spooky places by daylight, and sensible men had never thought that disturbing the dead was a good idea.

The tip of the dirk met with something that was neither soil nor rock.

Shifting slightly to ease the dirk back into his boot, he began to dig with his hands. His fingertips quickly touched cloth.

Brushing dirt away, he uncovered what was clearly a leg garbed in a man's leather breeks. His stomach clenched in discomfort, but finding boot leather next, he told himself to settle down, muttering, "Thank God, I'm not straddling his head."

"Joshua," he said then, his voice just loud enough for the two at the grave's edge to hear him. "Tell the lads to step well back and keep careful watch for any approach. I've had a sense of watchers everywhere for weeks but never stronger than right now. And I *don't* want anyone surprising us at this bit of work."

"You found something then," Tony murmured.

Without replying, Kirkhill inched his feet forward, keeping each to its own edge of the grave until he could brush soil carefully away at the other end. He knew what he would find but felt inexpressible relief to realize that although the face was the one he sought, only its left profile was visible.

Will Jardine was exactly where Kirkhill had expected to find him, but Will was *not* grinning up at him, so he had not grinned up at Fiona either.

⁓

Fiona woke Sunday morning to the sound of her son's cheerful gurgling. Opening her eyes, she saw that Flory had brought the baby into her bedchamber and was sitting with him in the window embrasure, making faces at him.

Flory looked up. "He smiled at me, my lady. Ha' ye seen him smile?"

"I have, aye, but 'tis rare," Fiona said. "Mayhap he will be a sober man, like Sir Hugh." She felt guilty, saying that, because Hugh had been kind to her. But still she thought of him as she had known him, a man of stern, unbending demeanor.

Flory was watching her. As Fiona met her gaze, the maid smiled and said, "He's sma' yet, mistress. He just be beginning to take note o' things around him. And soon now, he be a-going on a journey all the way to Dunwythie Hall. Ye be a-going to see some minstrels there, laddie." Her gaze slid away from Fiona's to the baby again. "I recall the minstrels at Lady Jenny's betrothal feast, Davy-lad. They gave grand entertainment. Mayhap these will be the same ones."

"We'll see soon enough if they are," Fiona said. She thought they might be the same, since Jenny and Hugh had spent time with the troupe that had entertained at Annan House on that occasion. But neither Mairi nor Jenny had said they would be the same people, so she did not want to speculate. She said, "I'll feed him now, Flory. Then I'll dress and go downstairs to break my fast."

"I brought ye a basket o' bread and sliced beef," Flory said, again seeming to avoid her eye. "The laird did say he thought ye'd want to breakfast in here today."

"Did he?"

"Aye, for he said ye'd ha' much to do. He be a-thinking, he said, o' riding to the Hall today, instead o' waiting, unless ye think ye canna manage it so."

"Today! Good sakes, Mairi does not expect us until Thursday, but I think she will be delighted if we arrive earlier. I'd like it fine, too. In troth, I have gey little left to do. We finished hemming the skirts she gave me, and I'd have few things to pack even if I were to take everything I own. David's clothes and such—"

"I packed them up afore ye awoke," Flory said.

"Then we can be ready whenever his lordship wants to go," Fiona said.

Her curiosity increased while she nursed the baby. Kirkhill had never objected before to her breaking fast in the hall. The men were nearly all outside by the time she went downstairs, so other than the gillie who served her and a few lads taking down trestle tables, she usually had the hall to herself.

She said nothing more on the subject to Flory, but as soon as she had dressed, she left David in her care and went downstairs to find his lordship.

To her surprise, he still sat at the high table with Tony. The trestles were already stowed away, and the lower part of the hall was empty.

"Good morning," she said.

They returned her greeting, and Kirkhill said, "That will be all, Tony. See that everyone who will ride with us is ready to depart after the midday meal. Evart will stay here with a small household staff, but he knows that I'm leaving most of our men-at-arms in the hill camps. He can send for them if trouble arises. We'll all be riding south if Archie summons us, so we can pick our lads up on the way, and spare their horses the extra distance."

"Aye, I'll see that everyone knows what to do," Tony said, getting to his feet.

Fiona stepped onto the dais. "I hope you won't send me away, too," she said.

"Nay, lass, I've been expecting you."

"I don't know why you changed your mind, but I have little to do, even if we left straightaway," she said. "I could easily have come down here to break my fast."

"I am glad you did not, for I must tell you about something that happened last night," he said. "I wanted to make sure that you heard it first from me."

"What is it?"

"I'll tell you, but I don't mean to reveal all the details just now. I told the lads who tidy up this dais to wait until we've left the table, but we'll have more leisure to discuss it all at length whilst we ride to the Hall."

"Good sakes, sir, what could we talk of then that we cannot discuss now?"

"Will *is* dead, Fiona."

"I am sure that he must be," she replied. "I have said so more than once."

He looked at her, his expression calm, as though he merely waited.

A chill trickled up her spine. "Mercy, do you mean you *know* he is dead?"

He nodded.

"*How* do you know?"

"I saw him," he said. "That is all that I mean to tell you now, and I'll ask you to keep even that to yourself until I let the others know. Don't even tell your Flory."

"Nay, I won't," she said. "Flory swears that she never gossips, but I know she does. She also learns things from others, though. News travels fast here, so if you *have* found him, doubtless others do know, sir."

"Aye, some others do, but only a few of my own lads, and they will keep it to themselves until I tell them they need not."

Remembering Flory's evasive looks earlier, she wondered if he might be mistaken in thinking that only his men knew.

"Where is he?" she asked.

"I'll tell you everything whilst we ride," he said. "I'm sending Tony ahead with some men to make sure that no one is lying in wait for us. And I'll have others riding behind. As we ride, you and I can put some distance between ourselves and those of our people who travel with us."

With that, she had to be content, but practicing patience was not one of her strengths, so the next few hours passed by at a frustratingly slow pace. She had little appetite for her midday meal and snapped at Flory for dawdling.

"Mercy, mistress," the maidservant protested, avoiding her eye. "Ye'd no be happy did I forget summat the bairn might need—nor yourself, come to that."

Fiona, wondering again if Flory might know that Kirkhill had found Will's body, was tempted to ask her straight out. But if Flory did *not* know, the question itself might reveal too much, so she resisted the temptation.

Shortly afterward, seeing Joshua in the yard, shouting orders to one or another of the men, she nearly ran out to ask *him* what he knew about Will. She resisted that urge, too, not only because she was certain that Joshua would not tell her but also because she knew he might tell Dickon that she had asked. That she might then have to endure another of Dickon's chilly scoldings deterred her. But had one more thing delayed their departure, she might well have taken that risk.

As it was, she chafed to be off. But not until they were on the Roman road that ran up the east side of the dale, and Spedlins had disappeared in the distance behind them, did Dickon finally say, "Shall we put some distance between ourselves and those behind us, lass?"

So eager was she that she gave her horse spur enough to startle it into a lope.

Kirkhill chuckled as she reined the animal in. "I doubt you want to race," he said. "This fellow I'm riding may not be Cerberus, but he's faster than your lad."

"I don't want to race," she said. "I want to hear about Will."

The look he gave her then warned her that she was not going to like hearing what he would say.

"Will was in Jeb's grave," he said.

She felt as if he had knocked the air out of her. He

said nothing further, giving her time to think. When she could, she said, "H-how can that be?"

"Will lived violently, lass, and he died the same way," he said. "Afterward, whoever killed him took advantage of the grave dug earlier that same evening for Jeb. He tipped Will into it and covered him with just enough dirt to hide him from view the next morning whilst they lowered Jeb's shrouded body to rest atop his."

"I'd think someone would have noticed him there even with a layer of dirt on top," Fiona said, shuddering at the thought of the two men in the same grave.

"Jane told me that that day began with as heavy a mist as the morning we buried Old Jardine," Kirkhill said. "She said that most folks were thinking more about breakfast and the warmth of the hall fire than aught else. After all, to most Borderers, burial is nobbut a chore that needs doing. Unless a priest is at hand to speak words over the grave, only the immediate family ever thinks to linger."

"I expect you're right, sir," she said, scarcely remembering Jeb's burial.

"Jane said you were there that morning, Fiona-lass. She said you looked almost as sick as Old Jardine was but that you got up whilst he stayed in his bed."

She grimaced. "I was not sure I'd get there, but I thought Will *would* be there, since he had never come to bed that night. I...I did not want him to know how badly he had hurt me. He was always apologetic after something like that, and I...I didn't want to hear it. Flory tried to keep me from going. She said that no one would expect me to be there. But in the end, she went with me. In troth, it was easier standing up and walking than I'd expected it to be. Getting out of bed was the hardest part."

When he did not comment, she said, "How did you find him?"

"Your dream suggested the likeliest place."

A shiver of fear touched her. "But how could it?" she demanded, aware that she spoke too loudly. More quietly, she said, "I did not recognize the place at all."

"Even so, when you described the hole into which you dreamed you had pushed him, it sounded like a grave and made me wonder if mayhap someone else had died around the same time. When I learned that Jeb had died the evening before and that they had buried him at dawn, just as they did with Old Jardine, simple logic suggested that they had most likely dug Jeb's grave the night he died."

"But I swear to you, I never thought of that, not for a moment!"

"Sithee, I'd been trying to imagine how a killer could have kept Will's body hidden so long. Dropping him in the river was one way, except that by now, his body would have surfaced and word of it would have sped up and down the dale as fast as the rumors about you did. If he had lain where he was, someone would have stumbled over him long before now. You had the information about Jeb in your memory, lass. I suspect that your dream simply put the pieces together for you."

"In a most dreadful way," she said, grimacing. "What did you do with Will after you found him? Surely, you did not leave him in there with poor Jeb."

"Joshua and some of my men shrouded Will properly and moved him to a decent grave of his own near Old Jardine's," he said. "We'll have to report finding him, of course, because people throughout Dumfriesshire and Galloway—and heaven only knows how much farther in every direction—know that he has been missing. But I saw no reason to raise such a dust about him before we must."

"Good sakes," she said as a thought occurred to her. "Do you think Will might have just fallen into that hole and broken his neck or otherwise died of it?"

"Nay, lass, I don't think anything of the sort. Nor will anyone else."

"But he may well have done that. He had been drinking, Dickon, heavily. Sakes, he was as ape-drunk that night as I'd ever seen him."

"Nevertheless, he did not fall into that hole," he said. "Someone shoved his body in there and took the precaution of covering it with just enough dirt to hide him from casual view. The likelihood of anyone's peering down into the grave—"

"But, mayhap some of the dirt they'd dug out of it just fell on top of him!"

"Someone clouted him hard enough to crush the back of his skull, Fiona."

The chill that she had felt earlier was as nothing to the ice that entered her veins at the vivid picture those words produced in her mind. Could she have—?

Kirkhill knew what she was thinking as surely as if she had spoken the words to him. Although he had assured her that she could not have murdered her husband, unless and until she knew all that had happened, she would go on wondering.

As if she were suddenly aware of his presence again, she looked at him and said, "Are you sure that I could not have done *that*, sir?"

"No one could know the answer to such a question absolutely," he said honestly. "I wish I could say that I'm certain you could not have struck him hard enough to kill him, but I cannot. I do think that with the injuries you had sustained, it is most unlikely that you could have picked up something heavy enough and struck him hard enough to do the damage I saw. But when the will is strong enough, people can do extraordinary things."

Her face paled and she swayed on her saddle, so he added hastily, "What I *can* tell you is what I said before. I could never believe that you moved him from that hill above the river around to that grave. Few women are strong enough to move a dead body so far. And *no* woman within a fortnight of birthing her child could accomplish that feat. Think back, lass. How easily could you bend over?"

For the first time in such a discussion, she smiled, albeit wanly. "Sakes, I could not even put my shoes on without Flory's help. Moreover, I keep forgetting the horrid pain I endured. Sithee, I don't remember feeling it that night, because I lost consciousness so soon after he knocked me down. But the next morning, trying to get out of bed for Jeb's burial...As bad as it was then, it must surely have been worse the night before. I doubt that I could even have got—"

When she stopped abruptly, he looked at her more closely. "What is it? Did you remember something new?"

"Nay," she said, but he could tell that she had somehow managed to distract herself. Whatever had just occurred to her was something that had occurred to her before and something that still worried her.

He let her ponder while his own thoughts roamed, seeking answers.

Fiona was afraid to look at him, lest he somehow realize exactly what fears had sped through her mind. The pain in her ribs where Will had punched her that dreadful night had been extraordinary. Without Flory's help the following morning, she was sure that she would have found it impossible to get out of bed.

Yet, somehow, the night before that, after Will had knocked her down and she had lost consciousness, she had somehow managed to get to her feet again and not only walk back to the tower but also up two flights of stairs to her room. And there, she had got undressed, climbed into bed, and slept until just before dawn.

How on earth, she wondered, had she managed to do all that without help?

The plain and obvious fact was that she hadn't.

So, who had helped her?

Flory was the one most likely to have done so, but she had not even seen Flory after supper that night. Old Jardine had angered Will even before they had supped. Afterward, Will had wanted to talk to her, and then Jeb had had his accident.

"Tell me, Fiona-love."

Only as her head snapped up did she realize that she had allowed it to sink nearly onto her chest as if her memories had grown too heavy to bear. But his voice steadied her as it nearly always did, and she turned toward him, seeking comfort.

"What is it, lass? You can tell me anything. Is it about that night?"

She nodded. "Sithee, it mostly started with Jeb."

"Your argument with Will?"

"Aye, because Will was already angry. Sakes, it seemed as if he was always angry about something those days. But that evening before supper, his father had said something that irked him. I don't know what it was, but I think Old Jardine may have told him that he had been spending too freely. They fratched often about money, because Will liked to spend it and Old Jardine liked to keep it. That evening, Will wanted to walk his anger off, and he said I should go with him, that it would be good for me. I think he wanted someone to tell him he was right or someone to blame. But when we got to the yard, one of his men told him that his favorite horse had got thorns in its hoof and Jeb was trying to pull them out."

"So you saw what happened to Jeb?"

"We did, aye. Will was practically running, pulling me along with him, and he shouted at Jeb, demanding to know how bad the damage was. Jeb's head jerked up, and the horse reared. A flailing hoof knocked Jeb headfirst into a post."

She shut her eyes, but the disturbing vision of that moment just grew clearer.

"Then what happened?" he asked, his calm voice banishing the image.

Taking a breath, she let it out and said, "Will flew into a rage. He said Jeb should have controlled the horse better, should have tied it more securely. I ... I took Jeb's side and ... and I snapped at Will. He was livid, but I was terrified for Jeb."

"Rightly so, as it turned out."

"Aye," she said with a sigh. "Neither of us realized that Jeb was so badly hurt, but as we argued, one of the men shouted that Jeb was not moving, that they did not think he was breathing. By the time they knew that Jeb was dead, Will was ready to blame me for everything that had happened."

"You!"

"Aye, sure. He said that my skirts, and not his haste or his shouts, had startled Jeb and spooked the horse. I lost my temper then and said that if he had trained his horse *out* of its ill manners ... aye, well, I doubt you need to hear the rest."

"Only if you want to tell me," he said.

"Nay, it was nowt but a spat. But like most of our spats, it soon grew worse. Will said his men could look after Jeb, because he had things to say to me and that I was going to hear every one of them. With that, he dragged me out onto the hillside path by the river. He dragged me along so quickly that it was all I could do to stay upright. In troth, sir, I don't recall all he said, or all that I said to him, but he slapped my face, and he must have kept hitting me, because I remember fearing for the babe. The next thing I remember is waking up in my bed the next morning."

"Is that all?"

She nodded before she realized that she had not mentioned what had come to her earlier, just before the disturbing memory of Jeb's death.

"You still don't recall going back to your room?"

"Nay," she said. It was on the tip of her tongue to tell him she did not think she could have gotten back on her own when a shout from ahead drew their attention.

Five riders approached, waving. She recognized her sister, her cousin, and Nan, followed by Sir Hugh and Rob Maxwell. The women were grinning.

Nan cried excitedly, "The men on the ramparts saw your advance party with Tony and warned us, so we ordered horses and came out to welcome you properly."

Fiona felt a surge of relief. Before she began exploring with Dickon the question of who might have aided her that night, she wanted to think carefully about what the consequences might be.

Chapter 17 _____

Their reception at Dunwythie Hall was a merry one, including music from minstrels in the courtyard and the sight of Sir James Seyton emerging from the keep with the lady Phaeline smiling beside him. The minstrel troupe included not only musicians, Nan told them, but also glee maidens, dancers, jugglers, and even actors.

Kirkhill knew that he would have little opportunity for privacy with Fiona at the Hall. One way and another, they had taken many such opportunities at Spedlins, but he was sure that the various members of her family would look dimly on such private moments between them at the Hall.

Moreover, Hugh and Rob clearly wanted to talk about news they had had from friends east of Annandale, where English raids had escalated. They told Kirkhill and Tony that Northumberland was gathering an army on the English side.

"The Douglas has sent for Archie to meet him and March soon," Rob said when the men adjourned to a room near the great hall that he'd claimed as his own.

"In Selkirk, aye, so it won't be long now," Hugh added. "Most of my men and Rob's are camped in woodlands southeast of here, as we had planned. You doubtless noted the minstrels' camp in the woods below the main gate."

Kirkhill nodded. "Your lads to the southeast have hidden all sign of their passage well. I saw nowt of any large company's tracks, and I looked hard."

Sir James said, "I've sent for the rest of our lads, Dickon. They'll arrive late tomorrow or by midday Tuesday. The English won't surprise us here."

"Most unlikely," Kirkhill agreed.

The Hall, sitting as it did on a hill above a sharp bend in the river Annan that faced west and north, and overlooking a long stretch of the Roman road a mile to the east, enjoyed a strategic location that precluded any surprise military attack.

Woodland covered much of the sloping hillsides around the Hall, but every approach remained visible from the ramparts, and a wide clearing separated the woods from the wall on every side. Moreover, signal fires would warn them of any significant attack from other dales or from England.

The Solway Firth protected most of south Dumfriesshire and Galloway, because its coastline was rugged and protected, too, by notoriously dangerous tides, and perilously unstable sand and shingle beaches where there were any at all.

Hugh said, "The men you brought should camp with the others, Dickon."

Rob added, "We have plenty of room inside the wall for your serving women and their bairns. Our people will be glad of their help in the kitchen and with the serving, and they can dine with ours in the lower hall, so they'll see the minstrels. The troupe will also provide an outdoor performance during our Lammas Day feast Saturday afternoon, so the local folk and the rest of our men can enjoy them, too."

"You will meet the fellow who leads this troupe after supper tomorrow evening," Hugh said. "He is called the Joculator, which means that he is skilled in nearly every art of minstrelsy. My Jenny and I met him before we married. In troth," he added with an infectious grin, "he arranged our marriage."

Kirkhill shook his head at him. "'Tis a grand tale, that, but we've all heard it, Hugh, even Tony here," he said. "At present, I'm more interested in hearing when you and Rob think Archie will want us to join him with all of our men."

"Nae doots ye are, but God alone kens that," Hugh said, switching abruptly to the common accent of the area.

Raising his eyebrows, Kirkhill looked at Rob Maxwell. "Sakes, does the man still mimic nearly any accent as quick as look at you?"

"Aye, sure," Rob said, grinning. "When Hugh tells a tale, you can hear the voice of every character that has a part in it."

"'Tis nowt but a bairn's trick," Hugh said. "And one that got me into trouble as often as not. However, it did allow me to serve Archie in some strange and fearsome places a few years ago, and it served well when I won my Jenny, too. But for those older tales, you'd be wiser to ask my man, Lucas Horne."

Rob chuckled. "Aye, Lucas delights in telling tales of his master."

To Kirkhill's surprise, since he had never before thought highly of any Maxwell, he was rapidly coming to like Rob as much as he liked Sir Hugh.

That Hugh trusted Rob was plain to see, and Kirkhill had great respect for Hugh's insight into people's characters. He knew that that ability, as well as his mimicry, had helped keep him alive in the days before he had won his knighthood, serving Archie the Grim.

The five men discussed their plans, but when Kirkhill realized that the others agreed with him, he let his thoughts drift back to Fiona. He wondered if she would confide her worries about a possible part in Will's death to her cousin or her sister.

It occurred to him that she might be more worried that he would confide all that he had learned from her to Rob Maxwell and Sir Hugh.

~

Fiona was trying to decide whether to be amused or annoyed with Nan. Since their arrival at the Hall, the younger girl had been doing her best, without any success whatsoever, to draw the attention of Sir Antony MacCairill.

Sir Antony, having arrived before them with the vanguard, had seen to his men first and then had retired with the other men to Robert Maxwell's chamber to discuss whatever it was that men discussed at such times.

After supper, abandoning the other four men, Sir Antony had sent a gillie to Mairi's solar to ask if he might pay his respects. She had welcomed him and had introduced him to Jenny, but Nan soon interrupted their conversation to ask him with fluttering eyelashes what had induced him to join the ladies rather than the men.

"Simple courtesy, my lady," he had replied with a disapproving look. "Something that you ought to strive to achieve. You have just interrupted your hostess in the midst of her sentence. Do try for a little conduct, lass."

Flushing deeply, Nan put her nose in the air, but when Sir Antony went on talking politely with Mairi, Jenny, and Fiona—and ignoring her—she finally declared that she was going to bed, bobbed a curtsy to Mairi, and left the room.

Sir Antony excused himself moments later, saying that he had better find the other men, lest they had received word from Archie and left without him.

"As if they *would* go without him," Jenny said on a gurgle of laughter when the door had shut behind him. "What goes on there?"

"God may know, but I do not," Fiona replied. "Kirkhill was negotiating a marriage with Sir Antony for Nan, but she swears she will have none of him. He seems to remain constant, but his notion of courtship is to tell her what she should wear and how she should behave, so I warrant it will come to naught."

"I don't know about that," Jenny said. "Nan seems far too interested in drawing his attention to have *no* interest in him."

"I think she just enjoys tormenting him," Fiona said.

"How are *you* faring, Fee?" Mairi asked then. "I can tell you that Sir Hugh has great regard for Kirkhill. He told us that Kirkhill is a man of action and one who thinks gey quickly in battle. Even more to his credit, from what I saw of him at Spedlins, he seems to be one who does not easily tolerate fools or foolishness, so I doubt that he believes any of the rumors about you. Do you get on well with him?"

Fiona felt heat creeping into her cheeks, so she said quickly, "In troth, I did not like him at first, because I saw no reason for him to act as my trustee. But he never did believe the rumors. You are right about that, Mairi, but I should tell you both that Will *is* dead. Kirkhill found his body."

"Faith, do you mean to say that he *did* die that night, and you have waited until now to tell us!" Jenny exclaimed. "You should have told us straightaway."

Uncertain that Dickon would approve of her telling them at all, Fiona said, "We have told no one else yet, so prithee do not spread the news about until he says that we may. Sithee, whoever killed Will hid his body most cleverly."

"Where?" Jenny demanded.

"I...I don't know," Fiona said, wishing she had never mentioned the subject and knowing that if she said that she must *not* tell them, Mairi and Jenny would insist that she *must*. "Kirkhill kept that to himself," she added, hoping to reinforce her denial. Then, remembering that Flory might already know about the grave and be telling others at the Hall, she wondered if she might be making matters worse.

Mairi's quizzical expression reminded her that her sister had once been able to tell when she was lying. She hoped that after two years of living with the Jardines, she was better at concealing her lies, but she had a sinking feeling that the guilt she felt for lying to Mairi and Jenny, two people she loved dearly, was obvious to both.

Accordingly, she excused herself soon afterward, saying that she, too, would get ready for bed. But she went outside instead to find Joshua, with Cerberus.

"Prithee, tell his lordship that I must speak to him before I retire," she said.

"Aye, sure, me lady," he said as he curried the horse Dickon had ridden. "Yon lad running toward us now be one I set to watch and tell me when the laird went upstairs, so chance be, he's in his chamber now. Shall I send him to yours?"

"Nay, he'll not want that. But tell him I may have done something he won't quite like and must discuss it with him. He will say how and where we can meet."

Joshua's eyes twinkled. "I'll tell him. I'll tell ye, too, me lady, that if he won't like it, it be gey better an ye tell him yourself afore someone else does."

Fiona, already wishing that she had kept her mouth shut, nodded and hurried away to her own old bedchamber, where she hoped to discover that Flory had been too busy putting away her clothing to have gossiped with anyone.

Instead, she walked in to find Flory and a chambermaid helping Nan dress.

Nan whirled about as Fiona entered, saying, "Just look at this wonderful dress, Fee. How Tony will stare when I wear it to supper tomorrow evening!"

"I should think that every man in the great hall will stare at you with so much of your bosom laid bare as it is," Fiona said. "What Sir Antony will think is surely less important to your well-being than what Kirkhill will think of it, however."

"Pish tush, I don't mean to let Dickon see it until I'm on the dais," Nan said. "He would never be so mean as to send me away in front of everyone. You'll see."

Fiona wondered about that, especially as she would likely stir Dickon's temper herself soon. She could scarcely admit that to Nan, however.

~⁀

Kirkhill received Fiona's message from Joshua with a slight frown but said only, "If you can waylay that Flory lass, tell her I would speak with her mistress if she will agree to meet me straightaway on the landing just below her own."

He dressed again quickly, thinking furiously as he did. He had said nothing to Rob, Hugh, or Sir James about finding Will Jardine, because he had yet to work out for himself just how he wanted to handle that. At present, he thought that the fewer people who knew of the discovery the better.

He was sure that finding Will's body would do nowt to put the rumors to rest and much to fuel them. Who else at Spedlins other than Will's wife might have wanted Will dead? Moreover, if Sheriff Maxwell was coming to Annandale—although he might be coming only as his brother and good-sister's guest for Lammas—if the rumors had reached his ears, he might feel obliged to investigate.

Doubtless, Kirkhill told himself, Fiona had been thinking along similar lines.

To his amusement, she was pacing on the small landing just below her chamber when he went downstairs from his.

"I know I should not have come down so soon," she said as he approached her. "But I—"

"Whisst now, lass," he said, nodding toward a gillie bounding up the stairs from the great hall. "I want you to take a turn about the yard with me. It is still light enough, the air off the river is cool, and we can talk a little."

"Thank you, sir, I would like that," Fiona said.

The gillie, hearing them, pressed hastily against the wall out of their way.

Once outside and a few steps away from the entrance, Fiona said quietly but with visible reluctance, "I told Mairi and Jenny that Will is dead and that you had *not* told me where you'd found him. I know that you said I should not, but—"

"I should have told them all straightaway," he admitted. "I did not, because Rob is, after all, Sheriff Maxwell's brother, and I had not had time to reflect on what the consequences might be if we let that news reach the sheriff's ears."

"He *is* coming here," Fiona said. "Mairi told me that she had invited Rob's brother, his good-sister, and his grandmother to come for the festivities. They will arrive Wednesday afternoon."

"Aye, I heard the same," he said, urging her toward shadows that the stable cast near the high wall. "I'll explain it all to Rob and Hugh tonight. They will agree that you could not have moved Will from the hillside above the river and over that ridge to the graveyard all by yourself. In troth, now that I have met Rob and seen how friendly Hugh is with him, I think we must tell the two of them, at least."

He could see that she was waiting for him to say that she ought to have held her tongue, so he said, "Fiona-lass, I should not have let you think that I meant for you to keep the news about Will from your sister or your cousin. You did well to keep the location of his body to yourself, though. If we can keep that quiet—"

"I doubt we can," she interjected. "I fear that Flory

already knows that you found him. And if someone else told her so, surely that person also told her where."

"Sakes, have you asked her?"

"Nay, for how could I without revealing more to her than I should? But she keeps looking at me as if she expects me to say something, and I cannot imagine what else it could be but that you have found Will."

"Well, if she does know, we can do nowt about it now," he said. "I would still keep the location of his body secret from all but your family if we can. It may be that someone who ought not to know will let slip that he does. If Flory has not admitted her knowledge to you, I'd guess she's not talking to others either."

The look on Fiona's face told him that she was not so sure about that. But the sun had been down for some time and darkness was descending on the land.

Glancing around, he saw no one else in the yard, and the lads on the wall would be looking outward, not into the courtyard. With a hand to her shoulder, he drew her deeper into the shadowy passage between the stable and the bakehouse.

He told himself that he meant only to reassure her, perhaps to give her a hug, but when she backed up against the step into the bakehouse, and stepped onto it, she was suddenly almost eye-to-eye with him. The temptation was irresistible.

The hand on her shoulder slid around to the hollow between her shoulder blades, seemingly of its own accord, and pulled her closer until his lips touched hers. They tasted of cinnamon, and lust stirred within him. Plunging his tongue into her mouth, he felt himself stir. Another part of him yearned to do its own plunging.

Although she responded as passionately as she had before to his kiss, she also felt the movement below and stiffened, breaking away with a little gasp.

"Fiona-love, this will all sort itself out," he said then. "It must, because I want you more than I have ever wanted anything."

"We must go in," she muttered, turning away. "Someone will see us."

His last ten words had been nearly the same ones that Will had spoken the day he had persuaded Fiona to elope with him, reminding her yet again how little she could trust her instincts with men. She did not try to speak as they walked back across the courtyard. It was all she could do not to run away from him, but common sense told her that haste on her part would merely draw attention to them.

Inside, as they passed the hall, she saw that many of the servants were still eating their supper, while men-at-arms who would spell those on the walls were laying pallets for sleeping wherever they could find space.

Dickon said nothing to her, clearly at a loss, and she could not blame him. What must he think of her, to have responded to him so easily each time he had hugged or kissed her, and now, to have stopped him and tried to hurry away as she had? He would think her demented, or worse.

He escorted her to her bedchamber door, and they both knew that Nan would likely be inside by now. He looked at her, his expression unreadable.

"I'm sorry," Fiona murmured with her hand on the latch handle.

"Nay, sweetheart, don't apologize," he said. "We'll talk tomorrow."

Whisking inside, she found that Nan was asleep, or pretending to be asleep. It did not matter which, because she was grateful for the silence.

Flory had David with her and would take him to Eliza when he wakened, so Fiona got herself quietly undressed and into bed. Her dreams were fitful and full of Dickon, so she awoke the next morning with an ache in her heart.

She did not see him when she and Nan went down to break their fast, and afterward, Mairi, Jenny, and Phaeline kept them busy all morning. At noon, they learned that Kirkhill, Tony, Rob, Hugh, and Sir James had ridden out to visit the camps to the east, to see that their men were alert and to invite half of them to come enjoy the minstrels that evening, while the others would wait until Tuesday night.

The men did not reappear until the family gathered on the dais for supper.

Fiona had left Nan in their chamber, scheming but certain that Tony would not miss seeing the minstrels perform. In truth, Fiona expected to enjoy Nan's antics and Tony's pretended oblivion even more than the promised entertainment.

The musicians were already playing when she entered the hall. She watched for Nan, but the moment she saw her, Fiona shifted her attention to Dickon.

Nan had waited until nearly everyone who was to sit at the high table had taken his or her place before making her entrance.

Standing at Rob's right with Hugh and Sir James next and Tony beyond James, Dickon clearly noted his sister's flamboyant attire, for his eyebrows shot up and his lips pressed tightly together. But he made no comment.

Fiona returned her attention to Nan. She saw disappointment on the younger woman's face but was unsure whether it stemmed from Tony's lack of attention or Dickon's. She could not help admiring Nan's demeanor as she walked boldly through the area cleared for the minstrels' performance and onto the dais. Nan was fully aware of her many admirers, because her eyes sparkled defiantly.

So admiring were some men that their comments were audible, but Nan held her head high, pretending to ignore them as she took her place beside Fiona.

Phaeline leaned across Jenny, her eyes wide as she said, "Nan, my dearest, such a dress! So low-cut!"

"Thank you, madam," Nan said with aplomb. "I am gey fond of it."

Phaeline blinked but said no more.

"It is magnificent, Nan, horrifyingly so," Fiona murmured. "If my wee David saw you now, he would think he was about to take supper. I wonder, have you any particular requirements for your burial ceremony? Lilies, roses, wildflowers?"

Nan grinned at her. "I do think that Tony noticed me, don't you? For all that he pretended not to look?"

"Every man here has noticed you. But are you sure that you wanted to invite the consequences that will surely come to you later?"

"Pooh, whatever Dickon might have done at home, he can hardly do here. I warrant he will have some things to say to me, and he may drone on longer than I'll want to listen. But that is all he'll do in another man's—that is, in Mairi's—house."

"But why do you do such things?" Fiona asked.

Nan shrugged. "In faith, I don't know. Some demon possesses me, I expect. Dickon wants me to marry Tony, and Tony says he wants to marry me. But he does not *care* about me, Fee, other than to tell me I ought not to wear what I like to wear, or should not do what I want to do. Sakes, even when I defy him, he does nowt!"

"But what *could* he do?" Fiona asked reasonably. "He is not your brother, father, or husband, Nan. He has no right to take you to task as one of them might."

"If he cared, he *would* do something," Nan said. Then, with a heavy sigh, she turned away as Rob held up his hands to silence the hall for the grace before meat.

After the carvers had carved and great platters of meat were on the tables, dancers and tumblers dashed into the open space, and the entertainment began.

Fiona enjoyed the fools who followed next. There were two of them, one tall and thin, and the other no taller than a child might be. Both wore whiteface. The short one, on long stilts, strode into the cleared space, haughtily guiding the taller one on strings like a puppet. The audience laughed at the sight and laughed even harder at the tall one's gangly antics as he unsuccessfully tried to free himself.

Jugglers came next, followed by an extraordinarily tall man in a long red coat, who juggled swords and daggers as easily as the others had juggled colored balls and large rings. Fiona had seen the tall one once before, at Jenny's betrothal feast. She expected him to fascinate Nan, too, but Nan was growing impatient.

"Mairi said there would be dancing," she muttered.

"Aye, sure, there will be," Jenny assured her across

Fiona. "Watch his hands now, both of you, as he throws that sword high in the air. That's the Joculator, and he is particularly deft. I have even seen him juggle lighted torches!"

Fiona tried to keep a close watch but glanced away from his hands when the sword flew almost to touch the high ceiling. The next thing she knew, the man was bowing and holding out a bouquet of white flowers. Where the swords had gone, or from whence the flowers had come, she had not the smallest notion.

The musicians began to play louder then as the acrobats and jugglers left the central area. Men moved to dismantle the trestles and shift benches to the sides of the hall. The dancers ran out then to begin a ring dance, inviting others to join them.

"Come on, Fee," Nan said, jumping to her feet. "Let us dance with them."

"Wait," Fiona said, looking toward the other end of the table. Mairi and Rob stayed where they were, but Sir James got up and moved to speak with Phaeline.

Kirkhill followed but passed them, stopping in front of Fiona.

"Would you like to join the dancers, my lady?" he asked Fiona.

"*I* would," Nan told him. "Why is Tony just sitting there?"

"He wants to finish his wine," Kirkhill said. "Do stop hopping about, Nan. If you want to join the ring dancers, you may come with us."

"But I don't *want* to go with you! I'd have some stranger at my other side. If Tony desires to marry me, I should think he would *want* to dance with me."

"And I should think that having done all you can to persuade him that you want none of him, you should be grateful that he is turning his thoughts elsewhere."

"Elsewhere! What can you mean by that?"

"Only that he can now concentrate fully on defending Annandale. If we can keep the English from supplying Lochmaben, March will have no reason to inflict his army on us, and Northumberland will quickly lose his remaining allies here. Then, mayhap, they will all bide at home."

"I don't care about any of that," Nan said. "And Tony is the only unmarried man here who is suitable to dance with me."

"Then be patient and let the man enjoy his claret," Kirkhill said. Extending a hand to Fiona, he said. "Come, lass, I can see that your toes are tapping."

Willingly, she went with him. But glancing back, she saw that Nan had not stayed in her place. She was walking behind Jenny, Mairi, Rob, and Hugh, and to Fiona's surprise, Nan carried a jug of wine that she must have taken from the table.

Tony had pushed his back-stool away from the table and was leaning back—wine goblet in hand, one leg crossed over the other—enjoying the entertainers.

Nan bent from just behind him and murmured into his ear.

"Dickon," Fiona said quietly. When he looked at her, she nodded toward the dais. "Look."

He did so just in time to see his sister empty her jug of wine over Tony's head and hurry on her way. She did not get two steps from him, however, before he reached out almost casually with his right hand and caught her by her left wrist.

With no visible effort, he pulled her back to him and with a dexterous twist of hand, dumped her facedown over his lap. Holding her in place with his left hand, he smacked her four or five times on the backside with his right.

She struggled fiercely but to no avail. And if she shrieked, the noise of the music and merrymakers in the hall drowned her out.

Fiona, aware that her jaw had dropped and that Kirkhill had gripped her arm and was urging her on toward the dancers, dug in her heels, unable to look away.

Tony—with no more effort than he had shown in capturing Nan—set her on her feet, spoke a few brief words to her, and returned his attention to the dancers.

Nan glowered at him, clearly furious. But when the glower elicited no response, she turned on her heel and stormed off the dais to an archway that led to the main stairs. Only after she had vanished did Tony reach for a napkin and begin to mop his dripping face, brow, and wine-soaked hair. Even then, he showed no emotion. He merely signed to a gillie to refill his goblet from another jug.

Turning to Kirkhill, Fiona said, "I should go after her, Dickon."

His grip on her arm tightened, but his voice remained low-pitched as he said, "Nay, lass, let her go and enjoy her sulks. She got no more than she deserved, and you want to dance. Moreover, you and I need to have a talk, and Nan will be in her bedchamber if you still think you must visit her after that."

"'Tis my bedchamber, as well," Fiona reminded him. "I would not like to find her utterly distraught, thinking that no one cares about her."

"She knows better than that," he said with a wry smile. "If I know our Nan, she is just hoping that Tony, and not I, will follow her upstairs. Doubtless, she told herself that I would say nowt about that outrageous dress she is wearing, despite the fact that she already knows that I strongly disapprove of it. Ah, so she said as much to you, did she?" he added when Fiona stared at him.

"She did, aye, but she did not tell me that you had already seen it."

"She wore it at Kirkhill the day that Tony joined us there. She knew that neither of us would like it, but that day, I made her change it before he saw it. I'm sure she thought she was paying us both back tonight, but she will learn her error."

"I expect she already has," Fiona said.

"Aye, and got more than she expected, but I still have something to say that she won't want to hear. The ring has begun, though, so dance with me, lass."

She agreed and much enjoyed herself, but the minute the music ended, her thoughts flew back to Nan. Even so, as Dickon escorted her to the dais, she felt his presence even more strongly than she had during the lively dance.

With him as her partner, she had felt safe and protected against any unseemly behavior, but she had understood Nan's reluctance to join the dance without a man she knew on each side of her. Most people behaved well at such events, particularly when they took place in baronial great halls. But occasionally someone with too much drink in him would take liberties with any pretty, young woman.

Dickon put a hand over hers on his forearm, and as they approached the dais, he gave it a squeeze. "You need not go to her, you know. It will do her no harm to have time to reflect on her behavior."

"I think she is unhappy," Fiona said. "She told me that Sir Antony only *says* he wants to marry her, that he does not really care about her at all."

"Sakes, the man has been crazy about her since her cradle days," Kirkhill said, shaking his head.

"Then mayhap he should tell her so," she said, catching his gaze. "Sometimes, a man believes a woman knows how he feels, but she wants to hear him say the words. I have only ever heard Sir Antony carp at Nan or correct her. Or else, he complains to you about her. I'll wager Nan has heard no more than I have."

"But the man can hardly prate nonsense in her ears before they are at least betrothed," he said sternly.

"Indeed, my lord?" She raised her eyebrows. "Do *you* think it wrong for a man to let his feelings show before the way is clear for him to do so?"

"You ken fine that I *think* that way, lass. The plain fact that I have not been able to conceal my feelings for you has weighed heavily on my conscience."

"Not heavily enough, thank the Fates," she said. "I know I confused you last night, but I made a terrible mistake two years ago and paid dearly for it. From the moment that we met, I knew that the way I felt about you was different from the way I'd first felt about Will but feared to trust myself. With Will, I felt only my delight that a handsome man was flirting with me. That was *all* it was."

"And with me?" His attention now was singularly intent.

"You irritated me at first, but I felt nonetheless drawn

to you. You filled my thoughts and stirred feelings deep inside of me that I'd *never* felt with Will. Sakes, I'd never dreamed a woman could *have* such feelings! Not just sexual desire but deeper sensations. With you, I feel warmth and a sense of safety and comfort—mentally as well as physically—that I've not known since my earliest childhood."

He said, "I felt desire from the moment you looked at me, sitting on the stone floor of the scullery." He hesitated, looking into her eyes. "I want to talk more of this anon, lass. Prithee, stay with me now and enjoy this fine entertainment."

"I will return shortly," she said. "But I must assure myself first that Nan is not too upset. I do fear that she is, sir. When I know she is not, I will come back."

"See that you do," he said. "Shall I send a gillie up with you?"

"Nay, none will harm me here. My father always kept servants on the stair landings whenever we had a company like this, and I'm sure that Mairi does, too."

He nodded, and she hurried upstairs to her bedchamber. But as she neared the door, it opened and Flory stepped out, closing it behind her.

"Flory, how is the lady Anne?"

"Och, mistress, I were just a-coming to find ye!" Flory exclaimed, looking past Fiona as if she expected to see Kirkhill at her heels. "The lady Anne were ever so upset, and angry withal. She said she wouldna stay another minute in such a place and was going to ride home straightaway."

Shocked, Fiona said the first thing she thought: "Not in that dress!"

"Nay, then, I did help her change and made her take a warm cloak."

"I must stop her. You look after David."

She doubted that Nan meant to ride as far as Kirk-hill House, because she could not hope to get there before dark. Praying that no one would even saddle a horse for her without consent from Dickon or Mairi, Fiona rushed out to the yard, expecting to find Nan fiercely debating such an order with a stable lad.

Instead, she learned that the lady Anne Seyton had flung herself on her horse with no more than a bridle and had galloped it out of the yard through gates still open after admitting a messenger, now dismounting in the yard.

Chapter 18 _____

Noting the red heart on the messenger's sleeve and recognizing it as the familiar device of Archie the Grim, the Black Douglas, Fiona knew he had likely come to summon the men. So she would have to go after Nan at once, herself, rather than try to speak privately with Kirkhill or any of the other noblemen just then.

"I'll bring her back," she said to the stable lad who had told her about Nan. "Fetch my gelding at once and then give me a leg up. If her ladyship just left—"

"A short while ago, but I canna say exactly how long, m'lady. Mayhap—"

"I must go! I want to catch her before she rides far," Fiona declared.

"Aye, my lady," the lad said. "Mayhap, though, I should go wi'—"

"I dare not wait if I'm to bring her back quickly," Fiona said, fearing that if he did not make haste, the men would be upon her. "Prithee, just do as I bid, and hurry!"

"Aye, sure," he said, running into the stable and returning minutes later with her bay gelding. Throwing her onto it and handing her the reins, he jumped back as she urged the horse to a trot and, once outside the still-open gate, to a lope downhill to the road. Shouting at two men-at-arms there, talking near the minstrels' camp, she learned that Nan was riding hard but had gone south, rather than north.

Hoping that Nan could not maintain the pace the two men had described for long, Fiona kept the gelding at a trot or a canter, alternating its paces and keeping an eye out for any sign that her quarry might have turned off the main road.

At last, she saw Nan in the distance and pushed the gelding to more speed.

Nan saw her and tried to outrun her but at last slowed and reined in, waiting until Fiona drew up alongside her before she said defiantly, "Why did *you* come after me? I thought it would be Tony!"

"Well, it's me," Fiona said. "I am sorry to disappoint you, Nan, but if you know what is good for you, you will turn around and ride back with me."

Nan tossed her head. "Why should I?"

"Because a messenger has come from Archie the Grim, so the men will all likely be too busy to think about us unless someone tells them what we have done. Then your brother, at least, will pay us more heed than either of us wants."

"I don't care what Dickon does," Nan said. "I won't go back to a place where I was so dreadfully humiliated."

"I chanced to glance back just before you upended the jug over Tony," Fiona said. "Dickon saw it, too, but everyone else was doubtless watching the dancers."

"Mairi saw what *Tony* did, and so did her lord husband, not to mention every servant on the dais," Nan said between gritted teeth as she urged her horse onward.

"Nan, please! You *must* come back with me."

"Nay, I must not! We will go to Spedlins, and that will teach Tony not ever to do such a thing to me again. I told your Flory that I was going home, but Tony will soon learn that I did no such thing. Then he will be wretched with worry."

"Not if he does not care about you, as you claim," Fiona retorted.

"Well, I think now that perhaps he does care. I just want to be sure."

"Why? What makes you think he does?"

Flushing deeply, Nan said, "I just do, that's all."

She shifted uncomfortably on her horse, drawing a smile from Fiona. "Nan, you cannot possibly want to ride all the way to Spedlins and back," she said quietly.

"Pish tush, as if I cared about a little pain. Forbye, I'll wager they catch up with us before we get there," Nan added confidently.

"They won't if they do not know that we have gone," Fiona said. "They will ride off to join Archie. That is what they have been waiting for, after all, and the gate was open for you only because Archie's messenger had arrived."

"But if they go with Archie and his army to fight the English, they may all be killed," Nan said, looking worried for the first time.

Hoping that her fears would make her more persuadable, Fiona said, "Aye, sure, they might. Just think how you will feel then."

Nan grimaced but recovered swiftly. "They are knights with much experience. Moreover, Dickon will not let anyone kill Tony. Nor will he let anyone kill him."

For the first time, Fiona felt a strong urge to slap Nan. But Nan chose that moment to spur her horse to a gallop again. Gritting her teeth, Fiona followed.

Dickon would be furious with both of them. It was the last thing she wanted, but she could see no way to avoid it. She could hardly let his sister ride on alone.

But as she followed Nan, Fiona was conscious of a most uncharitable hope that Kirkhill would flay his sister for her foolhardiness.

⁓

Kirkhill had just begun to wonder where the devil Fiona had got to when a gillie brought the Douglas messenger onto the dais.

The man went to Mairi and bowed. "Beg pardon, Baroness," he said. "I bring ye word from the Lord o' Galloway that your men and those o' these other lairds wi' ye should meet him just west o' Torduff Point, which lies—"

"Near the coast five miles east of where the river Annan meets the Firth," Mairi interjected calmly. "How soon does his lordship want our men there?"

"As soon as ever they can get there, m'lady. He's had word that the English Earl o' Northumberland means to invade Annandale afore the Earl o' March can do so. The Black Douglas rode to collect any men who be still besieging Lochmaben, and will ride from there to keep the villainous English from overrunning the dale."

Kirkhill began to rise but stopped at a gesture from Mairi.

She said, "A deep cleuch cuts through hills from about seven miles northeast of Annan town and runs southeast to the Firth. 'Tis called Riggshead Cleuch, and 'tis a perilous place with high, steep sides. The English have often used it to supply Lochmaben, and raiders use it, too."

"If that route is known, would they not seek another way to avoid meeting trouble there?" Kirkhill asked.

"Aye, sure, they might," she said. "But other routes also provide difficulty for a large force. They cannot simply follow the shore of the Firth, because it is too rugged, and quicksands there have swallowed horses and riders without leaving a trace. Moving north before they cross into Annandale will only alert folks east of us, who will set signal fires to warn us. My father said English raiders favor the cleuch because it is the quickest route and because no one lives within it."

Hugh said, "Mairi is right. I'll warrant that we've seen no signal fires yet because Archie got word about this from one of his spies in England and knows when and where Northumberland means to cross. We must get our men moving."

"Aye," Rob agreed. To Mairi, he said, "I ken fine that you'd like us to leave quietly, lass, but some of our lads are here in the hall. Just say that Archie has sent for our men-at-arms and tell the minstrels to go on entertaining. Then, the others can continue to enjoy the performance whilst we prepare to ride."

She nodded as Kirkhill said to Tony, "Get our men horsed and meet us on the road. We'll collect the rest at Spedlins. If you see Joshua outside, tell him to saddle our horses and... Well, he'll know what to do. I'll go up to tell Nan and Fiona that we're leaving, and then I'll join you in the yard."

"Tell that sister of yours to behave herself whilst we're away," Tony said.

Kirkhill raised his eyebrows. "Do you think I should tell her that the message comes from you?"

"I do, aye. I've waited long enough, Dickon, *and* put up with enough of her foolishness. When we get back, I mean to make that plain to her."

"You do that, but mind she doesn't lop off your head or aught else when you do," Kirkhill said, thinking that he would say much the same to Fiona *before* he left.

But when he reached the bedchamber that the two young women shared, he found Flory there alone, and she looked terrified when she saw him.

⁓

Fiona was trying not to think about Dickon, but her imagination kept presenting image after image of what he would look like, what he might say, and what he might do when he caught up with them, as surely he would. Not one of those images reassured her. Every one of them gave her the shivers, and thinking of the delightful things he had said to her the previous night made her want to cry.

He was the man she had always hoped to meet and marry, and the likelihood now was that he would be so angry he would forget that he had ever cared for her. And here *she* was, listening to his sister's foolish grievances and wishing Nan to perdition. That thought brought another, utterly unexpected thought of Mairi.

Perhaps this was simply what it was like to *be* an older sister.

With a sigh, she glanced at Nan, who had been muttering for some time now, mostly to herself or to the absent Sir Antony. Then, looking around, Fiona thought she saw someone in the forest west of them, which hid the river

Annan from view. She was unsure how far they had come, but they must be nearing Spedlins.

A sliver of ice slid up her spine at the thought of someone watching them, but the figure, if she had seen one, had vanished.

When they reached the next bend in the road unmolested, she decided that she had been imagining things. Nan was still in a hurry, pushing her mount harder than common sense would dictate. But if they had to stop, then Dickon and...

Shaking her head, Fiona told herself that it would be better not to imagine any more if she could avoid it. The road forded a trickling burn, and the river Annan chuckled along beyond the forest, cutting its path through the undulating dale on its way downhill to the Solway Firth.

Again, Fiona thought she saw someone in the woods, this time on the east side. It was common to see people by daylight, because the dale was well populated. But the movements she saw seemed furtive, as if people were hiding and watching.

"How much farther to Spedlins, do you think?" Nan asked.

"Sakes, how can I be sure?" Fiona said. "I rarely left there, whilst you have traveled this route from the Hall twice before. Do *you* not know where we are?"

"This road looks all the same to me. The river on our right, the hills yonder. Mairi knew where she was going, and so did the escort your mam sent with me when I rode to see you that day. I never had to heed where I was, exactly."

Fiona was about to admit that she rarely paid heed to

her exact location while traveling, either, when with a cacophony of shouts, whistles, and other cries, a party of men rode out of the woods and surrounded them.

"Look what we've found, lads!" a rider cried. "Better than horses, I say!" He grabbed Fiona's bridle. "Comely Scotswomen, young 'uns, too, and prime!"

"Unhand my bridle," Fiona snapped, trying to wrench her horse free.

"Nay, then, ye'll come with us," he said. "We've good use for ye, I'm sure."

"You're English!" she exclaimed. "What are you doing *here*?"

"Why, we're coming to claim our own, lass. Soon ye'll be English, too."

"Not I," Nan cried, slashing about with her whip so suddenly and furiously that she clipped a nearby horse under its jaw and set it rearing. The next slash caught the rider nearest her as he fought to control *his* mount. Seizing the opportunity, Nan lashed her horse's flank, and the beast reared up, whirling on its hind legs as it did, and bolted for the open road to the north.

Two of the men quickest to react reined their horses around to give chase, but a voice cried, "Let her flee, lads. I've been pondering how we'd get her brother and them to follow us, unsuspecting like. She'll do the job for us, and nicely, too."

Looking toward the familiar-sounding voice, Fiona tucked her own whip under her arm as she saw Hod approaching them on a fine-looking chestnut horse.

He gave her a mocking look as he said, "If you want to keep that toy, I'd suggest that you behave yourself, my lady. You have no protector here today."

His voice sounded different, and his demeanor seemed different, too.

"You don't sound like a household servant now," she said.

"At present, I am leading these raiders," he said. "We ride fast, so if you fear that that horse of yours cannot keep up, I'll take you up before me. What say you?"

"I say you can go to the devil," Fiona snapped, but a chill had filled her soul.

⟋⟍

Kirkhill cursed Archie Douglas's timing as he hurried out to the yard after his brief talk with Flory. The first person he met was Sir Hugh.

"We're nearly ready," Hugh said. "Getting word to the most distant camp will take more time, but as we'd planned, they'll catch up with us on the road."

"We have another problem," Kirkhill said. "Fiona and Nan are missing."

Hugh frowned. "Surely, they must both be inside."

"Fiona's maidservant said that Nan left in high dudgeon, vowing to ride home to Kirkhill House at once, tonight. Evidently, Fiona went after her."

"What's that you say?" Tony demanded, coming up in time to overhear Kirkhill. "How could they have got outside the gate?"

Hugh gestured toward the open gate. "It has been open much of the day. With so many of our men milling about, not to mention camping outside the wall, we've left it open. Moreover, the guards have no orders to stop anyone riding out."

"Sakes, then we must go after them," Tony said. "They cannot have got far. But, by heaven, Dickon..."

"Don't say it, Tony," Kirkhill warned. "We cannot chase them northward when we are duty bound to gather our men and meet Archie at the south end of the dale as soon as possible. The best we can do is to make sure those two *did* head north for Kirkhill, and then get word back to Mairi. She still has men enough here to send a party after them. But when we get back…"

He did not finish the sentence. Men were all around them, tending horses and weapons, and what he had been about to say was not for others to hear. He looked at Hugh, who met his gaze calmly. But he could feel Tony's impatience pulsing.

Kirkhill said, "Tony, I assume since you're here that you've got all our men mounted. We'll ride on ahead of these others to get our lads at Spedlins moving. Archie's messenger said he'd meant to deliver my message to me at Spedlins, but he met someone on his way there who told him I was here at the Hall, so he rode on, glad to avoid the extra miles. The men at Spedlins may ken nowt of all this."

Hugh said, "My lads are ready, but I do have more at Spedlins, as you know, so I'll ride with you. Rob and Sir James can follow us."

As their men sorted themselves into lines and Joshua scurried about urging them to greater haste before taking his place in the line directly behind his master, Kirkhill tried to estimate how long the women had been gone, and how far they might have ridden. As he did, a new thought struck him.

What if Fiona had simply decided to use Nan's flight as reason for her own? What if she still couldn't trust her own judgment? What if she just wanted to get away from him? Worse, what if she had feared that the sheriff's arrival might mean her arrest and trial for Will's murder? Such thoughts had terrified her before he had found Will's body. What if he had failed to convince her that he could protect her?

The thought that she might be trying to deal with his recalcitrant sister while fighting her own terrors unnerved him. He barely waited for the others to settle into place before he rode through the gates and down the hill toward the Roman road.

Just short of the road, noticing a man under a tree with a collie curled watchfully beside him, he shouted, "Did you see two ladies ride this way?"

The dog got up, wagging its tail.

"I did, laird, nigh half an hour ago," the man said, getting to his feet. "'Twas the lady Fiona a-following another lass. They went south on the big road yonder."

Kirkhill drew rein. "Art sure they rode *south*?"

The man nodded. "Could scarce miss their direction from here, could I?"

The dog was watching Kirkhill, its tail still wagging, its tongue lolling.

The animal looked familiar. "Are you from Spedlins?" he asked the man.

"Aye, sure, laird. We tend sheep there, me laddie here and me."

"But I don't think you traveled here with us, did you?"

"I ha' nae horse, laird, but 'tis nobbut a good stretch o' the legs, and we'll see the minstrels when they entertain outside here tomorrow."

Kirkhill nodded, thanking him, and continued to the

Roman road, where he turned toward Spedlins. The sense of urgency that Archie's message had stirred increased tenfold with the old man's news. *Why* had Fiona and Nan gone south? Nan had no reason to do so, and surely Fiona had not made such a decision?

Tony rode up beside him, saying, "I heard what that chap said, Dickon. But why would they ride south?"

"You can be sure I mean to ask them," Kirkhill said grimly. "Mayhap Nan recalled that Spedlins is only *three* miles away instead of ten, as Kirkhill House is."

Tony grimaced at the implication that Nan was just playing her tricks again, but he said no more.

Within Kirkhill, duty warred with emotion. He had a duty to obey Archie, but first he wanted to find Fiona and shake some answers out of her. He had to stop at Spedlins, anyway, to collect his men and Cerberus, as well as Tony's destrier. But he could not gallop his entire force down the Roman road at speed. Not only would that tire all the horses, but any horse coming up lame would be overrun.

Turning to the men behind him, he said to the one next to Joshua, "You there, ride back to Sir Hugh and tell him that Sir Antony and I are riding on to Spedlins. Then wait for Robert Maxwell and Sir James, and give them that same message. Tell them all to follow as quickly as they can. Joshua, you and the next two men will come with us. Now, Tony," he added, giving spur to his mount, "let's ride!"

The five men rode apace, but fifteen minutes later, Tony shouted irritably, "I thought we'd catch up with them before now. That sun will set within the hour."

"They are pushing their horses hard," Kirkhill shouted

back. "But they *are* heading for Spedlins. Nan knows of nowhere else to go, so we'll find them there."

They rode in silence after that, each man lost in his thoughts. A short time later, Tony said, "Dickon, look yonder. Is that not—"

At the same time, Kirkhill saw a bedraggled-looking Nan rounding the bend ahead of them, leading a limping horse.

Tony spurred toward her, and Kirkhill followed but soon held up a hand to halt Joshua and the other two men some distance behind them.

Tony had flung himself from the saddle and was already scolding when Kirkhill drew rein. "Enough, Tony," he ordered curtly. "Nan, where is Fiona?"

Bleakly, she said, "They've taken her, Dickon. A host of English raiders! I was riding as hard as I could to find you when my horse came up lame. He—"

"How long ago?" he demanded, fighting off the chill that swept through him.

"Sakes, I don't know. We had nearly reached Spedlins. The sun was still well above those hills to the west, and now it's touching them, if that is any help."

"It is," he said. "Tony—"

"I can show you where it happened," Nan interjected hastily.

"You will not. You are going straight back to the Hall, where you will stay until I come for you," Kirkhill snapped. He motioned the other three men forward.

Anticipating him, Tony said, "I'll take her back, Dickon. I have some few things to say that she deserves to hear."

"Nay, you will stay with me," Kirkhill said. "I cannot spare you just to look after my sister. Joshua will also stay, but these two men are utterly trustworthy." To Nan, he said grimly, "I will brook no argument, my lass, so do *not* try to start one."

"I won't," she said miserably. "Oh, Dickon, you *must* find her and get her back. This is all my fault."

"Aye, it is, but you won't help matters by delaying us now. These men will see you safely to the lady Phaeline's care until I come for you."

He did not add that she might not be so safe then, but Nan must have seen as much in his expression because she did not say another word.

⁓

"Where do we meet them?" one of Fiona's captors shouted to another.

"Across yon Firth, near Sandsfield," the other shouted back. "But not until we've taken care of our part o' this business."

"How many will be there?"

"Thousands, the old man said."

Fiona stifled a gasp. They had ridden hard, and she knew that her captors had taken her miles south of Spedlins. But she realized that what she had thought was just another English raiding party, one that Hod had joined out of spite or another such traitorous sentiment, was much worse. Thousands of men constituted an army!

She had lost sight of Hod after he'd turned her over to two of his men. One led her horse, the other rode beside her. Insultingly, they had let her keep her whip.

The men ahead turned off the road to follow a roiling burn uphill toward a low ridge, and the ruffian leading her horse gave its reins a jerk to follow them.

"Where are you taking me?" Fiona demanded.

"To England, lass. Ye'll like it gey fine there, may even choose to stay with us if your own folk refuse to take ye back. They won't though, will they?"

"But why take *me*? Of what use am I to you?"

The man's leer was plain enough to see. He threw back his head and laughed. The man leading her horse laughed, too.

Fear washed over her, but she fought it back, knowing it could not help her.

Recalling that she had often said that if only people would just talk with their enemies and make friends with them, there would be no war, she felt a nearly uncontrollable urge to laugh harder than the raiders did.

Surveying the men who surrounded her, forcing her on at a breakneck pace over the steep, uneven terrain, she tried to imagine having a civil chat with any of them, and failed utterly. Not one man among them showed any sign of civility. Certainly, Hod did not, despite his altered accent and demeanor.

What if, to entertain themselves, they decided to have sex with her when they reached their destination, to take turns with her? She doubted that Hod would stop them. And *she* had not been able to stop Will whenever he had wanted her.

A jolt of fear shot through her.

What would Dickon think of her after such an ordeal at the hands of such men…if she ever even saw him again?

He would tell you to stop being such a whining dafty, to stop wasting time worrying about something that has not happened yet and focus on what you can *do.*

After all, she reminded herself, *Nan got away from them.*

Her fears and the pounding hooves on the summer-hard ground made it difficult to think. But, knowing that she could depend on no one else to help her, she fought to suppress her fears and collect her thoughts.

Dickon was a man of action, a man who could think quickly on his feet in the heat of battle. Others had said as much of him, men who knew the value of such traits and recognized them when they met with them. Dickon had other valuable traits, too, traits that she had discovered for herself. He would have no use for self-pity.

She cudgeled her brain for advice that he might give her now. He had faith in her. He had said so. And he could not help her now. She had seen to that by the way she had left, dashing off in all directions, as Mairi might have said, just as she had done whenever she got angry or upset as a child.

To be sure, she had followed Nan. But that fact would only make things worse for them both, because Dickon would not be the only one to condemn their actions. Tony certainly would, and Sir Hugh. She did not know what Rob or Sir James might say, but Mairi and Phaeline would likely side with the men. They might understand why she had tried to spare Nan from Dickon's anger, but all of them would agree that Nan deserved his anger. And now, so did she.

Even so, Dickon would expect her to look after herself and she did not want to disappoint him. She realized that just thinking about him had steadied her.

Having left the main road, she knew she should heed her surroundings. The farther south they had ridden, the

more familiar the countryside became. But now they were
heading east instead of south and had entered a deep, rugged cleft or cleuch between two ridges in the tumble of
hills separating Annandale from Eskdale.

She had never been in the cleuch before.

A frothy burn ran down its center beside the track they
followed. In most places, the track was wide enough for
two riders abreast, but the walls of the cleuch jutted out
in places, so that Fiona could rarely see more than six or
eight horses ahead or behind. She soon lost her sense of
direction.

"Ha' ye nae more questions, bonnie one?" the one
leading her horse asked.

"My family is powerful," she said, thinking of things
that Old Jardine had said when Dickon had suggested that
Will might be a captive. "And wealthy."

"Are they now?"

His attitude taunted her, but she ignored it, trying to
think how to make herself sound too valuable to harm.

"My good-father was Old Jardine of Applegarth," she
said. "He oft took England's part in disputes, I'm told, as
did my husband, Will Jardine."

"What if they did?" the second of her two escorts
asked, glancing back. "Many Scots do so once in a way,
but the next time they remember they are Scots."

"Aye, sure, but your leaders will be wroth if you anger
men who might side with them. My sister is a baroness in
her own right, and *her* husband's clan has oft sided with
England. They will pay for my release, and pay more if I
am unharmed."

"Just who would this fine husband o' your sister be,
then?"

"Robert Maxwell of Trailinghail, in Galloway."

"Faugh, he'll be duty bound to follow the Lord o' Galloway, and that be the Black Douglas, Archie the Grim, as all ken fine."

About to dispute Rob's loyalty to Archie, Fiona decided against it and shrugged instead. "It is not for a mere woman to say what any man will do," she said. "But angering any Douglas can stir great trouble. Mayhap you do not know that I am also kin to Archie the Grim through my close cousin's husband."

"I'm thinkin' ye've been told more than any woman should be, and ye talk more than any should, too. So cease your prating. We dinna want to hear it."

"I do," another voice snapped. So intent had Fiona been on making her case that she had failed to notice that Hod had fallen back to ride just ahead of them, near enough to overhear them. "She may be worth more than we thought."

"Why, you are as English as these others," Fiona said. "And no peasant, either, I'll wager. Who are you?"

"You need to know no more than that I lead these men."

"Keep your secrets then. I ken fine that you're a villain."

"Then, mayhap you should keep that in mind before refusing to answer my questions," he retorted. "What do you ken of Old Jardine's gelt?"

She shrugged. "He had none. Kirkhill thought there would be some, but he has looked everywhere. Will must have spent it all."

He nodded, but a satisfied little smile tugged at his lips, as if he knew more than she did. He fell silent, and she looked ahead to see where they were going. Their pace had slowed. The sun had vanished below the rim of the cleuch, making her hope that the moon would rise before full darkness blanketed the land.

She wondered then if Dickon even knew that she had left the Hall. Even if he had not learned within the hour that she and Nan had ridden out of the castle yard, Nan would have returned by now, and she would tell everyone what had happened.

Dickon must be hot on their trail.

Even as the thought crossed her mind, they reached a place where the cleuch widened, and Hod shouted, "Take your places, lads! They cannot be far behind us!"

Fiona's breath stopped in her throat.

Hod had set a trap and expected Dickon to ride into it!

Chapter 19.

Having ascertained by the tracks they left that the raiders with Fiona were traveling south and consisted of at least a score of men—and knowing that they could do little by themselves to rescue Fiona—Kirkhill, Tony, and Joshua galloped their horses the remaining short distance to Spedlins. As they rode into the yard, Kirkhill said, "Joshua, get Cerberus ready and Tony's destrier, too."

Then, to Tony, as they dismounted, Kirkhill said, "I doubt that those riders were just English raiders."

"Agreed," Tony said. "'Tis more likely that Northumberland sent them to find out where Archie is and how many men he has raised. But why would such a party find itself so near Spedlins?"

"Mayhap as part of a wider attempt to cut Archie off from the Scottish forces east of us. There is another possibility, too, though," Kirkhill added thoughtfully.

Seeing a gillie running toward him, he said, "Help Joshua with the horses, lad. Nay, do not tarry," he added impatiently when the boy paused.

"But, laird, there were men here, many o' them! They went *inside*!"

"They are gone now, though, are they not?" When the boy nodded, Kirkhill added, "Is Evart here?"

"Aye, but he went inside, too, to see what devilry them villains ha' wrought!"

"Go and fetch him. Joshua will find other lads to help with the horses."

As the boy darted away, Kirkhill heard approaching hoofbeats and felt a surge of relief. He was impatient to be after Fiona, but it was increasingly clear that he would be unwise to outrun his reinforcements. His own men riding into the yard, followed by Sir Hugh and his, made a welcome sight.

"Rob is just behind me and Sir James, as well," Hugh said.

"Good!" Kirkhill caught sight of Rob Maxwell in the increasing crowd of horsemen filling the yard just as Rob dismounted and strode toward them.

"Your man said you'd met Nan, so we all hurried," Rob said. "Then we met Nan herself. She said that Fiona's captors were English raiders. Can that be so?"

"Aye, and I've just learned that they were here earlier. I don't know yet how much earlier, but recall that someone diverted Archie's messenger and sent him on to the Hall to find me, *before* he reached Spedlins."

"And that Old Jardine did side more than once with England," Hugh said.

"What if they did not know that Old Jardine and Will are dead?" Tony asked. "What if they believed they would once again find allies at Spedlins?"

"Everyone knows that Old Jardine has scarcely stirred from here these two months past," Hugh pointed out. "They would not expect him to ride with them."

"Nor would they expect Will to," Rob said sourly. "As far as I know, the English have never dealt directly with Will. Old Jardine ran everything. Still, the English may have expected to find men here willing to support them."

Kirkhill nodded, but his thoughts had taken a side track. "What if they sought something else, as well? Are you sure Archie still has spies on the other side, Hugh?"

Smiling slightly, Hugh said, "Being out of that game myself, I cannot be sure. But, knowing him as I do, I'd say Archie has spies wherever he needs them."

"I need to think more of this, but if you two and my uncle will collect the rest of our men here, I'm going to follow Fiona."

"By my troth, I don't know what to say about that lass," Hugh said. "She eloped with Will despite her father's enmity toward the Jardines, so she can be rash. But you said only that she'd followed Nan from the Hall. Why *would* she?"

Tony said grimly, "Doubtless to spare Nan from my wrath and Dickon's."

"She may have had other reasons for leaving without a word to me," Kirkhill said. "Some are private, I'm afraid, but I think she fears your brother, Rob."

Rob clapped a hand to his head, exclaiming, "Those damned rumors!"

"Aye, and worse," Kirkhill said. "Sithee, she dreamed that she buried Will in a hole that sounded like a grave to me. So I had my lads dig up a grave dug for another chap the evening Will went missing, and they found his body in it."

"Good sakes!" Rob exclaimed, gaping at him. "Do you mean to say that Fiona did murder Will and fears that the sheriff will arrest her?"

"I've never believed that she killed her husband," Kirkhill said. "But it *is* possible that she fears arrest." He explained what had happened that night. "I met her for the first time a fortnight later, and she still moved gingerly, thanks to the injuries he inflicted on her that night. If he weren't dead, I'd kill him myself," he added.

"With such injuries, and still with child, I doubt that she could have dragged him ten feet," Rob said thoughtfully. "How far were they from the graveyard?"

About to tell him, Kirkhill saw Joshua coming with the destriers just as Tony said, "Dickon, look yonder. There's old Evart rushing toward us."

"'Tis glad I am to see ye, laird!" the elderly steward exclaimed. "At first, I didna think ye'd come, but he were so fierce . . . See you, all your men camped hereabouts will join ye shortly, for Jeb's Davy did tell me ye'd be needing them."

"He did, did he? And when did you see Davy?"

"He were following her ladyship, he said, laird, but he galloped his pony here after he saw them English raiders take her and the lady Anne. He said the lady Anne had got away, but not our lady Fiona. I could do nowt, m'self, but he said ye'd be coming and would want all the men ye could gather to fetch her back."

"He was right. How long ago was this, and where is Davy now?"

"I dinna ken exactly but it may be nigh an hour now. Davy's still behind them, though. Another thing, laird." Kirkhill was taking Cerberus's reins from Joshua but nodded, so Evart went on, "Them English had already been here, inside the tower. That Hod were wi' them, and they broke up Old Master's bed . . . *your* bed, laird."

"Did they?" Kirkhill said, deciding he had been right to suspect a reason for the so-called raiders to pass by Spedlins other than just to seek Jardine aid. "Did they take anything?"

"Aye, sir, that Hod and another chap took sacks out wi' them. But they—"

"I'll look into all that later," Kirkhill interjected. "I mean to go at once to fetch the lady Fiona back. When those other men are ready, tell them we have ridden on and they are to obey Sir James Seyton's orders and do all that they can to catch up with us. If we turn off the road, we'll leave signs."

Turning to Rob and Hugh, he added, "I expect that you agree with me."

When they both nodded, he reined Cerberus toward the Roman road and urged him onward at a distance-covering lope that the destrier could maintain for hours.

Rob and Hugh fell in beside him after ordering their men to follow his. The three leaders had been riding in near silence at the head of them all for some time when Rob said, "You know, Dickon, I've been studying these tracks we're following, and one set keeps always just behind another. The second one could be a sumpter pony, but that would be an odd encumbrance for a raiding party in enemy country. I think someone is leading it."

Kirkhill, eyeing the tracks, agreed. When he looked up moments later, he saw something else. "That's Jeb's Davy just ahead, lads. Easy now."

Signing to those behind to slow, he reined in near the boy.

"They went that way, laird," Davy said, pointing. "I rode to the top o' yon ridge but didna think I should go farther, lest ye missed them turning off the road."

"Good lad," Kirkhill said. "Don't try to ride back alone, and *don't* follow us. You wait here until Sir James comes with the rest of our men, and keep out of sight until you recognize someone you trust."

"Aye, laird. But ye'll find her, won't ye?"

"I will." The sense of urgency that had nagged him the whole way turned to a chilling tension that he could not shake off. He fought to think logically. If they were making for England and had turned southeast at this point...

"They are making for Riggshead Cleuch as Mairi suspected," he said. "Tony, take some of these lads over the hills to meet Archie. Tell him to hie himself to the Sands near Eastriggs village. If the tide is out, he and his men can intercept these lads where the cleuch runs into the Firth east of the point. He'll know the safest way."

"Art sure that's best?" Hugh asked. "This might be nowt but a ruse to draw us *and* Archie into a trap."

"Aye, it might be," Kirkhill said. "I've been trying to think *why* English raiders would take Fiona. My first thought was that they'd hoped to hold her for ransom. But if they got what they came for at Spedlins and seizing her was just an impulse, they'd have little reason to fear pursuit yet or to travel at such speed. Hod may have taken her for devilment, and they are just trying to get out of the way of a larger force on its way to challenge Archie. Or they may be expecting to join it."

"Using the cleuch explains how they slipped into Annandale without exciting a hue and cry," Rob said. "Northumberland's army may come the same way."

"They may, aye," Kirkhill said. "But we'll give them a surprise if they do."

With approaching darkness, the cleuch had filled with dusky gloom. There were a few clouds, but moon-glow edging the cleuch's east rim promised moonlight. If clouds obscured it, riding through the cleuch in the dark would be madness.

But then, according to most Scots, the English were all mad.

Fiona, still mounted, was near the front of the waiting cavalcade now, with Hod and the man who had led her horse. They had asked no more questions.

As they waited, a stillness fell upon the company, so that all she heard was a noise now and again from horses and gear—a stamp of hoof, a metallic tinkle, or an occasional grunt. Whether that last sound came from man or beast, she could not tell.

Clearly, they had prepared to wait quietly for their unknowing prey. Hod had promised to kill her if she so much as squeaked, and she'd believed him.

With a sudden rattling sound that made her jump and her horse sidle nervously, a man ran toward them, apparently unheeding of the treacherous terrain.

"Sir," he cried. "They be a-coming! 'Tis an army they bring and gey more—"

"How many?" Hod demanded.

"Sakes, I didna wait to count them! There be riders as far as I could see."

"Then we'll lead them into the others," Hod said. "They'll not be hurrying through this cleuch."

They moved on, but slowly, wary of those following and of the gathering darkness. Fiona was just glad that her mount was sure of foot. The narrow, rocky streambed and numerous boulders made dangerous footing for any horse that stepped off the path.

For a time, the vagaries of the cleuch kept them in darkness, but at last, as they rounded a curve, she saw the flat gray-white Solway Sands still well ahead of them glittering in the moonlight. The tide was out.

In the distance, she could see the dark English coast outlined between the Sands and the moonlit sky, although the moon was not high enough yet to see it from inside the cleuch. The view was eerily beautiful, though, and frightening.

She wondered how long the tide had been out.

A full moon meant a spring tide, which swept in fast and high. As a child, she had often watched from Annan House as it rushed into the ever-narrowing, pie-slice-shaped Firth with spray flying high and a roar that people could hear for miles.

Would her captors have time to cross before it swept in again? Sakes, would they have time even to reach the Sands before the Scots caught up with them?

Just then, a shout echoed from atop the wall of the cleuch. The sound startled the men around Fiona as much as it startled her. Flickering lights drew her attention upward to the south rim. Torches were alight there...and on the north side as well.

"Ride for the Sands, lads," Hod shouted. "Hang on, lass!"

Fiona held on for dear life, and prayed. One moment she prayed they would leave her behind, the next that they would not leave her alone in the cleuch.

"A Douglas!"

The Douglas cry echoed through the cleuch and stirred the English riders to speed. "Won't they be waiting for us at the Sands?" someone shouted to the leader.

"Nay, there be cliffs all along this side hereabouts. They'll no touch us unless they want to leap to them from the cliff tops."

Fiona knew that the cliffs were not high along that part of the Firth, but she knew of no track down from them that was suitable for horses bearing armed men.

Then she heard cries, shrieks, and whistles behind them in the cleuch.

The raiders behind them were shouting now, and she was glad to be near the lead but frightened, too, that men behind her might ride over her in their panic.

Through the shouting, she heard one voice bellow, "There be thousands o' them, above and behind us. 'Ware arrows from above!"

Hod galloped on, and the man leading Fiona's horse rode faster, trying to keep up with him. Fiona had all she could do to hang on and pray that her horse would not break a leg. The Sands, and likely pitched battle, lay fifty yards ahead.

Kirkhill led his men through the cleuch at a pace that would tax the best among them. Hugh had sent some of his lads along the southwest rim with torches, and Rob had taken most of his onto the east rim.

The result was all they'd hoped it would be, as the English fled headlong out of the cleuch, across the river Esk channel, and on to the glittering Solway Sands.

"It will be grand if Archie is there to meet them," Hugh shouted to Kirkhill.

But Kirkhill shook his head. He knew that Tony would meet Archie at the village of Eastriggs just about the time *they* reached the Sands. His thought darted back to Fiona. He had scarcely stopped thinking about her since they had met Nan.

He was sure now that the English had taken Fiona and Nan, hoping to lure him and his men into ambush. That meant that Hod had likely identified the two young women, and that the English had let Nan escape on purpose.

That thought sent another jolt of unease through him. If they had taken Fiona only as bait, what would happen when they did not need her any longer? Even if Hod or one of the raiders saw her as a sexual prize, he would abandon her when battle loomed. If the man realized that she might fetch a good ransom, then he might try to get her safely to England, but—

Men above him on the rim were shouting; however, with pandemonium echoing through the cleuch, he could not make out their words. Beside him, Hugh had heard them, too. They exchanged glances.

"Either they see Archie coming or Northumberland," Hugh shouted, reaching back to seize the great sword from its sheath on his back.

Although Kirkhill also carried a sword, he kept a Jedburgh axe in a loop on his saddle. Like most Borderers, he preferred the axe to his sword for close work.

Thoughts of Fiona settled into the back of his mind where he kept personal thoughts when he needed all his wits for battle. A familiar sense of focused concentration took their place.

When they emerged from the cleuch onto the shore of the Firth, he saw that the so-called raiding party had forded the river Esk's narrow channel through the sand and was in all-out flight, spurring their mounts across the open Sands toward England. Approaching them from the other shore was an endless army of mounted Englishmen, thousands—doubtless with four times as many foot soldiers following.

The English army engulfed the raiders. As it did, Kirkhill thought he saw moonlight gleam on shining, long black hair amidst the sea of helmeted men.

Bellowing, "A Douglas, a Douglas!" he spurred Cerberus on, thirsting for battle and hungering even more to reclaim the lass he had come to love.

Fiona screamed at the sight of the vast army galloping toward them. For as far as she could see by the full moon's light, a sea of horses and men surged across the Sands. In minutes, the tide of riders engulfed them. As it did, she heard men screaming all around her, screaming that the Scots were coming, that the Black Douglas had raised an enormous army, many more men than Northumberland had.

Assuring herself that the English leaders must know how long the tide had been out and must believe that they had time to ride across the Sands and back, if necessary, she fought to stay calm despite the chaos on all sides. If the Scots were behind her, shouting the Douglas war cry, then Dickon must be with them.

She needed only to think of some way to make him see her.

For a time, her captors hauled her on toward England. But she soon lost sight of Hod, and the panicked voices soon led to more panic until she could no longer be certain which way her horse was going. Other riders pressed too close for her to see the English coast or the Scottish one, and men were wrenching their mounts around so abruptly that they reared and pawed the air. Panic threatened to overcome her, too, until a narrow leather strap snapped sharply across her right cheek.

Catching hold of it awkwardly with her whip hand, she stared at it for what seemed an eternity but must have been a split second before it began to slip away, and she recognized it as one of her reins. Her horse was plunging like so many others, but she had grabbed a fistful of its mane long since and managed to keep her seat.

Taking a breath, she realized that the poor beast's terrified plunging had made her captor lose his grip and that no one else was paying her heed. The panicked men behind her had panicked those coming toward them. The Douglas name and general pandemonium were having a potent effect. Every Englishman there seemed to believe that Archie the Grim was riding down on him with as many men as Northumberland, or more, chasing the English army back to England.

Moonlight glinting on steel ahead of her told her what to do. Glancing upward, noting the position of the moon, and recalling that it had risen in the east, she knew she must keep it on her right to get back to Scottish soil.

Leaning into her horse's neck, she flailed about with her whip to find the other rein. Catching it and talking to the poor, frightened horse, trying to steady it as the sea of men and horses swept past them, she fought to guide it against the flow.

Feeling the horse tremble under her as it withstood the

press of men and other horses, she held it steady until she detected a gap in the onslaught ahead.

The moon was on her right. Scotland lay ahead.

She kept her head down at first, fearing that if she looked any man in the eye, he might try to seize her reins or bridle. But she could not trust her sense of direction without keeping the moon in sight.

The tide! The thought flamed through her mind, threatening to ignite her panic again. Suppressing the fear, she peered ahead, seeking the Scottish coast.

In the mass of teeming horseflesh, she had drifted off her course.

Mentally scolding herself, focusing on where she wanted to go, she looked again toward Scotland and saw, straight ahead of her, a tall, broad-shouldered rider like so many of the others, but a man who was unmistakable on the powerful black destrier with its flashing teeth. The horse was equally unmistakable.

Dickon, on Cerberus, carved a path straight toward her through clashing swords, lances, and other weapons— lashing murderously about him with the largest axe she had ever seen, as Cerberus nipped at and kicked the English horses, forcing them to clear the path for him.

Confidence surging, Fiona kicked her horse, urging it on with a touch of her whip. Her gaze met Dickon's as an iron fist from behind clamped tight to her left arm.

⁓

Rage roared through Kirkhill when he saw the helmeted Englishman grab Fiona. Ridding himself of one foe with a deft swing of the axe, he knew Cerberus was doing his part, laying about the nearest horses with teeth and flashing hooves. When another adversary backed off, his mount screaming and plunging, Kirkhill urged Cerberus onward. Seeking Fiona in the mob of men and horses, he saw her lashing her whip at the wretch who had dared to lay his hand on her.

Forcing Cerberus through the crowd of panicky riders, hearing the Douglas war cry on every side of him, but with a murderous-looking fellow right in his path, he kneed Cerberus to the right and sent the Englishman flying from his saddle with a blow from the axe hard enough to make his own well-calloused palm sting.

Looking again for Fiona, he saw the villain dragging her from her saddle.

~

The man's grip was bruising Fiona's arm, his strength nearly jerking her from her horse, but she continued to fight him, clutching the reins and her horse's mane in one hand while she flailed at him with the whip in the other.

At the same time, she tried frantically to keep an eye on Dickon as he fought his way toward her. One moment, he was almost near enough to touch her horse, the next too far away. He was fighting for his life against at least two adversaries.

Concentrating on the villain clearly determined to pull her from her horse, and noting a wide tear in his jack above his elbow that had bared skin, Fiona leaned perilously toward it and bit him there as hard as she could.

He jerked away from her with an oath that she heard over the melee around her. As he did, a great axe blade passed between them. She heard a scream, hardly human, saw a spray of blood, and wrenched her gaze hastily away.

"Don't fail me now, lass!"

Dickon's voice steadied her nerves but did little else to stem the sick feeling awash within her. The Englishman was an enemy, but he had been a man, too, and now he was dead or soon would be. She doubted that anyone falling amid so many fighting men and plunging horses would have any chance of surviving.

"Come, lass, this way," Kirkhill ordered in an astonishingly calm voice, making her wonder if she heard him over the cacophony around them because his voice contrasted so to the panicky shouts and screams filling the night around her, or because her ear was especially attuned to it.

"Fiona, now!" he shouted with sudden urgency in his tone.

Gathering her wits, she nodded and spurred her horse after Cerberus, praying she would keep her seat. The Sands still teemed with men, horses, and wounded everywhere. Her gelding tossed its head and flared its nostrils as it tried to pick its way around and over the dead and wounded. The very sand ran with blood.

Nearby someone shouted in a voice that, but for its strong English accent, she'd have mistaken for Sir Hugh's, that the Black Douglas had fifty thousand men on the way. As it was, she saw many of Dickon's men, and others from Spedlins.

Some wore red hearts on their sleeves, denoting Douglas loyalty. Many had slowed and were turning back, satisfied that the English were in full flight.

Hearing a new note in the shouting beyond Dickon,

Fiona realized that the going had become easier, as if the troops still riding toward them were thinning.

Dickon had waved men past, urging them on, but some of those were slowing, too, glancing back toward the shouts.

"What is it?" she cried. "Why are they stopping?"

Just then a lull fell in the noise closest to them, and she easily heard shouts from riders on the open sands between them and the Scottish shore.

"The tide! 'Ware the tide!" Men were wheeling horses, turning back.

But Dickon hesitated and glanced back with a frown. "We're only a mile and a half, mayhap two miles, from the Scottish shore," he yelled. "These Sands stretch from its head for at least twenty miles, and there's no water in sight."

"'Tis a full moon," she shouted back. "The tide will be fierce."

"But, as near as we are—"

"Not so near, sir, we—" She broke off. Above the ongoing clash of weapons and shouts of men still fighting, she heard a distant, still-familiar roar. "Dickon, it's coming now! Warn the rest of our men, for they won't hear it. Sound the horns!"

"How far away is the water if we can hear it?"

She had narrowed the distance between them and, without slowing the gelding, could say without yelling, "No more than twenty minutes. But on these sands, it will take us all of that to reach a point where we can safely get ashore. In this bright moonlight, we'll see the spray first, because it flies high. When we see water, we'll have just minutes to save ourselves before the first huge wave strikes."

"Then ride on, lass! I'll be right behind you, but I must try to warn the others."

"Rob will *know*! Mairi said he has often sailed from Galloway to Annan."

"Rob is with Archie," he said. "But Hugh will know, too."

"Will he?"

"Aye, sure, for I doubt there is any way into or out of England hereabouts that our Hugh does *not* know. But go, lass, now! None will try to stop you, but when we blow the retreat, the English may follow us. Cut eastward, to shorten your ride, but keep clear of the marsh yonder and be wary of the Esk river outflow near shore. It may be deeper than you expect. Trust your horse!"

She nodded, knowing she had to obey him, that there was no time to argue, but feeling acutely uneasy to be riding on alone. She would be on her own until he could warn his men and catch up with her. But he *would* catch up. That she had to believe.

Urging her horse past Cerberus, she fixed her gaze on the Scottish shore, wishing there really *were* fifty thousand Scots awaiting her there.

She saw none but the men who had also heard the telltale roar of the incoming sea and were turning back toward the cleuch from whence they had come.

Wanting nothing to do with that cleuch, she did as Dickon had told her and cut sharply east, where the shore was nearer. Casting a glance to her right, she easily discerned the marshland he had warned of, because it was darker than the Sands and wore a shiny coating that reflected the moonlight.

Her imagination promptly provided her with an image

of what would happen if the tidal wave struck then and swept her and her horse into the muddy swamp.

⁓

Kirkhill caught sight of Sir Hugh's hornsman before he saw his own. In the tumult of the melee, his hornsman had apparently lost sight of him. He did not see Joshua either and hoped that both men would heed Hugh's hornsman and retreat.

"Lucas," he shouted when he saw Hugh's man, "sound the retreat! The tide is coming, and we must be off these sands before it sweeps us all away!"

Lucas nodded and deftly maneuvered his mount around an English soldier, who quickly took on another Scot instead. Lucas raised the horn to his lips and blew the Douglas retreat. Then, to Kirkhill's amusement and relief, he also blew the signal for Kirkhill's men to retreat, and another for the Maxwells.

Disengagement was not easy in the midst of battle, but many of the English were already trying to make speed for England, and the Scots were quick to heed the Scottish horn. As they turned toward home, however, many English riders took courage again and, jeering, urged their mounts to follow.

Shouting again to Joshua, Kirkhill ordered a speedier retreat.

Then, seeing Hugh still safely in the saddle with his sword at the ready, and catching his eye, Kirkhill indicated that he was going on ahead, and pointed toward Fiona, whose dark hair streamed behind her, gleaming in the moonlight.

Barely waiting for Hugh's nod, Kirkhill spurred Cerberus and followed her.

Chapter 20

Fiona slowed as she approached the river Esk, where it flowed through the sand near the Scottish shore. Her gaze swept the river channel's southern bank for puddles that warned of quicksand. As she looked westward, her breath caught in her throat at the sight of spray glittering brightly as it soared high into the moonlit sky.

Most of the men seemed to be heading toward the mouth of the cleuch.

Her gelding was splashing across the shallow river channel with yards yet to go when she heard thudding hoofbeats behind her on the sand and glanced back to see Kirkhill and Cerberus approaching the river's edge.

"Look yonder," she shouted. "You can see the spray!"

The tall, wide curtain of spray sparkled magically as it swept nearer, whirling in the steady breeze as if on an axis. She could smell the sea coming and fancied that she could feel its droplets caressing her face as she urged her mount onward.

The gelding was tired, but this was no time for it to rest.

"That spray's nobbut a mile or so off," Kirkhill shouted back.

"Then we've only minutes to get beyond its reach!"

Glancing westward, she saw a host of Scots now racing toward Riggshead Cleuch. "Should they not follow us?" she yelled. "You told me to cut to the east—"

"Aye, because your mount is tired! They'll make it easily enough!" Cerberus drew alongside the bay, and Kirkhill said in a slightly more normal tone, "The water will be shallow at first, will it not?"

"Some, but not rolling in, as on a beach," she said, spurring the gelding to keep up with the destrier. "It surges, as it does when you empty a pail into a corner! First, you see a long curve of white and flowing surf. Then, quite suddenly behind it, you'll see the swelling tide in a fearsome wall. By sunlight, it looks dimpled, with rainbows dancing in it. Even by moonlight, we should see some color."

"Faster, lass! Use your whip!"

She was riding as fast as she dared, but she glanced back and saw first the frothing surf and then the high wall of water, rushing inexorably toward them.

Kirkhill saw it, too, a glittering wall five or six feet high, a tumbling mass of dark sea surging and roiling beneath myriad white horses, awesome in its power.

"Ride, Fiona, and hang on tight! We'll make it easily enough."

She looked back at him, and to his delight, she grinned. It was a good thing, too, because after such a wild day and night, had she not felt the same exhilaration he felt whenever he pitted himself against Nature or any other force greater than his own, if she had seen glee in *his* expression, she might have thought ill of him.

But she was feeling just what he felt. He could see it.

"I'll race you!" she cried, spurring the gelding on.

Her horse was no match for Cerberus, but Kirkhill wanted her ahead of him and noted that Cerberus was content to allow it for once. Had another destrier ridden ahead of him, he would have done his utmost to pass it. The weary but still determined gelding, offering no challenge, was beneath the destrier's contempt.

Kirkhill kept a close eye on the approaching wall of water as it drew nearer, moving Cerberus up along the lass's left side, between the gelding and the danger.

She was still grinning, but she gave him a look and yelled, "Being protective, sir? I warrant that wall will send us all tumbling if it hits us."

"It won't hit us," he yelled back, hoping he sounded more confident about that than he felt. It was going to be close, and the gelding was nearly blown.

Eyeing the oncoming surge again, he estimated the distance to shore and decided he had time yet to decide if he should lift her off her horse. He doubted that the gelding could withstand the flood. He wasn't sure that Cerberus could.

Better for them all if they made it to higher, firmer ground.

She leaned forward, urging the gelding on, talking to it now, encouraging it.

He saw that most of the other Scots were ashore a half mile to the west, but at that distance, he could not identify anyone he saw.

No one had followed him and Fiona, but English riders were still chasing the Scottish stragglers. As he watched, a number of the English wrenched their horses to a plunging halt, wheeled them, and spurred them hard toward England.

Knowing they must have recognized at last the threat of the oncoming tide, he saw that the wall of water was nearly upon them. He saw, too, that the bluffs above the prominent point forming the west side of the mouth of the cleuch were swarming with men and horses, far more than had come with them. Easily visible in the moonlight, the Douglas red-heart banners waved wildly.

Archie the Grim had arrived.

~

Fiona saw the crowded bluffs and shouted, "Is that Archie?"

"Aye, 'tis himself," he replied. "He must have known the tide would come in, so he took his men upward, rather than brave the Sands with so many."

"Does he really have fifty thousand men up there with him?"

"Nay, that was our Hugh, I expect, seeking to increase the English panic."

Looking toward the fleeing English, she cried, "They'll never make it!"

"Watch where you're going, lass! Head up that hillside, where the trees are!"

The gelding was already going that way on its own, so she gave it its head but could not take her eyes from the sight of terrified riders caught in the flood of water sweeping them toward the marsh she had skirted. The screams of foundering horses and drowning men horrified her. All were in panic, terrified of dying.

Wrenching her gaze from the awful sight at last when

the gelding splashed out of the water and gave a mighty surge to reach higher, flatter ground, she called to him, "Should we not head west now, to join the others?"

"Nay, we should not," he yelled back. "Not yet."

She glanced at him but said nothing, merely nodding and urging the gelding on up the hillside toward the woodland Dickon had indicated.

When she looked again at him, he was watching the last of the Scots gallop their horses through rising surf. One horse stumbled, but its rider held it together, and she drew a breath of relief as the last Scottish horse scrambled from the river channel's eddying water—rising quickly now with the incoming tide—and found safe purchase on the steep shore.

She knew that Dickon had urged her into the trees because he had seen that the water was going to claim many lives and wanted to spare her the sight if he could, and she was grateful. She had seen enough already to keep her awake nights.

Not that Border women were unaccustomed to blood and gore, for they were well acquainted with such. But no one wanted to watch men and horses swept under by the tide. Still hearing their screams, and sure the memory would live in her mind for years, if not forever, she sent a prayer aloft that Hugh, Rob, Sir James, Tony, and the rest of their men who had survived the battle had survived the tide as well.

Drawing rein at the edge of the woodland, she said, "Will not Archie and the others look for you to join them?"

"Hugh saw us leave," he told her. "As for Archie, he has small claim on me now that we've sent the English home again. He has my men and Tony, and I'll wager that he has already sent word to Douglas and March. Neither will refuse to join forces with him whilst Northumberland has an army amassed at the border."

She did not care about Douglas, March, or Northumberland just then. She was just glad that he would stay with her. "Shall we stop here?" she asked.

"This tide will rise much higher, will it not?" he said, gesturing toward the tree line, still some twenty feet above them.

"Not for hours yet. Surely, you don't mean for us to spend the night here."

"Nay, but we'll be more comfortable if we need not think about a rising tide."

She grimaced. "Are you angry with me for following Nan, Dickon?"

"Nay," he said. "But we must rest the horses some, lass, and I'd liefer do it before we rejoin the others. Hugh and Rob will wait for us unless Archie orders them to ride with him. Even then, Hugh will wait until he knows we're safe."

"Will he?"

"Aye, sure," Dickon said, gesturing for her to ride ahead of him through the trees. Moonbeams shot down through the canopy, which was thin there, the trees not nearly as dense as the forests near Spedlins. "Ride just over that rise, lass. I recall a wooded hollow there with a burn. I'm thirsty, and the horses must be, too."

Now that he mentioned thirst, she recognized her own and was glad to see, as they topped the rise, that he was right about the burn. Except for its murmuring, the little glen was quiet. She could no longer hear any screams.

Drawing rein at the burn, she patted the gelding's neck

but did not dismount. Sudden tension filled her, making her heart pound. She no longer thought about horror but only about the fact that she was still alive and that Dickon was, too.

~

Kirkhill watched her pat her horse's neck as the beast stretched to drink from the burn. Fiona nibbled her lower lip, and he felt himself stir in response.

Dismounting, he dropped the reins and quickly unsaddled Cerberus. The destrier moved gratefully to drink from the burn, and would not wander. Moving to the gelding's side, he reached for Fiona and lifted her down to stand before him.

For a long moment, she stood, staring straight ahead at his chest. When she looked up at last, the moonlight caressed her face and gleamed in her eyes. Her gaze met his, serious now and wondering, and emotion surged through him as powerfully as the wall of water that had threatened them both just minutes before.

"Ah, sweetheart," he murmured, resting his hands gently on her shoulders. "I might have lost you before I even..." His throat tightened, and he dared not go on.

"But you did not lose me," she said. "Nor I, you. Could you just hold me, Dickon? I want to feel your arms around me, tight."

He looked upward, seeking guidance, but God did not deign to advise him. Swallowing, he said, "Lass, if I hold you...Sakes, I cannot just hold you. I want to wrap my arms around you and never let you go."

Her smile then was soft, warm, and filled with promise. "Hold me, Dickon."

He heard a moan from his own throat, but he did not hesitate, nor want to.

Embracing her, he pulled her so close that when she made no sound and seemed hardly to breathe, he wondered if he were holding her too tightly. But when he eased his hold, she wrapped her arms around him and hugged him closer to her.

Looking up again, she whispered, "Kiss me."

He felt himself stir again and knew that she must feel it, too.

"Is it wrong to kiss me now, after such a horror?" she asked.

"Nay, lass; it is natural for two people who care about each other to want to be together at such a time." He watched her eyes widen and her pupils grow even larger and darker than they had been before. Then he pressed his lips to hers.

She responded hungrily, opening her mouth to his searching tongue. Her body responded as well, tantalizing him more, as his fingers and hands caressed her.

"I do want you so much," he murmured.

"Me, too," she whispered against his lips.

"I meant to tell you so tonight," he said, straightening. "Before we left, I went upstairs to find you, to tell you, but you and Nan had gone."

"Don't talk; kiss me."

"Sweetheart, I want to do so much more than kiss you," he said. "I want to claim you as mine forever, to marry you. We should wait and—"

"But I don't *want* to wait," she said. "I want you now. I might never have seen you again after tonight. And Archie could take you away tomorrow."

"Nay, he will not. It will take time for the English to recover from their losses tonight, and Northumberland will be as sure as I am that the Douglas and March will join Archie. I ken fine that you want to be sure this time, sweetheart."

"I *am* sure, if you are. But it takes *weeks* to get married."

"Nay, I know the priest at Annan Kirk. We can wake him if he's asleep."

"Tonight?"

"Aye, sure, tonight if that is what you want. If you think your sister would not object, we can stay at Annan House tonight and ride back in the morning."

"I don't want to plan, Dickon, or wait. It is not as if I were a maiden, after all. I want you to make love to me. Now."

He held her close again. The clearing was softly warm, the murmuring water soothing to nerves still taut from battle. When she tilted her head up again, he kissed her hard and let his hands roam over her body, encouraging her to do likewise to him.

"Art sure about this, Fiona-love?"

"Aye, more sure than I've been about anything in my life before now."

They spread her cloak on the ground and lay down together. He rose on an elbow to look down at her, and his cock stirred sharply when she smiled up at him.

Her gaze was warm and unwavering. Her lips, when he reclaimed them, were soft and swollen and moist. Her darting tongue teased his. His fingers and palms caressed her breasts, soft yet firm, then moved to her bodice laces and deftly unlaced her. The silk ribbons of her thin cambric shift parted easily next, and its neckline opened wide, revealing the silken, rosy-tipped mounds beneath.

Her nipples were hard, and she gasped when his fingers touched them, and then moaned when he took each one between his lips and laved it with his tongue. Tasting her milk, he tasted again. "I could envy wee David," he murmured.

"You need not," she murmured back. "They are aching, overfull."

Her fingers touched the flap of his breeks, unfastened it, and touched him.

"You're not cold, are you?" he murmured.

She chuckled, a sound as soothing to him as the burn's murmurs and intensely stimulating, as well.

After a time, he moved over her and eased her skirt and underskirt up past her knees and soft, silky thighs until his palm could cup the parting of her legs and the velvety cleft it hid. His fingers explored it, finding it moist and eager for him. Easing his way, he gently inserted himself as she shifted to welcome him. He felt himself sliding into her warmth, and when he was fully inside, he kissed her again.

A small sob made him draw back to let the moonlight touch her face. To his dismay, it revealed the glint of moisture in her eyes.

"Fiona-love, what is it?"

"'Tis naught, but I've felt so alone for so long," she murmured as her watery gaze met his. "I did not realize until now *how* lonely I've felt."

"Ah, well," he said, kissing her again, "you are not alone anymore. We're together now, love, and I mean to see that we stay that way."

With that, Dickon eased almost out of her and back in, beginning a gentle rhythm that teased and delighted her. Never had she felt such sensations before.

Will's notion of coupling had centered on Will, and except for the first time, when he had given her a chance to accustom herself, first to his touch and then to his entry, it had always been quick, hard, and over as soon as he'd spent himself.

Dickon moved slowly, gently, and seemed more interested in her reactions than in his. If anything, he was holding himself back to give her pleasure, and his efforts were highly successful, because she felt as if every nerve in her was alert and responsive to the increasing pace of his movements.

Heat built within her to such an extent that her body seemed to take on fiery life of its own, arcing to meet his. So focused was she on every nuance of feeling that came from hitherto unknown depths in her that it was as well that Dickon asked nothing of her but to savor each new sensation.

Her body began pushing harder against his as the sensations grew more and more intense. Then, suddenly and without thought or intention, she arched and held herself, soaring higher until she thought she could bear no more. Release came just as abruptly but pulsed outward from the very center of her in waves of pure delight.

"Laird, laird, be that ye and our lady down there?"

The boyish shout from the top of the rise startled them both.

"God-a-mercy!" Fiona exclaimed, gasping, feeling the

fur-lined cloak and firm ground again beneath her, and struggling to reclaim her wits. "That's Davy!"

Dickon did *not* stop. The pace of his actions increased until she realized he *could not* stop. Seconds later, he collapsed atop her, gasping as hard as she had.

"Laird?"

The boy was closer. Fiona could hear his horse's hoof-beats.

Dickon heard them, too, for he rolled lithely off her and onto his feet in what seemed to be a single motion, one hand flipping her skirts back over her legs as his other first tugged to straighten his breeks and then moved to the flap to refasten it.

Grinning at him as she sat up, Fiona said, "You do that as if you have had much practice, sir."

His eyes twinkled. "Think what you like, lass. I've just learned over time to react quickly to an emergency. Davy, lad, over here!" he shouted.

Bending, he helped her up, and as she quickly tied her bodice laces, he snatched up her cloak and draped it over her shoulders.

"We're for Annan town now, sweetheart."

"Aye, sir," she said, reaching up to stroke his cheek. Feeling the roughness of his incipient beard, she realized that her cheeks were burning.

His hand clasped hers and moved it to his lips. He pressed it warmly against them before he said, "You *will* marry me, won't you, my love?"

"I must now, must I not?"

He grinned. "You will decide that for yourself, but you should know first that I'll not permit you to marry anyone else."

She chuckled. "I knew it would not be long before you were exerting your authority as my trustee, sir."

He shook his head at her, but there was no more time for teasing, because Davy emerged just then from the woodland.

"Where did you spring from, lad?" Kirkhill asked the boy. "I thought I told you to wait for the other men where the main road met the track into the cleuch."

"Aye, ye did," Davy agreed. "But, sithee, I soon saw that the English might surprise me there afore they came, so I rode on till I could see the Firth. Then I watched from the bluffs till the Black Douglas came, and the others. Dinna be vexed wi' me," he added hastily. "I kent fine that I could be off again and away did any o' them English villains make it ashore. They'd no ha' caught me."

"Then how did you find us here?"

"Sir Hugh rode up near where I was, and he sent me to find ye. He said he thought ye'd ha' ken o' this wee hollow. He said to tell ye the others left to join the Black Douglas, but he's a-waiting for us near the track west o' Dornock village. He said that ye'd ken the place and that the way back to the main road from there be gey easier than through Riggshead Cleuch."

"It is, aye," Kirkhill agreed. "What's more, that meeting place lies in just the direction that I want to go. What would you say, lad, if I were to tell you that the lady Fiona and I mean to marry?"

Davy grinned. "I'd say that be a fine thing, laird. But be our lady willing?"

"She is," Fiona said, smiling at him.

"I'll need a man or two to stand up with me," Kirkhill said. "Will you do it?"

"Me?" Davy's mouth gaped and his eyes widened.

"I don't know anyone better suited to the task," Kirkhill said.

"Aye, well, Sir Hugh and some others may think ye've gone daft, laird."

"We don't want to disappoint Hugh," Kirkhill said. "So mayhap I'll ask him to stand up with me, too. I do think a wedding is supposed to have two witnesses."

"Aye, sure, then, I'll do it," Davy said. "When?"

"As soon as I can waken a priest," Kirkhill said. "Art ready, my lady?"

⁓

The next hour passed quickly but not quickly enough to suit Fiona. The first part, before they met Hugh, was the most difficult. Her imagination produced different, negative ways that he might react to the news that Dickon wanted to marry her, but none of them matched the reality when they found Hugh with a half dozen of his men and Dickon's Joshua at the appointed meeting place.

When Dickon announced bluntly that he would marry Fiona, Hugh laughed.

"Do you dare to mock such news?" Dickon demanded before Fiona could express her own indignation.

"'Tis nobbut an expression of my delight at proving to be right about your feelings, my friend," Hugh said, still grinning. "Just ask my Jenny if you don't believe me. I told her before we left that if we found the lass, you'd marry her."

"What about me?" Fiona asked. "Were you so sure of me, then?"

"Lassie, I knew you'd not find a better man," Hugh said. "Moreover, after Tony told us about you dumping your food onto Dickon's trencher and—"

"He *told* you about that!"

"And about what followed, or as much as he knows about that. We both suspected then—aye, and Rob, too—that you two would make a match of it. Jenny and Mairi agreed with us, too, after they had seen you together."

"Never mind all that," Dickon said. "Davy here has agreed to stand up with me at Annan Kirk, Hugh, and I'd like it fine if you would, too."

Hugh grinned at the boy. "Aye, sure, I would. But won't the lass need someone to stand with her, too, and give her away? I'm her uncle. I should do that."

"I'd like that fine, sir," Fiona said. "Joshua can stand up with you, Dickon."

"I'd be honored if he would," Kirkhill said, glancing at Joshua, who smiled.

"He'll do that, aye," Hugh said. "We'll see it all done right, won't we, lads?"

"Aye, sir, that we will," Davy said, straightening his shoulders.

Since Dickon had seemed unsurprised to see Davy in the hollow, it occurred to Fiona only at that moment that Davy had no business at all to be so far south. Turning her gaze on the boy, she said, "But I don't understand, Davy. Surely, you did not ride all the way to Riggshead Cleuch with Kirkhill and Sir Hugh?"

"Nay, me lady. I followed ye and the lady Anne from the Hall."

"He did," Kirkhill said. "And he continued to follow

you after Nan got away. It was thanks to Davy that we knew where your captors had taken you."

She thought of Nan then, and guilt washed over her. "So you found Nan?"

"Aye, leading a lame horse," he said. "I sent her back to the Hall."

"She must be dreadfully worried. She was so fierce, Dickon. She fought those men off with her whip and rode away." Remembering that Hod, or another of them, had said to let Nan go, she swallowed hard. "They *wanted* you to follow me."

"We know that," he said with a slight smile. "They thought they were laying a trap for us, but we suspected as much, so Rob took one party of men along the north rim of the cleuch, and Hugh took another one south of it. We made as much noise as an army of banshees and scared the lights out of them."

"Out of me, too," she said, remembering. "I was terrified that my horse would break a leg or that the rest of Hod's men would ride right over me."

"So it was Old Jardine's Hod at the back of this, eh?" Hugh said.

"Aye, or the raiders he joined after he left us," she said. "He called them raiders, but he sounded different when he talked, like an English nobleman."

"There is one thing that you don't know yet," Dickon said to her. "The chap at Spedlins who told us that Davy was following you also told me that the English had been there and had broken up Old Jardine's fine bed."

"Broken the bed! Good sakes, why would they do such a thing?"

"I've been thinking about that. I'll want to see the

damage to be sure, but recall the key that I found and gave to you, and then took back again. I'm wondering if one of the carvings in that bed might have been a keyhole."

"Old Jardine's gelt!" she exclaimed. "If he hid it in that bed, and the English found it—" Recalling Davy's presence, she felt a wave of guilt, but when Dickon smiled reassuringly, she added, "How would they know to look for it, though?"

Joshua, who had been silent until then, said, "That Hod, of course."

"I agree," Dickon said. "If he is English, he was likely Northumberland's spy *and* his messenger. He said he'd been with Old Jardine for just three years, so I'd not be surprised to learn that much of that gelt came from England. If Jardine agreed to aid them again, be sure that he demanded a good sum for his help. Hod may have thought that with Jardine dead and Will missing, he could just take the money, either for Northumberland or for himself, with no one else the wiser."

"Mayhap he knew that Will was also dead," Fiona said. "Sakes, mayhap Hod killed him to get that money."

Kirkhill shook his head. "He *may* have known that Will was dead, but I doubt that he killed him. The English need all the support they can get in Annandale if they mean to take over the place. As it is, such support is fast waning. My guess is that Hod just wanted to take the money and clear out."

"If he did, then Old Jardine's gelt may be at the bottom of the Firth," she said. "Many of those raiders had sacks tied to their saddles."

"Most men-at-arms do," he said. "They carry small amounts of food and other supplies. They *may* have been willing to weigh themselves down with silver, but if they did, someone can look for it when the tide ebbs again. Such bags would be weighty enough to stay put for a while."

"Aye, well," she said with a sigh, "if they took any of it from the bed, they took all of it, so there will be nowt left for me. I'll *have* to marry you now."

⁓

Kirkhill looked swiftly at her but relaxed when he saw her mischievous grin. Hearing Hugh's chuckle, he knew that the other man had seen it, too.

Davy, wisely, kept silent.

Riding into the town of Annan, they discovered that although it was well after midnight, a number of its citizens were wide awake and in the streets, celebrating the defeat of the English army. With little delay, they made their way to the kirk and its adjoining manse at the center of town, where, dismounting at the manse entrance, Kirkhill hammered on the door.

A manservant answered, and Kirkhill demanded to know if his master, the priest, was asleep. "For if the reverend father has slept through the din out here, you must waken him and tell him that Kirkhill of Kirkhill requires his services."

Twenty minutes later—a mere ten minutes after promising a hefty donation to the kirk's building fund—Kirkhill was a married man.

He smiled at Fiona. "What think you, sweetheart? Shall we impose on the hospitality of Annan House now? Hugh, you must be our guest there if we do."

"Nay, Dickon, that moon will last until dawn, so I'm for

the Hall. Had the battle lasted longer, I might be ready for bed and a long sleep, but I'm still wide awake and likely to remain so long enough to get back to my Jenny."

"Aye, well, I'm wide awake, too, but this is my wedding night, so—"

"Prithee, sir," Fiona said. "It is my wedding night, too, but I've little desire to stay at Annan House and *every* desire for us to travel north with Sir Hugh. I'll need a fresh horse, and Davy will, too, but I'd much prefer to return to Spedlins for the night, or ride straight on to the Hall and my wee bairn."

He raised his eyebrows. "Faith, have I married a masterful woman?"

"Serve you right if you had," Hugh said.

"Well, he hasn't," Fiona told Hugh. "But Annan House has not been my home for two years and still feels like my parents' home, so it is not a place to enjoy my wedding night. In troth, though..." She glanced warily at Kirkhill.

"In troth, my greedy wife, you want to find out about the gelt," he said.

"Aye, my lord," she said. "I do."

*Chapter 21*_____

Leaving a messenger to request that Archie organize a search of the Sands for bags of silver—English or Scot—and temporarily exchanging Fiona's horse and Davy's for two from the priest's stable, they set out for Spedlins after the ceremony. Their journey was nearly twelve miles, but bright moonlight and the good Roman road meant they made nearly the same time that they might have made by daylight.

Kirkhill, Fiona, Joshua, and Davy parted from Hugh and his men at the Spedlins turning. The moon was still high when they rode into the yard.

The guardsman who greeted them blurted, "So ye found her, laird!"

"I did, aye," Kirkhill said. "I should tell you, too, that I have married her."

"Have ye now, sir?" the guardsman said with a delighted grin that banished Kirkhill's assumption that the people of Spedlins might demand reasons. "Pray, m'lady, will ye let me say straightaway that we'll all wish ye gey happy?"

"Thank you," Fiona said. "Tomorrow we must think about how we'll want to celebrate. We are all gey tired, though, and must get some sleep."

"Aye, sure, m'lady. Most o' our folks be still at the Hall, o' course, but I can stir up someone to aid ye wi' your—"

"That will not be necessary," Kirkhill said. "Joshua can see to my needs, and I will see to Lady Kirkhill's. You may return to your duties."

Glancing at Fiona, he saw her staring at him and realized that, as the priest had had no need to present them formally to their small audience, it was the first time she had heard her new title. He smiled and saw her relax as she smiled back.

Dismounting, they woke a gillie to see to their horses with Davy's help and went inside, where they skirted sleepers in the hall and went to the inner chamber.

"Good sakes," Fiona exclaimed as they entered, "what a mess!"

The lower section at the head of the exquisitely carved bed frame was broken, leaving a gaping hole that revealed a deep hollow inside.

Wood fragments littered the floor.

"It looks as if someone took a maul to it," Kirkhill said, sure now that he had been right, and kneeling to peer inside. "The space is empty, but it does look as if something had been in there. The dust inside is all streaked."

He straightened and said to Joshua, "I'll sleep in my lady's bed tonight. Tomorrow we'll decide what to do about this."

"Aye, sir," Joshua said, staring at the hole in the bed frame. "There be hinges there at the left side, for a wee door, like. That Old Jardine were a one, aye?"

"Go to bed, Joshua. Come along, lass," Kirkhill added, touching her shoulder. "We'll use the service stairs."

Weariness had caught up to Fiona miles before they'd reached Spedlins, but anxiety replaced it as she entered the bedchamber that she had shared with Will.

Moonlight spilled through the open window, illuminating the large bed.

When she hesitated at the sight, Dickon put his arm around her and said, "Look at me, lass." When she did, he said, "What's amiss?"

"I...I did not expect this," she said. "I thought we'd sleep in your bed. Will it not seem...? That is, will you not feel as if...?" She stopped, not knowing how to put her muddled feelings into words.

He moved to face her, touching her shoulders as he often did when he wanted to speak seriously with her. "Sweetheart, I know that Will must have shared that bed with you, but I have known it only as your bed and the bed where your bairn came into this world. It holds no ghosts for me, only two people I love and care for. If it makes you uncomfortable to sleep with me in a bed that you shared with him—"

"Do not say that you will leave! I don't want that. I only feared that you—"

"I don't care a whit about Will Jardine. You are mine, Fiona-love, and you were never truly his."

"Then take me to bed, Dickon."

By moonlight, he helped her remove all but her shift and took off his clothes while she brushed and plaited her hair, and watched him. Then, he returned to her, untied the ribbons of her shift for the second time that night, pulled it off over her head, and dropped it to the floor. Gathering her into his arms, he carried her to bed.

Their lovemaking was more tempestuous than before, and Fiona, reveling in the feelings he stirred, tried to imitate the things he did, to excite similar sensations in him. She wished she knew what else he'd like her to do but was reluctant to try some of the things that Will had demanded of her, lest Dickon disapprove of them.

As they lay back, sated, she drew a deep breath and felt more content than she could recall ever feeling before.

"That felt wonderful," she murmured.

"It did, aye," he agreed. Silence fell for a time before he said sleepily, "Still awake, sweetheart?"

"Aye."

"What are you thinking about?"

Her tongue seemed suddenly stuck to the roof of her mouth.

"Fiona?"

"I don't know how to say what I'm thinking."

"Just tell me what is in your head."

He said no more than that, although the silence lengthened until she began to fear that he had fallen asleep. Then she recalled that he had said she could tell him anything, and the one sure thing that she had learned about Dickon was that he meant the things he said. He would not be angry, and he would be honest.

Not knowing how else to begin, she said, "You are different from Will."

"Sakes, I hope I am!"

"You are, aye, in every way. So I don't know what you might like or . . . or dislike when you and I couple."

His low chuckle sent tremors through her body, stirring it to life again although she had thought she was exhausted.

"Sweetheart," he said, "you can do anything you like to me. Anything that you feel comfortable enough to try will delight me. Do you remember when I said that you had more power in one finger than most men have in their whole bodies?"

"Aye, but you do say odd things from time to time."

"I referred to the power that you have to ignite a man's passion. Sakes, if you only knew how often I have dreamed of lying with you, and feeling your hands, fingers, lips, and tongue on my body, even your wee white teeth."

"My teeth!"

"Fingernails and teeth are more than defensive weapons, Fiona-love. They can be effective in bed, too. I'd show you *how* effective, but if we don't sleep soon, we'll likely sleep right through the rest of today and Wednesday as well."

He leaned up on his elbow then and bent over her, claiming her lips, before he added provocatively, "But tomorrow, my love, we'll see just what they can do."

As he lay back, she smiled and snuggled against him, more delighted than he could imagine to hear that he had dreamed of her.

Sunlight had replaced the moonlight in the room when Kirkhill opened his eyes, telling him that the hour was much later than his usual rising time. He had not slept as deeply as usual those first couple of hours, though. The desire to savor all he felt, having Fiona beside him, had been stronger than his need for good sleep.

He realized that she, too, was awake, but as much as he wanted to take her again, he knew they should get up.

They had things to do. Hugh had told him the night before that Rob, Tony, Sir James, and the rest of their men would likely remain with Archie through the day and perhaps through the week, until Archie was sure that the English threat had truly diminished, at least for the time being.

But Spedlins was clearly undermanned if raiders had invaded it so easily, and he would have to ensure the safety of its people before he could leave again.

"Art awake, sir?"

"Aye, sweetheart," he said, moving to kiss her. She tasted good, even in the morning. "We should get up," he said, suiting action to the words.

They dressed quickly, and as he finished fastening the flap of his breeks, someone rapped on the door.

Glancing at Fiona to see that she was fully covered, he did not bother to ask who it was but said loudly, "Enter."

Flory came in, smiling. "I thought ye might want me, m'lady."

"Where is my wee David?" Fiona demanded.

"Wi' Eliza, downstairs, asleep," Flory said. "Joshua said to leave the wee laddie wi' her till ye'd broken your fast. He said ye'd be gey hungry."

"He was right," Kirkhill agreed.

"Aye," Fiona said. "But do not let Eliza nurse him if he wakens, Flory. I'm overfull of milk as it is, and I've missed my laddie."

"Faith, but I should think ye'd be fair aching by now," Flory said.

Meeting Kirkhill's dancing gaze, Fiona knew she was blushing, but she said only, "I am going downstairs to get food, sir. You may come along if you are ready."

Chuckling, he put an arm around her but said to Flory,

"I expect you've heard that I married your mistress, lass. Do you wish us happy?"

"Aye, m'lord, we all do," she replied with a grin.

"But when did you come back here?" Fiona asked her.

"This morning, early," Flory said. "It be nearly midday now, sithee, but when Sir Hugh said ye were back here at Spedlins, we thought we'd best come back, too. I'll just tidy up here whilst ye're downstairs."

Taking the main stairway, Kirkhill and Fiona entered the great hall to find that much of the remaining population of Spedlins had gathered there.

Cheers erupted as they appeared in the archway, and when they moved toward the small crowd, it parted and silence fell.

Sitting in the center of the chamber floor was a stout woven kist of the sort in which Kirkhill and most other people who could make or afford such things stored their clothing and linens. This one had rounded, stitched leather handles at each end, and leather loops and thongs to secure its lid.

Kirkhill looked from one grinning, expectant face to another. "What is this?"

Evart, the steward, stepped forward. His expression revealed little, but Kirkhill felt nonetheless that the old man was as pleased as anyone else there. Evart said, "Yon kist be a token o' our trust in ye, m'lord, and our esteem for our lady on the happy occasion o' which some o' us learned last night and others wi' the dawn."

Turning to Fiona, Kirkhill said, "Such a gift is most unexpected and likely intended more for you than for me, my lady. Mayhap you should open it."

She nodded, looking as puzzled as he felt.

As she moved to kneel by the kist, Evart said, "By my troth, sir, it be for ye both, equally, and for our young master, David Jardine, as well."

Frowning in his puzzlement now, Kirkhill moved nearer as Fiona unlooped the two thongs and opened the kist.

Inside were a dozen to a score of string-tied fustian sacks.

Fiona untied one of them, opened it, and gasped audibly as a sunbeam from one of the high, narrow windows glinted on silver.

⁓

Fiona stared at the coins, all silver groats and silver pence as far as she could tell at first glance. She counted the bags, fifteen of them, a small fortune.

"But how?" she asked. "I thought Hod must have taken whatever was here."

"And so he would have, aye, did he get the chance," Evart said. "But Hod were no the only one to ha' ken o' Old Master's gelt, nor he didna ken the hidey-hole for all that he did find the key. Old Master kept it till he died, m'lord," he added, looking at Kirkhill.

"But I found that key on the table in Jardine's bedchamber," Kirkhill said.

"Aye, sure, 'cause that Hod didna ha' ken o' what it fit. Not then." Evart frowned, then added, "I'd say that 'twere only when he'd had leisure to think on the matter that it came to him that Old Jardine might ha' hid summat in yon great bed o' his. Afore then, though, we'd got the old master's fortune safe again."

"Do you have a key, too, then?" Fiona asked him.

For the first time, Evart's expression revealed discomfort. "Nay, m'lady, not one o' my own. Sithee, Old Jardine had only the one key."

"Then how...?" She remembered the confusion she had felt when the key had seemed to be on the wrong ring of her chatelaine. "You took it from me!"

"Nay, not exactly," Evart said, looking beyond her.

Glancing over her shoulder, she saw Flory, her cheeks fiery red.

"He just asked to borrow it for a time and no to tell ye," Flory said. "He said it might be dangerous for ye to ken aught o' the matter."

Fiona saw Kirkhill frown and look from Flory to Evart, whose cheeks had also reddened. Hastily, Fiona said, "And you trusted Evart *not* to harm me."

"I did, aye," Flory said. But she was looking warily at Kirkhill.

"Easy enough, I expect, for you to slip into my chamber from the service stair and remove the bags from their hiding place," Kirkhill said. "But it might have been awkward had someone like Joshua caught you at it."

"Aye, sir, and I expect ye think it were me duty to tell ye all about it—"

"If you give me your word that Old Jardine's fortune remains intact for his grandson, that is all the assurance I need," Kirkhill said. "I begin to think that all of you have kept an eye on her ladyship, and on me, have you not?"

Fiona saw Evart's relief as he said, "This be the young master's inheritance, sir. We'd none o' us ha' touched it, save to keep it safe for him."

Kirkhill nodded. "Fair enough," he said.

"Tippy said Jeb told her that she and Davy should watch

over each other and those they love, that good people do that," Fiona said. "Is that how it was, Evart?"

"Aye, m'lady. Wi' respect, laird, we didna trust ye yet then to look after our bairn, his lands, and his mam as ye should. Until we could..." He spread his hands.

"I do understand, Evart," Kirkhill said. "After Old Jardine suggested that I might have killed his son, I could scarcely expect you to trust me straightaway."

Evart grimaced but did not debate the point.

"Laird, laird, the lady Mairi has come and she's brought a few o' them minstrels wi' her!" Davy was fairly dancing as he shouted the news.

Evart and one of the other men whisked the kist into the inner chamber, while Dickon and Fiona hurried to greet their unexpected guests.

"We came to help you celebrate," Nan cried as she flung herself from her horse. "What's more, Sir Hugh sent word to Rob and Tony and Uncle James that you'd married, so he thinks they may return as soon as this evening!"

~

Kirkhill turned to Hugh. "You sent a messenger to them from Annan?"

"Aye, sure, I knew they'd want to know about this turn of events, and Mairi would be disappointed if they don't get back by Saturday for her festivities."

"Mayhap so, but Archie—"

"Don't fret about Archie. I'll wager he has it all under control, and if he doesn't, he'll let us know soon enough. So, just welcome your nuptial celebration and cease your nattering."

Kirkhill looked at Fiona. "I begin to understand why

arbitrary orders irk you, lass. I'm acquiring distaste for them myself."

Nan exclaimed, "But you cannot turn us away!"

"Everyone is gey welcome," Fiona said firmly. "But if I had my way, the minstrels would entertain us this afternoon, after we dine. Then, if the other men arrive in time, we might take our supper this evening in the nearest orchard with just the family and mayhap a gillie or two to see to the serving."

"But if the other men don't come, that would just be dull," Nan complained.

Kirkhill's gaze caught Fiona's. He smiled at her, wishing he could send everyone else away but understanding, too, that she wanted to share their day. As it was, though, the afternoon passed quickly and the men returned before suppertime.

                         ◡

"Now see what you've made me do!" Fiona cried, laughing and wriggling to free herself from her husband. Aside from shaking her head at him, she spared no thought for the apronful of apples that he had startled her into dropping.

Slipping an arm around her waist, Dickon grinned at her and with his free hand pulled her around to face him. "Let Nan pick them up," he said, holding her strongly. "It will amuse her, and I want you. I've not had you to myself all day."

His face was close to hers, and his breath smelled of spices from the apple tart they'd shared after their meal under the apple trees. He held her so close that she felt him stirring against her. His expression was full of laughter and a loving hunger so fierce that it stirred her own and made her dizzy.

She wished fervently that they could be together like this forever. But she knew that duty would call him again, for such was the nature of things in the Borders. He would have to leave her then, but he would return, and meantime, he would remain faithful to her and would miss her as much as she would miss him.

Since the day they had met, grass and the leaves on the trees seemed greener, the sky bluer, and the colors of the flowers brighter. The world had become a warmer, more welcoming, and much more beautiful place.

"Happy, love?" he murmured close to her ear.

"Aye," she said softly. "Happier than I thought anyone could be." To her good-sister she said, "One apple rolled under that tree behind you, Nan." Then, smiling up at Dickon again, she said, "They will all be bruised now, you know."

"Aye, sure, and gey fine for more tarts," he said. "Take those to the cook when you've collected them all, Nan, or give some to the others first if you like."

"You'd get fat, eating so many tarts," Nan told him, laughing. She had her skirt full of apples and turned cheerfully away toward the others to share them.

"She seems happier now, too," Fiona said, watching her go.

"Aye, the naughty tease. Do you know whom she tells me she has decided she wants to marry, after having made such a great song about it?"

Fiona gave him a saucy look. "Tony, of course. I knew she would."

"But she said she would not have him no matter what anyone said."

"She did tell me, though, when I caught up with her after she rode off from the Hall, that she had decided Tony might care for her after all."

"Sakes, that was after he put her across his knee and skelped her good."

"Aye," she said. "There is no understanding it."

He frowned thoughtfully. "I may begin to understand. Sithee, I have told her that the reason I get so wroth with her is that I care so deeply about her."

"You said much the same thing to me," Fiona said. "But I don't advise you to skelp me to prove it, or to issue arbitrary orders to me, come to that."

He shook his head. "I would grant you almost any request, my love. However, I know better than to make promises that I know I won't keep. Art truly pleased to be a married lady again?"

"Aye, sir. I have never been more so. The only thing that could make me any happier would be to learn just what happened to Will. I am still cursed with that nagging feeling that I had a hand in his death and burial."

"Nay, then, ye did not!"

Dickon had opened his mouth, doubtless to reassure her, but his voice was not female and his lips had not moved. Shifting him aside, Fiona saw Flory behind him.

"Wherever did *you* spring from this time?"

"I were just walking in the orchard, me lady. I slipped behind yon tree when I seen ye two a-coming, for I didna want to spoil your time together. But I canna let ye think any longer that ye had aught to do wi' Master Will's death."

"But what can you know about it?"

"Nae one kens more," Flory said with a wary look at

Dickon. "Sithee, I did it m'self. Ye had nowt to do wi' it, 'cause ye was dead unconscious the while."

"You were not even there," Fiona protested.

"Aye, sure, I was," Flory said. "I'd seen that look in his eyes when ye left the stableyard, and I kent fine what it meant for ye, mistress." Turning to Dickon, she said, "It were Master Will's currish look, m'lord, like ye'd see on that snarling devil dog o' Old Master's or on the devil hisself. I'd followed ye both, m'lady, but I were afeard to get too close, and I kent fine that I couldna stop him hitting ye. Then he knocked ye down. He did nowt to help ye, though ye'd hit your head on the rock. Sakes but he looked as if he'd kick ye in the belly. I couldna let him hurt the bairn."

"Did you truly believe he would?" Dickon asked. "His own child?"

"He were thinking o' nowt save punishing her ladyship for back-chatting him," Flory said. "I'd seen that afore wi' him, sir, many a time, and I ha' me doots that he gave any thought to the babe. I didna ask him, though. I just grabbed up a stout branch and clouted him as hard as I could. I meant only to stop him from hurting them, no to *kill* the man. Must I hang for it, laird?"

"Nay, Flory, I'll let no one hang you," Dickon said. "But how did you get him all the way over the hill and into that grave? Surely, not by yourself!"

"Och, I did, aye," Flory said, looking him in the eye. "Took me nigh the whole night, that did, but I'd rolled him onto an apple sack whilst the mistress lay insensible. I were that scared for her, but even more scared o' being caught wi' his dead body. So, I dragged him off the path, amidst the trees, till I'd got her into bed. Jeb's grave be none so far from there, 'less ye be dragging a body. I kicked a rock in, tipped him in after it, and threw some dirt on him, so that if anyone saw him…"

"They'd think he got drunk, fell into the grave, and hit his head on the rock."

"Aye, well, he *were* ape-drunk, and it seemed gey fitting to make it look so after all he'd done to her ladyship."

"But I don't remember any of that," Fiona said, frowning. "Sakes, how did you get me to bed?"

"Ye were stirring when I got back from pulling him into the trees," Flory said. "I helped ye stand, and ye walked back wi' me to your chamber. Ye managed them stairs on your own, but I could tell it pained ye, and ye didna speak a word."

Looking at Dickon, Flory added glibly, "Likely, she were just a-walking in her sleep, sir, as ye might say."

"Doubtless, you're right," Dickon said gently. "I'm grateful to you, Flory."

She nodded and walked away, avoiding Fiona's eye.

Fiona stared after her. "Sakes, she cannot think that *I'm* angry with her!"

"Nay, lass, I think she just fears that you know more than you've admitted."

She looked at him searchingly. "Do *you* believe that?"

He smiled, easily meeting her gaze. "I just still think you may have seen or heard more than you remember."

"But what if I helped her?"

"You didn't," he said confidently.

"How can you be so sure? People can do extraordinary things when they fear for their lives or their children's. Otherwise, Flory couldn't have moved Will, either."

"Fear does give people strength," he said. "But I think Flory had help."

"Who?"

"I don't know for sure, and I don't want to know. But if I had to guess, I'd say that matters with Will progressed much as she described, except that I believe almost anyone here other than Hod and Will's most loyal men would have helped her, and that she knew they would. I think she sought help after she got you to bed."

"Then how could I dream that I'd put Will in a grave?"

"The same way that I realized where he must be after you told me about your dream. The *fact* of Jeb's open grave that night was just a piece of the puzzle, lass, a piece that I did not know about and that you had not consciously considered before you had your dream. But the knowledge was in your mind, so when neither Will nor his body showed up after so long a time, you fretted about the possibility that you might have killed him until the dream put that worry and Jeb's open grave together in as unlikely a tale as the one I first heard you telling the children."

"But do you really think so many people could have helped Flory?"

"I thought at first that your people all suspected you," he said. "But I kept seeing one or another watching me, and it is clear now that many are strongly attached to you. I think that they have guarded you well, whenever they could."

"Aye, perhaps, but if that is true..."

"Shall we go in now?" he said with a suggestive gleam in his eyes. "This is our celebration, after all, so I think our guests will forgive us for abandoning them. We can discuss this all night, if you like, although I might have some other ideas."

She glanced at the others, still gathered round the trestle table the gillies had set up for their outdoor midday meal. Sir James had an arm around Phaeline, Mairi and Jenny were laughing, and Rob was chatting amiably with Hugh.

"They won't miss us a bit," Fiona said, but she smiled as she said it. Everyone looked happy, and she knew just where she belonged.

With Dickon's arm around her, her baby safe in his cradle, and the rest of her family nearby, all was right with her world—at last.

Looking up into Dickon's eyes, she gave him another hug and let him take her inside and to bed.

Dear Reader,

I wrote much of *Tempted by a Warrior* on a laptop with my feet up on a deck chair, looking out over a beautiful lake in the High Sierras. It is the third and last book in the Dunwythie trilogy, which began with *Tamed by a Laird* (July 2009) and *Seduced by a Rogue* (January 2010). I hope you enjoyed it.

Archie the Grim did not rout the English from Annandale until 1384, when he besieged Lochmaben Castle and won submission and departure in just nine days. He might have done it sooner. Instead, though, he persuaded the English and other Scottish Borderers to honor and prolong the truce of 1369 until Candlemas (February 2) 1384, which, "coincidentally," was the day that he began his nine-day siege.

For those of you interested in knowing more about the fairy tale that Fiona is telling the children at the opening of this book, it is the ancient Scottish version of Rumplestiltskin and is called Habitrot. I came across it in *Scottish Fairy and Folk Tales,* edited by Sir George Douglas (Toronto, 2000). That Dover edition is an unabridged republication of the original text published in New York (no date, but its introduction was first delivered as a speech by the author/editor in January 1892).

Details of geography, towns, and dales come primarily from the *Ordnance Gazetteer of Scotland*, edited by Francis H. Groome (Scotland, 1892).

My primary sources for Douglas history include *A History of the House of Douglas,* Vol. I, by the Right Hon. Sir Herbert Maxwell (London, 1902), and *The Black Douglases* by Michael Brown (Scotland, 1998).

I must again thank the always astonishing Donald MacRae, who introduced me to the Dunwythies by asking if I'd be interested in a woman who nearly started a clan war. Little did he know that that one question would result in three books.

As always, I'd also like to thank my wonderful agents, Lucy Childs and Aaron Priest, my terrific editor Frances Jalet-Miller, production manager Anna Marie Piluso, master copyeditor Sean Devlin, Art Director Diane Luger, Senior Editor and Editorial Director Amy Pierpont, Vice President and Editor in Chief Beth de Guzman, and everyone else at Hachette Book Group's Grand Central Publishing who contributed to making this book what it is.

If you enjoyed *Tempted by a Warrior,* please look for *Highland Passion,* the first book in my new Highland trilogy, at your favorite bookstore in April 2011.

In the meantime, *Suas Alba!*

Sincerely,

Amanda Scott

http://www.amandascottauthor.com
    amandascott@att.net

Don't miss
Amanda Scott's
next Highlands
Scottish romance!

Please turn this page
for a preview of
her next novel,
available in mass market
in April 2011.

Chapter 1 ——————————

The Highlands, Spring 1400

The odd gurgling punctuated by harsher notes that was the Scottish jay's birdsong gave no hint of what lay twenty feet below its perch, on the forest floor.

The fair-haired young woman silently wending her way through the forest toward the jay's tall pine tree sensed nothing amiss. Nor, apparently, did the large wolf dog a few feet away to her right, moving like a graceful tarnished-silver ghost through the thick growth of pines, birch, and aspen. However, had the dog not been upwind of the pine tree, it might well have sensed something out of the way.

The breeze hushing through the canopy overhead and the still-damp forest floor beneath eighteen-year-old Lady Catriona Mackintosh's bare feet made keeping silent easier than it would be after warmer temperatures dried the ground. When a fat, furry brown vole scurried out of her path and two squirrels chased each other right past her and up a nearby tree, she smiled, feeling a stab of pride in her increased ability to move so silently that her presence did not disturb the forest creatures.

She listened for sounds of the fast-flowing burn ahead, but before she heard any, the breeze suddenly dropped and the dog halted, stiffening to alertness as it raised its snout. Then it looked at her and began to tremble.

Raising her right hand toward it, palm out, Catriona stopped, too, and tried to sense what the dog sensed.

The dog watched her. She knew its mind nearly as well as she knew her own and could easily tell that the scent it had caught on the air was not that of a wolf or a deer. The look it cast her was uncharacteristically wary, and its trembling likewise indicated wariness rather than the quivering, bowstring-taut excitement that it displayed when catching scent of a favored prey.

As their gazes met, the dog turned away again and bared its teeth but made no sound. She had trained it well and felt another rush of pride at this proof of her skill.

Moving forward, easing her toes gently under the mixture of rotting leaves and pine needles that carpeted the forest floor as she had before, she kept an eye on the dog, knowing that it would stop her if danger lurked ahead.

Instead, as she began moving, the dog moved faster, easing its way between trees and through shrubbery to go silently before her.

She was accustomed to its protective instincts. Once, she had nearly walked into a wolf that had drifted away from its pack and had gone so still at her approach that she failed to sense its presence. The dog had leaped in front of her, stopping her and snarling at the wolf, startling it so that it made a strident bolt for safety. She had little doubt that the dog would kill any number of wolves to protect her.

That it glided steadily ahead now but continued to

glance back reminded her that although it did not like what it smelled, it was just wary, not fearful.

Catriona felt no fear, because she carried her dirk and her brothers had taught her how to use it. Moreover, she trusted her instincts nearly as much as she trusted the dog's and was sure that no predator, human or otherwise, lay in wait for her.

The jay still sang. The squirrels chattered.

Birds usually fell silent at a predator's approach, and while squirrels sometimes shrieked warnings of danger, such alerts came in loud, staccato bursts as the harbinger raced ahead of the threat. The only odd thing now was that the two squirrels had grown noisier, as if they strove to drown out the jay's song.

As that whimsical thought struck, Catriona glanced up to see if she could yet spy either the squirrels or the jay. Instead, she saw a huge black raven swooping toward the tall pine and heard the larger bird's deep croak as it sent the jay squawking into flight. The raven's arrival shot a chill up her spine.

Ravens sought out carrion, dead things. This one perched in the tree and stared fixedly downward as it continued its deep croaking signal to others of its kind that it had discovered a potential feast.

The dog increased its pace as if it, too, recognized the raven's signal.

Catriona hurried after the dog, realizing only as she did that she could hear the rushing burn and that, had she not had her senses so finely tuned to the wolf dog and what lay ahead, she'd have noticed the sounds of the water sooner.

Following the dog into a clearing, she saw the turbulent

water beyond. The huge raven, on its branch overhead, raucously protested her presence. Others circled above, great black shadows against the overcast sky, cawing hopefully.

The dog growled, and at last she saw what had drawn the ravens.

A man wearing rawhide boots and a saffron-colored tunic with a large red and green mantle over it of the sort that Highlanders called a plaid lay facedown on the damp ground, unconscious or dead, with his feet pointing toward the tumbling burn. Strapped slantwise across his back was a great sword in its sling, and a significant amount of blood had pooled by his head.

The dog had scented the blood.

So had the ravens.

⁓

Sir Finlagh Cameron awoke slowly. His first awareness was that his head ached unbearably. His second was of a warm breeze in his right ear and a huffing sound. He seemed to be prone, his left cheek resting on an herbal-scented pillow.

What, he wondered, had happened to him?

Just as it finally dawned on him that he was on dampish ground atop leafy plants of some sort, a long, wet tongue laved his right cheek and ear.

Opening his eyes, he beheld two…no, four silvery gray legs, much too close.

Tensing, but straining to keep still as the animal licked him again, well aware that wolves littered Highland forests, he shifted his gaze beyond the four legs to see if there were more. He did see two more legs, but his vision seemed blurry, or else his mind was playing tricks on him.

The two legs were bare, shapely, and tanned.

He squeezed his eyes shut and opened them again. The legs looked the same.

Slowly and carefully, he tried to lift his head to see more of both creatures, only to wince at the sharp jolt of pain the slight movement shot through his head.

However, through the arch of the silver-gray beast's legs and body, he had glimpsed bare feet and ankles beyond, clearly human ones with bare calves, decidedly feminine. Now he saw bare knees, bare thighs, and bare . . .

A snapping sound diverted him, and the animal beside him backed off. It was larger than he had expected and taller, but it was no wolf. On the contrary . . .

"Wolf dog or staghound," he murmured.

"So you are not dead after all."

The soft feminine voice carried a note of drollery and floated to him on the breeze, only there was no longer a breeze. So, perhaps the voice was just in his head, and it had been the dog's breath he'd felt earlier in his ear. Coming to this conclusion pleased him. He hadn't lost his wits then, whatever else had happened to him.

"Can you not talk to me?"

It was the same voice again but nearer, although he had heard no movement, had not sensed her approach in any way. But other than the warm breath huffed into his ear, he had not sensed the dog near him, either. Recalling the shapely legs and bare feet, he realized with some confusion that his eyes had somehow shut themselves. He opened them to the disappointing revelation that her bareness ended midthigh, where a raggedy blue kirtle, kilted-up the way a man would kilt up his plaid, covered much of the rest of her.

"I can talk," he said, and felt again that odd sense of accomplishment. "I'm not sure I can move. And my head feels as if something tried to split it in two."

"You've shed blood on the leaves round your head, so you are injured," she said, her voice as soft and calm as it had been before, and still carrying a light note, as if she felt no fear of him or of anything else in the woods. "I can get your sword out of its sling if you will trust me to do that, and the sling and belt off you, too, but you will have to lift yourself a little for that. Then, mayhap you can turn over."

"Aye, sure," he said. If she had wanted to kill him, she'd have done it already, and she would not be able to wield the heavy sword as a weapon anyway.

She managed without much difficulty to drag the sword from the sling on his back, but when he raised himself to let her reach the strap's buckle underneath him, he had to grit his teeth against the pain and dizziness that surged through his head. Still, he decided by the time she had deftly unbuckled the stout strap and slipped it free of his body that little else was amiss with him *other* than an aching head.

"Now, if you can turn over, I will look and see how bad it is," she said.

Exerting himself, he rolled over and looked up to see a pretty face with a smudge on one rosy cheek and a long mass of unconfined, wild-looking, tawny hair. Despite the look of concern on her face, her eyes twinkled.

Fin could not tell their exact color in the shadow of so many trees with an overcast sky above, but they seemed to be light brown, rather than blue.

"Are you a sprite or some other woodland creature?"

he murmured, finding the effort to talk greater now. His eyelids drooped.

She chuckled low in her throat, a delightful sound and a most stimulating one. His eyes opened wide again, and he saw that she had dropped to one knee and was bending over him.

As he took in the two soft-looking, well-tanned mounds of flesh that peeped over the low-cut bodice so close to him, his head seemed suddenly clearer. Her lips were moving, and he realized that she was speaking. He had missed the first bit, so he listened intently to catch the rest, hoping thereby to reply sensibly.

". . . would laugh to hear anyone mistake me for a sprite," she said, adding firmly, "Now, lie still, sir, if you please. You must know that I was wary of getting too near until I could be sure that you would not harm me."

"Never fear that, lass. I would not."

"I can see that, but Boreus, my companion here, dislikes allowing any stranger near me. It was on that account more than any other that I hesitated to approach. Had you moved too suddenly or thrashed about as some do when they regain consciousness after an injury, he might have taken you for a threat."

Having noted how quickly the wolf dog had stepped back after the snapping sound he had heard—surely a snap of her slim fingers—he doubted that the beast would attack against her will but did not say so. His eyelids drifted shut again.

"Are you still awake?" No amusement now, only concern.

"Aye, sure, but fading, I think," he murmured without opening his eyes. "What is your name?"

"Catriona. What's yours?"

He thought about it briefly, then said, "Fin...they call me Fin of the Battles."

"What happened to you, Fin of the Battles?" Her voice sounded more distant, as if she were floating away again. He concentrated on her question, trying to think.

"I wish I knew," he said at last. "I remember that I was walking through the forest, listening to a damned impertinent jay squawking and muttering ruder noises at me for trespassing. The next thing I knew, your escort was huffing into my ear."

He drew a long breath and, without opening his eyes, tried moving his arms about more than had been necessary when he'd shifted himself. Pain shot through his head again, and he could feel the pain of some sort of scrape on his left arm, but both arms seemed obedient to his will. His toes and feet likewise obeyed him.

A hand touched his right shoulder, startling him. She had come up on the other side of him, and he had not heard her move.

He was definitely *not* himself yet.

"Be still now," she said, kneeling swiftly and gracefully beside him. As she bent nearer, he noted the bare softness of her breasts again before a cold, wet cloth gently touched his forehead and moved soothingly across it to cover his eyes.

He knew then that she must have gone to the burn that he could hear splashing nearby, and tried to decide if he remembered seeing that burn before.

Still uncertain, he murmured, "That feels good."

"It won't in a minute. You have a gash on the left side

Having ripped two pieces from her red f
skirt to soak in the burn, she'd used one to
the hope that it would soothe him and l
ing at her as she cleansed his woun
not for his sake but for hers, bec
be hurting him and would do
she did not keep seeing th

Now, however, she
waited until he look

To her surpris
to tell her tha
tickled his

"Do

All men, in her experience, disliked pain. Certainly, her father and brothers did, although all three were fine, brave warriors. The specimen of manhood before her looked as if he could hold his own against any one of them.

When he'd turned over, it had taken all of her will-power not to exclaim at his blood-streaked face. She reminded herself that head wounds always bled fiercely, and noted thankfully that all the blood seemed to stem from the gash in his forehead.

"Have you enemies hereabouts?" she asked as she gently plucked leaves and other forest detritus from the wound.

Instead of answering directly, he said, "I have not passed this way before. Are your people unfriendly to strangers?"

...annel under-
...cover his eyes in
...keep him from star-
...d. The latter hope was
...ause she knew she would
...a better job of the cleaning if
...e pain in his eyes as she did it.
...plucked the cloth from his eyes,
...ed at her, and said, "*My* people?"

...e, he smiled then, just slightly but enough
...t he had a nice smile and that her tone had
...sense of humor.

...you laugh at me?" she demanded.

...Nay, lass, I would not laugh at such a kind benefac-
...ess. I was just wondering if your people were human or
otherwise. Sithee, although you disclaim being a wood
sprite, I *have* heard tales of wee folk in this area."

"I am completely human," she said. "Keep still now
so you don't start bleeding again. Your wound is trying
to clot, but I want to rinse out these cloths, and if you
shift about whilst I'm doing that, you'll likely start leak-
ing again."

"Tell me first who your people are," he said as she rose
to her feet. His voice was stronger, and the words came
as a command.

Catriona eyed him speculatively. "Do you not know
where you are?"

"Aye, I am betwixt Strathdearn and Strathnairn, in
Clan Chattan territory. But that confederation boasts a
number of tribes within it—at least six, I think."

"Controlled by one," she said.

"The Mackintosh," he said, almost nodding. She saw

him remember and catch himself before he had moved his head more than a tiny bit.

Satisfied, she said, "The Mackintosh, indeed." Moving swiftly to the burn, she knelt and rinsed the bloody cloth in the churning, icy water. Then she dipped the other one, wrung them both out, and went back.

As she approached him, she saw Boreus go into the bushes a short way beyond the man's head. The dog moved with purpose, sniffing the air and then lowering its snout to the low, dense shrubbery. Moments later, it plucked an arrow from the shrubs and trotted back to her with it in its mouth.

Taking it, Catriona said, "I think Boreus found the cause of your injury, sir. If so, I can tell you that it comes from no Clan Chattan bow."

"Nor any Lochaber one," he muttered. "Do you ken aught else of it?"

"Nay, but I do wish Ivor were here," she said.

"Ivor?" He raised his left eyebrow, winced, and said ruefully, "I shall have to remember for a time *not* to express my feelings with facial gestures."

Chuckling, she said, "Ivor is the younger of my two brothers and the finest archer in all Scotland. He knows the fletching of most Highland tribes. But he, my father, and my brother James are away to the Lowlands with the Lord of the North."

"What makes you think this Ivor is the finest archer in the land? Scotland boasts many fine archers. I'm right deft with a bow and arrow myself," he added.

"No doubt you are, but Ivor is best."

"I know a chap who would likely beat anything your Ivor could do," he said.

"Aye, well, mayhap a time will come when they can pit their skills against each other," she said as she finished cleaning the area around his wound. "Lie still now for a few more minutes. The only thing I could bandage that with is more of my underskirt, and I fear the flannel would only chafe it and make it bleed more."

"I don't need a bandage," he said.

"How much farther must you go?"

"A day's walk, mayhap two."

"Then you should come home with me today and rest," she said.

His expression revealed strong reluctance.

Before he could voice it, she added, "Don't be daft enough to refuse. Someone wickedly attacked you, and that arrow knocked you headfirst against that tree, hard enough so that you bounced back and fell as you were when I found you."

"Sakes, lass, if you saw all that, did you not also see who shot me?"

"I saw none of that," she replied.

⌒

Looking narrowly at her, Fin said, "If you saw none of it, you cannot possibly know how I fell. Sakes, I don't know that myself."

"Nevertheless, that or something very like that *is* what happened," she insisted. "The arrow that Boreus found surely made the gash in your forehead, because the blood on it is still wet. You have a lump rising here by your ear"—he winced when she touched it—"and although you fell on these plants, I can see bark in your hair and down the collar of your shirt. Also, you have a tear in the sleeve of your jack and more bits of bark on your arm. The event depicts itself, sir. Moreover," she added, pointing, "your attacker clearly shot from yonder, across the burn."

He had to admit, if only to himself for the present, that she was right about the direction of the shot if she was right about the rest.

Deciding that he had had enough of lying on the damp ground, he sat up, then had to hold himself steady and concentrate hard to fight off the dizziness that threatened him without letting her see how weak he still felt.

Meeting her twinkling gaze, he grimaced, suspecting that her powers of observation were keener just then than his ability to conceal his feelings.

"The dizziness will pass if you just give it time," she said, confirming that suspicion. "You really should come with me, you know, because one can easily see that you are in no state to continue on your own."

The dog moved up beside her, eyeing him thoughtfully. Just looking at it reminded him that Highland forests sheltered many a wolf pack. The beasts would soon catch scent of his blood if he did aught to start the wound bleeding again.

"Would your kinsmen so easily welcome a stranger?"

"My lady mother welcomes all who come in peace," she said. "I warrant she will be glad to have a strong man at hand in my father's absence, even overnight."

He realized then that she was of noble birth and that he ought to have seen as much, despite her untidy appearance. Commoners did not usually own wolf dogs.

"How far from here is your home?" he asked.

"It lies in the glen just over yon hill," she said, pointing toward the granite ridge above them to the northeast. "We'll go through the cut above those trees."

"Very well, then I accept your kind invitation most gratefully."

Smiling in such a way that she made his body stir unexpectedly in response, she picked up his sword and sling and stood back to let him get to his feet. But when he reached for the sword, she said, "I can carry it."

"Nay, then, I do not relinquish my weapon to anyone, woman or man."

He saw a flash of annoyance, but she nodded and handed him the sword belt. He strapped it into place and took the sword from her, feeling its weight more than usual as he reached back and slipped it into the sling. But he did so, he hoped, without noticeable difficulty. She did not *seem* to notice, but he sensed tension between them.

The hill was steep, and it proved harder than he'd expected to follow her up through the forest to the ridge. She and the dog moved swiftly, and his dizziness persisted. Halfway up, he began to feel weary, almost leaden. To be sure, he had traveled far that day, but such profound weariness was abnormal for him.

When they reached the top of the ridge, he paused gratefully when she did. Although he assured himself that there was naught amiss with him but the dizziness and the strange weariness, he welcomed the respite.

"There," she said, pointing again. "We'll just row across the loch."

Staring at the island fortress in the midst of the long, narrow, brilliant blue loch below, he felt a jolt of recognition and a tremor of disbelief.

"Is that not Castle Moigh, the seat of the Mackintosh?"

"Nay," she said, "although you are not the first to mistake it so. That is my father's castle of Rothiemurchus. See you, my family likes islands for the greater safety they provide."

A different sort of tension radiated through him. "Who is your father, lass?"

"Most men know him as Shaw MacGillivray, war leader of the Mackintosh."

Stunned, Fin could think of nothing to say.

Her father was the very man he had sworn to kill.

THE DISH

Where authors give you the inside scoop!

♥ ♥ ♥ ♥ ♥ ♥ ♥ ♥ ♥ ♥ ♥ ♥ ♥ ♥ ♥ ♥

From the desk of Eileen Dreyer

Dear Reader,

Blame it on Sean Bean. Well, no, to be fair, we should blame it on Richard Sharpe, whose exploits I followed long before I picked up my first romance. If you've had the privilege to enjoy the Sharpe series, about a soldier who fights his way through the Napoleonic Wars, you'll understand my attraction. Rugged? Check. Heroic? Check. Wounded? Usually.

There's just something about a hero who risks everything in a great endeavor that speaks to me. And when you add the happy bonuses of chiseled features, sharp wit, and convenient title, I'm hooked. (For me, one of the only problems with SEAL heroes—no country estates).

So when I conceived my DRAKE'S RAKES series, I knew that soldiers would definitely be involved: guards, hussars, grenadiers, riflemen. The very words conjure images of romance, danger, bravery, and great posture. They speak of legendary friendships and tragic pasts and another convenient favorite concept of mine—the fact that relationships are just more intense during war.

So, soldiers? I was there. I just had to give them heroines. That was when it really got fun.

My first book is BARELY A LADY, in which a companion named Olivia Grace recognizes the gravely injured soldier she stumbles over on the battlefield of Waterloo. The problem is that this soldier is actually her ex-husband, Jack Wyndham, Earl of Gracechurch (You expected a blacksmith?). Worse, Jack, whom Olivia hasn't seen in four years, is dressed in an enemy uniform.

Jack and Olivia must find out why before Jack's enemies kill them both. Did I mention that Jack also can't remember that he divorced Olivia? Or that in order to protect him until they unearth his secrets, she has to pretend they're still married?

I didn't say it would be easy. But I do say that there will be soldiers and country estates and lots of danger, bravery, chiseled features, and romance.

It certainly works for me. I hope it does for you. Stop by my website and let me know at www.eileendreyer.com. And then we can address the role of soldiers in the follow-up book, NEVER A GENTLEMAN, not to mention my other favorite thing—marriage of convenience.

Happy reading!

Eileen Dreyer

♥ ♥ ♥ ♥ ♥ ♥ ♥ ♥ ♥ ♥ ♥ ♥ ♥ ♥ ♥ ♥

From the desk of Dee Davis

Dear Reader,

I have always loved run-for-your-life romantic adventures: *King Solomon's Mines, The African Queen, Logan's*

Run, *Romancing the Stone*, and *The Island*, to name a few. So when I began to conceptualize a story for Drake Flynn, it seemed natural that he'd find himself in the middle of the jungles of Colombia. After all, he's an archaeologist when not out fighting bad guys, and some of the most amazing antiquities in the world are hidden deep in the rain forests of South America. And since Madeline Reynard was involved with a drug dealer turned arms trader, it was also easy to see her living amidst the rugged beauty of the high Andes.

There's just something primal about man against nature, and when you throw two people together in that kind of situation, it seems pretty certain that sparks will fly. Especially when they start out on opposite sides of a fence. It's interesting, I think, how we all try to categorize people, put them into predefined boxes so that we have an easy frame of reference. But in truth, people aren't that easy to classify, and even opposites have things in common.

Both Drake and Madeline have had powerful relationships with their siblings, and it is this common bond that pulls them together and eventually forces Madeline to choose between saving herself or helping Drake. The fact that she chooses him contradicts everything Drake thought he knew about her, and the two of them begin a tumultuous journey that ultimately breaks down their respective barriers and leaves them open to the possibility of love.

So maybe a little adventure is good for the soul—and the heart.

For a little more insight into Madeline and Drake,

check out the following songs I listened to while writing:

"Bring Me to Life"—Evanescence

"Lithium Flower"—Scott Matthew

"Penitent"—Suzanne Vega

And, by all means, if you haven't seen *King Solomon's Mines* (with Stewart Granger and Deborah Kerr), Netflix it! As always, check out www.deedavis.com for more inside info about my writing and my books.

Happy Reading!

Dee Davis

♥ ♥ ♥ ♥ ♥ ♥ ♥ ♥ ♥ ♥ ♥ ♥ ♥ ♥ ♥

From the desk of Amanda Scott

Dear Reader,

Lady Fiona Dunwythie, the heroine of my latest book, TEMPTED BY A WARRIOR, was a real person, the younger daughter of fourteenth-century Lord Dunwythie of Annandale, Scotland. She is also the sister of Lady Mairi Dunwythie, the heroine of SEDUCED BY A ROGUE (Forever, January 2010) and cousin to Bonnie Jenny Easdale, the heroine of the first book in this trilogy, TAMED BY A LAIRD (Forever, July 2009).

Writing a trilogy based on anecdotal "facts" from an unpublished sixteenth-century manuscript about events that took place two hundred years earlier has been fascinating. From the manuscript, we know that Fiona eloped with a man from the enemy Jardine clan, and as I learned from my own research, the Jardine lands bordered Dunwythie's.

We also know that Fiona's sister inherited their father's title and estates, and that Lord Dunwythie died the day Fiona eloped, while he was angrily gathering men to go after her. Since we know little more about her, I decided that Fiona had fallen for her husband Will's handsome face and false charm, and had ignored her father's many warnings of the Jardines' ferocity, lawlessness, and long habit of choosing expediency over loyalty.

To be sure, she soon recognized her error in marrying Will. However, when she meets Sir Richard Seyton, Laird of Kirkhill, she is not interested in romance and is anything *but* eligible to wed. Not only is she married to Will and very pregnant with his child but also her father-in-law is dying, her husband (the sole heir to the Jardine estates) is missing, and his father believes that Will must be dead. Worse, Old Jardine believes that Will was murdered and is aware that Fiona was the last person known to have seen him.

Old Jardine has summoned his nephew, Kirkhill, because if Will *is* dead and Fiona's child likewise dies, Kirkhill stands next in line to inherit the Jardine estates. Old Jardine has therefore arranged for him to take them over when Jardine dies and run them until the child comes of age. Jardine also informs Kirkhill that he has named him trustee for Fiona's widow's portion and guardian of her child. Jardine dies soon afterward.

Kirkhill is a decisive man accustomed to being in

charge and being obeyed, and Fiona is tired of men always telling her what to do, so she and he frequently disagree. In my humble opinion, any two people thrust into such a situation *would* disagree.

The reactions of a woman who unexpectedly finds herself legally under the control of a man she does not know seem consistently to intrigue writers and readers alike. But in a time when young women in particular were considered incapable of managing their own money, and men with land or money were expected to assign guardians to their underage heirs and trustees for their wives and daughters, it was something that happened with regularity. I suspect, however, that in many if not most cases, the women and children did know the guardians and trustees assigned to them.

In any event, I definitely enjoyed pitting Kirkhill and Fiona against each other. The two characters seemed naturally to emit sparks. I hope you enjoy the results. I love to hear from readers, so don't hesitate to fire off a comment or two if the mood strikes you.

In the meantime, *Suas Alba!*

Sincerely,

Amanda Scott

http://www.amandascottauthor.com

*Want to know more about romances at
Grand Central Publishing and Forever?
Get the scoop online!*

GRAND CENTRAL PUBLISHING'S
ROMANCE HOMEPAGE

Visit us at www.hachettebookgroup.com/romance
for all the latest news, reviews, and chapter excerpts!

NEW AND UPCOMING TITLES

Each month we feature our new titles
and reader favorites.

CONTESTS AND GIVEAWAYS

We give away galleys, autographed copies,
and all kinds of fun stuff.

AUTHOR INFO

You'll find bios, articles, and links to personal
websites for all your favorite authors—and
so much more!

THE BUZZ

Sign up for our monthly romance newsletter,
and be the first to read all about it!

VISIT US ONLINE
@ WWW.HACHETTEBOOKGROUP.COM.

AT THE HACHETTE BOOK GROUP WEB SITE YOU'LL FIND:

CHAPTER EXCERPTS FROM SELECTED
NEW RELEASES
•
ORIGINAL AUTHOR AND EDITOR ARTICLES
•
AUDIO EXCERPTS
•
BESTSELLER NEWS
•
ELECTRONIC NEWSLETTERS
•
AUTHOR TOUR INFORMATION
•
CONTESTS, QUIZZES, AND POLLS
•
FUN, QUIRKY RECOMMENDATION CENTER
•
PLUS MUCH MORE!

BOOKMARK HACHETTE BOOK GROUP
@ WWW.HACHETTEBOOKGROUP.COM.